HUNTERS FOR HIRE

HUNTERS FOR HIRE BOOK ONE

JONATHAN YANEZ

CONTENTS

BOOKS IN THE HUNTERS FOR HIRE UNIVERSE

1. Hunters for Hire

2. Town Lore

3. All Valley Tournament

4. Godmothered

4.5 darkest Night

5. Devil May Care

6. Dying of the Light

ONE

LIFE SUCKS in more ways than one. Two years ago, if you told me I'd be in the prime of my life twirling "Tacos Culo Loco" signs dressed as a cheap imitation of Big Bird in downtown LA, I would have called you a dirty liar.

But here I am in a suit that smells like cigarette smoke and broken dreams, yelling at the top of my lungs. "Tacos Locos, Pollos Locos, Culo Locos!"

Every kind of car whizzes by, from Bentleys and Ferraris, to those that look like they've seen better decades. There was some kind of truck that passed and I swore there were bullet holes in the fender.

Downtown LA is the craziest mix of the rich and poor I've ever seen. But beggars couldn't be choosers. I needed whatever job I could take in order to fill the time between casting calls. At least at Tacos Culo Locos, no one could see my face behind the chicken mask.

My phone went off in my chicken pocket. At least I think it was a pocket. Its previous owner had slashed a hole on the inside of the costume. He might have cut himself in the process because there was dried blood everywhere along the interior.

Oh well, it served my purpose. I grabbed my phone, ringing with the familiar jingle of the original *Doctor Who* theme music. It was Tracy, the love of my life and woman who was sticking with me through thick and thin, or I guess in my case, castings and chicken costumes.

"Hey, Trace," I said into the phone. "Can't talk too long right now. Mrs. Gomez said she'd cut me if she caught me on the phone again. I think that's a joke, but she did take off her sandal and wave it super threatening at me while she said it. Come to think of it, there is a slash in this chicken costume."

"They made you wear the chicken costume again?" Tracy asked with a heavy sigh. "Please tell me you at least dry-cleaned it before you put it on today? Last time you came over after wearing that, you smelled like rotten spaghetti."

"Rotten spaghetti is highly unlikely," I told her. "They sell chicken here."

"Whatever. I was just calling to make sure we're still on for dinner tonight. I'm on this new low carb diet for the show I got casted to and I want to watch my macros," Tracy said into the phone. There was noise in the background like someone else talking. I thought I heard a man's voice. "Sorry, that's just Brad. He says hi."

"What? Brad Connolly? That's so cool," I nearly shouted. "Tell him I said hi. Ask him if I can get his autograph."

Tracy had just been cast for a supporting role in a new streaming drama. Brad Connolly was the lead. How the streaming service had gotten such a big name to play the main character was still a mystery to most.

"Shhhh," Tracy silenced me. "Take it easy. You don't want to embarrass me. It's my first day on set."

"Right, right," I whispered. "So cool. Tell him I said hi."

"Yeah, okay," Tracy answered. "So we're still on for dinner tonight?"

"Hey, chicken butt, do a dance! Pollo loco hermano man, shake it!"

I looked over to where a line of vehicles stopped at a red light. A balding man with dark sunglasses and yellow teeth leaned out of his vehicle window to address me. More grinning faces inside the vehicle told me his buddies were egging him on.

"John, John, are you still there?" Tracy asked on the other end of the phone. "I thought I heard someone yelling about a chicken butt."

"No, no, nothing like that," I lied to try and save face. "Yes, we're on for tonight's dinner. Seven o'clock at The Original Organic. I'll meet you there."

"Okay, see you then," Tracy said before ending the call.

"Hey, twirl your sign or do a dance or something, chicken boy!" the man yelled from out of his window.

"You leave my chicken boy alone!" Mrs. Gomez stormed out of Taco Culo Locos with that sandal in her hand. "My chicken boy dances for Taco Culo Locos and no one else!"

"Oh snap, that Mexican mom is going to come beat us with her sandal or something," the driver shouted amidst the roars of laughter of those inside the vehicle. "Light's green; let's go, let's go, let's go!"

The driver gunned the engine as the light changed and the car screeched off down the road.

"You okay, Jonny?" Mrs. Gomez asked in her thick Mexican accent. "They didn't bully you, did they?"

"Ahhh, nothing I'm not used to," I waved away her concern. "I'll be okay. I got a text earlier from my agent. I have another casting call to get to before dinner. This one's for a hemorrhoids campaign. It sounds super promising. My agent says I'm a perfect fit for the role."

"Oh, look at you." Mrs. Gomez placed her sandal back on her bare foot. "I know you're going places, Jonny. Now come on; pick up that sign and twirl it while we talk. You weren't on the phone when I came out, were you?"

"Oh no, of course not, who me? On the phone? Pshhhhh, please. I know the rules. I was not on the phone," I said, grateful to have the chicken mask covering my face. I've been told I'm a horrible liar. For some reason, when I lie I just can't shut up. "I know the rules. I play by the rules. You best believe dat. Phone, huh no, silly goose."

"Uh huh." Mrs. Gomez lifted an eyebrow that could have turned me to stone. "You still asking Tracy tonight? Tonight's the night, right?"

"Yep, I have the ring right here in this bloody pocket. Hey, is this blood in here or like ketchup or something?" I asked, patting the area over my chest. "It's kind of smelly. No offense."

"Official word is it was a nose bleed from Juanito, who used to wear it. Unofficially, someone got stabbed in it during a fight between two crack addicts here on 4th Street. Juanito wasn't too bright and tried to break them up," Mrs. Gomez rattled off as if it were nothing more than the latest gossip on the street. "But enough about crack addicts and their struggle for the last chicken wing. Let's see the ring, let's see the ring, Jonny!"

"Oh, right," I said, reaching into the costume through the neck with my right hand. The box the ring came in was right where I left it, next to my phone. "Are you ready to gaze on this beauty?"

"Oh yes." Mrs. Gomez clapped with delight.

I opened the box. The ring had eaten up nearly all of my savings. I had to add a few extra trips driving Lyfter at night to make it work plus all the money I made at my last job as an extra for a Life Alert commercial. I had played the son of an elderly woman, who came home to find her on the floor.

The woman who played my mother was a real sweetheart, except she cursed like a sailor and kept calling me "sweet cheeks" and inviting me back to the trailer for some one-on-one time to "practice" her lines. Fell for that one once and only once.

I presented the ring in my chicken-gloved hands.

Mrs. Gomez leaned in, squinting.

"Where's the—oh, oh, I think I see the diamond," Mrs. Gomez said with a long pause. "Jonny, are you sure they gave you a diamond in your ring?"

"Yeah, yeah, of course they did. It's riiiiiiiiiiiiiiiiight," I said, prolonging the word as I flipped the ring around to take a look, "there, uh huh, right in the middle; see?"

"Oh, yes." Mrs. Gomez patted me on the shoulder. "Sorry, my eyes just aren't what they used to be."

"No problem," I answered. "Hey, do you mind if I get off a bit early? I have a big casting call to go to and I don't want to be late."

"Of course, of course." Mrs. Gomez waved away the request. "You're one of the good ones, Jonny. You come and go as you need. I'll always have work for you. What did you say the casting was for again? Was it irritable bowel syndrome?"

"No, that one was last week," I said, heading inside the store with Mrs. Gomez. "This one's for a new hemorrhoid cream coming out. I think I have a real shot."

Turned out I would have had a real shot, but the casting got pushed back to a later date. Instead of heading there, I went back to the apartment I shared with my best friend, Evan Woods.

Evan was everything I wanted to be. At least career-wise. He was a working model, always getting booked on some of the biggest shoots there were. This year alone, he did work for GQ, Apple, and Sony. To top it off, he was one of the nicest guys I knew.

I met him on a shoot we did together a few years ago. Turned out we were both looking for roommates. The last one I had got married and moved out. Evan didn't talk about his last roommate much, just that the guy up and left one day. I guess he had had enough. Not a lot of people could take living with someone as successful as Evan while still struggling to make it on their own.

I was fine with it. I knew my time would come. I just had to pay some dues.

Home was an apartment complex called Haven in downtown Los Angeles. It was small but not in the worst part of town. We heard police sirens only once to twice a night, maybe the occasional helicopter providing support for a raid.

I pulled my old 1966 Ford Mustang into the rear of the square-shaped building. I bought it off its previous owner at a steal. It broke down on the way home from the purchase and still gave me problems now and again, but it just felt right.

Cracked paint and just as cracked asphalt surrounded the four-story apartment complex. There were three dozen units in all with the manager living on the ground floor. He was a crazy old man, always going on about creatures in the shadows and unnatural beings in our world, but I just figured he binged too many of those fantasy shows like *Supernatural* and *True Blood*.

I locked my car door and headed inside the back entrance.

"Hey, can you hold the gate?" a woman's voice I didn't recognize called out.

"Yeah, sure," I said on instinct, opening the gate wider and standing to the side so she could get through.

"Thanks, I'm just coming back from the grocery store and

I freaking refuse to make two trips carrying in the bags. I—ewwww, what's—what's that smell?" the woman asked. "It's like stale onions and—and chicken blood."

The woman was about my age, with brown hair and hard muscles that were easy to see past her tank top.

"What? I don't smell anything," I said, sniffing both underarms.

"I think it might be you."

"Oh, right."

"Sorry, that's really rude but, but, oh gosh, I can taste it in the back of my throat," she gagged, spitting to the side. "I'm your new neighbor, Shannon. I'd shake your hand, but..."

Shannon shrugged with both arms full of grocery bags.

"No worries," I answered, closing the gate behind us. "I'm John."

"John, great to meet you. I'm just going to stand over here to the side and get upwind of you," Shannon said with a polite smile. "I think I've seen you around. You live on the top floor, right? You have a roommate?"

It was record time, actually. All the female tenants in the building usually worked Evan into the conversation one way or another. Most just came out and asked if he was single.

"Yep, yep, Evan and I live on the fourth floor," I answered politely. "He's super nice if you want me to intro—"

A howl so primal it rattled my sternum ripped through the afternoon air.

TWO

SHANNON and I exchanged surprised looks. We both turned where the howling came from deeper into the complex and to the manager's unit.

To her credit, Shannon was the first to move.

"Come on, Stinky." Shannon turned with both grocery bags in hand and made a dash toward the noise.

Are you really doing this? I thought to myself, taking off after Shannon toward the screaming. *Maybe you should just call the cops or something.*

I was no coward, but neither was I in the business of running toward animalistic shrieks coming from my manager's apartment. Still, I wasn't about to let Shannon go by herself.

"Hey, hey," I said, gasping as I tried to catch up with her. She was fast, much faster than I expected, and she didn't even drop the egg carton hanging out of her bag. "Maybe we should call for help or something?"

We ran past the poorly kept shrubs and sparse greenery on the ground floor section of our complex. A pool with a wrought-iron fence surrounding it and questionably murky water rounded out the amenities our apartment complex offered.

We skidded to a halt at the closed door of unit one where the manager of Haven, Mr. Hyde, lived.

"Maybe he's just really pissed at a video game he can't beat; you know, everyone's playing *Fortnight* nowadays and freaking out when they die," I suggested, trying to come up with a reason not to knock on the door.

"*Fortnight,* really?" Shannon lifted an eyebrow. Her lips twitched into a grin. "You'll have to do better than that, Stinky."

"Maybe he's watching a political debate. You know how people get. He got triggered or something." I lifted my own brow. "And my name's not Stinky. I usually smell much better than this. Old Spice or Axe body spray is my go-to."

"Let's have a long, serious talk about your personal hygiene later," Shannon replied, lowering the bags to the ground in front of the door. "What's 'triggered' mean?"

"What, you don't know what triggered means?" I asked incredulously.

"Obviously not, if I'm asking," Shannon answered. "I'm not from around here. You people in LA talk weird and have all these new terms."

"Wow, first off, you can't say things like 'you people'." I raised both hands up toward her and took a step back. "That will definitely trigger people and is so not woke."

"Woke?" Shannon repeated. "Never mind that; let's start with 'triggered' first."

"You know, like 'hashtag triggered'." I racked my mind trying to explain the term for her. "When you hear or read something that sets you off or gets under your skin, it triggers you. Like, offends you."

"Oh, I get being offended," Shannon said with a shrug. "Why don't people just say that?"

"That's actually a good question," I said, rubbing my chin.

"Your stench triggers me," Shannon murmured to herself as if she were trying out the word for the first time. "Hmmm, I like it."

"Yeah, good use of it in a sentence," I complimented. "But hey, look. No more crazy yelling from Mr. Hyde's apartment. See, he's fine; he was listening to too much Rush Limbaugh or something that set him off. No need to go in and cause a scene. We can—"

The howl-like scream came a third time.

"That's it; I'm going in," Shannon answered, turning to the door.

I thought she was going to knock. You know, what any sane person would do. Press the doorbell a few times, do a funny rhythmic rap on the door like the *Terminator* soundtrack. That was a favorite of mine.

But not Shannon. She balled her hand into a fist and pounded her hand into the door three times. Each blow was so hard, it shook the doorframe itself. I thought she was going to break the door down if she did it again.

"Mr. Hyde!? Mr. Hyde!? Are you all right in there?" Shannon shouted through the door. "I'm coming in if I don't hear from you!"

"Coming in?" I repeated in a whisper as we waited in silence. "Like, break down the door? He's going to make us pay for that. I'm not exactly made of money here."

"Stand back," Shannon said, rearing her right foot high in the air.

The distinctive sound of a heavy lock being turned in the door sounded on the other side. More locks being opened, at least half a dozen slides and hooks being unlatched.

"This guy has more chains and locks than Azkaban," I muttered.

"Stinky, you're such a nerd," Shannon said, not taking her eyes from the door.

"But you understood the reference," I countered.

The doorknob finally turned. The door opened only an inch or two before it was caught by a chain still in place. I couldn't really see inside, but the vague outline of a man behind the door took shape.

"Yes, yes, what is it?" Mr. Hyde asked.

"We heard some screams coming from your unit." Shannon took a step toward him, trying to get a better view of the inside of his apartment. "We wanted to come in and make sure everything was all right."

Mr. Hyde gave off a hacking cough so full of phlegm, it made me take a step back.

"Yes, I'm fine. Sorry—I was uh—I was playing a game and lost; very frustrating," Mr. Hyde answered. "I'm fine now. I'll just restart the level."

"See, I told you," I said, turning from Shannon to Mr. Hyde. "Sorry for the inconvenience, sir. I know how frustrating those games can be. Plus all the trolls and bullies online. I was just playing the latest *Gateway to the Galaxy* game yesterday and those kids are not kind. They were teaching me new curse words. I felt like I needed to take a shower afterwards and rethink my life choices."

"What?" Mr. Hyde asked. "Never mind, okay. I'm okay. What's—what's that smell?"

"Are you sure everything's fine?" Shannon moved closer to the door while ignoring his question. "Those yells sounded pretty animalistic in nature."

"I'm—I'm okay. Thank you for checking," Mr. Hyde insisted.

"Okay, that's good enough for me," I said, picking up Shannon's grocery bags and handing them to her. "Let's go."

Shannon slowly followed.

The door to Mr. Hyde's apartment closed behind us.

We made our way to one of the stairwells in the corner of the square apartment complex. I'd already moved on from our encounter with Mr. Hyde. I had bigger fish to fry at the moment.

My hand instinctively went to the small, hard box carrying the ring in my pocket. A nervous sensation cascaded over me like a cold wave.

"Hey, are you even listening to me?" Shannon asked in a voice that told me this wasn't the first time she tried to get my attention.

"Yeah, sorry, what?" I asked.

"I said this is my floor." Shannon jerked her chin to the third-floor landing. "It was good to meet you. We should get together sometime. You, me, and your roommate. I don't know a whole lot of people since moving here. You know, I want to get woke."

"Nope, still not using that term right," I told her with a smile. "For sure, it was nice meeting you too. I'll talk to Evan and see when we can all hang out."

"In the meantime, you should take a shower." Shannon wrinkled her nose. "Seriously, though. It's like a skunk crawled into my mouth and took a sh—"

"I get it, I get it." I smiled as I left her for the stairwell once more. "I'm on my way to the shower."

I jogged the last flight of stairs to my own level. The floors were open on one side, looking down below at the courtyard and pool area. The opposite side was a long line of doors leading into different apartments.

I made my way to the apartment I shared with Evan. Although we were bachelors, we kept the place pretty tidy. Our apartment was small, two bedrooms each with their own bath, a kitchen and dining area with an attached family room. That was about it.

As soon as I stepped inside, I could hear a woman's laugh from Evan's closed door. A tie hung on his door handle.

"Oh, Evan, stop your teasing." The woman giggled. "You're such a bad boy."

"Say hello to my little friend," Evan answered.

I raised my eyebrows, heading to my room before I could hear any more of what was going on in Evan's room. I didn't want to have to bleach my eardrums later.

I spent the next half hour showering, shaving, and dressing in my best jeans and button-up shirt. I wanted the night to be perfect. I had been going out with Tracy for nearly a year and I knew she was the one.

I looked in the mirror once I was finished and let out a long breath of air.

"You got this," I told myself. "This is the night."

A light rap on my door interrupted my pep talk.

"Come in," I called.

Evan walked in naked from the waist up. A towel was wrapped around his lower half. Evan was tall and chiseled with a pale complexion. His high cheekbones and strong jaw made him a perfect fit for the modeling world.

"Hey, buddy," Evan said with a toothy smile. "I was wondering if you had any baby oil. Why are you all dressed up and—why are you wearing an entire department store's worth of cologne? Jonny, did you mix Axe and Old Spice together again? I thought we talked about this."

"Maybe," I told him. "Don't worry about it. I'm heading out with Tracy. Tonight's the big night. Remember I told you about it?"

"Oh right! Right." Evan looked around uncomfortably. He clicked his tongue a few times then took a seat on my bed. "Why don't you come and sit next to me for a minute? We can have a little roommate to roommate chat."

"What? Now?" I asked. "Don't you have someone waiting for you in the other room?"

"Don't worry about her." Evan patted the bed next to him. "She's a little tied up right now. Just—just come and take a seat for a second. I have something to tell you."

"All right, but I've got to get going," I said, sitting next to Evan. "I need to get there before Tracy. I don't want her to have to wait. She hates waiting."

"Riiiiiiight," Evan drawled. "It's kind of about that. You've only been going out with Tracy for what? A year now?"

"A little less," I confirmed. "But she's the one. I know she is."

"I just want what's best for you, man, and well, Tracy is a little, a little..." Evan searched for the right word, moving his head back and forth as if he were bobbing to some kind of beat. "Well, to be honest, she's kind of a selfish, conceited, elitist fame monger."

"What?" I asked, taken aback. "Why would you say that about her?"

"Just calm down and take it easy." Evan leaned over and wrapped his arms around me. His naked torso pressed against my chest. "Bring it in for the real thing for a minute. I want you to know this is harder for me to say than you to receive. I care about you, man. You're my best friend and I just want you to be happy."

Evan squeezed me so hard, it was difficult to breathe.

"Well, I'd—I'd be happier if your towel wasn't slipping right now," I said honestly, averting my gaze.

"Oh, right, sorry. Got to keep the anaconda in its cage." Evan let me go and readjusted his towel. "I swear that thing has a mind of its own sometimes. It's like an elephant's trunk holding a grapefruit."

"That's a weird analogy." I shook my head free of the

visual. "Listen, I appreciate you being worried about me, but it's going to be fine. You'll get to know Tracy better and see what I see in her."

"Uh, dude, I have gotten to know her pretty well, and I see her for what she really is." Evan stood up from the bed, securing his towel. "I hope it all works out the way you want it to, really I do. I just don't want to see you get hurt, man. I know how that feels. You're—you're like the younger, darker-skinned brother I never had."

"You know I appreciate that, but Tracy's different. You'll see. She's not what you think she is," I answered.

"Papi!" a woman's voice yelled from the other room. "Where's that oil?"

"Papi?" I asked. "On second thought, I don't even want to know. I don't use baby oil, but I have some lotion if you want. Bathroom, under the sink."

"You're the best," Evan said, heading for the restroom. He yelled out the door, "Be right there, Mami!"

THREE

THE ORIGINAL ORGANIC restaurant wasn't the fanciest or most expensive restaurant in town, but it held a special meaning to Tracy and me. It was where we had our first date almost a year ago.

I made sure to reserve the exact table where we first sat. I even ordered her favorite appetizer, gluten-free pita bread with non-fat yogurt dipping sauce, and organic pesticide-free baby carrots.

The restaurant was busy but not packed. The light chatter of other patrons filled the air and created the white noise I needed right now to keep me calm. The bulge in my pocket from the ring box felt like a brick at the moment.

I was pretty sure I was having heart palpitations just sitting there waiting for her.

"Are you okay, sir?" the waiter asked in a nasally voice. "Do you need anything? You look flushed."

"No, no, I'm fine," I reassured him. "Just a big date."

"Are you sure?" the waiter asked, eyeing me suspiciously. "There's no harm admitting if you need help. Is it drugs? Are you on some kind of drug, sir?"

"Drugs? What?" I asked, trying to decide if the waiter was serious or not. "No, no, I'm fine. Just waiting for my girlfriend."

I fidgeted with the napkin in front of me. With all the nervous energy pent up inside, I couldn't stop my right foot from tapping on the floor.

"Well, there's no shame in getting cleaned up and admitting you have a problem." The man poured me another glass of water. "I went to this hypnotist, Roger Fairbanks, and he set me straight. I can give you his information. Whatever it is you're on, he can help. What are you on anyway? Is it euphoria, the devil's juice, bang bang powder, damnation dust, pop rocks, skunk bump, brown sugar, black magic, monkey frost, panther acid?"

"Listen, I don't do drugs!" I said way louder than I intended.

The entire restaurant paused to stare at me.

"Well." The waiter rolled his eyes and gave me a finger snap. "Excuse me for trying to save your soul."

When he turned to walk away, I saw Tracy moving through the front door. Her head was down. She was texting someone on her phone.

"Hey, over here." I waved her over, standing up from my seat to give her a hug and a kiss. She turned her head to the side when I went in for the kiss. My lips brushed against her left cheek.

"Lips are super chapped right now," Tracy said, not looking up from her phone. "Just got to wrap up some last-minute work stuff. Brad is so funny, you know? The texts he sends. Who would have thought he'd be so down to earth?"

"Oh right, right, how was your day?" I asked, taking a seat across from her in the booth. "I want to hear all about it."

"Oh, you know, set life is so hard." Tracy finally put down

her phone on the table. "I'm starving." She picked up a piece of the pita bread. "Is this gluten-free?"

"You know it," I answered, flagging down the waiter, who came over reluctantly.

"Excuse me, can we get her a drink?" I requested politely, trying to keep my foot from tapping.

"Why are you so fidgety?" Tracy asked, taking a bite of her pita. "Are you okay?"

"I'm fine, I'm fine; just excited to be here hanging out with you," I responded.

"Drugs," the waiter whispered to her.

"What do you want to drink?" I asked her. "The usual?"

"I'll take one of your zero-calorie sparkling waters infused with herbal essence, but only if you have the Valhalla brand. They bottle their water straight from environmental-friendly waterfalls," Tracy said.

"Yes, of course we carry Valhalla," the waiter confirmed, turning to go. "I'll be right back."

Dinner was great. We talked about Tracy's new role in the streaming show that was yet to be titled but revolved around Brad, who played an out-of-work writer down on his luck who reinvented himself by performing as a clown for children's birthday parties.

Tracy said she was stuffed after a few bites of carrots and pitas. I didn't want to offend her by ordering meat, so I ordered the spinach salad with a side of hummus.

To be honest, I wasn't even that hungry. My stomach was in knots. As the night wore on, I knew I had to make my move. Tracy would have to go home soon to get her full eight hours of sleep in and apply her nightly routine of creams and lotions.

"Tracy?" I asked after chewing a mouthful of dry spinach. "You know I love you, right?"

"Ahhh." Tracy beamed. "I know you do."

"I'm so proud of what you've done and I know you're going to go far. We both are," I continued, trying to figure out a smooth way to get down on one knee. "We work so well together. We have so much in common from our jobs to where we want to be in the future. Well—well, I guess I'm trying to say I don't want to be with anyone else."

I slid out of the booth and withdrew the box from my pocket. On one knee, my heart beating a hundred miles an hour, I opened the box and presented it to her.

"Tracy Coach Prada, will you make me the happiest struggling model in Los Angeles and be my wife?" I asked, doing my best not to stumble over my words. My mouth was dry, hands clammy as I knelt there on the restaurant floor recently mopped with chemical-free jasmine soap.

For the second time that night, everyone in the restaurant went quiet.

I saw our waiter out of the corner of my eye shaking his head no. He was mouthing the words "drugs" and "high" over and over again.

Tracy looked at me, stunned for a moment. She pressed both hands over her mouth and started to cry. "Yes, yes, of course I will. Oh my gosh, oh my gosh. I need to put this moment on my Instagram feed."

A wave of relief hit me as everyone in the restaurant cheered. Tracy got her phone out and went live on her different social media platforms. I slid back into my part of the booth, so happy, I felt like I was going to burst.

It was all working out. Who said you couldn't have the American dream? I was living proof of it. Struggling model, with the love of his life and nothing but a bright future ahead.

"Jonny? Jonny? I think there's something wrong with the ring?" Tracy said, snapping me out of my joy-like trance. "There's no diamond."

"Oh, no, it's there," I said, pointing to the ring she placed on her finger. "I know, I know it's not the biggest diamond out there, but I'll get you a bigger one. I have a really great casting coming up my agent says I'm perfect for. I know I'll nail the audition tomorrow. I'll get you a bigger ring with that money. I promise."

Tracy shrugged then went back to snapping pictures and posting on Facebook, Twitter, Instagram, Snapchat, LinkedIn, Tiktok, and the rest.

We were both happy and I couldn't have asked for more. We talked about the future and the wedding for the next hour. I wasn't sure how I was going to afford it all, but I knew I'd figure it out.

Tracy had an early day at the studio, so we went our separate ways that night. The drive home was full of relief and stupid grins. By the time I got back to the Haven apartment complex, my face kind of hurt from smiling.

I needed to call my parents and tell them, of course, but it was late. I'd let them know in the morning. Boy, was Evan going to be surprised. I knew he had nothing but the best intentions, but he was wrong about Tracy. I just knew it.

I jogged up our steps and made my way to our apartment. I slid my key in the lock and let myself inside.

Light moaning from Evan's room told me he was still preoccupied with his guest.

"Man, he has the stamina of a marathon runner," I muttered to myself.

When the moaning became louder, I looked at his room. The door was only half closed.

I didn't want to be a creeper going to close the door, but neither did I really want to be serenaded with the calls of "Papi" and "Mami" the rest of the night.

Averting my eyes, I went to his door to close it the rest of the way.

A particularly sharp inhalation and painful moan made me look into the room before I could stop myself. What I saw that night would change my life forever.

My roommate, my best friend, stood in the dark room with a woman in his arms. They were both naked. The light was off and only the silver illuminations from the moon shone through an open window.

The woman had her back to me. Evan faced me with his mouth wrapped around the woman's neck. His eyes were black orbs. A thin line of blood ran down her neck where he punctured her skin.

My jaw dropped. I didn't know what to think. Was this some kind of kinky foreplay? Was this okay? Was I hallucinating?

Evan caught sight of me and raised his mouth from the woman's neck immediately. As if on command, his eyes reverted back to their pale blue.

"Oh, no, that's not good," he said, looking at me. "Jonny, I think we're going to have to have another talk."

FOUR

"NOPE, I don't—I don't even want to know," I stammered, trying to find the right words to fit the circumstance I found myself in at the moment. "Are you—no—I—"

"You're in shock right now, buddy," Evan said, dropping the woman's body he held in his arms. She fell to the ground with a hard thud, seemingly lifeless. "It's normal. Just let me explain. Don't freak out."

I had never had a panic attack before, but right now, with the motionless woman on the ground and Evan dripping blood from his mouth, I was on the verge.

Hold it together, hold it together, I coached myself in my head. *There's an explanation. This is all going to make sense. This is Evan, your best friend, the guy you watch football and gorge yourself on buffalo wings with without fear of judgment.*

"Can I get you a bag to breathe into or something?" Evan said, taking a step closer.

"Is she—is she dead?" I asked, looking at the woman on the ground.

"No, no, no, nothing like that, Jonny," Evan explained. "I'm one of the good ones. I wouldn't do that. She's alive.

She won't remember much when she wakes up. I just take what I need to survive. I don't turn them. I don't kill them."

I just stood there in the dark doorway trying to figure out my next move. I could run, call the cops, or try and let Evan explain what was going on.

"It's me, it's just me," Evan assured, looking into my eyes. "She's alive. She's going to be okay. I'll explain everything to you, if you just let me."

I took one more look at the naked woman on the ground. Her chest still rose and fell, slightly confirming what Evan said.

"Okay, all right," I said, extending both hands to the room in front of me. "But you need to put some clothes on before we talk and I need a drink or ten."

"Right, right." Evan nodded hurriedly as he donned his silk kimono. "I've always wanted to tell you, Jonny. I've thought about how this conversation would go a dozen times. I haven't said anything before because I didn't want to drag you into this life."

"What life are we talking about here?" I questioned, still not understanding what I had walked into. "What kind of kinky stuff are you involved with?"

"Not kinky; vampiric," Evan stated, motioning me out of his room and toward our family area. "I need blood to survive."

"Vampiric?" I asked, swallowing hard. Evan had to shepherd me to our couch. "Evan, are you sure you didn't hit your head or something? Are you telling me you're a vampire?"

I sat down, cracking a smile as everything made sense at once.

"Okay, okay, this is all very funny," I said, looking around the room. I stood up, craning my neck and searching for the hidden cameras. "Who put you up to this? Was it Tracy? My agent? Someone else? Where are the cameras? You got me.

What is this, some kind of staged casting for a show or something? Am I being punked? Is Ashton Kutcher here somewhere reviving his show?"

I went around the room, peering into our air-conditioning vents and in closets looking for the cameras and producers I was sure were there.

"Jonny?" Evan called quietly. "Jonny, it's nothing like that. This is all real."

"Right, yeah, okay," I said, my mind refusing to give in to this new insane reality. "Sure, you're a vampire living in Hollywood, right, nice try. I mean, I'm not the brightest bulb in the pack, but I'm not a dummy either."

I went back into Evan's room addressing the naked woman on the ground.

"Okay, ma'am, it's over. I know I'm being pranked. You can put some clothes on now," I told her, grabbing a blanket from Evan's bed and covering her. "You can get up now, seriously. I don't know how much they're paying you to do this, but you deserve every penny. You did great. You really had me. Ashton, Ashton, you can come out now."

"No one's coming, buddy." Evan sighed. "I know how you feel. I had to go through all of this myself, but it was worse for me. I was turned when I found out. It was a strange and awkward time for me, like puberty all over again."

Fear gripped the pit of my stomach laced with uncertainty. If this was for real, I wasn't sure I wanted to know at all. Could this be real? Was I dreaming? Was I hallucinating all of this?

"All right, come on." Evan ushered me once more to the family room. "I'm going to grab you a drink and then I'm going to tell you everything you want to know and probably some things you don't."

I went back to the couch. My mouth was dry, my brain working on overtime to make sense of my new reality.

"I've seen a lot of crazy stuff in my day," Evan started as he busied himself in the kitchen making a pair of drinks. "I know I look like I'm in my twenties, but the truth is I'm closer to a hundred and fifteen. I was born in 1905 and came out to Hollywood when I was in my twenties to find work. Young and naïve, I thought I could conquer the world. I found an agent, but he was more than I expected. A real sleazeball type, but he liked me and said he could find me work in early Hollywood. I believed him."

Evan walked over to me, handing me a glass with two ice cubes in clear liquid.

"I don't know if I should drink right now," I told him as a numb sensation spread from my head down. "I'm freaking out enough. Not sure alcohol is going to help."

"Alcohol helps everything," Evan replied with a shrug. He took a seat across from me with both drinks in his hands. He drained one and sipped on the other. "Ahhhh, that's the good stuff."

"And then what happened?" I asked, still trying to decide if I believed Evan or thought he was insane. Or maybe I was insane.

"Huh?" Evan asked, smacking his lips.

"I mean, once you came to Hollywood and found an agent," I said. "What happened next?"

"Well, he had me come over to his office to sign paperwork," Evan said, using air quotes to emphasize the word "paperwork." "I should have known something was up with that couch he had in his office and all the towels. I mean, who happens to have a leather couch in their office and a stack of clean, pressed towels? Oh well, like I said, I was young and naive with stars in my eyes. I figured something shady was going to go down, but I thought we all had to start somewhere."

Evan went quiet. He sipped on his remaining drink,

looking over my shoulder at the far wall. I could tell he was replaying the events in his mind.

"I'm sorry," I said quietly. I still wasn't sure how I felt about what I'd seen, but this was still Evan. This was the guy who bought me extra chocolate Yoo-hoos at the store, threw my laundry in with his, and always had an encouraging word when a casting didn't work out. "Did he—did he force himself on you?"

"Yeah, but not in the traditional sense," Evan explained, taking a last swig of his drink. "His teeth came out and his eyes went black. He latched on to me and I was sure he was going to suck me dry. He probably would have killed me right there, but we were interrupted. His secretary came in screaming about some airplane accident Howard Hughes had been in. When she saw what he was doing to me, she took her yelling to a new octave and ran right out of the building. My agent raced off after her to kill her, thinking I was already dead."

"But you weren't," I concluded the story. "And now you're something that sparkles in the sun and kisses Kristen Stewart."

"Not so much on the sparkling, but I would kiss Kristen Stewart." Evan winked in my direction. "How are you holding up? I know this is a lot. I haven't told anyone—human my story before. Between you and me, I think you're handling it pretty well. I mean, you didn't have to change your pants or have a mental break or anything."

"I was close to the mental break," I admitted. "Still might have to change my pants."

"I'm sorry you caught me like you did." Evan gave a long sigh. "I should have been more careful. The truth is, and I know this is selfish, but it feels good to talk to my best friend about it. I hated hiding it from you. It feels good to come out."

I nodded along with Evan's words. A cascade of unanswered questions raged in my mind from if the trope of vampires being burned in the sun was real to if Count Chocula had been based off a real person. I decided to start with the former.

"So you don't sparkle at all in the sun?" I asked, scratching the underside of my jaw. "What about all the other stories? Are you allergic to garlic, can you see yourself in the mirror, do I have to invite you in?"

"Please don't believe everything you hear," Evan said, reverting back to the normal cheerful Evan I knew, leaving the story of his past behind him for the moment. "Garlic is delicious, I probably spend way too much time looking at myself in the mirror, and I can go anywhere I want. The sunlight, though, is true."

"What?" I asked incredulously. "I've been out with you during the day plenty of times."

"Yes you have, but I've always been shaded as much as possible with sunglasses and clothing," Evan countered. "I have to wear a special cream that blocks out the sun's UV rays when I know there's no getting around it."

"I guess you are super pale," I allowed, taking in Evan's pasty complexion. "I've always thought that but just figured you needed more Vitamin D in your diet. I was going to suggest you get some sun but didn't want to come across as racist."

"Not all of us can have your bronze skin, Jonny boy," Evan said with a toothy grin. "Another thing is that I need blood to survive. Food is great, I mean, who doesn't love a triple cheeseburger with extra fries and a chocolate shake from Matty Too Fatty Burgers, but all it is, is taste for me."

"That's why you can eat whatever you want and still look like that," I said with a sigh. "You told me it was because you had a fast metabolism."

"Naw, that stuff goes right through me." Evan shrugged. "You should see the toilet after an all-you-can-eat buffet. It looks like a murder scene in there."

"Over share, man," I said with a grimace. "So you lure women back to our apartment and take what you need?"

"Don't make it sound so scum-baggy," Evan chided, screwing up his face. "I take as little as I need to survive. I've never killed or turned anyone. Their wounds heal quickly and they don't remember any of it."

"Are there more of you?" I asked. "I mean, more vampires, you know?"

"Uh yeah, a lot more," Evan explained, taking another sip of his drink. "Hollywood is chock full of vamps: Keanu Reeves, Johnny Depp, Madonna—you name it."

"No way, Neo? They got Neo?" I asked, astounded. "I always thought he looked the same from Point Break to John Wick."

"Oh yeah, they're all over the place," Evan answered. "A few like me take only what we need, but most of the others don't have a problem turning or killing their victims."

"Are there more?" I wondered. "I mean, more supernatural creatures like you?"

"You sure you can handle all of this right now?" Evan looked at me sideways. "You already have a lot to think about."

"No, man, this is like bingeing a Netflix series. I want it all right now," I answered, moving to the edge of my seat. "Werewolves?"

"Yep." Evan nodded. "Smell bad and usually act first and think later type. You'll see a lot of them in security, law enforcement, and the military."

"Zombies?"

"A lot of DMV employees, IRS types, and accountants." Evan shuddered a bit when he relayed the news. "I accidentally bit one once. I was starving and she was so cute. Tasted like week-old Kentucky Fried Chicken."

"Weird," I said with a shake of my head. "So vampires in Hollywood, huh?"

"Vampires in Hollywood," Evan agreed. "Your agent's one of them, mine is too. They control a lot of the strings here."

"My agent's one of them?" I asked, thinking of all the times I had been in his office. Taylor "Bubba" Reynolds didn't strike me as the vampire type. He did, however, wear dark glasses a lot. I thought it was just because he was practicing his poker skills, but if Evan was telling the truth, it was far more nefarious.

My next thoughts were cut off with some rustling from the next room.

"Papi?" a woman asked in a sleepy voice. "Papi, where did you go?"

"Papi, I think you're being paged," I told Evan.

"Right." Evan placed his drinks on the table between us and headed for his room. Before he disappeared, he stopped and turned around. "I'll explain more. I know this is all so new and hard for you. But you're doing a good job. Just don't tell anyone what you've seen until we can talk some more and you'll be fine."

Evan disappeared into his room with a series of "Mamis" and kisses.

I was left to my own thoughts. Today had been an emotional roller coaster from the high of Tracy accepting my proposal to the insane low of hearing that Evan was a vampire. If I thought things couldn't get crazier, I'd have been wrong. Dead wrong.

FIVE

DESPITE THE MADNESS of my day, sleep came fast and deep. When I woke in the morning, a line of drool glued the side of my face to my pillow. I stretched out in my bed, lacing my hands behind my head. I stared up into the ceiling.

The truth was I loved science fiction and fantasy stories and always wished I'd be the chosen one or be involved in an explosion that would give me abilities or transported to another time. Now that I was staring the impossible in the face, I was kind of excited. Scared but excited.

I ran through my normal morning routine of checking texts and emails. My agent had scheduled the casting call for me this morning. They never gave more than a day or so warning. But it was one of the sacrifices needed to make the castings. You had to be ready whenever they called.

I walked out of my room. Evan was already gone for the day, but he left a note on our counter that read: "Don't overthink it buddy. I have an all-day shoot, but we can talk about it more tonight when I get back. You can use my toilet paper if you want. I know you said that discount brand was making your anus look like Sloth's face from the *Goonies*."

I started my coffee when I realized I still needed to call my mom and dad and tell them about Tracy.

My mother picked up on the first ring.

"John, did you ask her? Tell me how it went. I want to hear everything," my mother gushed. "Where did you do it? Was she surprised? What did she say? Did she say yes? What am I saying, of course she said yes."

My mother knew I was popping the question soon, but I hadn't given her an exact date.

"Yes, Mom, I asked her and she said yes," I said with a smile. "You're going to have a new daughter-in-law."

My mother gave off half an excited inhale and half a laugh when I told her the news.

"He did it, he did it," my mother told my father on the other end of the call. "She said yes. Tracy said yes."

"Congratulations, son!" my dad called out from the other end.

"Thanks, Dad," I shouted back.

"Oh so is this public news now?" my mother asked. "Can I tell everyone?"

"Yes, go ahead," I said. "You can tell whoever you want."

"Oh my," my mother cooed. "There's so much to plan, dates to pick, flowers and a venue. I can't wait."

This was how most of our conversations went. My mother did ninety percent of the talking and I was there to answer questions and guide us to the next topic.

"John, you know I love you, right?" My mother switched gears like a racecar driver. Her tone quieted and all the joy in her voice evaporated. "So please take this the right way. I just want you to be happy."

"What is it, Mom?" I asked. "I told you I wouldn't do any more erectile dysfunction commercials. I'm sorry you got all those concerned calls from your women's Bible study. They don't have to pray for me like that. Everything's working down there. It was just a commercial."

"No, no, it's something else," my mother reassured me. "Norma's taken you off her prayer list for that. I'm talking about Tracy. It's just that she's a sweet girl who's still searching for who she is. I just don't want you to get hurt. Are you sure she's the one?"

"Yes, of course she is," I reassured my mother. "That's why I asked her. It's already done."

"Engagement isn't marriage," my mother reminded me. "It's not too late to part ways if you decide she isn't the one. You still have a way out, you know. There are plenty of fish in the sea. Why, when your father and I started dating, I was the filly many a stallion pursued."

"If we can never use that analogy again, that would be great," I told her. "I'm sure she's the one. I know she can get busy with work and her career, but that's life."

"Okay, I just want you to be happy," my mother answered. "I won't say any more."

"Thanks, Mom," I said.

The sound of knocking at my door signaled the end of our conversation.

"I got to go, but I love you," I told her.

"We love you too," my mother replied.

"Love you, son!" my dad shouted.

I hung up the phone and walked to the door.

The door jumped from its frame with a familiar force that nearly sent it inward as another staccato of knocks echoed in my apartment.

I was just going to open the door when I thought better of it and decided to look out of the peephole. I was living in a world of vampires and other supernatural creatures if I believed Evan. After all, one couldn't be too careful.

I leaned in toward the door, closing one eye. I looked out.

Shannon stood there with her hands on her hips staring straight at me.

"Hey, I'm not getting any younger out here," Shannon yelled. "If you're in there, open up."

"Man, this chick is aggressive," I murmured to myself. I unlocked the door and swung it open with a smile. "Hey, what's up?"

"Hey, is that coffee I smell?" Shannon asked, walking into my apartment without an offer. "Your place isn't that bad, Stinky. I was picturing more of a bachelor pad with lava lamps or cliché movie posters on the wall oozing single manhood."

"Please, will you come in?" I asked sarcastically as I moved to take the *300* movie poster of screaming bare-chested Spartans off the wall. I propped it against said wall backward. "What's going on? Are you okay?"

"Oh, just peachy," Shannon said, picking up my mug of still hot coffee and breathing in deeply. "Nectar of the gods passed down from our ancient ancestors generation to generation."

"If you want some alone time with your coffee, we can have a conversation later," I told her, going to make myself another cup.

"Nah. I'm good," Shannon said after a satisfying sip. "I came over because I heard some noise last night. Like something heavy thudding on the ground. I wanted to make sure you were okay."

"Oh, are you directly below us?" I asked.

"Yep." Shannon casually walked around the apartment checking things out as she enjoyed her—previously my—coffee. "I was going to come up last night but didn't hear anything else, so I thought I'd drop in this morning."

Shannon made her way to Evan's room and the closed door in front of it.

"We're good here—yep—I mean, what did you hear? What did you think you heard?" I asked, already starting to fumble my words with my lie. "I don't remember hearing a thud. Nothing dropped, like a body or anything."

I saw her move to open Evan's door a second too late.

"Hey, that's Evan's room. I don't think—"

Shannon was already in before I could stop her.

Hurry; what if she sees something kinky or vampirish! I screamed in my head.

I ran over, expecting the worst.

Shannon stood in the middle of the room looking around. Evan's room was vastly different from my own. I didn't have a lot of extra stuff. I was all about open space and bare necessities.

Evan, on the other hand, had the coin to spare a few indulgences like a black massage chair in one corner of the room and a bed with a full canopy in the other. His closet was open, packed with clothes and shoes.

Floating shelves lined one wall jammed with pictures of himself with celebrities he met on various shoots and films.

"Wow, can't wait to meet this roommate of yours, Stinky," Shannon said, making herself at home in the massage chair. She placed her mug in the holder on the arm of the chair. "I've always wanted my own massage chair."

My eyes immediately went to the place where Evan's last victim had fallen. I remembered the stains of blood. Lucky for me, Evan had scrubbed it out of the rug the night before, but it still looked damp and smelled like chemical cleaner.

"Yeah, well, I don't think we should be snooping around his room when he's not here," I admonished. "Come on; we should go."

"You're right, you're right," Shannon agreed, flipping on the controls for the massage chair that reclined and began to whirl with the electric motor starting up. "Just one second. I always wanted to—ohhh—ohhh right there."

Shannon's eyes rolled into the back of her head as she leaned into the massage. I didn't take much notice of it before, but I realized she was wearing a pair of tight yoga pants and a tank top that was probably a size too small.

What am I doing? I asked myself as Shannon continued to moan. *I'm already spoken for. I need to get out of here. Danger, Will Robinson, danger!*

My phone went off. It was my agent, Bubba. The thought of not answering crossed my mind, but if it was about the casting today, I couldn't miss it.

"Hey, Bubba," I said, taking a step out of the room and plugging my other ear with my finger. "I got your text about the casting. I'll be there."

"Great, great to hear," Bubba answered on the other end. "Make sure you wear a plain shirt and jeans. They want that everyman plain, defeated look."

"Got it," I acknowledged, trying to close the conversation before Shannon's moans were heard. "I—"

"Oh it's so deep!" Shannon practically yelled. "Oh my gosh, yes, yes, yes!"

I could feel the heat rush to my face.

"Jonny, Jonny, are you still there?" Bubbas asked. "You have the TV on or something? A little HBO before the casting?"

"Yeah, yeah, I'm here. I got it. I'll be there, everyman kind of defeated look, got it, thank you, Bubba," I replied.

"Okay, okay," Bubba said, ending the call with, "Knock 'em dead, kid."

I hit the button, hanging up just in time to avoid Bubba hearing Shannon say, "I'm going to be over all the time if you treat me like this, you dirty massage boy."

SIX

CASTING calls in and of themselves aren't bad. Really, you just check in, then wait for your name to be called like a doctor's office. If there are any lines for you to say, there are usually handouts at the check-in table or a dry erase board with your lines on them.

The bad part of going to these castings is that it's usually a full day in traffic maneuvering your way to downtown Los Angeles.

I rumbled in my old Mustang that smelled like gasoline and grease, making my way down the freeway. My mind wandered to the events of the night before. One option was that my roommate was crazy and actually just bit the woman in some kind of warped foreplay.

But I knew that wasn't the case. I had seen his eyes and teeth change in front of me. I'd been indoctrinated to another world that lived within our own. It was kind of terrifying and a little bit exciting if I was being honest.

I couldn't wait to talk to Evan that night and find out more about who and what he was. The unknown always intrigued me and it made life a little more interesting.

I pulled into the street I was given for the casting. There was no parking lot, so I had to park on a side street a few blocks down. It wasn't in the greatest neighborhood, but that was one of the few perks of driving a car that didn't look like it could run, even if anyone did want to steal it.

"It's okay." I patted the roof of my car as I closed the squeaky door. "I still love you."

I walked down the sidewalk to the building, enjoying the warm LA weather. Construction was going on across the street and other hopefuls with stars in their eyes were making their way to and from the casting building.

The structure was one I had been to before. It wasn't anything more than an empty office building rented out by various production and casting companies to use when they had to fill roles.

The offices could be casting for Cheerios one day and the NRA the next. Likewise, one group of hopefuls could be waiting their turn to recite lines for a Disney commercial while others waited in the same room to take headshots for an Adidas campaign.

I entered the building, going to my designated office space. When I entered the large waiting room, it was exactly what I suspected. A few dozen doppelgangers welcomed me.

Some were a little shorter, some wore glasses, some packed on a few pounds, but they were all varying degrees of me. Like alternate dimensions had spit out versions of myself that got changed a bit along the process.

When a casting call went out to agents, the casting usually read something like: desired hair color, build, age range, and ethnic preference.

What stood in front of me now was no less than two dozen men all between the ages of twenty-five and forty-five, taller with dark hair and brown skin.

Some looked nervous; other veterans of the game passed time on their cell phones waiting to be called.

I went over to the receptionist to check in.

"Hi, I'm here for the hemorrhoids casting at noon," I said with a smile.

She didn't even look up.

Instead, she pointed to two clipboards on the counter in front of her.

"One's to check in and the other is for the casting agency," she said in a nasally voice as if she were a pre-recording that hadn't picked up. "Write clearly and legibly."

"Got it, thank you," I told her.

I wrote my name on one clipboard then took the other to fill out my personal information. It was all standard protocol. Listed on the questionnaire were things like my agent's contact information, my own, and wardrobe sizes for everything from shoes to hats in case I got the role.

I took a seat in the spacious waiting room, not trying to overhear the version of myself who looked like he ate steroids for breakfast along with an attractive blonde.

"No, but seriously, when I did that last commercial for Euphoria cologne, I got in real well with one of the marketing members on staff there. They're always looking for new talent. If you want in, I can drop them your name," he said, shrugging in his shirt that was two sizes too small for him. Any tighter and I think it would have qualified as a wet suit. His nipples were so hard, I was surprised they hadn't cut their way out.

"Really, you can do that?" The woman's jaw dropped, eating up every bit of what the guy was selling. "That would be great. I just got finished with a Target commercial where they asked me if I could dance. I said yes, but when I got there, it was clear I had no idea what I was doing. I made it through the casting, but I don't think they're going to be calling me back anytime soon."

"Meh, I lie all the time about what I can do just to get the jobs: play the piano, sure, I know 'Chopsticks'; do you ride a motorcycle, I can learn; speak Spanish, *yo quiero* Taco Bell."

"Oh, you're so funny." The blonde adjusted her shirt seductively.

That was enough for me. I tuned out the chatter I had become so used to hearing on these casting calls and filled out the clipboard. I returned the paper to the receptionist, who didn't even look up when I passed it off, then took a look at the lines I was going to have to say into the camera. There were only two, so I wasn't alarmed at having to remember it all.

Hi, my name's Jimmy and I've battled with anal hemorrhoids my entire life. Now, thanks to Creamasol, I don't have to anymore.

"The things we do for money, right?" a familiar voice to my left asked. "I just did an AA commercial the other day. I showed up hungover to that one. Ironic, right?"

Jack Campbell was a tall, bearded, good-looking man in his late thirties. I had been on a few shoots with him before for Coors and Honda. He was a fast-talking high-energy kind of guy with a killer rear end. His butt was the same butt you saw in every Levi billboard or poster in Walmart.

"I should've known I'd see you here," I said good-naturedly. "Aren't you getting a little too old for these roles? I thought the casting call was for someone younger."

"Hey, when I see a casting for hemorrhoids, I come running." Jack grinned as he added his name to the list. He looked around the room to all the men waiting before addressing the secretary. "How many models were they looking for to fill this ad?"

"One man and one woman," she said, looking up for the first time. "Hey, don't I recognize you?"

"Maybe. I just did a commercial for Hallmark and a billboard for a men's aftershave—"

"No, no, no, turn around," the woman said with a smile, zeroing in on his rear end. "You're the Levi butt. I'd recognize that piece of meat anywhere."

"Guilty, guilty as charged," Jack confirmed, doing a spin. "Let me fill this out and I'll get it right back to you."

"Take your time, honey." The woman licked her lips hungrily as Jack and I walked away.

"Man, you get cast for all the cool stuff," I said in admiration. "I bet you'll get this one too."

"It's all a numbers game," Jack replied with a shrug. "You just have to keep showing up to castings. The new agency I'm with hasn't hurt either. They've been booking me for all kinds of gigs. Even direct bookings."

Direct bookings were when you didn't have to go to a casting call at all. Instead, your agent got you a job with the client with just your profile pictures alone. Those were the best. Simply show up at a certain place and time and work.

"You still with Bubba and his outfit?" Jack asked, jotting down his information on the clipboard. "Nothing against him, but he doesn't have the same connections as some of the other places."

"Yeah, yeah, I'm still with him," I answered. "He did get me a direct booking to a movie last year. I was poor outcast number two in a music video with Little Ray Ray. If you pause the video two seconds in, you see my back as the camera pans by. I'm the one wearing the blanket warming my hands over the fire we built in a drum."

"Hey, work is work, but if you're looking for something else, I can always introduce you to my new agent," Jack offered, looking up from his paperwork. "I have so many gigs now, I almost passed this one up."

"Who're you with?" I asked.

"V Model Management," Jack responded. "Mr. Bloodstone's the best. They've been in business for years and they have a long list of successful clients."

Warning lights went off in my head. V Model Management was the same firm that employed Evan. He had volunteered to get me in with his agent, but I had refused. Not because I didn't want the help, but because I didn't want him to feel like I was using him for his assets. I wanted to do this on my own.

Second to that was my newfound information about vampires running the ins and outs of the Hollywood scene. Now that I knew that, V Model Management run by a Mr. Bloodstone seemed like pretty obvious tells.

"I'm good now, but I might take you up on that offer soon if things don't get better with Bubba," I told Jack. "I want to stick it out a bit longer. You know, give him a real honest chance. He's been great."

"John Hunter." A woman opened a door to our left, reading out my name from a clipboard. "John Hunter? We're ready for you."

"Here." I popped up from my seat, looking over at Jack. "Good seeing you again, Jack."

"You too. Let me know if you want that intro," Jack said, scrunching his brow as he looked at the lines we were supposed to say into the camera one more time. "Actually, I might just leave this one."

I walked into the small room. On one side was a white backdrop, on the other a cameraman and assistant, along with who I assumed was the client sitting in a leather chair.

"Great, if we can have you stand right in front of the camera, and you'll just say your lines when we're ready," the cameraman instructed.

"Got it," I told him. I moved into place rehearsing the lines in my head. *Hi, my name's Jimmy and I've battled with anal hemorrhoids my entire life. Now, thanks to Creamasol, I don't have to anymore.*

"All right, this is how we're going to do this," the cameraman instructed. "You'll say your full name, give me a pause, then repeat your lines. Ready when you are."

I cleared my throat and looked into the camera. I ignored the other four pairs of eyes on me at the moment.

"I'm John Hunter." I did my best to channel the character I thought I was supposed to portray. Some poor soul that had battled his entire life with a serious issue. "Hi, my name's Jimmy and I've battled with anal hemorrhoids my entire life. Now, thanks to Creamasol, I don't have to anymore."

"Have you ever had anal hemorrhoids, Mr. Hunter?" the client in the leather chair, an older woman with straight hair and a severe look to her eyes, asked.

"No, I can't say that I have, at least not officially diagnosed," I answered. "I've had rashes and issues down south before, but I'm not one hundred percent sure it was hemorrhoids. I did try to WebMD it, though. That was a nightmare. Some things you just can't unsee."

"Yes, be that as it may, try again, with more emotion," the woman directed. "I want to feel your grief and then jubilation at finding a product that frees your inner butterfly."

"Inner butterfly," I repeated, psyching myself up. "Okay, I got this."

Inner butterfly, inner butterfly, I repeated to myself. *You're a butterfly, free of hemorrhoids for the first time. Be free.*

"Ready when you are," the cameraman said with a laugh he tried to disguise by coughing.

"I'm John Hunter," I said, really getting into character, this time showing a man who was dejected and defeated until he found hope in the form of anal cream. "Hi, my name's Jimmy and I've battled with anal hemorrhoids my entire life. Now, thanks to Creamasol, I don't have to anymore."

SEVEN

"GIVE me a call when you get a chance," I told the voicemail on Tracy's phone. "I know you're shooting right now, but I just wanted to give you a heads-up on my casting—I think—I think I blew it again. Anyway, call me when you can."

I pressed the hang-up button on my phone and placed it on the seat next to me. My vehicle wheezed to a stop at Haven Apartments. I thought about going to the gym to relieve some stress.

Truth was, I was usually a pretty optimistic guy. After this casting, I didn't feel too hot. Like all the other castings, they don't tell you if you have the role or not right away. That phone call either comes or doesn't come in the next few days.

I made the walk to my apartment, opening the door to find Evan inside in his silk kimono. He looked up at me with a smile.

"Hey, man, how did the casting go?" Evan asked. "I bet you nailed it."

"Well, I don't know. I just don't feel great about this one," I grumbled. "I mean, I've never had anal hemorrhoids, at least not for sure, so it was really hard to get into character. I tried freeing my inner butterfly, but I'm not sure if it flew or not."

"Well, that's weird and confusing, but turn that frown upside down, little guy." Evan slapped me on the shoulder and went to the refrigerator. "I bet you did great and you're just overthinking it."

"Maybe," I allowed, catching a Yoo-hoo Evan tossed me from the open refrigerator. "Hey, I forgot to tell you, we have a new neighbor downstairs. She pretty much invited herself in and gave herself a tour of our apartment and your room."

"Oh, did she?" Evan waggled his eyebrows as he opened his own bottle of chocolaty goodness. "The joke's on her. If she brought a black light into that room, she would have never stepped foot inside. I mean, that massage chair has seen its fair share of use, if you know what I mean."

"Yes, I get it, I get it." I grimaced. "I'm also never using that chair again. She's a handful, our new neighbor Shannon, I mean."

"Can't wait to meet her." Evan tossed his head back and began to chug his drink.

"Hey, maybe it's time for me to take you up on that offer to work for V Model Management," I mused, thinking about what Jack had told me at the casting. How nice would it feel to be able to walk out of castings I didn't really want? "He said a Mr. Bloodstone owns it. That's who represents you, right?"

Evan choked on the Yoo-hoo going down his throat. It sprayed out in a brown mist all over the counter.

"Sorry." Evan coughed.

"What? I thought you offered to introduce me to your agency anyway," I asked with a raised eyebrow. "I mean, if that's not on the table anymore, I get it."

"No, no, no." Evan wiped his mouth with the back of his hand. "It's not like that. Of course the offer still stands. It's just knowing what you know now about my kind. Mr. Bloodstone is the top of the food chain around here. He's the head vamp. If you start working there with the knowledge you have, you need to be careful. You can't let anything slip that you're hip to the game."

"When did you start saying things like 'hip to the game'?" I asked with a frown.

"I know, I'm not sure why I said that." Evan shook his head. "But to answer your question, yes, of course. I'll still make the introduction; you just have to be extra cautious not to let anything slip. If they knew that you know, without being one of them, well, they'd either kill or turn you."

"That idea is still so crazy to even try and wrap my brain around," I told him. "I can't believe you're a vampire. I mean, I can because I saw it, but it's like part of my brain won't accept it. Hey, can you do that thing where your eyes go black and your teeth grow again?"

"I'm not a sideshow attraction at a circus, Jonny," Evan said with a deadpan stare. "I'm a real person too."

"Come on, Dracula," I pushed. "Just one more time. I didn't see it really well in that dark cave of wonders of yours last night."

"All right, just this once because you're my best friend." Evan stood back from the table and cleared his throat. "Here we go; don't freak out."

The familiar jingle of the *Doctor Who* theme song vibrated in my pocket.

"Whoops, hold on just a second," I said, checking the phone to see if it was either my agent or Tracy. It was Tracy. "Hey, my fiancée. How are you?"

"Hey, baby," Tracy responded, trying to shush someone in the background. "I'm good, I'm good; just a long day on set. I think I'm going to call it an early night, though. Can we hang out later? I know you wanted to see me tonight, but I just really need my full eight hours."

"Yeah, yeah, of course," I replied. "We have the rest of our lives, right? Let's hang out tomorrow when you're off."

"Okay, great," Tracy answered. "See you tomorrow."

"See you tomorrow, Tracy Coach Prada," I said. "Love you."

The phone went dead.

"Still can't believe she changed her middle and last name to Coach Prada," Evan said with a raised eyebrow. "You don't think that's a bit much?"

"People change their names all the time," I reasoned, defending her. "Besides, she'll be Tracy Coach Hunter soon enough."

"Did she even ask you how your casting went?" Evan prodded. "Did she say 'I love you' back?"

"Hey, she has a lot going on right now." I chugged the rest of my Yoo-hoo before continuing. "Besides, don't try and change the subject now. The eye and teeth thing. Let's see it."

"All right. I'm just looking out for you." Evan slapped his hands together, rubbing them vigorously before jumping up and down a few times on his toes as if he were warming up. "Here we go."

Evan's change wasn't gradual or subtle in any sense of the word. One second, pearly white teeth and baby blue eyes were looking at me. The next, completely black orbs stared in my direction. Pointed teeth filled his mouth with the canines being the most pronounced.

"Tada," Evan said with a shrug. "This is me all vampired out. What do you think?"

"I think this is crazy," I said, standing up not because I really needed to, but I felt like I needed to do something with my racing heartbeat. "How have vampires stayed hidden all these years?"

"Because whether we're good or bad, we all agree on one thing; we need to remain undetected," Evan explained. "There's only four options when we show someone who we really are. They're killed, turned, sworn in as a follower, or in my case, wake up with a sore neck and no memory."

"And then there's me," I said.

"And then there's you," Evan agreed. "You're an exception. That's why it's so dangerous for you now."

"I get that you need blood to survive, but have you tried animal blood or maybe bags of blood from a clinic?" I asked. "You know, like an all-natural substitute or something else less straight from the vein?"

"Oh, I've tried it all," Evan said, reverting back to blue eyes and straight teeth right in front of me. "They work, but I need it a lot more often. When I tap someone directly, I can be filled for a full month."

"You're like a vampire camel," I breathed out loud.

"First time I've heard that one." Evan grinned. "What are you going to do tonight?"

"Oh, I don't know, maybe play some video games or watch reruns of *Golden Girls*." I shrugged, plopping down on the sofa. "Maybe I'll get real crazy and order out."

Evan crossed his arms over his chest, pursing his lips together as if he were debating something with himself. "Come on, Cinderella, we're going out tonight. V Model Management is having an event for its models, celebrating a hundred years in business. You're coming with me as my plus one."

"I thought you said it was too dangerous for me now?" I asked. "You said Mr. Bloodstone was one of the worst."

"I'd rather you get introduced with me watching out for

you," Evan answered. "You know how you get when you start lying, all tongue tied and obvious about it."

"Who me?" I asked as if I were actually offended. "I don't do that at all. No way. I think you're thinking of someone else. I'm not like that, no way, boo boo."

"See." Evan shook his head. "You have some time to take a nap if you want and shower. We won't go out until tonight."

I took Evan's advice and passed out for a few hours. When I woke, it was a hurried dinner of whatever wasn't moldy in the refrigerator and getting dressed. I decided on one of my two suits, a blue one I had bought for a wedding years ago, brown shoes, and a white shirt.

"I'll meet you by the car," Evan called, heading out the door. "I'll grab the mail on the way."

"Right behind you," I replied. I closed and locked the door to our apartment no more than two minutes after Evan left. Our apartment had elevators, but they were always hit or miss if they worked and the stairs were closer.

I jogged down the first flight to the third floor, pausing when I heard a woman grunt and a heavy thud. Normally, I would have kept going, but I realized the sound was coming from Shannon's apartment. She said she lived right below us. Her door was open at the moment.

EIGHT

I WALKED OVER, hearing the sounds of deep exhales and thuds over and over again. I peeked in to see Shannon taking it to a punching bag like the thing owed her money.

She wore a pair of black short-shorts and a sports bra. Her hands were wrapped with black fabric so as to not rip open the skin over her knuckles.

The sounds came from her lungs when she let out a strike. The bag made the heavy thud sounds as it swung from side to side. The bag itself was supported by a large metal hook connected to the ceiling. Four heavy bolts anchored it in place.

Shannon wore her hair in a braided ponytail. Sweat trickled down her face and upper body.

"You going to just stand there, Stinky, or are you going to come and hold this bag for me?" Shannon asked without even looking at me. "Nice suit, by the way."

"Nice use of your family room," I said, walking into her apartment. "Very Rambo meets Bruce Lee meets being on some kind of government watch list."

Like our apartment, the kitchen opened to the right.

Unlike ours, the family room area had no actual furniture in it at all. It looked like some kind of makeshift gym with the punching bag in the middle and a rack of weights against the wall. Her small dining area didn't have a table at all. Instead, it was filled with boxes. What looked like the butt of a rifle stuck out of one, a sword handle out of another.

"Should I be worried about you?" I asked. "I mean, friend to friend."

"Just hold the bag, will you?" Shannon asked as she placed a left-right-left combination that resulted in the heavy bag swaying from side to side.

I was no professional fighter, but I could tell Shannon knew what she was doing. Her movements were well-placed, her balance perfect, and when she hit the bag, it moved.

I stood on the other side of the black bag, holding it in place for her. My eyes drifted up to the ceiling once more where she had anchored the bag. "Mr. Hyde's going to be pissed that you drilled into the ceiling."

"He can take it out of my deposit," Shannon said, slamming her right fist into the bag so hard, I felt a tremor of force ripple through the bag and into my body. "Where are you going all dressed up? Out on a date?"

"No, not with the fiancée tonight," I told her. "I'm going out to a party with my roommate."

Immediately, Shannon's focus broke. She stopped staring at the bag and looked over at me. "Evan?"

"Yep, Evan and I are heading out," I told her, not surprised she was interested in my good-looking roommate. Although now that I knew he was a vampire, I wondered if I should be more selective in introducing women to him. "It's kind of a work thing."

"What kind of work do you do?" Shannon asked, going over the kitchen counter where a water bottle and towel waited for her. "Are you a salesman or something?"

"No, I'm a model," I answered. "Well, struggling model-actor."

Shannon took a long draw from her water bottle, looking me up and down like a piece of meat she might throw in the oven or not. "I can see that."

I felt uncomfortable being weighed in her mind. I looked over to her open door.

"If you're going to go all Creed in your apartment, that's your business, but you should really close your door. You're going to freak out your neighbors," I told her. "I'm not sure how they do things where you're from, but in North Hollywood, we keep our doors closed."

"Air conditioning sucks," Shannon commented with a shrug. "In the Midwest, we leave our doors open all the time."

"What do you do?" I asked, looking around at the place again. "I'm guessing interior decorator is out of the question."

"Personal trainer," Shannon shared, directing the conversation somewhere else when she caught me eyeing the boxes again. "But you better get going, Mr. Engaged. We don't want you to miss your big party."

"Right," I told her, eyeing the open door again. "I would insist that you keep your door closed, but something tells me you'd be just fine if you had an unwanted guest."

"A girl can handle herself," Shannon said, winking at me. "But seriously, tomorrow, me, you, and Evan should all get together. Bring the fiancée too. A new city can be lonely."

"For sure I'll check their schedules," I told her, showing myself out the door.

The cool night air brushed against me as I headed out to meet Evan in the parking lot. It was dark now and the city of Los Angeles was just coming to life.

Evan's car looked like it didn't belong at our apartment

complex at all, maybe not even the entire block. His new black BMW practically glimmered underneath the parking lights.

Evan sat in the driver's seat going through our mail with the window rolled down. He looked up when he saw me. "I was about to send out a search party for you."

"Sorry, got caught up with that new neighbor I was telling you about," I said.

"Oh right." Evan waggled his brows. "Shannon."

I walked over to the passenger side and opened the door. Leather seats greeted me in a comfortable embrace. The air conditioning in the car was on low with the Bad Boys theme song thumping in the background.

"Although now I'm not so sure if I should introduce you to girls," I said honestly. "I mean, if you're going to just do your vampire thing on them. Am I assisting in some kind of crime?"

"I'm just doing what I need to survive," Evan answered, looking down at a piece of mail with a shake of his head. "Why do they keep sending me mail addressed to a Shayne Silvers? I've returned to sender a dozen times and I still keep getting someone else's mail. Like I'm trying to be a productive citizen over here and it's just one thing after the other."

We clipped on our seat belts and headed out for the night. Like most nights, traffic was heavy. It took us half an hour to get to a nightclub called After Hours where the party was being held.

Evan ignored the valet, choosing to park his own car. He was particularly picky where he chose to park his ride. Unluckily for me, Evan was the type to park farther away from other vehicles in order to avoid nicks and scratches.

That meant in this massive parking lot, we were a good city block away from the entrance to the nightclub.

That was when my nerves started to kick in.

Should you really be doing this? I asked myself. *Knowingly going to where there are other vampires that—that kill people? How badly do you want to make it as a model? What are you willing to do and not do?*

These and more questions forced their way into my mind as we exited the vehicle.

"I got you, buddy," Evan said to me over the roof of the car. "Trust me, it's better you do this with your best friend to guide you than by yourself. If you're serious about being in this industry, it was bound to happen sooner or later."

"All I'm saying is my drug dealer and I are going to have to have a serious talk." A pair of hard-looking men walked by Evan's car. "He stiffed me on the last buy and now he wants to charge double."

The other man caught sight of us and jerked his chin our way.

I couldn't tell if the pair were homeless or this was the latest fashion trend to hit the street. One could never tell in LA. Both men wore baggy clothes that looked as though they'd seen better days. One had tattoos creeping up his neck, the other crooked gold teeth that looked like they were throwing gang signs at me.

"Hey, nice ride," the man with the neck tattoos who had been talking about his drug dealer addressed Evan. "How much one of those cost you? I bet I could get me one of those cheaper than you got yours."

"Highly doubtful, my friend," Evan said, stepping up to the man with a smile. "I got this one at a steep discount. The power of negotiating with cold hard cash."

"Yeah, I could use a little cash about now," the thug said with a smile of his own. He reached in his waistband, pulling out a knife. "Why don't you hand me the keys and you won't have to bleed out in this parking lot."

Evan looked at me with a raised eyebrow.

"Hey, man, we don't want any trouble," I said, rounding my side of the car to back up Evan. The other thug stepped in my way, blocking me from being able to offer aid.

I had never really been a fighter. I mean, a few school yard fights in middle school and bullying in high school, but that was about it. I wasn't sure what kind of weapon the thug with the golden teeth in front of me carried but he also reached behind his back.

"No, no, no." Evan waved me away. "Jonny, I got this. I didn't tell you that along with my special diet comes certain physical perks. I don't need the help, but thank you."

"What're you talking about, you pale stick figure?" The thug in front of Evan grabbed his attention by waving the knife in front of his eyes. "Give me your keys. You stupid or something?"

I tracked the knife along with Evan. It was a short blade, serrated on one end and smooth on the other. I'm sure it had a name, but I was no knife expert. I had a Swiss army knife once. My dad gave it to me one Christmas. I cut my thumb on it the same day testing the blade.

"I don't usually give warnings or second chances," Evan told the man as he searched the parking lot for witnesses. The closest people were far enough away not to notice. They were probably already drunk or high and facing the opposite way as they parked and headed away from us toward the nightclub. "But Jonny's already been through a harsh revelation in the past twenty-four hours. I don't want him to have to see more."

"Peso, we should get going, man," the thug in front of me said nervously. "This is taking too long."

"I'm going to enjoy cutting you, you privileged piece of sh—"

I watched in slow motion as Peso lunged at Evan. I moved

forward to help, but I was stopped at the front of the car while Evan was on the driver side.

Evan moved so fast, he was a blur. One second, Peso was lunging for him; the next, he was caught looking at his thug counterpart, the blade of his own knife in his friend's stomach.

Both thugs shared my same expression as we all looked at one another for answers we didn't possess.

"Pe—Peso, what th—what the hell, man." Peso's friend sank to his knees, gripping his stomach. "Why—you stabbed me?"

Peso's mouth was open in shock. In a second, he had been turned around, moved a few feet over, and his hand forced to stab his friend. Evan stood by me, shaking his head.

"Real friends don't stab their friends in the middle of a robbery in questionable night club parking lots," Evan tsked by my side. "Shame, I hope that knife blade was clean. Tetanus is nothing to joke about."

I looked at Evan, still trying to process what happened. I'd seen him. At least I thought I did. My eyes were still trying to catch up with what my brain told me had happened.

"Oh man, oh man," Peso groaned, pulling the knife free with a spurt of blood.

"You should run now while you still have legs to take you," Evan said, his eyes going black and teeth elongating. "I'm getting tired of trying not to kill you."

"Oh! Oh snap!" the one who had been stabbed yelled in panic, trying to get to his feet and run.

"Sweet Mary protect me!" Peso yelled, backpedaled, and fell over his friend. Both men went down in a tangled mess before helping each other up and making a run from the parking lot.

"Sweet Mary?" Evan shrugged, reverting back to his

normal human-looking state. "That's a new one on me. You think he was Catholic or something?"

"No idea," I said, still half shocked myself at how fast Evan moved, how smooth he seemed in a deadly situation where most people would have frozen or panicked. "How fast are you?"

"Probably twice as fast as the normal human." Evan shrugged like it was nothing. "A little stronger too and I can heal at an incredible rate. Perks of the affliction. It's not the first time I've been in a dangerous situation. I mean, come on we live in North Hollywood, I'm driving a BMW. Plus, I'm super old, remember? I've seen and been through a lot. Hey, were you about to get stabbed for me?"

"I mean, that wasn't the plan. I like my spleen where it's at, but I wasn't going to let you fight off those guys by yourself," I said, feeling the surge of adrenaline ease.

"That's why you're one of the good ones, Jonny." Evan slapped me on the shoulder and jerked his head toward the rhythmic bumping of the music coming from the club. "Come on; let's go. I have some vampires to introduce you to."

NINE

THE CLUB DOORS were guarded by three large men dressed in black suits. Each man looked like he wanted to hurt me. A line of men and women stood down the side of the building penned in by steel stands and red velvet rope.

For some reason, the image of a herd of cattle hit me as I looked at the girls in their short skirts and the guys with too much gel in their hair, waiting in their pen to get in.

Excited chatter sounded from those gathered as the bumping trance music from inside teased at them with promises of ecstasy and freedom.

Evan bypassed the line altogether, making his way to the largest bouncer.

The man was a mountain, easily a head taller than I was and a good eighty pounds heavier. In a different life, he could have started as the center for the Seattle Seahawks.

"Tiny, what's up, my man?" Evan went over to him without pause and raised a friendly hand in greeting. "I didn't know you were going to be working tonight."

The man named Tiny didn't bother to return the greeting. Instead, all six foot six of him reared up and scowled at Evan.

"You have a lot of nerve coming back here after what you pulled last time," Tiny growled.

Everyone within earshot quieted. The other bouncers behind Tiny looked up, ready to step in at a moment's notice.

For the second time that night, a rush of adrenaline hit my system. I was all about being loyal to my friend, but Evan wasn't making it easy.

"Tiny, Tiny," Evan crooned, extending both arms wide. "I didn't know she was your sister. I swear. And I treated her with nothing but respect. You can believe me when I say that."

Tiny curled his hands into fists, looking Evan up and down before cracking a smile. "She said you took care of her, made sure she got home safe. Thanks for that."

I let out a long sigh of air I didn't know I was holding.

With the promise of a fight no longer on the table, those in line went back to their conversations. The other bouncers stepped back and returned to their work.

"Come here." Tiny clapped Evan's hand with his own and brought him in for a one-armed hug. "Who's your friend?"

"Oh, this is my roommate, John, Jonny Hunter," Evan introduced me. "Jonny, this is Tiny."

"Good to meet you, Tiny," I greeted, extending a hand.

Tiny's hand was more like a paw, his grip crushing.

"Any friend of Evan's is a friend of mine." Tiny flashed a smile. "He's been coming here since even before my time and I've been here for a while myself."

"Big group today?" Evan asked, trying to change the subject. He eyed the number of people still in line waiting to get in the club.

"Oh yeah, there's a large private party tonight," Tiny answered, producing a pair of neon green wristbands for us. "A lot of coin. They reserved all the tables. You two are good to go in."

"You're the man," Evan said.

"Thank you," I stated over the noise inside the club as one of the other bouncers opened the doors for us.

Tiny nodded.

Inside After Hours, the lights were dimmed with laser displays sweeping their way across the floor and up the walls and ceiling in sporadic motions. The dance floor was packed with people about to make bad decisions. A massive square bar rested in the center of the room.

It was shoulder-to-shoulder standing room only as soon as we stepped in. Bouncers dressed in all black with earpieces tried to keep walkways clear, but there were just too many people.

Evan, apparently having been a regular here, knew the way to the private VIP section of the club. He jerked his chin to me and began maneuvering his way through the press of people like some kind of salmon swimming upstream.

"Excuse me, sorry, excuse me, pardon me," I said with every step as we made our way to the left of the building and up a short flight of stairs. I shouted to Evan's back "This place is crazy!"

"You haven't seen anything yet," Evan said with a twinkle in his eye. "Come on, they're up here."

We finally made it to a second-story room overlooking the dance floor with a railing that reminded me of a balcony. Another pair of bouncers stood here and checked our wrist-bands before we were permitted to enter.

When we were finally allowed into the private area, I decided Evan was right. I hadn't seen anything yet.

White tables were set up in the expansive second story with ice sculptures and so much food and booze, I wondered how the tables could hold it all. A private bartender stood behind a bar at the corner, serving drinks like some kind of wizard.

There was actually room to walk around as a few dozen beautiful people chatted away. Even the music was dampened in this room so you could actually have a conversation.

"Come on, I'll make some introductions." Evan waved me to join him.

I followed him through the room as he exchanged waves and smiles with faces he recognized. I got a few sideways glances myself but nothing unwelcoming, more curious.

Some of the faces I thought I recognized from billboards and commercials I'd seen.

"Hey, is that Jon Hamm?" I asked with my mouth open. I knew it was, but I still had to ask.

"Yep, he's not one of us but runs in the same circles," Evan explained, waving to the actor, who returned the gesture with a smile of his own.

I was just getting the sense that maybe this was a bad idea when my imposter syndrome went into high gear. I didn't belong here. This was a place for the elite. I had no business stepping into this room. What if they found out? What if they knew I was trying to make ends meet doing whatever jobs I could take? What if they could smell the chicken suit on me?

We passed beautiful face after beautiful face and a woman I thought was Ellen DeGeneres. I didn't want to confirm her identity with Evan. If he responded in the affirmative, then I was really going to freak out.

At the back of the room was a series of booths set into the wall. An older heavyset man with thin hair sat in the largest of these booths with a woman half his age draped over each arm.

"Evan." The man smiled as we approached. "How goes it? I heard you're nailing that new Amazon commercial we have you on."

"Always grateful for the work, Mr. Bloodstone," Evan replied.

"Evan, how many times have we talked about this? You can call me Winston." Winston turned to the dark-haired beauty on his right who had to be high on some kind of drug with sunken eyes and a flush across her skin. He whispered something in her ear. She giggled nervously.

"I just wanted to thank you for all the work and introduce you to a friend of mine." Evan stepped to the side and motioned to me like some kind of prize up for grabs on a game show. "This is John Hunter. He's an up and comer at the moment."

Winston Bloodstone looked up from the young woman and eyed me curiously.

"Haven't we met before?" Winston asked.

"No, no, I don't think we have, Mr. Bloodstone," I said, reaching across the table with an extended hand and what I hoped wasn't a nervous but approachable and friendly smile.

Don't screw this up, don't screw this up, I yelled to myself in my head. *This can be your big shot. Just make a good impression.*

"No, I'm sure I have," Mr. Bloodstone returned, accepting my hand and pumping it before letting it go.

His hands were cold and clammy. I had to force myself not to wipe my palm on my pants leg.

"He looks like that guy on the Life Alert commercial," the cute redhead on the other side of Mr. Bloodstone's arm cooed. "You know, he steps in because his mother's fallen and can't get up."

"Oh, right, right!" Mr. Bloodstone cackled, throwing his head back to the ceiling. "You're the Life Alert guy! I always thought in that commercial your pretend mother looks a little too happy she's getting help from you."

"Yeah, she was kind of frisky in the dressing room too," I replied with a shudder. "She kept on calling me 'sweet cheeks' and asking me to bend over to pick things off the ground."

Mr. Bloodstone got a good one out of that. His belly shook with laughter like some kind of dark interpretation of Santa Claus.

"I like you, John," Mr. Bloodstone said after his laughter subsided. "What agency are you with?"

"I'm with Bubba from—"

"Bubba," Mr. Bloodstone interrupted me with an eye roll. "Please, that guy's a bottom feeder. Come work for me. I'll have one of my assistants contact you for the paperwork and we'll start booking you on shoots next week. You've got a good complexion, strong fit kid. You'll do well."

I didn't know what to say. I was sweating because I was so nervous. Was it really that easy? All I needed to do was make him laugh with a few minutes of conversation and he was willing to take me in and give me work?

"Um, yeah, thank—thank you, Mr. Bloodstone," I stammered, trying to find the right words. "That would be great."

Mr. Bloodstone looked over my shoulder at someone approaching. He actually got up from his seat for whoever it was.

"Awww, and there they are, the newest power couple in Hollywood," Mr. Bloodstone said, opening his arms in welcome for whoever it was.

I turned in time to see Tracy, my Tracy, walking toward the table arm in arm with her co-star Brad Connolly.

My face must have said it all. A look of panic washed over Tracy's before she quickly recovered. Her eyes never left mine.

"Tracy, Brad." Mr. Bloodstone moved from his seat and embraced them both. "So glad you could both make it. Please grab a drink."

"I'm only interested in one kind of drink tonight." Brad

eyed the two young girls in the booth, who stared at him starstruck. "If you know what I mean."

"Of course, of course," Mr. Bloodstone cackled. "There'll be plenty of time for that later. Tell me about the shoot."

The two men continued to talk, but their conversation was lost to me.

I locked eyes with Tracy, my gaze making its way down to her left ring finger. She wasn't wearing her ring.

TEN

"JONNY." Evan put his hand on my shoulder.

"I'm good, I'm good," I said as my right eye started to twitch. "I'm fine, perfectly fine. Why wouldn't I be fine?"

"What are you doing here?" Tracy asked, sidling up to me with a nervous smile.

"What am I doing here?" I repeated, trying to keep my voice down. "You said you had to go to bed early tonight. Where's your ring?"

"I uh—I uh, I forgot it," Tracy answered. "I can't wear it on set and forgot to put it back on."

"You are a horrible person and Jonny deserves better," Evan stated, giving Tracy a deadpan stare. "Seriously, you're the seed of Satan as far as I'm concerned."

"Can we just talk about what's going on here privately?" Tracy pleaded, ignoring Evan. She walked away from us toward the balcony of the second-story VIP lounge.

"You deserve better, buddy," Evan said with a shrug.

I felt numb. I'm not sure if it was loyalty or love or something else that made me follow Tracy to the opposite side of the room where the music was louder and we could see the dance floor below thanks to the wide balcony.

Seal, the singer not the animal, was in the corner talking to Terry Crews. They were both laughing and having a good time. If I wasn't so confused at the moment, I would have been starstruck again.

"Why did you lie to me about staying in tonight?" I asked Tracy.

"Listen, the most important thing is that we don't make a scene, okay?" Tracy said, turning to me with a stiff stare. "I've worked really hard to get to this point and I don't want you to screw it up."

"Me?" I asked incredulously. "Why don't you just answer the first question? Why did you lie to me about staying in tonight? You could have just told me the truth. And why are you walking arm in arm with Brad Connelly? Is that just some kind of show promo thing?"

"I just don't think there's room for a lot in my life right now," Tracy huffed. "Things are just moving so fast and I thought you'd want to come with me tonight if I came to the party."

"So you're just ashamed of me like I'm some kind of pimple!?" I don't know why I used that analogy. Or why at that exact moment the one song cut out before the next began.

Everyone in our immediate vicinity looked over at us. I could feel heat rise in my face.

"Hey, is everything okay over here?" Brad Connelly walked up, looking at Tracy and then back to me. "Tracy, is this man giving you a hard time?"

"No, no, it's fine, Bradley," Tracy reassured. "I'm fine."

"Yeah, Bradley," I added. "We're fine. I'm Tracy's fiancé, by the way. Nice to meet you."

"Fiancé?" Brad looked at Tracy, confused, before looking

back at me. “She never mentioned you. Never even said she had a boyfriend. I don’t want to make you feel bad, but I didn’t even know you existed.”

“You can’t just say, ‘I don’t mean to make you feel bad’ and then say whatever you want,” I growled. “Because you did hurt my feelings, Bradley.”

“I just need a minute,” Tracy said, placing her hand on Brad’s chest. “Just give me a minute.”

“Okay, I’ll be right over here if you need me,” Brad said, giving me a confused look of recollection. “Hey, don’t I know you from somewhere? I mean, not through Tracy—she’s avoided talking about you like the plague apparently—but you look familiar to me for some reason. Aren’t you the—”

“Yes, yes, I’m the Life Alert guy,” I said, doing my best to remain under control and calm.

“No, no, I wasn’t going to say that.” Brad pursed his lips. “Erectile dysfunction, right? Yeah, that’s where I know you from. You did that erectile dysfunction campaign. Well, I can see why Tracy wouldn’t talk about you.”

A group of gorgeous people to our right erupted into laughter at hearing Brad’s comment. Flashbacks of my high school experience hit me like a bucket of cold water. In my twenties, I only had to deal with imposter syndrome and rejection, but now PTSD from the years of being bullied reared its ugly head like some macabre zombie long dead.

After the laughter died down, Brad backed out of the conversation, going over to a young woman with a dress two sizes too small and a drink in her hand that looked like it weighed more than her.

I turned back to Tracy, who was scrolling through her phone.

“Are you seriously checking your Instagram right now?” I asked in disbelief. “I’m trying to have a serious conversation with you here.”

"See, that's what you don't get." Tracy gave me an eye roll. "I'm a working actress now. I have to connect with my audience twenty-four/seven. I think I just need some space, Jonny, honestly."

I closed my eyes, taking a deep breath. The last thing I wanted to do was take a break, especially when we just got engaged. Something tickled the back of my mind, something important. It hit me like a lightning bolt.

"Tracy, I didn't know you were getting in with V Model Management," I said, getting in close and talking directly in her ear. "You need to be careful. These—these people aren't what you think they are."

I hesitated there. Should I tell her everything? Would she even believe me?

"I told you it is the erectile dysfunction guy." Brad came back with a group this time that included John Cena and Adam Driver. "See, he's here, I wasn't just imagining it."

More laughter erupted from the group. I looked back at Tracy, about to ask her if we could go outside or somewhere else to talk. Before I could begin, she shook her head.

"I just need some time, Jonny," she said, putting her phone back in her small black purse. "We can talk about this tomorrow, please?"

All of a sudden, I felt like I was in the wrong here. Tracy looked at me, begging me with her eyes not to make a scene. That was the last thing I wanted.

"Come on," Evan called, pushing his way through the crowd gathering around us. He leaned into my ear. "She'll be safe; they aren't going to kill her. We should go before this becomes a larger issue."

"Okay, okay," I said, allowing myself to be led away by Evan.

I followed him out of the VIP room down the flight of steps and outside. I felt like I couldn't breathe. My head was spinning and I was sweating. I didn't even know what to make out of everything that had just transpired.

Are you wrong about all of this? I asked myself. *Do you need to give her space? She is the one, though, right? We two love each other. Is this just something all couples go through?*

"Sorry about that." Evan sighed. "I mean, I didn't do anything wrong. I've been a great friend, but I can't imagine how you feel. I'm sorry Tracy did that to you. You want to go get a drink or something? We can—"

"Yeah, yeah, I think I need a drink or twenty," I answered.

A short ride later, Evan and I were parking at a dive bar close to our apartment called Bad Decisions.

I'd never been to the bar myself, but I'd seen it before. Unlike the club, this place was more of a local's joint off the freeway. Rock music played and the dark lit room smelled like cigar smoke and alcohol.

The place was about half filled with people joking and laughing. The crack of a pool stick on a ball snapped me back into the moment.

Evan had been uncharacteristically quiet on the way to the bar. I wasn't sure if he felt responsible at all, but I just didn't have it in me at the moment to try and make small talk.

Evan found us a place on the far side of the bar. A curvy bartender came over to us with a grin. "What can I get you two?"

"What's the strongest drink you have?" Evan asked as if this were a question he was used to asking. Before the bartender could respond, he held up four fingers. "We'll take four and keep them coming."

"You got it." The bartender looked over at me with a frown. "Is your friend going to be okay? He looks like he just got hit in the balls."

"More like his heart got kicked in its tiny heart balls,"

Evan said, slapping a credit card down on the bar top. "Like I said, keep them coming."

"Oh, got it." The bartender gave me a look that I hated. A look I had seen before by so many bullies in high school. The look that said, "I'm sorry you're such a loser. You have my pity."

She went to work pouring god knew what into four glasses.

"You don't have to pay for all of it," I told Evan, snapping out of my dazed state long enough to reach into my pocket. "I should have enough to pay for my own."

"Stop." Evan pushed my hand and the offered credit card away.

"Stop what?" I questioned.

"Stop trying to always do the nice or right thing and just let me do something nice for you," Evan said, motioning to the glasses the bartender placed in front of us. "Now bottoms up, little guy. You'll feel better after you get a few of these into your system."

"Do I want to know what's in this?" I asked the bartender as I picked up the first glass.

"Do you want me to be honest or do you want me to tell you that you want to know what I put in there?" the bartender asked me with an upturned eyebrow.

"Never mind." I shook my head.

"Cheers to forgetting about tonight and a harsh hangover tomorrow." Evan clinked his glass against mine. "And, hey, at least the music in here's decent. I think that's some Beastie Boys playing now."

I took down the drink like the pro I was not. It felt like pure fire draining down my throat. I couldn't help but cough as I grimaced and slammed the cup down on the counter.

"Woooo!" Evan shouted beside me, draining his own.

"That'll put hair on your chest. Let's do another. I'm really digging the upbeat vibe of this pl—"

"I Will Always Love You" by Whitney Houston blared over the speakers as I started to feel the lightheaded effects of the first drink.

"Oh great!" I shouted. "How do they even have a song like that in a place like this? This is Tracy's and my song!"

"Less talking and more drinking." Evan shoved another glass into my hand. "I don't want to hear another word about Tracy until you have this in your system."

I took down the second drink and the third and maybe fourth before things started to get hazy. I remembered some kind of drive-through and fast food coupled with stumbling in and out of Evan's car with his help.

There was definitely vomit at some point and I was back at our apartment and then finally bed. I fell into my bed dead to the world. I wish that could have been the end of the night for me, but my subconscious had other plans. It was time for me to relive the events of my nightmarish high school experience all over again.

ELEVEN

"COME ON, JONNY," my mother called from my bedroom door. "You're going to be late for your bus. I have to leave for work in a few minutes and I want to make sure you're awake."

"Hmmm—what?" I mumbled. "I don't think we should feed the beaver ice cream all night."

"What?" My mother almost laughed. "Jonny, come on. Wake up."

"Oh, sorry, Mom. I'm up, I'm up," I said, sitting straight up in bed and rubbing sleepy eyes.

"How late did you stay up last night?" My mother raised an eyebrow. "Hold on. I take that back. I don't want to know. Just make better decisions. All those video games and such little sleep isn't going to do you any favors during the day."

"I know, I know," I said, throwing off the covers and swinging my legs out of bed.

"Oh." My mother turned to leave then hesitated. "You might want to skip a shower this morning. We've had trouble with the hot water. It's going to be turned back on today."

I was about to complain then bit my tongue. I knew my

parents were trying their best. Saying anything right now wouldn't help and only serve to make my mother feel worse.

"Okay, okay, thanks for letting me know," I told her as I shoved my legs into my only jeans. A used pair of Converse and a simple white shirt with the GI Joe logo rounded out my clothing for the day.

I shoved my schoolbooks into a tattered backpack and headed to the bathroom to brush my teeth and see what I could do about my hair.

When I got there, I didn't even recognize the person staring at me in the mirror. Puberty had not been kind and that was putting it mildly.

Acne crossed my cheeks and forehead as if it were caught in a holy war with my face. I badly needed braces, but at the moment, there just wasn't money for that. I wore thick glasses and had managed to put on a good forty pounds thanks to all the sedentary video game time and lack of motivation.

I remembered that adorable little kid stealing teachers' hearts growing up. What happened to him?

"High school and puberty happened to him," I said out loud to the version of myself in the mirror as I spat out the peppermint suds. "Life can be so cruel."

I finished up in the bathroom, washing my face as best I could and brushing my long hair. Looking back, I didn't really know what I was thinking with the long hair. I was going through some ancient Spartan phase, thinking it would make me look cool or tough or something.

I bounded down our rickety stairs to the pantry. Wooden boards creaked underneath my feet as I grabbed my favorite sugary cereal, Taffy Clouds, and poured a double serving into a bowl.

My mother was on her way out the door.

"Jonny, your father will be home late tonight and so will I.

If we miss dinner, there's some soda in the fridge and a frozen pizza you can put in the microwave." My mother came over and planted a kiss on my head. "Have a great day at school, my dear."

"Thanks, Mom, love you," I said.

"Love you too." My mother gave me a wink and a smile that brightened up the entire house before she left.

I opened the fridge to discover there was no milk. It looked like water or soda were my two options unless I wanted to eat the cereal dry.

"I like cereal," I justified in my head. "I like soda. How bad can it be?"

I reached for a can of Orange Explosion that boasted twice the amount of normal sugar on the label and poured it all over my bowl of Taffy Clouds. I brought my bowl back to the table and went to town.

"Not that bad," I said out loud. It seemed these days I was talking to myself out loud more and more. I wasn't sure if that was a good thing or not.

I noted the digital clock on our oven. If I was going to make the bus, I'd have to finish my bowl of diabetes quickly. Slamming spoon after spoon of fizzing sugar into my mouth, I felt it was a shame no one was around to witness my speed-eating record in effect.

I placed the bowl in the sink and ran out the door. The morning air was crisp, making me think I should run back for a sweater, but I had come too far. Plus, just with the run from my front door to the sidewalk, I was already winded. I still had another block to run if I was going to catch the bus.

I hustled down the block just as the bus turned a corner and came into view. Breathing was difficult. The characters in my video game always made running look so calm and effortless.

I huffed to a stop as I waited my turn with the other kids

to get on board. For a freshman, the bus ride was always a crap shoot. Sometimes no one said anything to me, other times I was dragged into some kind of joke or bullying experiment.

"Hey, hey, Jonny." My one and only friend Dillon sidled up next to me. "Hey, you have a little soda or spit or something on your second chin, right there."

"Oh, thanks," I said, still trying to catch my breath. I was feeling lightheaded from my run, my chest tight with the exertion.

"You going to pass out or something?" Dillon asked. "I've told you not to try and run before. Physical activity of any kind is dangerous for people like you and me. We're supposed to be the ones behind the computers taking calls or something."

Dillon was my same age but taller and skinnier, which was really frustrating since we ate pretty much the same thing. Well, I wasn't sure how much cereal and soda he was consuming, but I had been with the guy as we downed bags of chips and energy drinks.

Dillon was my only friend after moving to the area. We shared the same interests, and if it wasn't for him, I'm not sure if going to school would have been bearable at all.

"Hey, did you get the latest DLC for *Quest of Champions?*" Dillon asked as we boarded the bus. "I just downloaded it last night, and let me tell you, the ultimate versions of the heroes are super overpowered. I mean, it's like Darth Vader taking on Bilbo Baggins. No offense to Tolkien intended, I love Middle Earth and elves are hot, but it's just not fair."

Dillon had the unnatural gift of projecting his voice at the worst times. We walked down the narrow aisle of seats, passing girls I knew I'd never have a chance with but still didn't want to ruin my reputation even if I had one.

Most girls didn't even look our way or know we existed,

for that matter. The ones who did look up from their phones just rolled their eyes or grimaced before looking back down.

"Elves and hobbits are the best," a voice mimicked Dillon from our left. "I dream about them at night. Oh no not my no, no spot!"

I didn't have to look up to know what section of the bus we had crossed into. Traveling down the bus toward our seats meant we had to pretty much take the one ring to Mount Doom if we were still using Lord of the Rings analogies.

The front of the bus were the popular clicks, your cheerleaders, hot girls, and cool kids, the middle were the jocks, rebels, and goths, and the back was reserved for nerds, outcasts, and this one kid named Billy who always smelled like old cheese for some reason and wanted to talk about politics.

The voice mocking Dillon at the moment came from Eric Ortiz. I wasn't really into football, so I wasn't sure what position he played, but I knew he was big and popular around the jocks.

"Actually, I do not get aroused by elves," Dillon corrected him. "I'm more into the amazon women if you get my drift. You know, a little Diana of Themescura, am I right? Say what? Give me some."

Dillon extended a hand for a high five toward Eric.

Eric grimaced at us both like he tasted something foul in his mouth.

"Whatever, freak," Eric said with an evil glimmer in his eye. Instead of giving Dillon a high five, he balled his hand into a fist and slammed it into Dillon's unsuspecting hand. "Get to the back of the bus with your kind and shut your stupid mouth."

The punch landed with an audible smack.

Pain exploded across Dillon's face as he recoiled his hand to his chest.

"Hey!" I yelled, pulling Dillon back. "You didn't have to do that."

The bus lurched forward. Our large bus driver Mrs. Salmon looked in the rearview mirror. "Hey, you kids sit down! Don't make me pull this bus over again because I will and there'll be hell to pay. I didn't have my coffee this morning and you know Mrs. Salmon needs her coffee to act right in the head. I'm feeling a little unstable right now and I will bust a cap in a teen if I have to, you feel me?"

Eric gave me another wicked smile but didn't say anything. All his buddies around him were laughing at us and the painful expression on Dillon's face.

"You heard her, pimple face," one of the other jocks taunted me. "Go sit your poor tubby gut down."

I guided Dillon to the back right where we usually sat. My friend was flexing his hand, opening his palm and closing it over and over again.

"It hurts, but I don't think anything's broken." Dillon pressed on the joints of his wounded hand. "You think maybe I have adamantium or something? I mean, he hit me pretty hard and I'm all right. Maybe I should have Miss Turly check me out when I get to school."

"How many times have you been to see Miss Turly already this year?" I asked Dillon with an eye roll. "It's going to start getting weird."

"I don't know. I don't track my love journeys to her," Dillon said as if he were offended. "Don't judge me."

"I'm not judging anyone," I said, pursing my lips. "I'm just wondering how it's going to work. She's probably triple your age."

"Love has no age, my close-minded friend," Dillon reassured me. "The bond we share for one another is timeless and plentiful."

"The love you share for each other?" I asked. "Does she know she loves you too?"

"Not yet, but she will." Dillon gave me a knowing smile. "It's just a matter of time before I break through the walls she's set for herself."

"You kind of sound like a stalker," I told my friend. "I'm not sure if this relationship or lack thereof is healthy for you."

"The heart wants what the heart wants, my young padawan learner." Dillon sighed, then perked up as he remembered something. "Hey, did you bring your four bucks so we can go to the party?"

"I did, but are you sure it's a good idea?" I asked him. "I mean, you just got punched on the bus. If we go to a party, these guys are sure to be there and things could get worse."

"Naw, adamantium bones, right?' Dillon reassured me. "It'll be great and good for us to get out. My mother keeps telling me I need to spend more time away from the computer screen, and to be honest, I think she's right. You know, like two Pokémon trainers on an adventure into the unknown."

If I had known how the rest of the day was going to go, I would have never stepped foot off of the bus.

TWELVE

SCHOOL WAS PRETTY MUCH JUST a repeat of life on the bus, only on a larger scale. I tried to be inconspicuous as I walked down the halls. Making eye contact with anyone was a serious no-no.

Head down, I traveled from one class to the next with Dillon talking about the latest sci-fi movie or fantasy game. If I could keep this up for three and a half more years, maybe I would be able to get through high school alive.

True to his word, Dillon insisted on seeing Miss Turly before lunch.

"Come on, man, just come with me," Dillon urged. "I'll be in and out in a few minutes. I just want to go in and say hi and let her check on my hand. She won't admit it, but she misses me. And then we'll go pay for the party."

"The things I do for you," I said with a sigh. "Just don't get all awkward again around her. It makes me feel ten times more weird when you do all that lovey-dovey stuff."

"You should take notes," Dillon said, opening his backpack and extending a book in my direction. "I've been reading a book called *Love Language,* and it's seriously chock full of great information. I'll let you borrow it. Who knows? At the party, you might find someone."

"Unlikely," I told him as we reached the nurse's office.

"Your loss," Dillon said, placing the worn book back in his bag and opening the door.

The nurse's office was probably one of the nicest places in the rundown school. Clean with bright white lights and a white countertop, it was a room I visited probably too often between my asthma and being dragged along with Dillon for what he called his "love visits."

"Hello, my darling," Dillon crooned to Miss Turly, who sat behind the counter. "I have returned."

Miss Turly was an older woman with a slight hitch in her gait and a fake left eye that always pointed in the wrong direction. At times, I had trouble remembering which was her real eye and which was the prosthetic.

"Dillon, we've talked about this," Miss Turly said playfully. "It's not appropriate to call me that. Now, do you actually have something wrong with you or is this a social visit."

"Oh, my dove, I have wounded my hand in battle this yon morning." Dillon extended his right hand for inspection. "I knew you to be the balm for not only this hand, but for my very soul as well."

Miss Turly took Dillon's offered hand, inspecting it, and turned a raised eyebrow to me.

"And how about you, Mr. Hunter?" Miss Turly asked. "How's the chaffing?"

"Oh, much better, thanks for asking," I said from my seat. "The rash is gone too."

"Glad to hear it," Miss Turly said, examining Dillon's hand. "Well, nothing seems broken. It does look slightly discolored. You might have a bruise. What did you say happened to it?"

Dillon's eyes were closed in a moment of ecstasy.

"Dillon, what happened to your hand?" Miss Turly asked again.

"Oh, I cut it shaving," Dillon answered, opening his eyes. "It already feels better just being held by you."

"Not appropriate again," Miss Turly said with a chuckle. "I'll get you an ice pack for that, but you should be fine. I have aspirin as well if it starts to act up."

"Will you still be chaperoning the after school party today?" Dillon asked, not taking his eyes off the woman. "I heard you might be there."

"Yes." Miss Turly placed a cold pack in Dillon's hand. "I'll be there and it's not a party; it's a fundraiser for the after school music program."

"Right, right, that's what I said." Dillon moved to take her hand and give her a kiss on the back of it, but Miss Turly pulled away just in time. Dillon ignored the action. "If it's meant to be, maybe we'll cross paths again."

"You take care of yourself now, Mr. Hunter," Miss Turly said to me with another of her amused smiles. I had a sneaking suspicion she actually liked Dillon. Not in any kind of romantic sense, but that she found him sweet and amusing.

"Thank you." I waved to her as I headed for the door. "And thanks for the extra inhaler last week. My asthma was really going crazy with the winds."

"Anytime." Miss Turly turned back to her work as Dillon blew her a kiss.

"So when were you going to tell me that this party we're going to is actually a fundraiser?" I questioned

"Party, fundraiser." Dillon shrugged. "You say tomato, I say ketchup. You say potato, I say French fries. It's all the same."

"That's not how that saying goes," I told him.

"I'm pretty sure it is," Dillon answered. "I heard it in a movie."

"It's you say tomato and I say tomoto, and you say potato and I say pototo," I continued. "It's not about ketchup and French fries, although I am getting hungry."

"I still think you're wrong since those aren't even words, but let's just agree to disagree." Dillon took a turn down the hall, following the herd of students to the cafeteria. "I know you need some protein to bulk up, but let's pay for the party first and then we can go eat. It'll only take a few minutes."

A table had been erected right outside the cafeteria doors where a pair of students were selling tickets to the "party" for four dollars apiece. I couldn't bring myself to ask my parents for money for something extra, so I opted to break into the good old piggy bank and count out some change.

I knew money was money; still, I wish I had cash, a card or even a check to use right now. The cheap zip-lock baggy full of change felt like a brick in my pocket.

A short line formed in front of the table as students supporting the band paid for their tickets with twenty-dollar bills and even credit cards.

"Hey, maybe I'll let you go solo on this one," I told Dillon nervously. "Parties aren't really my thing."

"Come on, man, don't bail on me now." Dillon's shoulders slumped. "You said you'd come. You've always been a loyal comrade in arms."

"I've known you for six months, since moving here," I corrected him.

"Exactly my point." Dillon stuck a pointer finger into the air. "And in those six months, you've been a trustworthy journeyman. Don't let me down now."

The line moved a few feet. There was no one I knew in line thus far. A few familiar faces and I already counted out the change at my house. With any luck, I'd be able to slap down the bag of change and they'd give me my ticket before anyone else noticed.

"Okay, okay," I told Dillon. "You're right; I did say that I'd go with you. I won't let you down."

"My man!" Dillon shouted loud enough to draw all eyes to us.

I hung my head, doing the primal beta submission act of avoiding eye contact.

"You'll love it and I owe you one," Dillon continued. "You need the latest Pikachu card, I got you. Having a hard time passing the next level in *World of Warcraft,* you have my sword. Missed the last episode of *Doctor Who,* then—"

"Thanks," I interrupted, trying to shut him up. "I get it, I get. You owe me one."

My heart rate picked up, which didn't take much these days. I noticed no one was paying with cash. One kid even took out his own checkbook and took his time writing a check like some kind of CEO.

Kids could be cruel. I knew that. What was I about to step into here? Any high school was deadlier than a battle royale and more political than an episode of *West Wing.*

"Next," one of the two kids at the table called. He had to be a senior. He wore a soul patch on his chin and a severe look in his eyes. "You, Freshman, let's go."

"Right, right," I said, fumbling into my pocket. "So funny story—I, uh—you see, my girlfriend needed to borrow some money, so I gave her all my hundreds and, uh—my check-book's at home, so—"

"Listen, we're not running a charity here," the guy said, looking over at the painfully pretty girl sitting next to him. One look from her and my armpits started to sweat. "If you don't have the money, you're not getting a ticket."

"No, no, I have the money right—right here," I mumbled, removing the dirty zip-lock bag from my pocket. The plastic bag ripped right as I was about to place it on the table. I slapped my hands down on the change before they could roll all over the place. "I just have it—in change."

The two seniors traded looks again.

"I already counted it." I did my best to shield the table from any unwanted eyes. "It's four dollars. I promise. Can I just get my ticket now?"

"Really?" the girl asked, smacking the gum in her full lips. "You brought change? I didn't know people even carried change anymore. Do we have to accept this?"

"Hey, come on; hurry up!" someone yelled from down the line.

Dillon shoved his way next to me. "I can help you out if you need—"

"No, no," I insisted. "I'm good. It's all here. I swear I just need my ticket."

My heart pounded out of my chest. I just wanted to get out of there, go find my usual empty bench in the cafeteria, and eat my delicious pizza squares.

"Yeah, I guess money's money," the guy announced, mad-dogging me like he wished our paths had never crossed. "We'll take it."

"Great, thank you," I said in a gush of relief.

"But I'll need you to count it," he continued.

I looked down at the pennies, dimes, and nickels, all the tiny judging eyes of dead presidents looking back at me. I was sweating for sure now. I could feel the beads coming down my forehead. I wanted to run away.

"Does that guy have change?" more voices asked in line.

"Hey, I've had to pee for like the last ten minutes over here," someone else said. "Kick the underprivileged kid out of line already."

"Here, here," I said, moving my finger around the table like a maniac separating the coins and placing them in piles.

"What in the name of the New York Giants is going on here?"

I heard the voice and my heart sank to the pit of my stomach. It was Eric Ortiz. I knew, given an opportunity to bully, he wasn't going to pass anything up.

I could feel him looking over my shoulder.

"If you want a ticket, you'll have to get in line," the pretty senior told Eric, flipping her hair to the side. "But you should come. We could use the support of the football team."

"Yeah, not so much interested in band camp," Eric said, shoving Dillon to the side and standing right next to me. "Holy crap, are you paying in change? Look at all those pennies! Twenty-nine, ten, five, seven, forty eight; does that mess up your counting?"

I wanted to cry, but I forced myself to ignore Eric and keep going.

Like most days, Eric traveled in a pack. All his buddies behind him started shouting numbers.

"Hey, poor nerd, I'm talking to you," Eric sneered, placing both his hands on the table. He used them like a broom, swiping all the coins to the ground. They fell in a cascade of spinning tinkling noises, and I broke.

Falling to my hands and knees amongst the laughter of all those around, I manically began picking up my change. I felt sick, hot, anxious, depressed, and like crying all at once.

I woke up from my dream in my own bed in my apartment. A cold sweat covered my body and then I vomited all over my chest.

THIRTEEN

THE PUKE that drizzled down my chin and onto my chest and stomach was warm and smelled sour.

I lay there for a moment as memories of the night before faded in and out. I remembered drinking at the bar, Evan taking me home after a late night drive-thru run, then puking my guts out in the toilet before sinking into my bed.

I winced, looking out the blinds now at a full sun, high in the sky. The digital display on my phone read ten thirty. No texts or calls from Tracy.

It felt like a tiny dwarf had climbed into my ear and now used my brains as a forge, hammering along with my heartbeat.

Stumbling out of bed and to the shower, I recalled my dream from the night before as if I had actually relived it again. It was a memory that haunted me wherever I went. I was still that kid inside. As much as I hated feeling weak and insecure, maybe I'd always be that freshman version of myself.

After cleaning myself, clothes, and sheets, I went to the kitchen to hydrate and grab some food. My phone rang.

I grabbed it immediately, hoping it was Tracy. Evan's name shone in bright letters along the top of the display screen.

"Hey, man, sorry about last night," I said into the receiver as I answered the call. "I'm not sure if you paid for all the drinks and I think I tasted Taco Bell this morning when I threw up. I can pay you back for—"

"Stop with all the money and your weird fetish with paying people back," Evan interrupted me. "I'm just worried about you. How are you feeling? You were

sobbing up a storm last night and shoving bean and cheese burritos into your mouth like you were in some kind of eating contest."

"Oh, that's what I was tasting in the vomit, beans," I said with a sigh, trying to remember more about the events of the night. "Hey, did you drive us back after taking all those drinks with me?"

"Yeah, but my metabolism burns off alcohol way faster than I would like. I can get drunk for a few minutes after I take something hard back, but I was sober by the time we left. Any word from Satan's favorite daughter?"

"Don't call her that," I said, tired and confused. "She's Satan's step-daughter."

"Ahhhh." Evan sighed. "So you're beginning to see the light as well?"

"I don't know, man," I exhaled. "I mean, something's definitely up and things need to change, but I'm just not ready to give up on her yet. Are you sure she's going to be safe working with Mr. Bloodstone and V Model Management?"

"They won't kill her," Evan said, sure of himself. "She's too high profile now that she has her own streaming show. If anything, they're grooming her."

"Grooming her for what?" I asked, already knowing the answer. Blood rushed from my whole body down to my feet, leaving a cold sensation in its place. "They're going to turn her?"

"I can't say for sure, but I've seen them do it before," Evan answered. "Either turn her or let her be one of their human pawns. Either way, she'll be safe."

"I've got to call her and warn her," I said, shuddering at the possibility of Tracy being turned into a vampire. "I can't just let her walk into this."

"It looks like she already has and through no fault of your own," Evan said, pulling the phone away from his lips and shouting to someone else. "Okay, I'll be right there."

"On the same shoot?" I asked

"No, this one's a commercial for Ryan Reynolds' new gin company," Evan told me. "You know, he's actually a super nice guy in real life. I bet you if he ran for president, he'd win. Anyway, glad to hear you're feeling better. I've got to go."

"Thanks for everything, man," I told him. "I owe you."

"You don't owe me anything," Evan denied before hanging up. "That's what friends do."

Evan has to be the nicest vampire in existence, I thought to myself. *He's like the Mr. Rogers of vampires.*

Before I could over think my next decision, I went into my contacts, pressing Tracy's name to dial her number. The phone rang once and she picked up.

"Oh, hey," I answered, not expecting her to even be able to answer the phone while she was on set. "I thought I'd be going to voicemail. Are you at work?"

"I am, but we're on break," Tracy answered. "Listen, Jonny, we need to talk."

Never in the history of any conversation do the words "we need to talk" proceed something positive. I braced myself for what was coming next.

My pause was long enough to give her permission to continue.

"Life's been a roller coaster lately, with the show, getting engaged, and now everything that comes along with it," Tracy said, clearing her throat. She was trying to hide her sadness, but I could hear it in her voice. "I need some space right now to figure things out. It's not you. It's me."

"I really wish we didn't have to do this over the phone," I said, trying not to panic. I felt sick all over again. "Let's talk in person. I can come over to—"

"No, no, I think this is the best thing," Tracy cut me off. "Over the phone is fine."

Panic mode set in.

"Well, if you need some space, I can give you time," I said. "What if we take the next few days to think about what we want together and how we can move forward?"

"No, Jonny. I don't think you're understanding me." Tracy's voice carried an edge to it now. "Like, I need space, as in a break. I'm breaking up with you. I'll mail you the ring with anything I had of yours at the apartment."

"Tracy—how—I understand you're under a lot stress, but you don't mean this." I fumbled over my words, racing to find an answer that didn't plummet me into another serious depression. "Let's just take a breather."

"No, I've put a lot of thought into it. *Cosmo* had an article with exercises to do on your relationship written by JLo and I have to agree with her. Right now, my career comes first."

"Jennifer Lopez!" I shouted over the phone. "Why are you taking relationship advice from Jennifer Lopez? She's been married and divorced more times than the New England Patriots have won the Super Bowl and Tom Brady has won a lot. He's the G.O.A.T."

"Listen, I trust my girl Jennifer on this one and I don't need that kind of negativity in my life. Besides, I don't know what goats have to do with this conversation," Tracy huffed. "Listen, I'm done. We're over."

"G.O.A.T. is an acronym for Greatest Of All Time," I said as an empty feeling filled me from the inside out. "Whatever happens to you and me, there's something you should know about Winston Bloodstone, V Model Management, and the entire industry here in Hollywood. Tracy, they're controlled by vampires."

The line was silent.

I didn't really blame her. I understood what I sounded like, insane. Insane is what I sounded like.

"I can prove it," I told her, trying to think of a way to back up my crazy claim. "You just have to be careful. I don't think they plan on killing you but maybe turning you into one of them."

"Oh my gosh, you would say anything to try and keep me right now, wouldn't you?" Tracy laughed. "But vampires? Come on, Jonny, this is kind of dorky, even for you. Have you been diving back into your *Twilight* books again? I thought you were over that phase of your life."

"Is anyone ever over *Twilight*?" I asked. "That was an epic love triangle. I'll always be Team Jacob. But that's not the point. The point is that you need to be careful."

"Listen, we're over, Jonny," Tracy said in a deadpan voice. "Don't call or text me anymore. Jay Lo also says that the first no is the cleanest. It's not healthy for either of us to drag this out. This is good-bye."

The phone went dead.

Life felt like I was moving in slow motion. I put the phone on the kitchen counter. The pounding in my head took a backseat and that same numb feeling descended on me.

I sat down right where I was on the kitchen floor, trying to process it all. Evan and even my mother tried to warn me about her, but I was just too blinded. I had brought this all on myself. The only woman I ever thought I loved had just thrown me away after consulting a Jennifer Lopez article in *Cosmo*.

I didn't even know Jennifer Lopez wrote articles, but that seemed beside the point.

I spiraled.

FOURTEEN

BEFORE I KNEW IT, I was walking out of my complex to the grocery store mini mart at the end of our block. Alcohol didn't seem the best way to deal with my feelings since I was still hung over, but my stomach was empty and I was hungry.

The glass panes on the store wall facing the street were covered in stickers and advertisements from cola-flavored energy drinks to hot Cheetos.

A table was set up outside the store where a couple of younger girls sat with who I assumed was one of their mothers selling Girl Scout cookies.

"Would you like to buy some cookies today?" one of them asked me with a genuine smile. "We were able to take a day off school to raise money for our chapter."

"Yes," I told the small girl in uniform. "Yes, actually, I want to take two—no better make it three boxes."

"Oh wow!" the other girl said, jumping to attention. "Which ones do you—"

"This one's fine," I said, grabbing the closest box and ripping it open with abandon. I worked my way through the plastic wrap inside the box and pulled out the cookies, trying to shove two in my mouth.

As a working model, there were things you had to sacrifice to have a certain look. Things like sugar and bread were two of the things I missed the most, and to be honest, all willpower had left me in the middle of my depression.

"That's going to be fifteen dollars for three boxes." The girl's mother, who had been eyeing me seductively before, now looked at me like I was about to run off without paying.

"I'll just take one," I said, offering them my credit card. "You girls going to high school soon?"

"What are you, some kind of pervert?" one of the girls asked.

"Nope, just someone who's been through all of that, chewed up, and spit out the other end," I said around a mouthful of Thin Mints. "Let me give you some advice. Run. Run for your freaking life or join the cheerleading squad and be popular. Because if you have a bad high school experience, that trauma sticks with you into your adult years. Who knows, maybe even forever. It's a dark journey, ladies."

Both girls looked at me with wide eyes, their mouths contorted into deep Os.

The mother tried frantically to jam my card through her chip reader to get me out of there.

"And I'll tell you something else," I said after shoving three more Thin Mints into my mouth.

"Please don't," the mother hissed, jabbing at her screen to complete the payment and get me on my way.

I ignored her.

"All the sports and grades you get are supposed to give you value in who you are; your friends, your status are all supposed to be summed up into this imaginary algorithm to give you value." I poked a finger toward each of the girls.

"Nobody should give you value and let you decide how you feel besides you."

The mother looked up from her phone.

"Oh, that actually wasn't that bad." The mother almost gave me a smile. "I thought you were going to say something crazy and mildly inaprop—"

"And another thing," I continued, ignoring the mother. "If you don't want to go to college it's not the end of the world. Don't fall in love with any good shows based off books; the show will rarely live up to the series in novel format. What happens in Vegas does not stay in Vegas. That stuff comes back with you."

"Please leave," the mother snapped, handing me back my card. "Or I'm going to call the police."

"I have decided, I will be on my way now," I said, accepting my card and stumbling into the store.

The bell rang to the mini mart. Rami, the owner of the shop, was someone I knew well. Anytime I needed anything, short of full grocery shopping, I'd stop by.

"Hey, there he is, Mr. Model Man. How goes it?" Rami asked from behind the counter. "Oh, Girl Scout cookies? Nice choice, but should you be eating that? What about all those fancy jobs you have lined up?"

"It's a cheat day, Rami," I said over my shoulder. "Where's your ice cream?"

"Last aisle in the back," Rami instructed. "Jonny, you feeling okay? Your eyes look kind of crazy right now."

"I'm a new man. I'm a new man, Rami," I said, zeroing in on the ice creams. Unfortunately, all Rami had were the one-gallon buckets, not the five gallons I had thought of purchasing. "Hey, do you have any cake icing?"

"Aisle two on the left," Rami said quietly. "Jonny, what's going on? You're very clearly not all right, my friend."

The store was small with only five aisles to navigate.

There was one older woman in the store shopping. She didn't even pretend she wasn't interested in our conversation. She stopped shopping completely with a can of dog food in her hand.

I grabbed the container of chocolate frosting off the shelf then back-tracked to grab a cola-flavored energy drink I'd seen advertised on the window.

"Love, love happened to him," the old woman said quietly. She looked me up and down. "Love lost."

I did a double take, examining the woman closer. I had seen her before, but I was sure we'd never spoken.

"Do I know you?" I asked.

"You don't, but I've been watching you." The older woman gave me a sad smile.

"We all live in Haven Apartments," Rami offered, clearing up the confusion. "Mrs. Grundy lives on the bottom floor, across from you and next to me."

"Oh right, that's where I know you," I said, grabbing a container of cream cheese then backtracking toward the flaming hot Cheetos. "Well, good to see you again, neighbor."

"It gets better," Mrs. Grundy advised, making her way to the cash register and paying for her items that ended up being nothing but a rawhide dog chew and a dozen cans of dog food. "I know that doesn't help you now, but know the pain will stop and it will get better."

"Right, right, thanks," I said, not wanting to be rude but also not needing to take advice on my love life from a complete stranger. My hands and arms were full now. I was crushing the ice cream in the crook of my left elbow.

I started doing math in my head, trying to calculate how much money I could spare for extra food against how much I had in my bank account.

Mrs. Grundy finished her purchase and walked to the

door. Before she left, she stopped and looked me right in the eye. Her thick glasses magnified her pupils to double their size.

That stare stopped me in my tracks. It was like she was looking not just at me but through me, reading my very soul itself. Or maybe that was just the feeling all the sugar in the Thin Mints gave me. I was sure it had been months since I had this much sugar in so short a time.

"You are a special young man." Mrs. Grundy gave me a small, knowing smile. "This is not where your story ends. This is just the beginning."

"I'm not really sure what to say to that," I told her, searching her armload of dog food. "I hope you and your dogs have good health and a pleasant New Year."

Mrs. Grundy smiled wider before pushing out the door.

"Would you like to buy some Girl Scout cookies?" the voices outside wafted into the store.

"No you, panhandlers!" Mrs. Grundy griped at them. "I've got diabetes. Can't be eating any of that poison you're peddling."

The door closed behind the woman, cutting off anything else she was going to say.

"Mrs. Grundy," Rami said with a smile and a shake of his head. "She's a good woman but a bit harsh and opinionated at times."

"She seems like a real gem," I said, bending over and depositing the goods in my arms on the counter. I fished my credit card out of my pocket. "I might need a bag to carry all of this stuff. If this ends up being more than twenty bucks, don't ring me up for the rest."

"No need to pay." Rami smiled, bagging my purchases.

"What do you mean?" I asked with a scowl. "You don't have to give me this stuff. I'm going to pay you."

"Wow, partner," Rami said with a raised eyebrow. "Pump

the brakes. As much as I would like to give free handouts to my friends, I'm a capitalist at heart. I've got bills to pay too and more child support letters coming in by the month."

"Well, then let me pay for my stuff," I insisted.

"No can do." Rami pushed the full plastic bag of sugar and fat toward me. "Mrs. Grundy paid for you when she paid for her own stuff. It was amazing, to the penny. She must have been keeping an eye on what you were grabbing and knew exactly how much it was going to be with tax. She's one smart cookie. Smells like dog piss half the time, but one smart cookie."

"Oh—thanks," I said, accepting the bag. I didn't really know what else to say. No one had ever bought my groceries before.

"Well, I didn't do too much, partner." Rami shrugged. "Mrs. Grundy should be the one you're thanking."

"Right," I acknowledged, grabbing my bag and heading for the door.

I pushed the door open, making eye contact with the two Girl Scouts and the mom. The mom immediately looked down like she hadn't seen me and started talking to the girls about making better life decisions.

That was fine with me.

I headed toward Haven Apartments, hoping to catch sight of Mrs. Grundy in the distance. I mean, she was an older woman and left moments before Rami packed up my groceries. She couldn't have gotten far.

Still, she was gone. No sight of her knitted sweater, nothing.

"How did she get back to her apartment so fast?" I asked myself out loud.

I pondered the question walking back to my own apartment. I opened the black wrought-iron gate of our complex with my key and made the trek to the fourth floor.

I looked across the open area of our square-shaped complex, wondering if I should go over and try to figure out which apartment she lived in. At the very least, I wanted to thank her for the kindness. My past scars wanted me to thank her and let her know I didn't need her help, but deep down, I knew I just needed to say thank you.

I was lost climbing the stairs still partially hung over and looking over across my complex when I nearly collided with Shannon.

"Wow, easy there, Stinky," Shannon warned, grimacing at me as if I smelt like some kind of dead carcass. "Why do you always have some kind of new terrifying smell on you when I see you?"

"What? I smell fine," I argued.

"You kinda smell like puke." Shannon wrinkled her nose in disgust. "I mean faint puke like you tried to wash it out, but still puke."

I took a deep breath, settling myself so that neither anger or sadness seeped through. Hiding either one of those emotions was a chore most days. Today, coupled with depression, it was nearly impossible.

Shannon must have caught on. Whether it was my silence or the look on my face, something told her what was wrong.

"Oh no," Shannon said, eyeing the clear plastic grocery bag I carried. "What happened? Girl problems?"

"Listen, I don't really want to talk about it right now," I said with a sigh. "I know you're trying to help, but I just need some time."

"Did you break up with her?" Shannon pressed, eyeing the bag closer. "Wait a minute, an entire gallon of ice cream and frosting? Did she break up with you?"

I nodded.

For the first time since I'd known Shannon, her abrasive

nature disappeared. She put a gentle hand on my shoulder and looked in my eyes.

"I'm sorry," Shannon told me. "I really am. I know what that feels like. I mean, I don't personally because I've never been broken up with, but I hear it sucks. The guys I've broken up with always cried. If you want to cry, it's okay."

"I don't want to cry," I insisted.

"Shhhhhh," Shannon said, pressing her pointer finger against my lips. "Let it out. You don't have to be strong anymore."

Her finger was cold against my lips. We shared yet another awkward moment on the stairs as we gazed into each other's eyes. I had to turn my head to get her finger off my lips.

"Well, thanks for the talk, I think," I said with a fake smile. "I'm going to go to my apartment and drown myself in calories now."

"I'm here for you," Shannon told me. "I have a training appointment at the gym I can't miss, but it's only an hour. Do what you need to do, and as soon as I get back, I'm coming in to check on you."

Shannon gave me a hard nod as if her words were scripture then bounded down the steps.

"Really, that's nice of you but not necessary," I called to her.

"I don't have a lot of friends here," Shannon said without looking back. "The few I do have I'm going to look out for."

With that, the ball of muscle and energy was gone.

I stood there for a moment trying to sort out how I felt about it. The bottom line was that I couldn't control her. If she wanted to come by later to see how I was doing, maybe that wasn't so bad.

I let myself back into my apartment, laying out my horde of food bought by Mrs. Grundy in front of me.

I really need to figure out which apartment she lives in and go thank her. Rami said she lived next to him and he's the middle apartment, so I have a fifty-fifty shot, I thought to myself as I flipped on our TV. *I'll go thank her today.*

It just so happened that my favorite episode of *Golden Girls* was on. I plopped down on the couch, threw caution to the wind, and dove headfirst into my self-imposed therapy session.

FIFTEEN

I STARTED with the hot Cheetos dipped in cream cheese and washed down by my cola energy drink. The soft block of dairy complemented the crunch of the spicy cheese chip like something I'd expect to greet me in heaven.

I couldn't remember the last time I had a soda or an energy drink. The carbonation made me burp with a familiar satisfying sting.

Next, I moved on to the ice cream and can of frosting, alternating between the two without pause. I was a madman, searching for food to support my emotional state just like I had been in high school.

By the time the first *Golden Girls* episode was over, I felt bloated and uncomfortable. I switched the channel to a WWE rerun and kept eating.

Before I knew it, there was a knock on the door. I felt sick and so bloated, it looked like I was about to go in and deliver a tiny Baby Yoda.

Never one to leave my door unlocked, I went over and opened it. Shannon walked in with wide eyes, staring at the table full of half empty containers.

"Don't judge me," was all I could manage before going back to the couch and throwing myself in front of the TV. I popped my top pants button for extra comfort.

"You probably just consumed enough calories to last five days," Shannon said, dipping her finger in the chocolate frosting and sucking on it. "Oh, is this the latest WWE episode? I missed it this week. I heard they were going to have a table, ladders, and chairs match for the intercontinental championship."

"You watch WWE?" I asked with a raised eyebrow.

"Hey, girls can like WWE too. Don't put me in a box," Shannon scolded, making her way over to Evan's room and sneaking a peek inside. "I like football too. I heard the G.O.A.T. is making another run at a Super Bowl with his New England Patriots."

"He's gone, working," I answered her unspoken question. "Which is probably where I should be if I could land a job. I need to go back and twirl the sign more."

"What?" Shannon asked, joining me on the couch.

For a second, I was going to try and change the subject, but I was too tired to care what she thought at the moment.

"I wear a chicken costume and twirl a sign when I'm not going to castings. I drive Lyfter when I can too." I looked at her, ready for her to break into a grin.

She didn't.

"Gotta do what you gotta do to survive, right?" Shannon said, surveying the carnage of fat and sugar on the table in front of us. "I can't believe you ate that much cream cheese. I'm not even mad; that's impressive."

"You're not going to laugh at me?" I asked.

"For what?" Shannon wondered. "For working to be able to make ends meet?"

"Yeah, I mean, it's not exactly glamorous work," I said.

"Trust me, I've done worse for money." Shannon wiggled

her brows. "One time, there was a stench from the house next door. Neighbor didn't want to crawl underneath the house to check it out. Paid me twenty bucks to crawl underneath there and deal with it."

"What was it?" I asked. "I mean, the smell."

"Oh man, you should have seen it." Shannon actually looked excited as she told her story. "So there I am crawling on my hands and knees under this house. There's maybe ten inches from the ground to the floor above me. Everything's dark and it reeks like worse than you the first night we met. So anyway, I make it to the end of the house and see this crazy big possum, dead but still juicy. That thing had to weigh seventeen or eighteen pounds."

"I feel sick," I mumbled, putting a hand on my stomach.

"The tail slipped right off in my hand; the skin, I mean," Shannon said, shaking her head. "That was pretty crazy. I wouldn't have been able to get it out by myself, but my sister helped me."

"Enough with the details," I said with a burp. "I didn't know you had siblings."

"Just a sister," Shannon said uncomfortably.

Shannon would never be accused of being tactful. It was clear talking about her sister made her uncomfortable. Without a natural segue, she jumped up from the couch.

"Well, come on; let's get to it," Shannon said, beckoning me to follow. She headed for my room.

"Hey, where are you going?" I asked, following her.

"You can't work out in jeans and a t-shirt," Shannon said, making a beeline for my room and opening my dresser drawers. "You need some shorts and maybe a sleeveless shirt. Come on; you have workout clothes."

"Listen, I just ate a lot of food and I don't really feel like working out," I told her. "I appreciate you coming over, but—"

The rest of what I was about to say was cut short with a black pair of shorts and a sleeveless shirt that read "Cobra Kai" thrown at my face.

"Come on, put that on," Shannon ordered, passing me and turning her back. "I'll give you some privacy, but I might decide to sneak a peek or two. Just going to be honest. You're a single man now."

I stood in my room for a minute deciding whether I was going to go or not. The main thing that made me move into action was the fact that I knew Shannon wasn't going to take no for an answer. For better or worse, we were friends now.

I stripped down to my Marvel Comics boxers, putting on my gym clothes and shoes. True to her word, I saw Shannon turn her head a few times in my direction.

"All right," I said, stretching as I joined her in the family room. "What are we doing? Heading to the gym or out for a run? My cardio's pretty weak after a heavy meal."

"Nothing like that." Shannon motioned me to follow her. "Come on; I'll show you."

We headed down the stairs to the third floor and Shannon's apartment. I wasn't sure how someone like her could afford a two-bedroom apartment on her own, but that wasn't really any of my business.

Heck, maybe I should ask her for career advice. She seemed to be doing pretty well as a personal trainer. Maybe I should get into that business as a side job while my modeling career took off.

We entered her sparsely decorated apartment, one of those wooden striking dummies I recognized from martial arts movies had been added to the room.

"Where do you eat?" I asked her. "I mean, you don't have a table, chairs, couch, or a TV."

"I usually eat on the go or standing up." Shannon walked over to her heavy punching bag and leaned over, picking up a pair of boxing gloves. She tossed them to me. "Strap up, Buttercup."

I caught the gloves in the air. I'd taken a few martial arts classes growing up, but nothing serious, nothing that stuck long term. I held the gloves, just looking down at them, wondering if I was really going to do this.

"You've got a lot of issues to work through," Shannon said with her hands on her hips. "We all have a lot of issues to work through. You can do that behind a bottle or bury yourself in donuts or you can use that anger and hurt and channel it into something good."

"That's probably the wisest thing you've said since I've known you," I answered, putting on the gloves.

"Yeah, well, don't get used to it." Shannon approached the heavy bag hanging from her ceiling with bare knuckles. "This is how you stand, left leg forward, legs bent at the knees. Hands are always up by your face. We'll start with a jab, jab, cross combination."

Shannon demonstrated the strikes as she coached me. Each time she struck the bag, it quivered under the onslaught of her power. Her moves were fast and efficient in a way that reminded me of some kind of snake striking out for a lethal bite.

"Now you try," Shannon said, stepping to the side.

"Okay," I said, doing my best to mimic her stance and moves. It felt like I was making enough contact with the bag, but it was clear I was much slower than Shannon.

"Good." She coached me despite my thoughts. "Left, left, right. Left, left, right. Let's just work on that combination for now. We'll switch it up in a second. As hard as you can, now. Don't get lazy on me."

I nodded, saving my breath for the blows. I had to admit it felt good. It was a fun and safe way to get rid of some of the anger I carried. Not just anger at Tracy but frustration at the entire situation, struggling to make rent, still dealing with the stupid trauma from high school.

"Breath out through your mouth with each blow," Shannon told me. "Let me hear you."

I gave off short exhales through my mouth each time I sent a blow into the bag.

"If you don't want to talk about it, that's fine but this is like confessing your sins to the priest right now," Shannon expressed as I worked. "Think about what's pissing you off and you let it go. You use that fuel to propel you forward instead of holding back."

"You're making too much sense," I said, pausing for a moment and breathing hard. "Thanks for this. You're right. It is helping."

"Eyes on the bag," Shannon instructed. "I know the breakup sucks, but what's really bothering you."

"I've got baggage and I'm not talking about a carryon," I said, hammering my hands into the bag as hard as I could. "Money was tight growing up. It was the freaking Gulag in high school."

"Awww, there it is," Shannon said, looking at the bag that swayed now with every right hook I threw. "Time your punches so that the bag swings toward you when you hit it. Here, I'll just hold it."

Shannon placed herself on the other side of the bag, steadying it for me.

"Kids can be mean," Shannon agreed, going back to my therapy session. "I'm sure they worked you over pretty well. But you're not that person anymore. You let that person go every time you hit the bag. Dig deep, Dig deep, Jonny; get it all out. Come on, you can hit harder than that. Harder!"

Every time I hit the bag, flashbacks exploded in my mind. Kids laughing at me, the coins spilling all over the ground, the expressions of disgust on their faces when they looked at me all drove me forward.

"Come on, Jonny, let it go," Shannon yelled. "Harder, let it go!"

My right hook carried a yell instead of just an escape of air from my mouth. I hit that bag with everything I had, throwing my body behind it. The force of the strike rippled through the bag and into Shannon. She lost her grip and stumbled backward.

"Wow," I exclaimed, looking through the sweat dripping into my eyes. "I'm sorry, I'm sorry. Are you okay?"

Shannon looked at me as if she were seeing me for the first time. "Yeah, I'm fine, Stinky. That's one heck of a right cross you have there when you want to."

"Yeah, yeah," I heaved. "I guess you're right."

"Feel better?" she asked.

"You know what?" I marveled with a smile. "I think I do."

"Good." Shannon jerked her chin to her gear. "You're welcome to use it any time you'd like to work out your demons."

"Thanks," I answered, looking around the place again. All the boxes had been moved out of the dining area. One of the bedroom doors was closed, the other slightly cracked. If I craned my neck just right, I could see in. "Hey, is that a—"

Something hard struck me across my right temple.

I fell to the floor, confused. Pain exploded behind my eyelids. On hands and knees, I looked up to see Shannon above me.

"I'm sorry about this," she apologized with a look of genuine sadness in her eyes. "But I don't want you to get hurt tonight."

She brought her right foot to the underside of my chin. I was out like an obese kid at an all-you-can-eat vegan buffet.

SIXTEEN

BLACKNESS GREETED me on the other side of that kick. More darkness waited for me when I opened my eyes. My head felt like how the punching bag must after a training session.

I winced, trying to see through the darkness. I tried raising my hand to my head to see how bad the damage was. I couldn't move my hands at all, I couldn't even feel them, come to think of it.

Both arms were tied behind my back to the weight set behind me. I sat in Shannon's dining area. The events proceeding my unconscious state hit me like a sledgehammer. I looked out the windows to my right to see silver moonlight shining through.

"I already patched you up," Shannon's voice said from somewhere in the dark.

I screamed in fright like some kid getting a jump scare from *Friday the 13th*. In any other circumstance, it might have been funny.

I craned my neck forward, squinting through the darkness. I could see Shannon's form across the kitchen, near the front door.

"Shannon, what—what's going on?" I asked, still coming out of my daze. "What are you doing?"

"I'm trying to save you from turning into collateral damage," Shannon said through the darkness. "You're the kind of guy that's going to rush into a situation you don't understand, thinking you're protecting a friend and end up hurt or worse."

"Well, Chuck Norris, if you haven't noticed, I'm already hurt," I told her, trying to pull free of my bonds behind me. It was no use; rope or tape or something barely allowed circulation to my fingers.

"I stopped the bleeding and took care of you while you were out," Shannon said as if that was enough to absolve her from her actions. "You know you talk in your sleep? Why do you need to teach Girl Scouts? You kept going on about how they needed to know the truth of this cold hard world."

"I think I should be the one asking questions," I stated, changing the subject. "You owe me that much, whoever you are."

"You know who I am," Shannon said. "I haven't lied. Only withheld some of the truth. Your roommate's not who you think he is."

A bulb lit in the inside of my head.

"Evan?" I asked rhetorically. "This is all about Evan? That's why you always ask about him? I thought you wanted a date."

"Yeah, the blood-sucking kind isn't really my type," Shannon answered. "I prefer my dates actually warm and living. But you wouldn't know anything about that. To you, he's just your roommate and best friend. That's why I needed to take you out of the equation."

I closed my eyes, trying to put all the puzzle pieces

together. A burp that tasted half spicy Cheetos, half chocolate icing escaped my lips. If I was being honest, it wasn't half bad.

"All of this training, the weapons in the boxes," I said, opening my eyes. "You're going to kill him? What are you? Some kind of supernatural police? You go out and hunt vampires?"

"You knew?" Shannon asked a question of her own before answering mine. "You know what he is?"

A wave of relief washed over me.

"Oh, Shannon, you're going to feel so silly when I explain things to you." I sighed. "Evan's a vampire, but he's one of the good ones. He doesn't turn or kill anyone. He didn't even want to be a vampire, but he was turned anyway. He's just doing what he has to, to survive. This has all been a misunderstanding. If you let me go, we can go upstairs and talk to him and have a cup of tea or something."

"And you believe him?" Shannon challenged with ice in her voice. "You just take as gospel whatever he tells you?"

"I saw it firsthand," I informed her. "He could have killed a girl the other night and he didn't. I mean, I'm not saying the system he has is perfect, but until we can figure out another way for him to survive, at least he's not killing or turning anyone."

"The only good vampire's a dead vampire." Shannon walked closer to me, the rays of the moon revealing her attire. She was dressed completely in black with body armor over her chest and a neck guard that went as high as her ears on the sides. A sword hilt poked over her right shoulder. She looked like a badass from the future.

Fear creeped into my veins.

"Don't kill Evan," I grunted, struggling harder with my bonds. "You don't know him. Give him a chance."

Shannon shook her head.

"Someone!" I shouted. "Anyone, help! This chick is out of her mind—"

Shannon slapped a thick piece of tape over my mouth.

"I'll come free you when it's done," Shannon said, crouching next to me. "Also, I removed your phone from your pocket while you were unconscious. You didn't get the hemorrhoid cream commercial. I'm sorry about that too. I know you could use some good news. Hang in there."

Shannon stood up and walked out the front door.

I tried yelling, but thanks to the tape, the noise came out muffled at best. I violently jerked on my bonds. They didn't give. I worked my way up to my feet in a deep squatting position. The weight rack I was connected to carried weights from ten pounds all the way to fifty. I wasn't sure how much that weighed, but it was more than I could lift.

Think! Think! I screamed inside my head. *Evan's about to get decapitated by some crazy Kevlar-wearing psycho hunter. Come, on, come on, come on!*

I took air in through my nostrils hurriedly. I had minutes maybe less before Shannon broke into our apartment and killed Evan.

The bench holding all the weights wasn't bolted to the ground, but the thing had to weigh two to three times what I did. I was almost sure what was holding my wrists secure was the same kind of thick duct tape covering my mouth.

Frantically, I found the edge of the weight set behind me. It was cold metal. The corner wasn't sharp, but it would have to do. Back and forth, I sawed the tape against the metal corner.

Come on, come on, come on! I screamed in my head. *If you can't do this for you, then you can do it for Evan and a very dangerous but still attractive Shannon.*

I stopped myself in my thoughts. Was she attractive? I mean, of course she was, but was it okay to think she was? I was just engaged yesterday. But Tracy broke up with me. Could I move on? Did I need some time to heal? I mean, I was practically damaged goods.

Breaking glass from somewhere upstairs tore me from my insecure thoughts. Like a maniac, I went to town on my bonds, sawing up and down.

There was only one thing in my mind at that point, break free. My shoulder muscles cramped and screamed in pain. Hot agony raced up and down my arms. I ignored it all, feeding off that same sense of piss and vinegar I had found while training with Shannon.

I must have made quite a sight, squatting on Shannon's floor in the dark like I was some animal in the woods about to defecate.

I ignored the pain, focusing on one thing, getting free of the tape. Along with my up and down motion, I also pulled apart my wrists with every ounce of strength I possessed. The tape wasn't tearing, but the good news was with all my straining, I actually moved the entire weight set a few inches.

If you can move it a few inches, maybe you can tip it over, I thought. *Come on, time to channel your inner Hercules and get this job done.*

More crashing came from upstairs along with a yell I thought was Evan.

With a silent scream of effort, I stood up, bringing the set with me. The weight toppled from the weight rack, making heavy thudding sounds on the carpeted ground. My hands slipped from underneath the leg of the weight rack. Without a second thought, I was off.

Still bound with my hands behind me, I had to turn around and grab the door handle to let myself out of Shannon's apartment. The cold night air hit my sweating body like a bucket of ice water.

Air came in and out of my nose in heavy forced contractions. The tape covering my mouth was more of a pain than I anticipated. Memories of my high school years and the asthma attacks kicked in.

Shoving those memories to the side, I headed for the stairs, taking them two at a time. I raced toward my open apartment door and burst inside.

The apartment was a mess. All the lights were off, chairs were overturned along with the kitchen table itself. Shannon and Evan barreled out of his room locked in mortal combat.

Shannon brought a katana down in a two-handed grip on Evan's head. Evan caught her hands in his and the two battled for dominance.

"I don't know who you are," Evan huffed. "I don't want to kill you."

"Like you've killed so many before?" Shannon said from underneath a mask that covered her from the bridge of her nose down to her neck. "You're dead, bloodsucker."

Shannon sent a kick to Evan's nuts that had to obliterate them altogether, vampire or not. Evan squeaked, sinking to his knees. For a split second, Evan lost his grip on the katana handle.

Shannon took the opportunity to tear the weapon free and lift it high for a killing blow.

"No!" I screamed. Under the tape, it came out more like a muffled shout from Hodar from *Game of Thrones*. I raced forward, not really sure what I was going to do, but I sure as heck wasn't going to stand by while Evan had his huevos rancheros curb-stomped by some vampire hunter.

The noise at least did enough to break Shannon's concentration as I charged her. She sidestepped my clumsy attack, tripping me, and sent me flying into the wall head first.

I saw stars again as red blurred my vision from an open cut.

I turned on the ground to see Evan recover enough to

deliver a wicked uppercut to Shannon's own crotch. Her eyes went wide. Evan grabbed the katana by the hilt again, flipping Shannon over his hip. He landed on top of her, forcing the blade lengthwise and down on her throat.

Shannon released her left hand from the hilt, creating a barrier between herself and the blade with her armored forearm.

My date with the wall and sliding down it had loosened the tape from my mouth. With abandon, I rubbed my mouth on my left shoulder, slowly breaking my lips free from the sticky tape.

"No," I shouted to Evan as soon as I was free of the tape. "Evan, no, don't!"

"This heathen is crazy!" Evan exclaimed, looking at me with a face of disbelief. "She tried to castrate me while I was sleeping; probably believes in a flat Earth too!"

"I don't know who she really is, but I know she thinks you're a monster," I told Evan, reaching his side. "I know you're not. Prove to her that you're not the monster she thinks you are."

It was kind of weird telling Evan he wasn't a monster at the moment. His eyes were all blacked out, his teeth razor sharp.

The expression on Evan's face did not bode well for Shannon. He turned back to her. There was nothing I could do to help; he was too fast.

SEVENTEEN

"IF I LET YOU GO, are you just going to try and kill me again?" Evan asked, pressing down on Shannon. "Or try kicking me in the balls?"

"I don't know. I guess we'll have to see," Shannon challenged.

Just then, there was a knock at the door. All three of us looked up at the closed apartment door. In my rush to get inside, I must have hit the door so hard, it swung back in on itself and closed.

"Jonny, Evan?" Mr. Hyde's voice came through the door. "It's Thomas Hyde, your landlord. Is everything okay in there?"

All three of us looked to one another like little kids on the verge of getting in trouble.

"Don't try and kill me again," Evan hissed at Shannon, getting off of her, sword in hand. "I'm going to be so pissed if you murder me. Seriously, I'm going to do all the creepy kind of haunting on you—showers, mirrors, you name it. I can be vengeful. It's not something I'm proud of, but watch yourself."

Shannon lifted herself from the ground, staring daggers at Evan in the dark room.

"Well, look at us all getting along now." I awkwardly turned to my side and motioned to my still bound hands. "A little help here?"

"Evan? Jonny?" Mr. Hyde struck the door again. "I can hear voices in there. If that's not you, then I'm going to call the police."

"I've got to get the door," I said as Evan used Shannon's katana to free me of the tape. "You two behave."

"Wait," Shannon said, "you're still bleeding. Let Evan get the door."

Evan handed me the katana then hurried over to the door, flipping the lights on along the way.

Shannon and I stepped to the right, getting out of the line of sight of the door. The living room was a mess with the broken table in front of the TV and a lamp on the ground.

Together, Shannon and I listened to the conversation.

"Mr. Hyde," Evan greeted as if he were seeing a long lost friend for the first time. "How are you? I've been meaning to stop by and say hi."

"I'm okay," Mr. Hyde answered with a cough. "Just a little sick, but I'm fighting off the cold. Your neighbors reported breaking glass and some loud thuds. I wanted to come over and make sure everything was okay."

"You know what, I appreciate that so much," Evan thanked him. "I mean it. Neighbors should look out for neighbors and there's less and less of that going around these days. We're totally fine. Thanks for asking."

"You sure?" Mr. Hyde didn't sound like he believed him. "Jonny okay as well? Jonny, you in here?"

My eyes went wide. I didn't mind talking to Mr. Hyde, but Shannon was right. I was bleeding from a cut by my scalp.

Shannon was faster than I was. She removed a red scarf

that acted as her mask and tied it around my head like the Karate Kid.

"Go," she hissed. "He's not going to leave until he sees you're okay."

I knew she was right. Even now I could hear Evan trying to convince Mr. Hyde I was in the restroom and our landlord not buying it.

"Evan, who's at the door?" I said, stepping forward to the doorway. "Oh, Mr. Hyde, hi."

Both Evan and Mr. Hyde looked at me like I was some kind of freak.

"Why are you dressed up like Rambo?" Mr. Hyde asked, trying to get a better look inside.

Both Evan and I moved to place our bodies in his line of sight.

"That's a good question." Evan looked at my red bandana. "Why are you dressed—"

"I was just practicing my late night karate in the way of the ancient Iron Fist," I said, channeling all the improv classes I had taken over the years. "Evan was helping me."

"Right, Iron Fist." Evan nodded along with my words. "You see, Jonny was getting bullied by some girl and I wanted him to be able to stick up for himself."

"A girl was bullying you?" Mr. Hyde raised a brow. "Like a kid?"

"They're small, but they can be mean and they have a ton of energy," I answered, trying to keep myself from rambling on like I always did when I lied. I couldn't. "She goes by little T.T. on the streets. She's only ten, but she's built like an NFL linebacker. I don't know what her parents are feeding her, but she needs to be checked for steroids for sure. I think she might be Russian actually. You know, those Russian gymnasts are no joke—"

"Thaaaaat's eeeeenouuuuuugh," Evan said in a low singsong voice without breaking his gaze or smile on Mr. Hyde.

We all stood there for a second, Evan and me nodding like idiots and Mr. Hyde clearly not believing us but not knowing how else to push the subject.

"Okay," Mr. Hyde finally relented. "But please keep it down. Your neighbors are trying to sleep."

"Yes, of course," Evan said as he closed the door. "Our apologies."

I breathed a deep sigh of relief; that was, until we turned around. Shannon pointed a handheld crossbow at Evan's heart, loaded with a wooden stake.

"Oh, not this again," Evan huffed.

"Shannon, please stop," I implored, placing myself in front of Evan. "Just talk to him for a second. Whatever you think vampires are, I'm sure you have good reason to do what you're doing, but at least let's talk about this before you pull the trigger."

Maybe I should have been scared at having a weapon like that pointed at my face, but to be honest, I was just pissed.

"Listen," I said with a growl that impressed myself and took Shannon's eyes from Evan to me. "In the last few days, I've found out vampires are real, been dumped by my fiancée, knocked out, tied up, and this morning vomited all over myself in my bed."

"You did what?" Evan asked from behind me. "I thought you got it all out last night."

"That's not the point," I said, taking a step closer to Shannon with outstretched hands. "Just please, I can't take anymore crazy right now. I'm not sure who you really are, but I know you'll give Evan a chance to talk before you continue to try and kill him."

"How do you know that?" Shannon asked. "Also, it's hard to take you seriously with that bandana still around your head."

"Because you saw me hurting today and you helped me," I reasoned, tearing the bandana off my forehead. "I think that was the real you."

Shannon chewed on her lower lip for a moment then peeked over my shoulder at Evan.

"I'm not going to promise I won't kill you ever," Shannon told Evan. "But I'll give you a minute to talk for Jonny's sake and the fact that I still feel bad for knocking him out. But I still might kill you later."

"Hey, no one lives forever," Evan said then thought about his words. "Unless they're a member of *Supernatural,* then maybe. The main characters on that show have stayed alive forever."

Shannon lowered her weapon and holstered it on her right thigh.

I felt like things were calm enough now to step to the side. The three of us stood in our trashed living room staring at one another. I hadn't noticed it with the lights off, but Shannon had a deep cut of her own along the left side of her face where her hairline started.

"You're going to need stitches for that," Evan told her, nodding to her wound.

"Oh, don't you worry about me, vamp," Shannon replied. "Why don't we start with you. So you're not a bloodsucker like Jonny says?"

"I was turned and not given a choice about it." Evan shrugged. "I only take what I need now to survive. I don't kill or turn anyone. It's not a perfect life, but I do what I can. I fell into work with the other vampires in Hollywood and here I am."

"And the blood you still take?" Shannon asked with a

raised eyebrow. "What about the innocent victims you prey on?"

"I already said it wasn't a perfect scenario, but until we find a sustainable alternative, this is what I am." Evan slumped his shoulders with a sigh. "If you have any suggestions, I'm open to them."

"Yeah, a sunbathing appointment or your head off your shoulders," Shannon sneered.

"Easy, easy," I told her. "We'll figure something out for him. He only needs to feed once a month for now and he just did. We can find a different way for him to live before it happens again."

"Great, now we're having a conversation on rehabbing vampires." Shannon sighed.

"And how do you know about all of us?" Evan asked. "Most humans that have an inkling into the supernatural don't live to talk about it."

"Oh, there's more of us out there than you'd like to think bloodsucker," Shannon countered. "Most of us just keep our mouths shut so other people don't think we're crazy. When people do talk about it, they're just written off as coocoo for Cocoa Puffs."

"Is that what happened to you?" I asked. "Did you see something and no one believed you?"

"I would have killed you too," Shannon continued, ignoring my question and looking at Evan. "I had you if your roommate hadn't stepped in."

"Maybe, maybe not." Evan shrugged. "We'll never know now that we're friends."

"Don't push it," Shannon warned him. She pressed a hand to the side of her head and winced for the first time. "I'm going to go take a closer look at this. I might need stitches."

Classic Shannon; she didn't wait to be invited or feel

awkward in our apartment. She just walked off to the bathroom and mirror in my room.

Evan and I stood alone staring at one another for a moment.

"Your new girlfriend's crazy," Evan said with a heavy sigh. "But she does have a *Punisher* kind of charm to her. I like her."

"Wow, she's not my girlfriend," I stated. "I'm damaged goods here. Tracy just broke up with me this morning."

"You know, I'm sorry to hear that, but also super relieved." Evan shrugged. "She was bad news. Like the Queen of Hearts from *Alice in Wonderland* bad news. Real talk, there were a few times I considered killing her just to take her out of your life. You know, set it up like an accident."

I gave him a deadpan stare.

"Just a joke." Evan extended both hands toward me, palms up. "Just trying to lighten the mood. But seriously, now you should go out with Shannon. I don't know, this might be because she just tried to kill me, but I like her for you."

"What? Are you insane?" I half shouted then lowered my voice. "Are you insane? I'm still recovering from having my heart put in a blender on high. I'm broken, damaged, Humpty Dumpty, might never love again. I'm not going to ask Shannon to go out on a date with me."

"Who's going out on a date with you?" Shannon asked, rejoining us in the room. "Are you about to download Tinder?"

"No, what?" I asked with a shake of my head.

"There's a lot of weirdos out there. Be careful," Shannon advised. "I'll admit it; I gave it a try when I got here. Not worth it. Way too many freaks in LA. Anyway, the vamp was right."

"Evan," Evan corrected her. "My name's Evan."

"Whatever, Bloodsucker," Shannon continued. "I'm going to need stitches. I'm headed to the ER."

EIGHTEEN

I HAD NEVER HEARD of any talk about stitches or the ER in such a nonchalant way. Shannon might as well have been talking about going to go grab a cup of coffee.

Evan looked at me wide-eyed then jerked his head in her direction.

"What?" I asked out loud as Shannon grabbed her katana and made herself somewhat pedestrian by removing her Kevlar vest and neck plate.

"Go with her," Evan hissed with a roll of his eyes.

"This chick is crazy," I whispered back in a hurried tone. "I don't really know anything about her. Like where did she learn how to fight like that?"

"You know I can hear both of you," Shannon interrupted, holding her vest in one hand and her neck plate in the other. She still looked far from someone you'd pass on the street with the katana poking over her shoulder and her arm and leg armor, but in the dark, she might pass just as someone headed home for the night.

"Jonny should go with you to make sure you get there," Evan volunteered.

"I don't need anyone," Shannon said before leaving. "And I'm watching you, Bloodsucker. One false move and I'll be there to take your head from your shoulders."

"No killing or turning for me, ma'am." Evan crossed his heart. "You'll see. We're going to be friends one day."

Shannon rolled her eyes and left.

She doesn't have anyone to go with her, I thought in my head under Evan's judging eye. *She probably doesn't even know where the ER is.*

"Hold up, Shannon," I called, exiting the apartment. "I'm coming with you."

Shannon was already at the end of our level, heading down the stairs.

"I don't need any charity or pity," Shannon told me, not breaking her stride. "I'll be fine. I'm wearing my big girl pants today."

"Well I'm wearing my big girl pants today too. You're not going to do anyone any good if you pass out behind the wheel from blood loss or get lost on the way," I told her, catching up with her quick strides. "Deal with it. I'm coming with you."

Shannon didn't say anything, dropping her armor and weapons off at her apartment then grabbing her keys.

I waited for her like an awkward third wheel, even though there were only two of us.

"Why are you doing this?" Shannon asked, locking her door as we headed to her car together. "If I were you, I'd hate me right now. I knocked you out. I befriended you just to get to Evan."

"That's a good question," I agreed, ignoring her question and asking one of my own. "How did you know Evan was a vampire at all?"

"Anonymous tip," Shannon answered. "I got a phone call one day saying there was a vamp in this complex."

"So what are you? Some kind of vampire killer for hire?" I asked.

We reached her car, an outdated black Mazda 3.

"I'll drive," I said, holding out my hand.

"I haven't lost that much blood," Shannon stated with a deadpan stare. "I'm fine."

"Great, you can be fine in the passenger side seat," I insisted. "Don't make me put the Rock Bottom on you right now. I owe you for knocking me out. I don't know karate, but I know crazy."

"You're ridiculous." Shannon ran her tongue around the inside of her mouth in thought. She slowly handed me her keys before pulling them back. "Answer me one thing, though. Why are you being so nice to me when you should hate me right now?"

"Because I know what it's like to be alone," I told her in a moment of honesty. "I know what it's like to feel like a stranger to everyone you see. I know what it's like to have to tell yourself every day that you're better off alone anyway when you know you're just lying to yourself."

Shannon swallowed hard. In the light of the street lamp in our apartment parking lot, we just stared at one another. Shannon opened her mouth as if she were going to say something non-sarcastic for once, but then thought better of it and tossed me her keys instead.

"Try not to scratch her," Shannon jerked her head to her old Mazda. "She's a classic."

"Oh, I bet," I said, letting myself in the car and unlocking the door for her.

The ride to the ER was quick. In Los Angeles, the hard truth was that clinics and ERs were in high demand. I had been to the one I took Shannon to once before when I cut my toenail wrong and it grew back ingrown like some kind of demonic pain from the other side.

We pulled up to a full parking lot, but thanks to the fact that the left side of Shannon's face was covered in a sheet of blood, the nurses pushed us to the front of the line.

I got more than one angry scowl from the passersby as if I was the one who had injured Shannon.

We were shown into a small exam room that smelled like hydrogen peroxide after check-in, where we waited.

"So are you even a personal trainer at all?" I asked, deciding to push my luck a bit. "Or was that all a lie?"

"Nope, it's all true, actually," Shannon answered. "I personal train as much as I can and when I get a lead I go out at night and track vampires."

"Just vampires?" I asked. "Evan told me there were other creatures out there too."

"Just vampires for now," Shannon said. "One killed my sister. Everyone thought I was crazy when I told them what I saw. No one believed me, not even my parents. Eventually, I found answers to what I was searching for. Those answers have turned me into what I am today."

"A personal trainer slash hunter," I said for her. "Who doesn't blink at pain and sucker punches grown men."

"Yeah, something like that," Shannon answered with a rueful smile. "I am sorry about hitting you. Personal training just seemed like a good fit for staying in shape for what I really wanted to do anyway."

Shannon stared at the wall across from us in our tiny room. The white paper lining the table she sat on crinkled underneath her weight as she shifted uncomfortably.

"We were still teenagers," Shannon said, more to the wall than myself. "Louise was older than me, already eighteen and working her first job as a waitress at a local diner. She was gorgeous. All the guys in town wanted to go out with her, but she was fiercer than even me."

"Really?" I asked with a sad smile. "That seems hard to imagine."

"Oh yeah." Shannon laughed out loud. "She'd send boys home crying. One time, she gave this kid who wouldn't leave her alone a purple nurple that darn near ripped his nipple clean off. I had forgotten about that."

The room quieted again. The smile on Shannon's face disappeared. I wasn't a counselor or psychiatrist, but I knew enough to know when to keep my mouth shut and just let Shannon tell me her story in her own time.

"One day, this guy comes into the diner. He's all dressed up with a Mercedes and says he's visiting from Hollywood just out for a few business meetings and looking for new talent." Shannon swallowed hard. "My sister bought it all. She starts seeing him during the few weeks he's in town. One night, she goes with him and stays out past curfew. My parents are freaking out."

Shannon paused again, taking in a deep breath and letting it out slowly. I could see her hands turn into fists.

"I didn't want her to get in trouble. We always looked out for each other like that," Shannon's voice quivered, not in sadness but growing rage. "I went to the hotel he was staying at to get her to come home. Through the window, there's a part in the curtain and I see him—I see him, eyes all black, teeth in her like some kind of animal. There was blood everywhere. I started screaming for help. People began to take notice. The man who turned my sister ran out of his room and to his car, knocking me over."

"Did you say turned?" I asked, not expecting this twist in the story. "He turned your sister into a vampire?"

Shannon nodded.

"The sun was just coming up. I sat on the ground just outside the room, dealing with the concussion the door handed me when the man burst out of his room," Shannon continued quietly. "I thought Louise was already dead, there was just so much blood. Then Louise gets to her feet and walks toward me as if she were seeing if I was okay. As soon as she stepped outside and the sunlight hit her—she started flaking in some kind of supernatural heat. She turned to ash right in front of me. Just like that, she was gone."

A moment of heavy silence rested on the room like some kind of physical weight. Nothing that came to mind felt right to say at the moment.

"So I promised myself I'd find him," Shannon finished. "When no one believed my story, I took it upon myself to seek answers to what I saw happen. Long story short, here I am hunting vampires in Hollywood."

"I'm so sorry," I told her. "I know that doesn't seem like enough, but I get it. Thank you for sharing that with me. I get why you want to kill all vampires now."

"If Evan's what you say he is, he'd be a first." Shannon relaxed her hands. "All the ones I've killed have been bad news."

"How many have you killed?" I asked incredulously.

"Seven," Shannon said without blinking. "They all deserved it. I'll kill triple that number if that's what it takes to catch my sister's killer. Heck, I might keep up this gig even after I find him. There are too many of them out there and no one's regulating them at all."

"But other people must know," I said. "I mean, if you and I know plus whoever tipped you off about Evan. If there are other people out there that know what's going on, maybe they'll start doing something about it too?"

"Yeah, those people are called crazy when they start speaking out." Shannon rubbed her tired eyes. "Some of the people who have actually seen the paranormal have AA type meetings if you know where to look."

"What?" I asked. "Like, hi my name's Jonny. My roommate is a vampire type AA meetings?"

"Yeah, well, most people there aren't living with a supernatural, but, yes," Shannon responded. "You can come with me if you want. They have another meeting tomorrow night."

"That might be good," I told her. "It's nice to have someone to talk to about all of this."

"I know what you mean," Shannon added. "If you ever tell anyone I told you this, I'll have to kill you, but it felt good talking about Louise. I mean, remembering what a fireball she was and the whole purple nurple incident. I had forgotten about that."

"Wow, did I come in at a bad time?" A young male doctor opened the door. "I heard purple nurple. Is that what you're in here for?"

"Nope; cut myself shaving," Shannon answered, pointing to the side of her face.

"I've heard that one before." The doctor gave me a friendly smile and nod before snapping on a pair of gloves and taking a closer look at the cut. "This looks really clean. What were you using to shave, a katana?"

Shannon and I traded a look.

"Oh." The doctor looked between us. "I was kidding, but —okay. You see some pretty weird stuff in here working the late night shift at the ER."

"Let me get something to take the edge off and then we'll get it cleaned and stitched closed." The doctor moved over to a tray he brought in and started filling a syringe from a bottle. "If there's any kind of abuse going on here, we can talk alone. Just say the word."

Both Shannon and I couldn't help but chuckle.

"Domestic violence is not a joking matter." The doctor skewered both of us with a firm stare but lingered on me. "I'm serious."

"No, no, I agree," I told him. "It's just that she knocked me out and tied me up, so if there was any kind of abuse going on here, it's not what you think."

The doctor looked at Shannon to corroborate my story.

"I have issues." Shannon shrugged. "I'm working on them."

NINETEEN

SHANNON TOOK the stitches like a champ. I shouldn't have guessed anything else. The ride home was actually pleasant. We even had a laugh at her kicking Evan in the balls and him returning the favor.

When we got back to Haven Apartments, it was already in the early hours of the morning. I opened the gate for her and we walked through the courtyard area to the stairs that would lead us to our respective apartments.

"So what are you going to do next?" Shannon asked.

"What do you mean?" I questioned.

"I mean, your eyes are opened to a whole new world and you're handling it like someone sane," Shannon answered. "You should really come with me tomorrow night to the meeting."

"Oh right, the AA meeting for the supernatural," I responded, wrapping my arms around myself against the chill of the night. "I really need to work my other jobs to bring in some money, especially now that the hemorrhoid cream gig didn't work out. But if it's at night, I can make it."

"Great, meeting starts at seven, so we should head out about six thirty," Shannon said as we reached the third level of the apartment complex and her floor. "Sorry again about the whole knocking you unconscious thing and tying you up to my weight rack. How did you get out from under that weight rack anyway? I mean, that thing has to weigh a few hundred pounds."

"I just hulked out on it," I answered, rubbing my tired eyes. A yawn escaped my lips.

"All right, go to bed, Mr. Male Model. Cinderella needs her sleep," Shannon teased.

I was too tired to argue. I stayed just long enough to watch Shannon cross her floor and get into her apartment safely. I climbed the last story of steps to my own apartment and immediately came to a halt.

My hairs stood on end. It was already cold, but an unnatural chill raced down my spine. Something was watching me. I wasn't sure how I knew, but I could feel it.

All the way down my hall in the corner of the unit of apartments, two yellow eyes close to the floor blinked at me from the shadows.

My mouth went dry as the moonlight reflected off something massive and the teeth that belonged to said creature.

We just stood there staring at one another. My mind immediately raced for a rational explanation.

It's a dog. It's just a big black dog with impossibly large teeth, I lied to myself. *Someone who lives here has a massive black dog you've never seen before.*

A whistle touched my ears as I stared at the impossible creature. The sound the whistle made was low and barely audible to me. The dog or whatever it was seemed to be able to hear the sound and recognize it as a call. Like a blur of darkness, it was gone, racing down the other side of the U-shaped level and disappearing in the stairwell beyond.

"My heart can't take this," I muttered to myself as I made my way to my apartment door.

Evan, being the great roommate he was, had already cleaned up the apartment from the battle royale he and Shannon hosted. I went to my room and fell asleep, dead to the world. Lucky for me, there were no more dreams of my past waiting for me.

WHEN I WOKE, it was business as usual. It seemed my life was getting back to normalish despite the insane turn it had taken. I went to Tacos Culos Locos to twirl signs in the morning and planned to drive Lyfter in the afternoon before the supernatural AA meeting.

When I arrived at Tacos Culos Locos, Mrs. Gomez wore a look of horror when she saw my face.

"Ay, Jonny." Mrs. Gomez came out from around the counter with both hands extended in my direction. "What happened to your face, mijo?"

"Oh right," I said, allowing her to take my cheeks in her hands like some kind of veterinarian inspecting an animal. She turned my head from side to side. "I had an accident with a door jamb. Ran right into it. I don't know what I was thinking. There's a lot on my mind right now: global warming, politics, bigfoot sightings."

"And of course the wedding," Mrs. Gomez added. "What did she say? I didn't get a text the night the big question was popped. Shame on you, but I know you're busy."

"Oh yeah, about that." I sighed, trying to sift through my feelings. I still felt numb, depressed, and empty. "Tracy broke up with me."

"Oh, Jonny!" Mrs. Gomez screamed, wrapping her arms around me in a tight bear hug. "Jonny, mijo, I'm so sorry!"

The few patrons who were already inside the restaurant all turned in their seats to look at me, including the workers.

"I can't imagine how you feel right now," Mrs. Gomez went on, wailing each word. "To be rejected like that, thrown to the side of the curb like a moldy tortilla. I saw this coming. I should have done more, said something to help."

"I'll be all right," I said. "I'll figure—"

"Jorge, Jorge." Mrs. Gomez broke our embrace and headed for the kitchen. "Jonny needs to sit down and eat. His girlfriend he was in love with, about to be his wife, broke up with him. His dreams have been dashed. He is a mess of emotion."

Everyone in the restaurant stared at me with that same look of pity I used to get in high school. My blood boiled, but what was I going to do?

"Sit, mijo, sit." Mrs. Gomez waved to me to take a seat at a small table with two chairs on either side. "You twirl the sign soon. Just sit for now and I'll get you something to eat."

I knew arguing with her wasn't going to get me anywhere, so instead, I sat down and ate a breakfast burrito the size of my face. To be honest, it tasted wonderful and it was the first real food I had eaten and kept down in a while.

After breakfast, it was a morning full of sign twirling and impromptu dance moves in the smelly chicken suit. Now, having seen more blood than I would have liked to recently, I was almost positive it was in fact bloodstains in the chicken suit.

As lovely as Mrs. Gomez was, she was also a shrewd businesswoman. I wasn't allowed to work more than my designated hours or else she would have to offer me benefits.

That meant my afternoon was free to work my second job as a Lyfter driver. Lyfter was a great way to earn some extra money in between casting calls and sign twirling. I was on my way to my first pickup when I checked my email on my phone at a red light.

A message from someone named Amber at V Model Management was wedged between some prince in Nigeria stating he had family jewels he needed me to protect and an advertisement to grow my nether regions.

I clicked on the V Model Management email:

Hi Jonny,

My name is Amber. I work at V Model Management. Mr. Bloodstone asked that I reach out to you and get you to fill out some preliminary paperwork so we can start getting you sent to castings. Please feel free to call and schedule a time to come in at your earliest convenience.

Thank you and talk soon,

Amber

"Oh great," I said, scratching my head. A horn blared behind me, signaling me to move. The light in front of me had turned green somewhere between my internal debate of everything I ever wanted at the largest casting agency in Hollywood and the fact that they were run by blood-sucking real life vampires.

I gunned the engine, moving forward with the flow of afternoon traffic. So here I was. On one hand, I could work with the enemy and fulfill my dream or refuse and go back to sign twirling.

These thoughts weighed in my mind as I traversed through traffic following the pickup of my next passenger. The address took me to a rundown strip mall with stores ranging from laundry to smoke shops.

I pulled up at the address where a woman wearing jeans so tight, I thought they might burst at any moment, walked up to my car. Her eyes were huge as she took in my less than impressive vehicle.

Without electronic controls, I had to lean over and manually roll down the passenger side window.

"Hello, were you waiting for Lyfter?" I asked.

"Mmm hmmm, mmm hmmm." The woman ran a hand full of nails so long they could be knives through her hair. "I'm waiting for a Lyfter vehicle, not some death machine from the sixties that's not going to make it down the street. I have an important meeting to get to, do you feel me?"

"I feel you," I answered, inwardly biting my tongue. "I know it's an older car, but it'll get you where you need to go. It doesn't look like you're headed that far. I can have you there in fifteen minutes."

"Mmm hmmm, mmm hmmm." The woman weighed her options in her head. "Listen, I'm not trying to be rude here, but—I don't think Priscilla's going to be comfortable riding in this, Mmm mmm. I just feel a lot of strange Ju-ju emanating from your aura right now like some dark or supernatural type stuff. Mmmm mmmm, Priscilla, don't touch that. You feel me?"

"Who's Priscilla?" I asked, confused.

The woman blinked at me like I was stupid.

"Oh, right, that's your name." I sighed, ready to try and placate her to get in my car without seeming desperate or stalkerish. The truth was I needed the money. "Well, Priscilla, all I can promise you is a safe and quick ride. If you have to call another driver, you might be late for your appointment. Look at my reviews on Lyfter."

While Priscilla mulled over my offer, I caught movement in my rearview mirror. A large black dog, maybe even a wolf, sat in the shade at the far end of the strip mall.

If it wasn't the exact same animal I had seen the night before, this was its twin. Even though it rested in the shadows, I could see it much clearer now. It had to weigh a hundred or more pounds. Yellow eyes and a pink tongue, licking its canines.

I turned in my seat to get a better look at the strange

beast. In the second it took me to shift my weight and look behind me, it was gone.

"Okay, okay, then," Priscilla acquiesced, opening the rear door that squeaked on its hinges like some kind of popping bones in an old body. "I'll take a chance with you, then, Mr. Classic Car. Your aura is pure, but the auras you've been picking up around you, well, let me tell you, you need to rethink who you've been hanging out with."

"I feel you," I said as Priscilla closed the door and we entered the stream of traffic. I looked out the rearview mirror one more time. The dog, wolf, or whatever it was, was gone.

TWENTY

I WAS able to fit in another four rides after Priscilla. One was some guy who smelt like hand sanitizer and wanted to be taken to the adult store and another a young kid who kept asking me if I knew where to buy drugs.

I pulled back into Haven just in time to go with Shannon to the AA meeting for supernatural survivors or whatever it was. Evan's BMW was still gone. I wanted to talk to him about the offer from V Model Management before I made a decision. I knew what I wanted, but after hearing Shannon's story about what the vampire had done to her sister, I wasn't sure which direction to go.

Making my way through our courtyard, I noticed Rami heading out from his apartment. He looked like he was in a hurry to get back to the Kwiki Mart. A burden of guilt hit me like lightning bolt as I remembered Mrs. Grundy and the kindness she had shown me. I still had yet to thank her.

"Hey, Rami?" I called, catching up to the store owner before he exited the front gate. "Wait up."

"Hey, Jonny, got to get to the store—what happened to

your face?" Rami asked, concerned. "Are you okay? Did those Girl Scouts work you over?"

"Yeah, I didn't know they made brass knuckles for fists so small," I joked. "I'm fine, though, seriously. Tripped over my own feet down a flight of stairs and ran into—I'm fine. You said Mrs. Grundy was your neighbor? Which unit does she live in? I wanted to thank her for picking up my tab and offer to pay her back, if I can."

"Oh, right." Rami pointed to the unit on the right side of his own. "That's her. But seriously, you're not inflicting harm on yourself, are you? Sometimes I worry about you creative types."

"No, no, seriously," I reassured him. "I'm good. The breakup's been rough, but there's so many other things going on right now, I think my mind has been too busy to really focus on just the negative."

"Keep your chin up," Rami said over his shoulder. "You know I got to get back to the store, but I'm here if you want to talk. Swing by and Slushy's on me. Or at least I'll give you a discount."

"Thanks, Rami." I waved as he took off down the sidewalk.

I made my way over to the unit Rami pointed out and rapped on the door. A mat under my feet greeted me with a language I had never seen before. It looked like runes or some kind of ancient text. The words by my shoes shimmered for a moment and glowed.

I blinked hard, shaking my head from side to side. When I refocused on the words, they were plain black writing.

"I got to lay off Mrs. Gomez's horchata," I mumbled to myself.

The door swung open without a sound. Mrs. Grundy stood there blinking at me through massive glasses, a purple knit sweater over her stooped shoulders.

"Jonny, how are you?" Mrs. Grundy asked as if she had expected me. "Before you offer, the answer's no. I'm not taking back any money you try to give me. Your fatty foods weren't that much and we all need a hand every so often. We should, however, talk about your diet and how you deal with your emotions."

I opened my mouth then closed it again. Then repeated the act.

"Well, come on now, spit it out." Mrs. Grundy gave me a sly smile followed by a motherly purse of her lips. "Say, what happened to your face? Did someone sucker punch you?"

"Sorry, I'm just having a hard time talking to you," I finally managed. "It's like you know what I'm going to say before I say it. Thank you for the groceries. If you won't let me pay you back, let me help you out some other way sometime."

Before I could continue, a dog rounded the corner. It wasn't the same black dog I had seen over the course of the last twenty-four hours, but this one was the same size. A Rottweiler so large its head nearly came up to Mrs. Grundy's own sniffed the air and padded toward the door.

I wasn't afraid of dogs but neither was I used to being this close to animals so large.

"Easy," Mrs. Grundy said. "He's a friend."

"Who are you talking to?" I asked, taking a tentative step back.

"Both of you." Mrs. Grundy chuckled. "Jonny, this is Warden, Warden, this is Jonny."

The large dog sniffed the air again then let off a low growl.

"He's a friend, my boy, he's a friend. I'm sure of it." Mrs. Grundy scratched the big animal behind his ears. She turned to me. "Sorry, he has a rather great sense of smell. He may be catching a whiff of something else on you. But you should probably get going. Don't you have a meeting to get to?"

I wagged a finger at her, not knowing how she could have known I was on my way out.

Mrs. Grundy waggled her eyebrows, clearly enjoying my confusion.

"How have I not seen you before?" I asked instead of any of the other dozen questions I wanted to know. "I've lived here for a year now."

"I've been here much longer than that," Mrs. Grundy remarked with a shrug. "There are always people moving in and out of Haven. Maybe we've never crossed paths. Or maybe now that your eyes are open to new possibilities, you're able to see me for who I am. Like when you own a white car all of a sudden, you see nothing but white cars on the road."

I caught more movement in the house; another dog, this one larger than Warden came to the door wagging a tail so hard, I thought it might shake completely off its butt. This dog looked like pictures I had seen of a St. Bernard.

Unlike Warden, this animal practically shook with excitement at seeing me. It looked from Mrs. Grundy to me and back again as if seeking her permission.

"No, not yet, Cerberus, not yet. He's not ready yet, but soon," Mrs. Grundy soothed the large animal.

"How many dogs do you have?" I asked.

"Oh, they come and go as they like." Mrs. Grundy shrugged. "This is more like a layover for them if you will."

"I don't understand that at all," I said honestly.

"I know." Mrs. Grundy chuckled. "You're not supposed to. For now, you and I are two ships passing in the night."

"Isn't that a sexual reference?" I asked.

"Yes, indulge an old woman her inappropriate jokes." Mrs. Grundy waggled her brow. "I'm old. I get to say stuff like that every once in a while and get away with it. Your girlfriend is waiting."

"Who?" I asked.

Mrs. Grundy gestured with her chin over my shoulder.

I turned around to see Shannon coming down the stairs.

"Oh, she's not my—" I said, turning around to address the old woman. Without a sound, the door in front of me was closed. "—girlfriend."

"Hey, Stinky," Shannon said, reaching the bottom floor. "You ready?"

"Yeah, I think so," I answered, still confused at the conversation I just had with Mrs. Grundy.

"You look like you just read a word in the dictionary you don't understand," Shannon said, tossing me a bottle.

I caught the cold beverage in the air. It was a protein drink.

"Something like that," I told her, falling in step with Shannon as we exited the rear of Haven apartments complex. I shook the protein shake in my hand. "What's this for?"

"Figured you'd forget to eat dinner or run out of time," Shannon answered. "Was I right or was I right?"

"You're not wrong," I agreed, snapping the top off the carton and taking a long pull of the chocolate liquid. "Mmm, tastes like Yoo-hoo."

"Like what?" Shannon asked. "I'll drive."

"You know, Yoo-hoo," I said, getting into Shannon's vehicle. "Chocolate drink, glass bottle, yellow container?"

"Nothing," Shannon admitted, pushing her lower lip out. "That must be a weird Hollywood thing too."

"No way," I answered, buckling my seatbelt in place. "Yoo-hoo is a delicious drink-like treat enjoyed by millions of people across the globe."

"Whatever you say." Shannon started the vehicle and merged into traffic.

Talking with Shannon was easy. We joked about sports, playfully argued about the best movie, and even touched on something serious.

"How are you holding up?" Shannon ventured the question out of the blue as we pulled off the freeway and into an industrial section of the city. "I mean, with the whole breakup thing. Did you dive face first into a dozen donuts today or snort a line of Cheez Whiz?"

"I thought about shooting up with some pudding, but I got too caught up with work," I answered. "Honestly, I've been trying not to think about it. You know, deal with it nice and healthy by burying it down deep and not talking to anyone about it."

"Awww, this is the way," Shannon teased.

"This is the way," I agreed with a smile.

The car grew quiet as each of us thought about what we weren't talking about. I guessed Shannon was remembering her sister, while I dwelt on my failed relationship.

As luck would have it, we pulled up to an abandoned-looking warehouse on a street of abandoned-looking warehouses. There wasn't much in the way of traffic.

"Are you sure this is the right place?" I asked, looking the place up and down. "I mean, it doesn't look like the most crowded street in LA."

"Oh, this is the place," Shannon said, getting out of the car.

I joined her, looking up at the cloudless sky. There was a bite in the wind that any Midwesterner would have called me a baby for complaining about.

Shannon led the way to a chain-link fence that stood guard around a white warehouse building that had seen better days. Rust now ate at the sides of the building and the roof itself, calling into question the structure's integrity.

There was a light inside spilling from the interior and

through a window. Calm chatter could be heard from within as we walked closer.

"It's a small group; there's coffee too," Shannon said. "It'll be good to talk with other people about what we know."

"How did you find this place again?" I asked. "I mean, who's advertising meetings like this?"

Shannon dug her phone out of her pocket, flipping to Facebook. She pulled up a group for an Urban Fantasy book titled *We Need to Talk*. The tagline for the book was "When no one will listen, where do you turn?"

"What, are you serious?" I asked incredulously. "There's coded messages for these meetups?"

"People are out there searching for answers." Shannon shrugged. "Messaging the admin of this group led me down a rabbit hole and eventually here. There are chapters of W.A. across the country."

"W.A.?" I asked.

"Witnesses Anonymous," Shannon answered.

We finally made it up the long driveway to a massive sliding door Shannon rapped on without hesitation. The booming sound reverberated inward in typical Shannon fashion.

The talking inside stopped.

A second later, a short stocky man with wide shoulders and a heavy beard slid the heavy door open as if it weighed nothing. He appraised us through thick eyebrows.

"Shannon." He nodded. "Who's the noob?"

"John Hunter," I greeted, extending my hand toward the man. "Nice to meet you."

"Ryan." The man grabbed my hand, nearly ripping it from my socket. I could feel hard calluses across his palm. "Ryan Michaels. Always glad to have another face in the group. You a witness to something unnatural or you just a looky-loo?"

"He's seen some stuff," Shannon responded for me. "You know I wouldn't bring a nonbeliever to a meeting like this."

The edge in Shannon's voice made Ryan take a step back and raise his hands in front of him to calm Shannon.

"My bad, my bad," Ryan stated. "Come on in, then. It's getting cold outside."

Shannon and I stepped inside the warehouse. The place must have been used as some kind of machine shop during the day. Heavy apparatuses and materials lined the walls with a large open space in the middle.

A circle of folding chairs had been set up along with a long table holding a pot of steaming Black Rifle coffee and a pink box of donuts. I immediately recognized the brand of coffee with the bag sitting there next to it. It was one of my favorites. The smell of machine shop grease and rich coffee mixed and assailed my nostrils like some kind of heavenly aroma luring me farther into the warehouse.

There were already a half dozen people present who ranged from a teenage girl with a nose ring to an older man losing his hair.

"Hey, everyone," Ryan addressed the group. "We have a new visitor today. Let's make him feel welcome. His name's John."

"Hi, John," the group said in unison and my first meeting at W.A. began.

TWENTY-ONE

"AND THAT WAS my first time being felt up by the Sasquatch," Delores said, shivering slightly in her seat, although her face wasn't one of anger or disgust. She actually smiled a bit at the memory. "His hands were so strong. When he finally found the leftover candy bar in my pocket, he took off into the night, but I wish he would have kept going."

"My gosh, is this a W.A. meeting or some kind of R-rated romance narration?" The teenager whose name tag red Sue said exactly what I was thinking. "Delores, you need a man."

"I do," Delores agreed without complaint. "I really do. My Grinder app is downloading now. Hopefully, I'll find someone online."

"Sue, please," Ryan chided. "This is a safe place for all of us to come and talk about our supernatural experiences."

My eyes were so wide, I thought they were going to fall out of my head. Delores was actually slouching in her seat now, fanning herself.

Shannon jabbed me hard in the ribs.

"And why don't we move over to our newest member."

Ryan waved to me with a meaty hand. "John, would you like to share?"

"Uh, yeah, sure," I said, clearing my throat. "This whole thing is still really new to me. I was introduced to the world of vampirism a few days ago when I found out my best friend was one of them. It's still hard to really wrap my head around. I've been dealing with a lot since then. It's strange, though, it's terrifying and exciting all at once, like the world can still be new and hold secrets. It doesn't seem so boring anymore."

"I know what you mean, if I may intrude." The older man who had to be in his early seventies gave me a hard nod. "Name's Nate by the way."

"Go ahead, Nate," I said. "I was done anyway. That's pretty much it."

"I've seen and done a lot in my days from my time in Nam serving our country to my career as a boxer. I thought I had seen it all," Nate said, smacking his lips. "Then up comes my unwanted guest, and all of a sudden, I started back to square one like you said. I have no problem saying it's a bit scary, but more interesting, like I'm on some kind of journey of discovery."

"Nate has a creature under his house," Shannon added. "He's not exactly sure what it is yet, but he's convinced it's supernatural."

"It hardly makes any sounds under the house, but it smells gaud-awful," Nate said. "I'd go down there myself, but my back isn't what it used to be. The crawl space is too low for old bones like mine. Plus, I don't necessarily want whatever is down there killed, just moved out."

"What makes you think it's something supernatural and not just some kind of cat or possum?" I asked. "I mean, it could be anything, right?"

"It could be, but it ain't." Nate whipped out his smart

phone like some kind of weapon. "You see, I installed a camera above the opening of the crawl space so I could see what I was dealing with."

"Not the video again," Sue mumbled.

"You two can show and tell when the meeting's over," Ryan said, keeping us on track. "We're almost done now."

The rest of the stories were fascinating. Sue told about a zombie strain at her school that was spreading faster than a virus on crack. Other stories were of werewolves, fairies, and even a talking gnome. Although Steve, who shared about his encounter with the gnome, smelt like he bathed with marijuana, so I wasn't sure his story was entirely accurate.

Neither Shannon or Ryan chose to speak about their experiences. It wasn't that mysterious that Shannon would opt out of speaking about her dead sister. I did, however, find it interesting that Ryan, who led the meetings, decided to pass.

After the last member shared, Ryan wrapped us up.

"Well, a big thank you to everyone who came out tonight," Ryan said, standing from his folding chair. "I want you all to know that you are not alone out there. We are here for you and we believe you."

That seemed to be the cue for everyone to get up and head for one last round of Black Rifle coffee and donuts.

"I'm telling you, man, that little garden gnome was having a conversation with me and everything," Steve said before I rose from my seat. "I mean, he was like professor status and stuff. Talked like Einstein and Neil deGrasse Tyson had some kind of super smart love child raised by Steven Hawking."

"Easy, Steve," Nate said, coming over to Shannon and me. "He believes you. We all do."

"Oh, show him the video, man, show him the video," Steve urged Nate. "Wait until you see this. This is some trippy stuff right here."

Nate moved to stand between me and Shannon, extending his arm as far as he could and squinting at the screen before he hit the play button.

The screen transitioned to a nighttime scene. The colors were black and a bright green indicative of some kind of night camera.

We were looking down from a vantage point that I guessed was the roof into a side yard. A square opening where the house met the ground couldn't be more than a foot, maybe a foot and a half high.

We waited, watching. Something poked out of the crawl space. At first glance, it looked like a big cat. Like the head of a small mountain lion. As it moved out further, I could see the body was covered in what looked like feathers and there were even wings on its back. It moved low to the ground and on all fours. A pair of long tails rounded out the strange creature's appearance.

Altogether, I guess it had to be two feet tall, since it crouched to get out from under the crawl space and weighed around fifty pounds.

"See, what do you think of that?" Nate asked.

"Trippy man, trippy as heck." Steve bobbed his head in time with his words. "You got to take care of that thing. man. You can't let that thing have babies under your house. Next thing you know, it's ripping through the floorboards trying to make a midnight snack out of you and the missus."

"Yeah, but who do I call?" Nate asked, looking to any of us for answers. "It's not like the city is going to believe me. A private pest control company would come out, but they're not equipped to deal with this. I don't want anyone getting hurt."

"Shannon could do it," I blurted without thinking. "She has experience climbing under houses and getting possums."

All eyes swung to me then to Shannon.

"That was once a long time ago." Shannon shook her head. "I'm not here for that now."

"But I mean, you have the armor and weapons and everything," I pressed. "If you went one on one with Evan, you could take this thing out for sure."

"And you don't have to kill it," Nate said, jumping on the bandwagon. "I just need it out. I could pay you, of course. Whatever you want. I just want that stench gone from under my floor and I can't do it myself. John could help you."

"Whoa, let's not get too crazy here," I argued, raising both hands up in a sign of surrender. "I don't have the extensive training Shannon does. I'm just a fan."

"Monster hunting, so baller," Steve agreed as he walked off to grab some donuts.

"You could name your price," Nate insisted. "I'm retired from the military and the boxing ring, where I've done well for myself."

I thought of all the hours sign twirling and Lyfter driving. I remembered how hot it could get in that chicken suit. How I always had to convince people I was picking up that my vehicle would make it from point A to point B.

"We'll do it for eight hundred," I said, pulling the number out of my rear end.

"Done." Nate grinned from ear to ear. "I'm telling you, it'll be easy money. I'd do it myself, but like I said, these old bones won't fit under there."

"Sorry, Nate, sorry," Shannon interjected, grabbing me so hard by my arm, I felt like I was being taken by a teacher to the principal's office. "I just need a minute with my psychotic friend here."

"Take all the time you need," Nate said with a smile.

Shannon walked me back a few steps farther into the machine shop. Her grip was vise-like.

"Ouch, I bruise easily," I tried joking with her. Shannon wasn't having any of it.

"What are you doing?" she hissed, finally releasing my arm.

"What do you mean, 'what am I doing'?" I asked her. "I'm getting us paid. Eight hundred bucks. You know how long it would take me to earn money like that sign twirling or driving Lyfter? We'll split it. Six hundred for me and two hundred for you."

Shannon raised her eyebrow and gave me a look that would have made Medusa shudder.

"Okay, five hundred for me and three hundred for you," I tried to negotiate. "That's tax free. I mean, I should earn a little bit more since I found the job. Come on, you're telling me you couldn't use the money? I'm sure you do great as a personal trainer, but who couldn't use a few extra dollars?"

I could tell I was finally getting through to her. The look on her face was going from a "hell no" to a "no way."

I saw that as progress.

"There has to be a new sword or something dangerous used for killing that you've been wanting," I urged. "Maybe some new gloves or a punching bag?"

"I do want to up the arsenal," Shannon said to herself. "Okay, four hundred, four hundred right down the middle."

"Would you be willing to take—" I cut off the next words I was about to say under the death stare I got from Shannon. "Four hundred for each of us sounds great, partner."

I extended my hand.

Shannon took it and pumped it firmly.

We turned to rejoin Nate, who waited to hear what we decided with eager anticipation.

"My associate and I," I began, motioning to Shannon, "agree to take the job."

"Oh, this is wonderful news." Nate slapped me on the

shoulder. "You've made an old man's day. I can't tell you how tough it is to be sitting in the old La-Z-Boy watching *MASH* and an odor comes through the floor like someone mixed vomit with rotten eggs. When can you start?"

I had to swallow the bile that came to my mouth at the mere mention of the disgusting combination.

"Give us tomorrow morning to get things together and then we'll come take care of your problem in the afternoon," Shannon told him. "We should do it while it's still light out and most people are at work. Let's say two o'clock."

"Two it is, you got it," Nate said with another side grin. "See you tomorrow for a little adventure."

TWENTY-TWO

SHANNON HAD training appointments the next morning she couldn't move. That meant I got to sleep in for a few hours anticipating a workout from hell of my own she promised to give me when she came back.

That gave me dangerous downtime to think about Tracy and what I was going to do about V Model Management. I scrolled through my social media accounts, looking at pictures of Tracy and wondering if she had ever loved me at all.

Maybe it wasn't even her fault. Maybe she thought she loved me, but it turned out she loved her career more.

Multiple times I thought about calling her or sending her a text, but what would that solve? Yeah, I was hurt, but did that mean I wanted to get back with her? To be honest, I wasn't sure what I wanted for the time being.

A rap on my door in the cadence of the *Terminator* theme song interrupted me from my thoughts.

I set down my phone and rolled over in bed. "Come in."

Evan opened the door dressed in his silk kimono with two steaming cups of coffee.

"Thought I'd drop in to see what you were up today," Evan said, placing my cup on my nightstand for me. "Can't have you in bed feeling bad for what the ice queen did to your heart."

"Thanks," I said, sitting up. "No, I'll be okay, but I'm glad that you came in. I got an email from V Model Management. They want me to fill out some paperwork so I can start working."

"Well, that's great news, isn't it?" Evan asked, surprised I wasn't more enthused. "They're the top modeling agency with all the connections. They'll get you work for sure. Why am I sensing you haven't told me everything already?"

I decided to spill my guts. Evan, as the one friend who had stuck with me through everything and as a member of both the supernatural and human world, might understand.

He spit his coffee out when I told him about Shannon's past and then again when I mentioned the creature we were supposed to capture.

When I finished, he was wide eyed, shaking his head.

"Man, Jonny, trouble comes to you like fake news to the media." Evan sighed. "You've got a lot to handle."

"First I need to decide what to do about Mr. Bloodstone and V Model Management," I said, sipping on my coffee. "I mean, here it is. The 'in' I would have jumped at last week without thinking twice. Why is it so hard now?"

"Because you know who it is, you know who controls the power," Evan stated as if it were the simplest thing to understand. "You have to decide if you want to get in bed with the vampires running Hollywood or not. I can't answer that for you. It's easy for me since I'm already one of them."

"But you're different," I told him. "You don't turn or kill."

"It's not easy." Evan shrugged. "Sure, I don't agree with what other vamps do, but I understand where they're coming from. It's hard to go against your very nature day in and day out."

"Why do you?" I questioned. "I mean, why did you choose to be different when everyone else is killing or turning left and right?"

"We're getting pretty deep here, Jonny." Evan shifted in his pink fluffy slippers uncomfortably. "I came in to have coffee, not be interviewed on the Doctor Phil show or is it Doctor Oz? I get those two confused."

"You don't have to answer," I said, already knowing Evan would. "You've been a great friend through all of this and done more than enough."

"I guess I never had the chance to want to be turned or not," Evan said, thinking back to his own encounter. "That choice was made for me, so how could I make that choice now for others? As far as the killing thing goes, I just don't have it in me. I know I'm not human anymore. I'm something else. But maybe, just maybe if I can keep myself from killing anyone out of pure greed for their blood, I can retain a sliver of my humanity."

The room grew quiet.

Evan stared down at his coffee in a gloomy, very unlike Evan way.

I could see the hurt in his eyes, the hate for what he was and the hope for redemption in his own story.

"So I'm pretty sure Shannon still wants to chop your head off, but I do think she's warming up to you," I said, changing the subject. "She could have come in last night and tried to ambush you again, but she didn't."

"Right?" Evan lit up like a light bulb. "Aw man, she's perfect for you. I know, I know you're working through your PTSD with Tracy, but just keep an open mind. I mean, how many women do you know carry body armor and a katana with them when they go out?"

"I might have left out an important side note," I said, remembering how Shannon told me she found Evan. "Shannon got an anonymous tip about you being a vampire. Someone out there knows."

To my surprise, Evan seemed unfazed.

"A lot of people out there know about me." Evan shrugged. "Perks of the job having my face everywhere and other petty models hating on my success. The real question is who knows Shannon's a vampire hunter."

We both took a moment to mull that one over.

"But seriously, we should talk about this creature you're going to go hunt." Evan was the first to break the silence. "You might be in over your head here. It's a strange world and even I don't know everything that goes bump in the night."

"Do you know who might?" I asked.

"There are historians of the supernatural called Watchers, but they're only whispered about. They have to find you, not you find them." Evan scratched the underside of his jaw. "Sorry, I know; not very helpful."

"It's okay," I said. "The thing didn't look that big and we're only trying to get it out from under the house not kill it."

I spent the morning with Evan. It was great not to have to worry about sign twirling, Lyfter driving, or casting calls for the time being.

When ten o'clock rolled around, it was time for me to head down to Shannon's for my crash course in combat training.

"Come in," Shannon called as I rapped on her door.

Walking into her apartment, I immediately felt all the blood rush to my face. Shannon stood facing away from me putting a sports bra on over her head.

"Oh, I, ugh, should I come back?" I asked, averting my

eyes to the floor. "I didn't know you were changing. You said to come in."

"Take it easy," Shannon answered. "You're fine. I'm already done. I just wanted to change into some cleaner clothes from the gym before I get these clothes all sweaty again. You ready?"

"Yep," I said, looking up.

Shannon wore a pair of tight shorts, a sports bra, and her dark hair in a ponytail. She failed to put on any footwear, leading me to believe this was intentional.

"So you have plenty of strength," Shannon began, going to a corner of the room and coming back with two sticks the right size and shape to resemble a pair of swords. "What we need to work on now are combat skills. Have you ever trained with a weapon before?"

"Well, when I was little, I used to play laser tag..." I said, letting my voice trail off under Shannon's stare. "Ooooookay, not the time to joke. I get it. Honest answer, no. I have never trained with a sword. I have been to the shooting range a few times, but that's been it."

"Well, eventually, we should work our way up to firearms, but I'm not trying to get shot under some old guy's house because you get trigger happy," Shannon stated, tossing me one of the sticks. "Let's start with something like a sword and work our way up."

"Right," I said, proud of myself that I had caught the offered weapon in the air. The section of Shannon's apartment that would have been the family area was clear with everything with the exception of the punching bag.

We moved to the right of the heavy bag. A narrow lane of free space before we ran into the wall was all we needed to train.

What followed for the next three hours was a master class in bladed weapon training and hand-to-hand combat.

Shannon was a great teacher; brutal at best, violent at worst. She threw me over her hip a few times. By the time we were done with the sword training, I was sure I was going to look like I had been in a full-on fight. I could feel bruises forming on my forearms and shins where she struck me.

Our wooden swords cracked over and over again as we practiced. Eventually, we went to smaller wooden knives and then hand-to-hand combat.

It was near the end of our session that I started getting pissed. Shannon wasn't taking it easy on me at all during the hand-to-hand sparring section of our session.

Sure our hands were wrapped, but it still hurt like the dickens when she nailed me in the ribs or side of my head.

"Come on," Shannon half goaded, half encouraged me. "We're almost done. Don't slow down. They don't slow down. They'll be faster and stronger. We need to be smarter and last longer in a fight."

Sweat dripped from my hairline down my face. Oxygen came in heavy burning gulps.

Shannon kicked out at my stomach. I dropped my arms to block the blow, leaving my face open for a quick strike to my jaw. I wasn't sure if she was holding back, but it didn't feel like it when she hit me, that was for sure.

"Active," Shannon coached. "Always active. Come on; where's that same intensity I saw when you were hitting the bag the day of your breakup? Where is that same strength when you spilled all my weights from the rack? I'm not holding back. Neither will your enemies. Don't you hold back on me! Come on, Jonny, come on. I know you have more."

I didn't know how she still had enough oxygen to talk in the middle of training. I was saving any breath to suck in as much air as I could. My lungs burned nearly as badly as the muscles in my arms. Keeping them up in front of my face was a real chore.

Shannon came in again with a kick to my leg.

This time, I stepped to my right, putting the heavy punching bag between us.

"Good thinking, but what are you going to do now?" Shannon asked. "You can't hide behind the bag forever."

I balled my right hand into a fist and slammed my arm forward with all my weight behind the blow. The bag moved, swaying toward Shannon.

My instructor was too smart to get hit by the bag, but that was what I was counting on.

Shannon moved to the side, ready to engage around the swinging bag.

I wasn't there.

Moving to the opposite side of the bag, I rounded on her flank, grabbing her from behind in one massive sweaty bear hug.

"Gotcha," I wheezed.

I should have known better.

Shannon drove her feet into the ground, forcing us both back. With every step, we picked up speed until the wall stopped us. We crashed into the drywall with enough force for me to not totally lose my hold on her but loosen my grip.

Shannon jerked to the side, ripping free from my clutch and turning to face me. I struck out with a right to her stomach that connected with an audible gasp as she lost air and dropped to her knees.

"Yes!" I shouted, slumping down next to her, exhausted. "Student, one. Master, fifty or however many times you dropped me."

"Not bad," Shannon praised, recovering from having the wind knocked out of her. "But how did you know which side of the bag I would have gone to? If you had chosen the wrong side, we would have met head on."

"I guess you'd follow the way I retreated around the bag,"

I shared. “You also have a tendency to go to your right when you’re attacking, like a poker player’s tell.”

Shannon blinked at me a few times then jutted out her lower lip and nodded.

“Not bad, Kemosabe, not bad at all.” Shannon lifted herself from the mat and offered me a hand up. “Ready to go test your skills out against the real thing?”

TWENTY-THREE

"HEY, so you having any kind of second thoughts about this or anything?" I asked Shannon, squirming in my seat. "I mean, I'm still going to do it. I need the money. But I can't kick this little voice in my head that says we're about to get mauled by a supernatural creature. It's going to bury our bodies under the house and we're never going to be heard from again."

Shannon kept her eyes on the road as she maneuvered the streets to Nate's house. After cleaning up, we had packed armor and enough weaponry to start a small war into the back of her Mazda 3.

"I mean, it's an animal," Shannon said, talking herself through it. "We don't have to kill it; we just have to get it out of there. I'm pretty sure it's going to be more afraid of us than we are of it, plus the armor I'm packing can take a beating. We'll be okay."

Shannon didn't sound too sure of herself as she talked. It was like she was trying to convince herself of the idea.

I kept my mouth shut. I mean, this had to be better than

wearing a chicken suit or negotiating with strangers to get into my car like some kind of creep.

Nate lived on a nice street in a suburb of Los Angeles. Traffic was never good in LA, but right now at 2 pm, it was bearable.

Shannon pulled right into his driveway.

Nate's home was white with grey trim. An SUV and a sedan were parked on the street. No one was out.

Good, no witnesses, I thought to myself. *It's going to be okay. In and out and you'll be four hundred dollars richer, no tax.*

Nate opened the door to his single-story home with a wide smile. He stepped off the porch and came to greet us as we unpacked our black duffle bags from the Mazda.

"So glad you didn't get cold feet and actually decided to go through with this. I was just thinking anyone in their right mind would have probably turned me down. Thank god for W.A., right?" Nate said, grabbing one of the bags and shouldering it. "Say, what do you have in here? Steel maces and 50. caliber machine guns?"

"Yep," Shannon answered, shouldering her own bag.

Nate teetered under the weight for a moment but regained his balance and took the lead.

"I opened up the side gate over to the right," Nate instructed. "We can walk through the backyard and to the other side of the house. The missus is out getting her hair done. She's not exactly a believer in the supernatural, so I thought it best she be out while all of this was going on."

I carried a black duffle on each shoulder, the weight of the bags crushing my skin and muscle.

We followed Nate through a nicely kept backyard with manicured green grass and fruit trees on the opposite side of his house.

As soon as I saw the size of the opening to the crawl space, I wanted to go home or call for my mommy.

The opening was something you'd expect a large cat or a small dog to fit through.

Don't freak out, don't freak out, don't freak out, I repeated in my head like some kind of mantra. It didn't seem to help much. Imagine that.

I dropped the bags I was carrying next to Shannon's. The thick duffle bags made dull thuds on the grass underneath us.

Getting down on all fours, I peered into the daunting crawl space. Even though it was a warm sunny day in Los Angeles, a cool dampness came from underneath the house. I couldn't see far into the crawl space, perhaps ten to twenty feet in front of me. The darkness and a series of pipes and supporting beams blocked my sight to the far end of the house or anything to the right.

"Here," Shannon said, dropping beside me. She handed me a heavy-duty flashlight.

The beam pierced the darkness. I was mentally preparing myself for anything at the moment. I was ready to witness things from the Chupacabra to some kind of mutated possum.

Nothing.

I wasn't sure if that was better or worse. Part of me was relieved at not finding anything. The other half wished I saw it already, taking away the icy finger of fear held by the mystery of not knowing.

"Well, I don't think we're going to see whatever it is from out here," Shannon said, sitting back on her heels. "Time to gear up and get in, Stinky."

"You sure there's something down here?" I asked Nate. "I mean, I don't see anything and sure don't smell anything."

"Oh yeah, it's down there." Nate's back popped as he to tried to get down on all fours. It was a long, painful process like watching an old rusted crane move in slow motion.

"It's okay, it's okay. You don't have to get down on all fours," I told the veteran. "We'll go in."

Shannon unzipped the bags and began to unpack our goodies. She brought *everything* from our Kevlar vests to headlamps and extendable poles that would act like spears.

"Where did you get these things?" I wondered, grabbing one of the spears that extended out like an expandable baton. "Aren't these illegal?"

"Don't ask, don't tell," Shannon said, handing me a taser. "We'll try to guide the thing out using the spears. Remember, we're not trying to kill it; just get it out of there. The taser is just if it charges you."

I looked down at the small device in my hand. It was about the size of my palm. A button by my thumb promised an electric current at the end of two prongs if I pressed it.

"And let's just say this Chupacabra creature isn't fazed by my magic trick; what then?" I asked, pressing the button on the taser.

A blue current formed between the metal prongs.

"I'll be carrying something just in case," Shannon reassured me, strapping a handgun to her hip.

"Hey, maybe I should carry a gun too, just in—"

"No way," Shannon cut me off.

"I mean, what if—"

"You're not trained with one." Shannon shook her head as if it were out of the question. "I'm not trying to get shot in the butt when you get trigger happy. This isn't tickle fights and lollipops anymore; this is the real thing."

"Okay." Nate walked up to us with his phone so close to his eyes, I thought his nose had to be touching it. "So I've done a little digging on the interwebs and the best guess I can come up with as to what this thing is, is a chimera."

"Bless you," I answered.

"Who, what now?" Nate asked, confused.

"He's trying to lighten the mood with comedy," Shannon said, giving me a playful smile. "Go ahead, Nate, continue."

Nate presented the phone to us. On it was the picture of a beast with the head of a lion, the body of an eagle, and two snake heads for tails. The creature looked menacing, something straight out of a Greek legend. The only problem was the creature Nate showed us had to be the size of a small vehicle. There was no way it was going to fit underneath the house.

Shannon had to be thinking the same thing.

"I don't think a beast that size is crawling under your house," Shannon told him with a frown. "But that video you showed us of whatever's down there does look like a smaller version of a chimera. Guess we're not going to find out until we get there."

"Right." Nate nodded emphatically. "I mean, what I really want to know is how does something like this go so unnoticed? I'm the only one talking about it as far as I can tell. I mean, there are chat forums and internet threads about them, but they seem loonier than a bunch of kids high on Monster energy drinks."

"Maybe those kids aren't as crazy as we think." I shrugged on my Kevlar vest, tightening the straps around my sides. "But that doesn't answer the question of where they come from and how they've remained fairly hidden this long."

The three of us grew silent. Not a single one of us could offer a helpful solution.

Shannon placed her headlamp on her forehead and flipped on the light. I pocketed my taser and extended my spear. As dangerous as this moment was turning into, I felt an adrenaline rush of excitement. I mean, I was about to go into the unknown to wrangle a creature of mysterious origin. If this didn't get the geek in me excited, I didn't know what would.

"I should go first," I volunteered as Shannon and I approached the opening of the crawl space.

"No, and that doesn't have anything to do about pride or going first to be tough," Shannon answered. "I'm smaller and have years of training in close quarters combat. You were dipping Cheetos in cream cheese a few days ago."

"I told you I'm damaged goods from my breakup," I said, deadpan. "Don't judge me."

"Hey, no judgment, Stinky." Shannon gave me a wink. "I'm just saying right now I should be the one to go in first."

Without waiting to hear what I would have to say, Shannon dropped to all fours and shimmied into the darkness.

"She's a firecracker," Nate said with a grin. "Reminds me of my missus twenty or thirty years ago. You want some advice, John. You keep her close. She's the real deal."

"So I've been hearing," I remarked, also dropping to my hands and knees and heading under the house.

The cold darkness surrounded me now. Vents placed every few yards around the perimeter of the crawl space let in some light through metal mesh but not enough to fight back the gloom. A deep earthy smell assailed my nostrils, now along with something else.

I couldn't quite place the smell. It was soothing like burnt hair with old artichoke hearts.

There was barely enough room to crawl on my hands and knees if I bent my elbows and sank my back. With every hand or knee forward, the back of my Kevlar vest rubbed against the supporting wooden beams above.

Shannon was right in front of me, moving deeper into the underground space like she had been doing this her entire life.

That same sense of excitement and wonder overtook me,

increasing my heart rate. One thing was for sure, this was no casting call.

Other than our moving, the space under the house was deathly quiet. A large wooden beam to our right supporting a series of water pipes with metal brackets made it so we didn't have a clear line of sight to what was on our right or ahead of us.

When we rounded the corner, eight hundred bucks for this job didn't seem like enough.

TWENTY-FOUR

A CREATURE not of this world blinked back large green eyes at us. If I had only seen the face, I would have said it was some kind of large feline in its adolescent life.

The head and neck was where the similarities to any kind of cat I had ever seen stopped. The rest of its body was covered with some kind of dark feathers. A pair of wings sat on its back.

All three of us just stared at one another.

I sneezed once, twice, then three times. A cloud of dust filled the small space with every sneeze. My eyes watered and itched.

"Easy, easy, little guy," Shannon said in a calm, soothing voice. "We just need you out of here. We—ugh, god, that smell. I can taste it."

I directed my gaze to the spot in front of the creature. Sitting on its paws was the carcass of some kind of large rodent, maybe a possum or raccoon with its guts spilled open. The remains of a few of these carcasses lay littered around the creature.

"It's in the back of my throat," I groaned, dry heaving. "Like old cheese and skunk."

"Don't breathe through your nose," Shannon consoled me. "Although, at this point, I think all my odor receptors have me strangled to death."

The creature cocked its head to the side, eyeing us curiously.

"Okay, little guy," I said, moving to my left along with Shannon to create a lane for the animal to escape. "We just need you out of here. No reason for anyone to get hurt. Come on, let's go."

The creature's green feline eyes flashed with a sense of understanding. I couldn't be sure it knew exactly what we wanted, but I got the sense that at least it knew we were talking to it.

The animal lowered its head closer to its kill as if it were afraid we were going to take it.

"Nope, nope, we don't want your food," Shannon told the animal. "We just need you to get out of here. You can take your snack with you."

"It's a to-go meal, buddy," I told it. "Just take it to go."

"I'm going to try to guide it out of here with the spear," Shannon told me. "Maybe I can even hook its meal and it'll follow us out of here if we drag it out first."

"Be careful," I warned. "If it is a baby chimera, then it has snakes for tails. I can't believe I just said that seriously."

"Well, it's a pretty strange world we live in now," Shannon said, extending her spear. With the blunt end, she reached the six-foot stick forward, trying to grab on to the dead rodent.

The blunt end of the spear sank deep into the open intestinal tract of the animal with a squishy sound like someone stepping on a wet sponge.

The baby chimera hissed and latched razor sharp claws into its meal.

Then two things happened at once. Shannon jerked back the spear to try and placate the animal. A squirt of dead carcass juice came with the action, painting me across the face. It just so happened I was in the middle of opening my mouth to say something. The flavors of sour and salty but not in a good way ran down my throat.

The second thing that happened is our shifty friend decided to make a run for it. The chimera bolted from its spot, racing past Shannon and heading for the lane we created for it to escape.

The animal brushed by me, and for a moment, I thought we had succeeded. A pair of thick tails that looked like snakes had other plans. Both those hateful little snake jaws decided to take a bite out of me on the way out.

Two pairs of fangs sank deep into my chest piece, right where the Kevlar was positioned to protect me.

I'm no expert on supernatural creatures or the strength of said creatures, but what I did know was that the chimera was a lot stronger than it looked. Without breaking stride, I was dragged along the bottom of the house toward the exit. My head bashed against pieces of supporting wood and pipes not once or twice but three times.

Stars exploded in my vision as I lost the grip on my spear and fumbled in my pants pocket for the taser.

Shannon was yelling something I couldn't hear.

The next thing I realized, I was outside. Bright sunshine beat down on me, blinding me from the dim light my retinas were used to moments before.

"Oh sweet Mary, have mercy on my soul!" Nate shouted, leaping or more like falling to the side and out of the way.

With my left hand, I grabbed on to the snake heads, trying to dislodge the creature from my Kevlar vest. That was when I got the sense they were stuck more than they wanted to keep on biting on to me. I could feel their jaws working, trying to let go of the thick fabric.

Left hand holding on to the snakes, right hand fishing in my pocket for the taser and being dragged across the back lawn, I got the briefest flash of the house to my right. The two-story building had wide windows above.

An older woman with a fake spray tan in her robe and acrylic nails the length of short knives stared out at me with an open mouth.

You and me both, lady, I thought to myself.

Finally, the finger on my right hand wrapped around the cold plastic of the taser.

At the same time, we ran out of real estate in Nate's backyard. This didn't seem to faze the baby chimera in the least. With a powerful bound of its back legs, it spread its brown wings and vaulted over the six-foot wall, taking me with it.

My body slammed against the cinder block wall that separated Nate's backyard from his neighbor's. My vision went from a perfectly blue sky to a dirt ground in a matter of seconds.

Blood spurted from my nose like a sprinkler.

We landed on the other side. I was so out of it from the hit, I wasn't able to take in my surroundings. I did manage to press the button on the taser and shove it up the chimera's butt.

The chimera hissed, more pissed off than in pain. At the same time, the shock was enough to allow the snake tails to lose their grip on my Kevlar vest.

I came to a skidding stop in a heap, my vision covered in blood. Everything hurt at the moment. It was like I had done a brutal workout at the gym and every single one of my muscles was screaming at me to stop the madness.

Breathing hard, I sat up, wiping blood from my eyes. I

was in the middle not of someone's backyard, but of a construction site. It seemed Nate's backyard butted up against a new strip mall being planned. There were work trucks, tools, and supplies everywhere.

It must have been some kind of break because only two construction workers were in the general area. One dropped the sandwich in his hand and did the sign of the cross over his chest.

The other must have also been religious to a certain extent because he yelled out with an, "Oh lord have mercy!"

I turned back to see what they were staring at. The chimera had recovered from its shock and looked at me as if it were trying to decide whether to fly away or go in for the kill.

I could hear Shannon and Nate yelling my name, but they weren't going to get to me in time to help.

I struggled to my knees then feet, brandishing the taser.

"We're done here." I waved off the chimera. "We're done. Go, go back to your mom and dad."

I felt the presence of something large next to me. Hot breath tickled my hand.

The chimera looked beside me then tucked its snake tails and launched high into the air.

I was already having a rough day. The last thing I wanted to do was look to see what stood next to me. Heavy panting and the hot breath were my only clues.

Forcing myself to look to my right, ready for anything. I saw the same black wolf dog that had been following me for the last few days.

The animal looked up at me with what I swear was a smile. Its thick pink tongue lolled out of the side of his mouth. For the first time, I noticed its collar. A thick brown piece of leather had a red medallion on it. I couldn't make out the words because it was in a different language, but I recognized the writing. It was the same symbols used in Mrs. Grundy's doormat.

"Jonny!" Shannon yelled, vaulting over the fence. "Jonny, are you hurt?"

I looked up at her from the wolf dog, nodding like an idiot.

"Did you see—did we really—this dog came to save me," I told her at once, motioning to the animal.

As if he had overstayed his welcome, the dog moved into action, sprinting away from the construction site, lost behind pallets of wood a moment later.

"Yeah, yeah, I saw it," Shannon said, coming over to me and looking me in the eyes. "I think you may have a concussion. Do you know what today is?"

"It's pay day," I said, nodding. "That's what today is."

A rush I had never felt before dulled the pain seeping through my body. I wasn't sure if I was good at monster hunting, but I knew I liked it.

"Seriously, Jonny," Shannon murmured, looking at the construction workers who had their phones out now, ready to start snapping pictures. "We should go."

"Right," I said as we both turned our backs and vaulted over the wall to meet a waiting Nate.

"Oh my word, I thought you were dead for sure," Nate said, catching me in a hug that made everything hurt all over again. "When I saw you being dragged behind it like some kind of rag doll and then that horrific scream, I thought you were a goner."

"I didn't scream," I denied with a confused look at the two. "Did I?"

"I didn't want to make you feel bad," Shannon said with a playful slap on the back. "But you sounded like a little girl who stubbed her toe or something."

"Never mind that," Nate said excitedly, slapping his

hands together. "You two did it! You did it! We need to celebrate with a beer. You two like Broken Skull IPA?"

"Sure," Shannon agreed, looking at our filthy state. "Maybe we should take them out here. We'll take off our gear too."

"You got it," Nate said, entering the house. "Three beers and your money, of course. Well, hotdog, I'm not sure what I'll be happier with: the smell being gone or the fact that I saw a real life chimera. I can't wait to tell the group at W.A. about this!"

Nate disappeared into the house like some kid who was just told he was going to Disneyland.

"You sure you're okay?" Shannon asked me again. "Your nose is still leaking blood."

"Yeah, yeah," I said, pinching my nostrils together and tilting my head back. "My head's still spinning on what just happened. Did a supernatural creature really just drag me across the yard and over a wall?"

"I think it did." Shannon laughed. "Sorry, I'm not laughing at you. How ridiculous is this? I mean—this is crazy."

"I'm glad you think so," I told her. "You're keeping it pretty mellow and I'm freaking out inside."

"Are you kidding me?" Shannon said, shaking her head and exhaling. "I'm no pro at this. I mean, a vampire, sure but other creatures of the paranormal? I'm just pretending I know what I'm doing."

We stood there like two idiots, chuckling. Me with my bleeding nose and Shannon dusting herself off from all the dirt we had been crawling through under the house. I could only imagine what I looked like, but for the first time in a long time, I was genuinely happy.

TWENTY-FIVE

ON THE WAY back from Nate's house, I decided to tell Shannon everything. Not just about what I suspected about Mrs. Grundy, but about V Model Management and the vampires that ran the place.

Shannon remained quiet in a very unlike Shannon way. I did see her grip the steering wheel so tightly, her knuckles turned white when I mentioned Winston Bloodstone.

When I was done, I was afraid I had made the wrong decision. The muscles in Shannon's jaw line trembled with rage.

"Well, maybe that was a bad idea." I laughed uncomfortably. "I just thought you should know. I don't want you to think I'm hiding things from you. To be honest, I don't even know what I'm going to do about the V Model Management offer. I mean, four hundred bucks for a half hour of work seems pretty legit to me. Photoshoots usually pay double or triple that, but the work is so sporadic. I'd be lucky to get cast for something once every two to three months."

Shannon remained quiet. We pulled into the parking lot behind Haven Apartments.

She still looked pissed.

Holy crap, I think she might kill me, I thought to myself. *Yep, I'm pretty sure she's going to kill me.*

"So then, good talk, hope you have a nice night, partner." I attempted a smile, grabbing the car door to let myself out of this coffin. "See you soon."

"Wait," Shannon said, grabbing my left forearm in a vise-like grip. "Just give me a minute."

Her voice was calm enough. Maybe she wouldn't decapitate me after all.

I sat in the car, ready to sprint out the door at a moment's notice.

"Thank you," Shannon said, looking at me. "Thank you for telling me about V Model Management. You should take the job."

"I should do what now?" I asked, raising my eyebrows in surprise. "Sorry, the chimera must have hit me harder than I thought and damaged my eardrum. It sounded a lot like you said I should join V Model Management."

"I did." Shannon ran her tongue round the inside of her mouth. "You should go in, get the lay of the office building and as much intel as you can find. I'll do the rest."

"Shannon," I said, shaking my head. "I'm not doubting your skills, but this wouldn't be one vampire; this would be a building of them or at least mixed with humans that were loyal to them to an extent."

"I'm not interested in the reasons why it can't work," Shannon said, grabbing her phone as an epiphany hit. She jammed her finger tips on the glass screen of her phone so hard, it was like she wanted to break it. I couldn't see what she was searching for. But she stopped when she found it.

Shannon's face drained of blood. She stared at the phone's screen as if it were something from another planet.

"That's him," Shannon breathed. "That's the man who killed my sister."

Shannon turned the phone to face me. A picture of Mr. Bloodstone's smiling face and double chin greeted me.

I didn't know what to say. On one hand, I wanted to congratulate Shannon. Her hunt for her sister's killer was nearing an end. On the other hand, I wanted to tell her to stay away from Mr. Bloodstone and his coven of vampires. Not only was he a supernatural being surrounded by other supernatural beings loyal to him, he was the head of the largest modeling agency in Hollywood. With that kind of influence came power.

"Go to the office," Shannon began, nodding slowly as if she were agreeing with herself. "Go to the office, get all the intel you can, and I'll do the rest. I'll go in at night to minimize casualties."

"Shannon—" I interrupted, trying to talk her down.

"If I take them by surprise, I can rip through half of them before they know I'm there," Shannon cut me off. "I finally found him."

"Shannon, it's too dangerous," I told her. "There'll be too many of them."

"I'm doing it, Jonny," Shannon said, looking over at me with eyes so cold, I thought they might freeze me on the spot. "With or without your help, I'm doing it."

I knew she wasn't bluffing. Walking away now wasn't an option for me, not after I supplied her with the information that might get her killed.

"I'm not letting you go in there alone," I told her. "I'll figure something out. You're not alone anymore in this fight."

Shannon gave me a confused look. For a second, her features softened and either some lint or a tear reached her eye.

"Ugh, thanks, thanks, Stinky." Shannon cleared her throat, breaking eye contact. "But first thing's first, let's go talk to this woman about her dogs that are following you around. We can get the gear out of the car later."

Shannon and I walked into the Haven Apartment complex just before dinner. Most people were out at their jobs, but we did pass a middle-aged woman who looked at me open-mouthed.

I had cleaned up as best I could from my battle royale cage match with the chimera. Still, my face was bruised and my nose was twice its normal size.

"I beat him," Shannon confessed to the open-mouthed stranger as we passed. "He should have listened the first time. Am I right?"

The woman sped up her walk and hurried on.

"You know her?" I asked.

"Nope." Shannon winked. "With the thirty-six apartments in here, all I know are you and Evan, oh, and Mr. Hyde."

"And now you're about to meet Mrs. Grundy," I said, directing us over to the older woman's door. My eyes looked down at the welcome mat in front of her door. I was sure of it. The same kind of runes or symbols on the mat were also on the black wolf dog's collar.

Before I could think of the many reasons I shouldn't, I lifted my closed fist to rap on the door.

Right as my closed hand descended on the wood, the door opened. Mrs. Grundy looked at us through her thick glasses and gave out a manic cackle.

"Jonny, Shannon, please, please come in." Mrs. Grundy turned her back, not waiting to see if we would join her. "We have much to discuss and not enough time. Never enough time."

Warden and Cerberus rounded the corner, stopping both of us in our tracks. Warden eyed us suspiciously while Cerberus threw caution to the wind. The big dog galloped right next to us, licking our hands and asking for pets.

"Oh, look at this big girl," Shannon said with a smile as she dropped to a knee and rubbed the dog's jowls. "You're a good dog, aren't you? Good dog."

"Cerberus is a big baby," Mrs. Grundy informed us. "Don't mind Warden either. He's an old soul like me. He'll warm up to you. Jonny, would you be a dear and close the door behind you? We wouldn't want a draft getting in."

"Sure," I said, closing the thick door. It wasn't until the door was closed behind me that the musty smell of the place hit me. It didn't stink, per se, but you could tell dogs definitely lived in the apartment along with a thick heavy odor that reminded me of old books.

The apartment, like all the others, opened to the kitchen with the family room and dining areas in front of us. I knew to the right held one bedroom and bathroom and to the left the other.

Mrs. Grundy took a seat in the family room area, where an overstuffed recliner sat in the corner of the room. A love seat sat across from it. There was no TV in place that seemed to be the centerpiece of so many family living spaces.

"Please, please take a seat." Mrs. Grundy waved us to sit down across from her. "I can practically read your thoughts, your minds are running with so many questions. So what would you like to know first?"

Shannon and I looked at one another before taking a seat on the small couch.

Warden went over to Mrs. Grundy and lay down next to her. Cerberus kept her head in Shannon's hands, enjoying the love bestowed on her.

"Either you know everything and just aren't saying or there's been a big miscommunication and you're about to think we're crazy," Shannon offered. "You do know about the —the other beings in our world."

"Yes, yes, yes." Mrs. Grundy laughed. "Just come out and say it. We all do. Ask away, my dearies, ask away."

"That big black wolf dog following me," I blurted so fast it came out in a single rush of words. "He's yours?"

"Mine as much as any other hellhound I care for," Mrs. Grundy corrected me. "They come and go as they please, although Warden has chosen to stay by my side for years now."

"Exactly what is a hellhound?" Shannon beat me to the question.

"Creatures of the supernatural that live among us in disguise," Mrs. Grundy informed us. "They walk among us as canines we are used to seeing, only showing how different they truly are when the need arises."

"Where's the other one?" I asked, looking to the right and left. "Where's the black dog that looks like a wolf?"

"Ahhhh, yes, Odin is a bit more of a loner," Mrs. Grundy explained. "He came to me looking for shelter but comes and goes as he pleases. He's chosen to follow you over the last few days."

"Why?" I asked, remembering how he stood by my side encouraging the chimera to run instead of attacking again. "Not that I'm not grateful. He saved me today."

"Oh yes, you were lucky." Mrs. Grundy pointed a gnarled finger in my direction and shook it. "You need to be more careful, young man. A single bite from a chimera, even one as young as the creature you tangled with, would have been enough to cause paralysis and, within hours, death."

I swallowed hard. My right hand went to the area where my Kevlar vest protected me from the bite, right under my collarbone.

"Wait, how do you know that?" Shannon asked, standing up from her seat so abruptly, it made both dogs jump. "That just happened and we didn't tell you."

"Now you're asking the right questions," Mrs. Grundy said, nodding her approval to Shannon. "You're a bright one. The one I believe was chosen to help police this world."

"Don't change the subject just to confuse us," Shannon insisted. "So you're some kind of supernatural witch or something?"

"'Or something' to use your own words," Mrs. Grundy answered. "I am in tune with the goings on of the supernatural world. 'Witch' is such a pedestrian term. The order I hail to is known as the Court. I am a Watcher in said Court."

It was my turn to stand up. All this crazy knowledge being dropped on me required some pacing.

"So you've just been living here and watching the goings on of the supernatural in the human world?" I asked, trying to fit the puzzle pieces together in my mind. "How long have you lived here? Why are you just revealing yourself now?"

"I've lived here longer than you," Mrs. Grundy replied. "It was not yet time to reveal myself. You and Shannon both had to be ready. You are ready now."

I traded frustrated looks with Shannon. I felt like a kid asking my parent "why," only to have my parent say, "Because I said so."

"Wait a minute; your voice," Shannon said, pointing her finger at Mrs. Grundy. "You're the one that tipped me off about Evan being a vampire over the phone. You're the whole reason I'm here."

"And so the plot thickens." Mrs. Grundy gave us both a devilish smile, sinking deeper into her armchair. "You both may want to retake your seats for this. Things are about to get, how the young people say, YOLO."

TWENTY-SIX

"I AM GOING TO SIT DOWN," I said. "But I don't think you're using that term correctly. Don't feel bad; Shannon's not great at this kind of stuff either. YOLO is an acronym for You Only Live Once. You're probably looking for something like 'cray cray' or 'lit up in here'."

Both Shannon and Mrs. Grundy looked at me as if I had grown an extra head.

"Okay," I said, taking my seat on the couch. "I'm going to shut up now and just enjoy this nightmarish story time my life has become."

"I did call you and tip you off about Evan Woods living in Haven Apartments," Mrs. Grundy stated. "I've been watching your growth as a hunter of the supernatural. Both myself and the Court approve of your actions hunting and slaying the supernatural that are getting out of order. One of the main reasons Watchers exist, such as myself, is to keep the worlds of the human and supernatural separate."

"Did you even get to know Evan before you ordered his death?" I challenged, sticking up for my friend. "Listen, I'm not saying the man's an angel, but he's doing the best he can with the hand he's been dealt. Did you ever think about that?"

I didn't mean to raise my voice at the old woman, but the last part came off as a shout.

Warden growled at me, lifting the top of his lips to show off an impressive arsenal of sharp pointed teeth.

"He's still a friend." Mrs. Grundy reached down to stroke the back of the dog's ears. "He's a loyal friend. Our world is in short supply of those these days."

Warden settled down, placing his head between his paws, although he never took his eyes off me.

"I am woman enough to admit I was wrong about Evan," Mrs. Grundy answered. "However, he was only part of the reason it was important for Shannon to come to Haven. The other part was for you two to meet. In the history of our order, hunters never hunt alone."

"So there are other people out there doing what I do?" Shannon asked incredulously. "I mean, other people staking vampires and chopping off heads?"

"Far too few, I'm afraid," Mrs. Grundy admitted. "Most hunters don't make it past their first hunt much less years into the profession."

I could feel a migraine coming on. Hunters, the Court, hellhounds; it was all enough to make me want to go back to my gallon of ice cream and chocolate icing.

"Listen, I'd love to be part of this Court you have going on and own a hellhound and all of this, but I'm just picking up the pieces of a life that's been shattered," I told both women. "So just unsubscribe me from all of this, okay? I need some time to think about it all and—"

"What about Mr. Bloodstone, at least?" Shannon asked. "What about all that talk that I wasn't alone anymore?"

"You're not," I told her. "I'm not letting you go alone, but that's as far as I'm committing right now. I'm not trying to get initiated into this Court and do the whole mask and black robe thing as we burn a chicken liver and chant Kumbaya on a full moon."

"It's not like that at all when you join." Mrs. Grundy rolled her eyes then gave me a wink. "We do all that on your first anniversary if you live that long."

"See that, right there," I said, shaking my head. "That's the kind of crazy I'm talking about. Yeah, today was fun and we made some great money, but—"

"If you were to decide to join as hunters, the Court has deep pockets." Mrs. Grundy waggled her brow. "You'd lack for nothing when it came to housing, food, or other."

"Go on," I encouraged, perking up at the promise of a bank account that wasn't overdrawn on a monthly basis.

"You'd of course work for the Court and go on the missions assigned to you, but they would be far and few between," Mrs. Grundy explained. "More often than not, you would be responsible for finding and executing your own hunts."

I looked over at Shannon.

"Don't look at me, Stinky," Shannon said with a Cheshire smile. "She had me at 'deep pockets'."

"Take some time to think about it," Mrs. Grundy told us. "However, if you lack for anything when it comes to the hunt you're about to take on, you have only to ask. We've had our eye on Winston Bloodstone and V Model Management for a while now. We wouldn't be disappointed if he were to accidentally get his head chopped off or burned to ash."

"Noted," Shannon said, heading for the door. "Thank you."

"Of course." Mrs. Grundy rose from her seat with a grimace of effort. "Those who wish to keep the balance are too few these days. We need to stick together."

Shannon and I took our leave of Mrs. Grundy's house under the watchful eye of Warden and the licks of Cerberus.

We walked in silence around the gated-off pool and to our side of the apartment complex.

"Listen, this is my fight," Shannon said as we climbed the stairs. "You don't owe me anything. I'm going tomorrow to end Bloodstone. Maybe it's better if you—"

"Stop," I told her. "I'm going with you. Let me talk to Evan about it and he'll shed more light on the building, I'm sure. Bloodstone's luring in my ex anyway. Regardless of how I feel about her, I don't want to see her dead or turned."

"You're a good friend, Stinky," Shannon said as we reached her level. "Whatever this chick was thinking letting you go, it's her loss."

Without another word, Shannon walked down the hall and into her apartment.

I was too tired to consider what that comment could have meant. My nose was starting to throb again. The ibuprofen Nate gave me was wearing off.

I climbed the last flight of stairs to the fourth floor and went into my apartment.

Evan was sitting on the couch playing *Gears of War Five,* trash talking opposing players on the other side of his headset.

"Oh, you're a big man, real big man threatening me over a video game?" he shouted into the microphone. "You want some of this? Come get some!"

One look at my face and he hit the pause button on the game.

"Let me get some aspirin and I'll tell you everything," I told him.

And I did; I told him about the chimera bashing in my face, Mrs. Grundy, Shannon's plan to kill Mr. Bloodstone, everything.

"I was just waiting for you to get back to see if you wanted to go to Matty Too Fatty's for a burger," Evan muttered in a daze. "Holy goodness, Jonny, how are you managing to get yourself into all of this?"

"I don't know." I shrugged. "It's like as soon as I found out that you were a vampire, the supernatural floodgates opened and now here I am."

"You're not actually going to go through with it, are you?" Evan inquired.

"Go through with what?" I asked.

"I mean, trying to get to Bloodstone is going to be darn near impossible." Evan shook his head. "Let alone killing the guy. He's been around for a long time, Jonny. This isn't going to be as easy as Shannon getting the drop on him like she did me."

"I know, I know," I acknowledged. "But I can't let her go alone. She will if I don't go with her."

Evan let a long breath of air escape his lips.

"I know you're one of them," I told him. "But you're my friend first and I wanted you to hear it from me. If you can't help, then I understand. I don't know what kind of loyalty you have to them or Mr. Bloodstone specifically."

"I hate them," Evan ground out, not looking at me. "I hate them all. I hate myself for what I am, but I've stopped trying to imagine it could be different. I don't care what she does. I like Shannon, but I just met her. I'm telling you as my best friend, don't do it. That place is locked up like Fort Knox with both human and vampire security. She'd be going up against six maybe eight guards easy. Plus Bloodstone himself. I'm sorry for what happened to her sister, but Shannon's death isn't going to solve anything."

We sat in the family room in silence for a moment.

"You're going anyway, aren't you?" Evan asked me. "I know that look on your face. It's the same look you get when you're letting a silent but deadly fart out. You think you're being sneaky about it, but your face contorts like someone who pirates movies listening to a sermon about theft."

"She's all alone, Evan," I told him. "I'm all she's got."

"I was afraid you'd say that." Evan sighed. "Come on; get me a piece of paper and a pencil. I'll show you the layout of the building."

Evan was precise and detailed of what I would encounter going to V Model Management's office. From the guards on the bottom floor to the receptionist who was a vampire herself to the sixth floor penthouse where Mr. Bloodstone handled his affairs.

"If you're going to do this, then tomorrow night's the night," Evan explained. "They have an initiation meeting for any new vampires into the coven the first Friday of the month. That's tomorrow. Bloodstone will be there for sure."

I nodded along with Evan's words. I knew he felt conflicted giving me all of this information when it was clear what I was going to do with it. Sure, he had no love for his own kind, but still, like it or not, he shared a bond with them.

"Decapitation or some high-powered UV rays will be the best way to put them down for good," Evan instructed. "Stakes to the heart will incapacitate them, but if you want them gone, they won't do the job. You need to put them down quick. You saw what happened in the fight with Shannon and me. We're too strong and fast to be taken one on one in a fair fight."

"Thank you—I mean it," I told Evan. "Thank you for all of this. I know this isn't easy for you."

"Just come back safe," Evan stated, holding my eye. "Just get back and we can put all of this behind us like some bad dream."

"You're not pissed that I'm planning to kill your employer?" I asked him. "I mean, once we do this, you'll be out of work."

Evan shrugged.

"I've been pretty smart with my money over the decades, always living below my means. I mean, no offense, but we live in Haven Apartments and we split rent, soooooo." Evan gave me a toothy grin. "Who knows, maybe this is the kick in the pants I needed to start my own agency. I've always played around with the idea. Also, and I know this is a bit off-topic, I feel like you're going to have two black eyes to go with that broken nose. They're already swelling."

"How does it look, though?" I asked. "Do I look tough?"

"You look like Rocket Raccoon from *Guardians of the Galaxy*," Evan answered honestly. "V Model Management should get a kick out of that when you go in tomorrow for your paperwork."

TWENTY-SEVEN

THE NEXT MORNING, the soreness in my face felt worse, if that even was possible. The irony that I looked like I was on the losing end of a martial arts match with Bruce Lee and headed to a modeling agency was not lost on me.

V Model Management was located in downtown Los Angeles in the middle of a business section of the busy town. Trying to sneak in later that night was not going to be easy.

I parked my car in a parking lot behind the building where the attendant sat in his guard shack with his feet up, scrolling through his phone. A pair of cameras monitored the parking lot.

The bottom floor of the building was all glass walls, making it even more difficult to sneak in unnoticed. Two guards sauntered around without a care in the world. A smiling receptionist with short strawberry-blonde hair greeted me with a puzzled expression.

"Hello, can I help you?" she asked.

"Yes, I'm here to fill out some paperwork," I answered, bringing a few fingers to my nose to make sure I wasn't bleeding again.

"Riiiiiiight," the woman drawled, staring at my swollen nose and black eyes like I was from another planet. "What's your name, sir?"

With my peripheral vision, I could see the two guards take notice. They eyed me, muttering to one another.

"John Hunter," I said, showing my ID. "She knows I'm coming."

"John Hunter, John Hunter, John Hunter," the woman repeated, looking at her computer screen.

The guards began walking toward me. I could see one press the communications piece in his ear and say something into it.

Maybe coming to the agency looking like I had just been dragged through the dirt by a chimera wasn't the best idea I'd ever had.

"There you are," the receptionist said just as the guards reached the front desk. "Yes, you have an appointment with Stacy, who runs our HR department. You're free to go up and meet her. She'll be on the second floor."

"Thank you." I nodded, looking over at the two guards, who remained silent. "Gentlemen."

"What happened to your face?" one of them asked me.

"Amateur boxing," I responded without blinking. "You should see the other guy."

I made my way over the white marble floor to a set of four elevators.

Don't look like you're checking everything out, I reminded myself. *Act naturally.*

I turned my neck this way and that, hoping to anyone who looked at me like I was just working a kink out. There were cameras everywhere, at least two on the front door, one on the reception desk, and another two monitoring the elevators.

I pressed the circular button near the elevator doors with

the arrow pointing up. A second later, a light dinging sound caught my ears and the elevator to my right opened.

Stepping inside, I was greeted with "When a Man Loves a Woman" by Percy Sledge, classic. I studied my options for floors, one through six. I knew I was supposed to go to the second floor, but Evan told me Mr. Bloodstone's floor was on the top level.

"Hey, can you hold that elevator," a familiar voice shouted.

I reached out a hand to stop the door on instinct.

Tracy stepped in.

We both stared at each other in shock.

Say what you want about her, but in my eyes, she was still the same woman I had gotten to know and love over the last year.

"Oh, Jonny," Tracy said, shifting her Starbucks white mocha nonfat latte with almond milk and an extra shot of espresso between her hands. "What are you doing here? What happened to your face? Maybe I should take another elevator."

"It's fine," I said, feeling a stab of pain in my gut as I looked down to her finger. The ring I bought her wasn't there. "It's a short ride."

Tracy seemed to weigh her options on getting out or not, but the doors were already sliding closed.

She pressed the number six button on the inside of the elevator. The irony of the music stabbed me in the heart and twisted.

Before she could ask me what floor I was going to, I answered her questions.

"Mr. Bloodstone invited me to come and work for him," I said as the elevator moved into motion. There was so much I wanted to tell her. So many feelings I didn't have time for in that moment. Whatever she had done to my feelings aside, I didn't want to see her dead or turned. "Tracy, do you know what you're getting into here? Do you know what this all really is?"

"This is everything I've ever wanted," Tracy said with a heavy breath. "I'm sorry. I know that stings. I'm not trying to hurt your feelings even more, but this is what I want. All of it."

The way she said the words, the way she looked at me when she said them, I knew she already understood what V Model Management really was.

"They promised me a long life and a successful career," Tracy continued, reinforcing the fact that she knew they were vampires. "What more could I want?"

The elevator slowed and the doors dinged open. The level we were on now looked like an apartment more than an office building. Two more guards dressed in black suits flanked the elevator doors.

Tracy stepped out.

"Oops, looks like you forgot to press the floor you wanted," Tracy said.

"Silly me," I answered, looking past her to try and see anything else I could on the level that might help. There were no cameras or obvious extra security measures. Most of the walls making up the level were glass, giving away a breathtaking view of the city. To the right of the room was an emergency exit and stairwell beyond.

The doors closed and Tracy walked out of my life for the second time.

THE MEETING with Stacy from the HR department of V Model Management was a quick process. She said they usually would take a new headshot then, but given my current situation, they'd just use one of my older photos.

Stacy informed me to call her when my swelling and bruising went away and they would send me on some jobs. No casting required; we were talking about direct bookings, the crème de la crème here. No more auditioning for hemorrhoid cream.

My head ran wild with ideas while driving back to Haven Apartments. Was I really going to do this? I was going to throw away the opportunity of a lifetime and start decapitating supernatural creatures instead?

At that same time, "Fight Song" by Rachael Platten came on. I knew what I had to do. I knew what the right thing was to do. Singing the lyrics along with Rachael gave me a sense of resolve and empowerment.

"This is my fight song, Take back my life song, Prove I'm all right song!" I belted as loud as I could. "My power's turned on, Starting right now I'll be strong!"

At that same time, traffic stopped at a red light. My windows were rolled up, but the rubber edging around them was cracked and did little to mute noise. The car to my left was an Asian family who stared at me as if I were from another planet.

A younger girl I guessed was their daughter took out her phone and started recording me.

The rest of the way home, my resolve went from unsure to pretty sure I was doing the right thing. After parking at Haven Apartments, I went straight to Shannon's unit. If we were going to do this, then we needed to gear up. Thanks to LA traffic, it was just past lunch. My stomach was rumbling and I knew we needed to prepare.

Shannon's door to her apartment was open again.

"Hey, you really should be more careful about leaving your door open. This is North Hollywood. You're not in

Nebraska any—" I cut myself off as I ducked out of the way of the muzzle to the rifle Shannon held in her hands. "Wow, point that thing somewhere else."

"It's not loaded," Shannon reassured me. "I'm just getting ready for tonight."

"How'd your intel run turn out?" Shannon asked, cleaning the inside of the rifle barrel with a wire brush. "Anything good?"

"It just confirmed everything Evan told me," I answered. "I think the hardest part will be the cameras."

"Don't worry; I've got something for that," Shannon divulged. "Hey, are you hungry at all?"

"Starving," I replied.

"I'll order some Matty Too Fatty," Shannon told me, exchanging the rifle for her phone. "What do you want?"

"I'll go pick it up," I volunteered. "If you have it delivered, they charge a fee."

"It's on me." Shannon jerked her head to the counter, where the stack of cash from Nate sat. "We're rich now, remember? Straight ballers. How's that for LA slang?"

"Better," I said, taking in the cash and the stock of weapons present. "I feel like we're in a rap video or some kind of weapons dealers."

"Ha, I wish," Shannon said, punching in the order for us. "What do you want? What do you models even eat, like a salad or something?"

"What are you getting?" I asked.

"Double fatty burger with chili cheese fries and an extra-large molten lava chocolate shake," Shannon answered. "If this is my last meal, I don't want to mess around."

"Last meal!?" I asked incredulously. "I plan on getting out alive tonight. Do you have a death wish or something? Because I don't have a death wish."

"Kidding, Stinky, just kidding." Shannon offered me a

grin. "But seriously, what do you eat? Like lemon water and a side of air?"

"Very funny," I answered. "I'll take a double double fatty burger, extra-large fries, and a cherry Pepsi."

"All right, all right," Shannon said, nodding. "I can get behind that. Mr. John Hunter living large over here."

Shannon placed the order, going over the weapons we wanted to bring for the night.

"We don't know who there's going to be a bloodsucker and who's going to be human," Shannon told me, going over to one of her bedrooms. Before she opened the closed door she looked at me with a serious expression. "Don't freak out when you see this. You're the only one besides me to know what's in here."

"Listen, in the last few days, I've seen some pretty messed up stuff," I told her. "I'm sure whatever you have behind that door isn't going to be worse than..."

Shannon opened the door, revealing a scene straight out of *John Wick*. Her spare bedroom was an armory. The walls were lined with both firearms and bladed weapons. The far wall also had a computer atop a black desk.

Crates that I guessed held more equipment or ammunition were neatly stacked in the corners of the room.

"Holy crap," I whispered. "What are you going to do with all of this? Start a demilitarization of Panama?"

"I was thinking about doing that next week," Shannon teased me. "But a girl has to be prepared for whatever may come her way."

"What the heck is this one?" I asked. I played my fair share of *Call of Duty* in my day, so I knew the weapon was some kind of grenade launcher. "I want this one."

"Yeah, not so much, Terminator." Shannon took the weapon from me and placed it back on the wall. "We want to kill the vampires, not take down the entire building with us inside."

"The plan tonight will be me taking point and you covering my six," Shannon explained. "We'll give the humans every chance to escape. Those that try and fire on us, I'll be able to put down with non-lethal rounds. The vampires will only be slowed down by regular rounds. Daylight isn't going to be an option, but we'll have blades and I can bring some incendiary—"

A knock on Shannon's apartment door interrupted our conversation.

"Matty Too Fatty's?" Shannon asked, surprised.

"No, that's too fast," I told her, taking the grenade launcher from the wall again. "Something else."

TWENTY-EIGHT

SHANNON PICKED up a pistol and approached the door. My grenade launcher wasn't loaded, so I wielded it like a club instead.

We approached the door, each of us on one side.

"You can put the weapons down." Mrs. Grundy's familiar voice penetrated the door. "And, John, that's really not the right way to hold that weapon."

Shannon and I exchanged puzzled looks.

"She's not wrong," Shannon murmured, stuffing her weapon into her lower back waistband.

"But how does she know that?" I asked, not expecting Shannon to have an actual answer. "That's freaking me out."

Shannon opened the door for our elderly neighbor who also happened to be a Watcher for the Court.

Mrs. Grundy stood there with a shawl over her stooped back. She wore sweatpants and a shirt that read "Baby Yoda is my spirit animal."

In her right hand, she carried what looked like a gift basket wrapped in pink cellophane. She gave me a knowing grin.

"A little gift basket for the two newest hunters to join the Court," Mrs. Grundy said, handing me the basket.

I nearly pulled my hernia carrying the basket. I was no slouch when it came to the gym either. The basket had to weigh near eighty pounds. Mrs. Grundy made it look like a bouquet of daisies.

"What the heck do you have in here?" I asked. "Grenades?"

"How did you know?" Mrs. Grundy waggled her grey eyebrows. "A pair of special grenades equipped with a UV flash that will even the odds tonight against the forces you'll encounter. Along with that are some snuf as well as a weapon more suited for your skill set, John."

"What skill set?" Shannon asked. "No offense, Jonny, but you're a male model."

"None taken?" I asked more than told her. I was trying to figure out if I should be offended by her comment. "Hey, wait a minute."

"Exactly," Mrs. Grundy continued before I could get into it with Shannon. "Anyway, I should let you two prepare. You have a big night ahead of you."

"We do and thank you for the gift basket, but we didn't agree to join your Court," Shannon reminded her. "No offense, at least I haven't."

"The last time I committed to anything, I had my heart ripped in two, put in a blender, then lit to a pile of ashes," I told her. "I'm with Shannon on this one. I haven't agreed to anything."

"No, but you will," Mrs. Grundy said with a knowing nod. "Now there's a young man with a case of acne trying to get into the apartment complex carrying a large order of Matty Too Fatty's. I'll let him in on my way down. You young people should really watch what you put into your bodies."

Without another word, Mrs. Grundy left.

THE REST of the evening was spent gorging on fat and calories while preparing our equipment for the night to come.

Shannon packed a large black duffle bag for each of us. Inside were body armor as well as her patented neck shields meant to keep us safe from those pesky unwanted vampire bites.

There was enough weaponry and ammunition to make Scarface approve as well as the new items Mrs. Grundy dropped off. The UV grenades were easy enough to understand. My weapon and what she called snuf was not.

"How did she fit that axe in the gift basket?" I asked, still doing mental backflips to figure that one out as I sat in the passenger side seat. "I mean, it looked large, but when I lifted it out of the basket, it grew, right? Did I have a psychotic break or did it grow as I lifted it out?"

"It definitely grew," Shannon confirmed. "Your axe is cool, but what about that stuff she called snuf? Did you read the directions? We're supposed to snort it one at a time and it only lasts a short period. I mean, I experimented with drugs when I was younger, but after waking up in a ditch with a coyote staring at me, I was done."

"Maybe we save the snuf for a last-ditch effort, like only if things get really bad," I concurred. "I'm not about sniffing magic mystery powder."

"Agreed," Shannon said, maneuvering through late-night traffic. "Hey, you want to throw something intense on? Listening to the right song can really pump me up before a hunt."

"Oh, say no more. I got you," I said, plugging her AUX cord into my phone. "I came across the perfect song earlier today."

The lyrics to Rachael Platten's "Fight Song" came on and I started bobbing my head to the beat.

"You've got to be freaking kidding me, Stinky," Shannon said, eye rolling at me so hard, I thought her eyes were going to fall out of her head. "I can't believe you're doing this to me right now. Have you heard of the term cruel and unusual punishment?"

I channeled all the anxious pent-up energy into the words coming out of my mouth as I wiggled my shoulders and danced in my seat.

"Come on, you know the words!" I shouted to Shannon as I put a pretend microphone under her mouth.

"No, no, I really don't." Shannon fought back a smile.

It was too late. I saw her about to crack.

"This is my fight song, take back my life song," I wailed away, going even crazier in my seat until the dam burst.

Shannon laughed out loud then joined in.

Like two idiots, we traveled down the freeway to V Model Management, but for at least the space of that song, we could forget about what had been done to us, what position we found ourselves in, and what we were about to do next.

I wish that song could have lasted forever. We arrived at V Model Management much too soon.

Shannon parked behind the building's parking lot in an alley Evan had pointed out. It was almost eleven now. Most people should be in bed or at least powering down for bed and not looking out their window at the two hunters arming themselves for battle.

The alley smelled a little like pee and a lot like mildew. A cement wall to our right paralleled a line of apartments and garages to our left.

"You said you had something to take care of the cameras?" I asked, fitting the Velcro straps on the side of the

Kevlar vest tight. "What is it, like are you a hacker or use some kind of cool EMP tech or something?"

"Nothing that fancy," Shannon said, screwing on a silencer to her handgun. "I'm going to shoot the ones that are in our way. By the time whoever's monitoring them comes out to take a look, we'll already be inside."

"But what about the cops?" I asked, holding a UV grenade in one hand and the steel neck guard in the other. "I didn't sign up for that."

"What cops?" Shannon looked at me like I was a child asking if Santa were real. "You think someone like Bloodstone's going to call the cops? The last thing vampires want is police around them. When ish goes down, they're going to try and handle it themselves."

"I hope you're right," I muttered, fitting the neck guard around my throat. It felt like putting on a neck brace but a little more comfortable. Shannon padded the inside that fit snug against my neck. A steel outside started just below my ear and fit under the shoulder harness of the Kevlar vest.

"All right," Shannon said, going over the plan again. "Let me take point. I've done this before. You're our UV grenade guy; you have the snuf and your axe."

"I really feel like I should have a gun," I grumbled, shaking my head. "It just doesn't feel right going in there without a gun."

I held Shannon's gaze in the darkness. The cold night air sent goosebumps up and down my exposed arms.

She leaned in so close, I thought she was going to kiss me for a second. Instead, she leaned closer to my ear and whispered, "No, stop asking. I'm not trying to get shot tonight."

"Okay." I shrugged with a sigh. "You're the professional."

"If all goes well, you won't have to do much but stand back and watch the show," Shannon said, looking at the axe in my hand. "Plus, you have that monster Viking axe and the drugs Mrs. Grundy gave us."

"Right," I said, hefting the axe in my hands. The black wooden handle was marked with runes all the way up the shaft. At the top, dark grey metal turned into an axe blade on one end and something like a sledgehammer on the other. Shannon fitted a strap to it so it fit on my back.

The snuf was something straight out of a drug cartel movie. Paper packets with blue powder sat in my right pocket. The only instructions printed on the gum-sized paper packet were: "Inhale one through nose deeply. Effects last seconds and try not to piss yourself."

I thought that was a little overboard, but what in the last few days of my life wasn't?

"Let's go," Shannon said, jumping onto the seven-foot stonewall separating the alley from the V Model Management parking lot.

Shannon looked like a badass in the light of the moon and stars overhead. Like me, she wore her Kevlar vest and neck shield. Unlike me, she carried her katana over her right shoulder, a rifle in her hands, and a handgun on her hip.

She was up and over in a second's time. I followed suit, thanking myself for all those pull-ups I hated but forced myself to do anyway at the gym.

I dropped down heavily on the other side behind a row of parked cars. The entrance to the building was ahead of us. We had to cross about fifty yards of parking lot and the guard booth with the attendant inside.

"We'll have to move fast," Shannon told me, taking a red bandana out of her pocket for herself and then a black one for me. "Extra precaution in case we miss a camera."

"Good thinking," I said, taking the bandana and wrapping it around the lower half of my face. My heart was pounding in my chest so hard, I could hear it in my ears.

"Let's go," Shannon said, rising from her position behind a parked Tesla. I followed close behind as Shannon crossed the quiet parking lot so fast, I had trouble keeping up. Whoever was in charge of sound production for movies with silencers had it wrong. Sure, the silencer helped muffle the noise, but by no means was it quiet.

Shannon pulled the trigger twice, rewarded with sparks each time as the cameras exploded on impact. We passed Porsches, Cadillacs, and Range Rovers on the way to the building.

"Hey, what the—"

Shannon released the hold on her rifle, letting it fall and be supported by the sling around her shoulder. She drew her handgun in one fluid movement and placed a round to the young man's head.

The kid went down without another sound.

Shannon holstered her sidearm, bringing the rifle to her shoulder again.

We were already next to him by the time I could make a sound. Cold dread filled my gut. This isn't what I signed up for. I came to kill vampires preying on the weak and innocent, not to kill kids.

I felt like I was going to vomit when a second look at the teenager told me he would have one heck of a headache when he woke, but he wasn't dead. A welt was already forming on his forehead the size of a baseball.

"Non-lethal rounds, remember?" Shannon asked. "Get him inside the booth. Let's move."

I obeyed, dragging the kid inside. That double Matty Too Fatty cheeseburger still threatened to exit my stomach.

"Moving," Shannon said as soon as I closed the door to the booth. The bottom floor of V Model Management was glass doors and also faced a street. We ran the half block to the front doors, passing only a homeless person on the sidewalk who looked at us with a toothless O-shaped mouth.

I ran ahead, opening the door for Shannon, who hurried in, dropping her rifle again and allowing the sling around her shoulder to carry it. She drew her pistol as both guards on duty jumped to attention.

TWENTY-NINE

THE RECEPTIONIST WAS GONE for the day; the two guards remaining had been sitting behind the half circle desk.

Two trigger pulls from Shannon's weapon and both men slumped to the ground unconscious. Five more rounds fired and the cameras in the lobby were out. Shannon was a pro behind the trigger.

We half speed-walked, half ran toward the elevators, only stopping briefly to make sure both targets were down. The pair of guards lay on the ground with welts already forming on their faces.

These guys were only doing their jobs; how much they knew about what was really going on at V Model Management was a guess. But this was better than ending them permanently.

Shannon reached the elevators and pressed the button.

"They know who they're working for," Shannon told me as she caught me eyeing the pair of men. "They have to at this point. Probably serving Bloodstone under the promise that he turn them one day."

I didn't say anything. Adrenaline coursed through my

body so fast, I didn't trust myself to speak. The craziest most illegal thing I had done at this point was skip an item at the self-checkout line at Wal-Mart. Even then, it had been a mistake. I tried to go back and pay for it, but the worker on duty told me just to take it. I still felt bad about that.

The elevator doors dinged open.

"Hey, guys, we have some cameras out in the parking—"

One of the largest men I'd ever seen stood in the elevator gaping at us. This guy could have been a pro wrestler in another life. I wasn't sure how his arms fit in his black uniform. His legs were the size of my torso and I wasn't little.

Smooth Jazz, maybe some Miles Davis or Louie Armstrong, serenaded our ears from within the elevator.

Shannon lifted and fired her weapon at his forehead. The nonlethal round struck him then fell off.

The man's eyes went black like Evan's. Pointed teeth sprouted from his mouth.

"Oh shi—"

Shannon's suppressed rifle filled the lobby with dampened thunder as she emptied her clip into his head and chest. Dark blood painted the inside of the elevator doors. For a moment, I thought she had him.

The elevator doors started to close.

Shannon's rifle clicked dry.

The bloody vampire missing sections of his face and chest reached out, gripping the edge of the elevator doors to stop it from closing then charged forward, sending a straight kick to Shannon's chest that sent her flying backward.

I removed the battle-axe from my back and swung for the fences. The vampire was fast, ducking below my first wild swing then backing into the elevator for the second. Like an idiot, I pursued him, entering the elevator.

The third strike to his chest, the vampire actually

accepted, allowing me to sink the axe's blade deep in his sternum.

The wounds from Shannon's rifle were already healing across his face and the rest of his body.

My axe sank so deep, I couldn't pull it out.

"You idiot." The vampire ignored the blow, grabbing the shaft of the weapon with one hand and my throat with the other. "An axe to my chest isn't going to stop me."

At that moment, something strange happened. The dark grey axe blade had some kind of slow reaction to the vampire. The blade heated red as if it were on fire.

The vampire howled in pain, ripping the weapon out of his chest and throwing me across the elevator.

"The steel of the gods!?" The vampire held the stinking charred wound on his chest with one hand. "How did you come across such a weapon?"

"It was in a gift basket!" I yelled, seizing my opportunity to finish him. I brought the bright red axe head down on top of him.

The vampire twisted out of the way of the blow, and hit me in a tackle, slamming me against the elevator wall.

The doors of the elevator were trying to close but were stopped by Shannon's abandoned rifle.

The vampire used his weight to crush me. My head banged off the elevator wall. I saw stars explode across my vision.

I lifted the axe to no avail. The vampire used his left hand to control my wrist that held the axe. He pinned it to the wall. With his right hand, he grabbed my throat.

"Who are you?" he shouted in my face with flecks of saliva hitting my nose and eyebrows. "Where did you find this weapon?"

"Your—your mama gave it to me," I choked out past his crushing grip on my throat. I was proud of myself for that one. If I was going to die, then at least I'd go out saying something cool.

Instead of death, I saw a steel blade sprout through the giant's throat. He gagged, losing control of me. I slumped to the ground, coughing.

Shannon maneuvered him to the elevator doors, sliding her blade to the left half, severing his head from the rest of his body. The giant fell to the ground, still trying to fight.

Shannon picked up her rifle from where it lay next to his spasming body. To his credit, the man managed to turn around and tried to attack us again. With his head half falling off his shoulder and vertebrae and nerves cut, it was a clumsy attempt.

"You okay?" Shannon asked me.

"Yeah," I coughed, getting to my feet.

"He's going to kill you," the giant gargled. "He's going to kill both of you."

Shannon pressed the button to the fifth floor before kicking her boot into the vampire and forcing most of his body out of the elevator.

The elevator doors closed on his neck.

The elevator moved upward, ripping the vampire's head from the rest of his body. His head rolled into the elevator with us with a thick spray of blood making the small square chamber resemble a Pollock painting.

I coughed, gagging on the substance. My stomach churned as I did my best to spit it out of my mouth.

"You really should learn to shut your mouth when bodily fluids start flying," Shannon scolded, releasing the magazine on her rifle and jamming a new one in place.

"Yeah, you're telling me," I said, spitting one last time for good measure. "How are you doing? You took his kick like a champ."

"Ribs aren't too happy about that," Shannon said as the

elevator doors dinged open on the fifth floor. "Probably bruised but not broken. Come on, same plan. We'll move to the stairs then go up to the sixth floor."

The bloody elevator doors opened for us, revealing a clean office space with lots of glass offices and small cubicles.

A woman wearing headphones danced to her silent music as she vacuumed the carpet on the other side of the office.

Shannon lifted her handgun.

"Hey," I whispered to her. "Really? You're going to shoot the janitor? Is that necessary?"

"Never can be too careful," Shannon said, holstering her weapon. We hurried on in a hunched run for the door to the stairwell. "Hey, what's the deal with your axe? Why is it glowing red like a lightsaber?"

"No idea," I told her. "As soon as I sank it into the walking mountain, it lit up like a sparkler. I think it might detect vampires or something like that? It hurt him. But when we get to the party, let's use the UV grenades agreed? That was one vampire that nearly ended us. I'm not eager to go up against a few dozen."

"You and me both," Shannon said, reaching the door leading to the stairs.

She nodded to me.

Axe in my right hand, I slowly opened the door with my left.

Shannon stepped in, looking down the barrel of her weapon, first pointing it up and then down the stairwell.

"We're good. Let's go," Shannon whispered.

We stepped into the stairwell, moving upward to the sixth floor. The door to the floor looked like any other. I wasn't sure what I was expecting it to look like, knowing this was where the vampire leader of Hollywood lived; maybe made out of bones painted blood red?

Shannon pressed a finger to her lips. A steel bar ran across the center of the door.

I nodded, pressing on the door slowly. A faint click came from the locking mechanism as the door opened ever so slightly.

Shannon and I peeked in.

A few feet from us, the back of a guard in a black suit stood sentry. The massive living-room-like space the luxury apartment opened up to was filled with figures wearing dark red robes.

There were twenty or thirty of them present. One man wearing a silver mask addressed them all. I recognized his voice. It was Mr. Bloodstone.

"In the long-standing tradition of our coven, it has been up to us to introduce only the best and brightest in the industry to join our ranks," Mr. Bloodstone said in a booming theatrical voice. "As such, it is my honor to introduce to you the newest member, Miss Tracy Coach Prada!"

I felt my heart stop as a slender figure next to Mr. Bloodstone took his hand and joined him in front of the rest of the group. She also wore a silver mask with the eye holes cut out.

"I'm sorry," Shannon whispered in my ear. "But this isn't the time for second thoughts. You have those UV grenades ready?"

I put my axe on my back with my head spinning and took the grenades from my belt.

"She is your sister now," Mr. Bloodstone continued. "There has never been a greater time to belong to the coven. We feast where we live and our chapters across the globe only grow in strength. The Count himself has sent word that our time to rule the humans draws nearer."

"Three," Shannon started, gritting her teeth. "Two."

I wasn't ready to kill Tracy. I knew that much. I wasn't

willing to kill the woman I loved just last week, vampire or not, without giving her another chance.

"One," Shannon finished, bursting through the doors.

"Tracy, turn away!" I yelled, rolling both UV grenades into the room.

I closed my eyes and turned my head, taking my own advice.

Two massive explosions shook the room.

Even with my head turned and eyes closed, I saw the brilliant flashes of light the UV grenades sent off. As soon as they detonated, I turned around, opening my eyes and trying to blink my pupils back into focus.

Screams erupted from those present as their vampiric bodies met the light penetrating through their robes and the eye sockets of their masks. They deteriorated into ash in front of my eyes.

Nearly every red robe fell to the floor with the silver mask clanking to the ground beside it.

In a last ditch effort to protect Bloodstone, a group of vampires closest to their leader threw themselves on him. They also shielded Tracy, who stood next to him at the time, by default.

They all paid the price, dying from the UV grenades, but they had succeeded in saving their leader.

Bloodstone stood up next to a trembling Tracy. He ripped off his mask and robe, staring daggers at Shannon and me.

"Bloodstone!" Shannon roared. "Do you remember me? Do you remember my sister?"

Bloodstone snarled with rage. "I'll see you burn for this."

What I had assumed to be an empty room now filled with more guards who had fallen but weren't dead. They stumbled forward, lifting their weapons toward me and Shannon.

There were six of them all dressed in suits, and blinking

to try and readjust their vision. They were as human as Shannon and I.

"It pays to employ humans as well as vampires for an event like this," Bloodstone growled. "Take the man alive. I want to know everything he knows. I'll deal with the woman."

All six men still blinking from the flash holstered their handguns and started toward me.

THIRTY

TRACY TOOK off her silver mask, horrified at the scene in front of her. Dozens of vampires had just been turned to ash that most likely included new friends of hers and acquaintances.

"Today you pay for what you did to my sister!" Shannon roared, pumping rounds into Bloodstone as she stalked forward.

Half of me wanted to tell Tracy she needed to get the heck out of here; half of me wanted to go and help Shannon take down Bloodstone, but at the moment, I had my hands full.

The six black-suited human men surrounded me and moved in at once. This wasn't like in the movies where the bad guys came at the hero one at a time and he then took turns knocking them out.

They came at me in a circle and began turning that circle into a closing noose.

"Hey, guys," I said in my best tough-guy voice. "I don't want to kill any of you. Stop now and I'll spare your souls."

It didn't work, but I had to try.

Needless to say, each one of these muscles for hire had

more hand-to-hand experience than I did. The battle-axe helped to even the odds for a few seconds as I swung the weapon wide, keeping them at bay.

One of the guards dove in, trying to catch me after a particularly wide swing. I let go of the axe handle with my right hand, bringing my elbow sideways, and cracked him across the nose so hard, I heard a crunch.

The next second, I was bombarded by the other five. One guy grabbed my axe handle, trying to rip it from my grip. Another put me in a chokehold from behind. The remaining three laid into me with a series of punches and kicks to my legs, torso, and face.

I knew if I let go of the axe, it was all over. Heck, it might have already been over and I was too stubborn to admit it.

Left hand with a death hold on the axe, I raised my right and found the guy's eye who had me in a chokehold.

This is so gross, I thought to myself as I jammed my thumb into his eye's socket so deep, I swore I felt his brain. His eyeball popped like a pimple then felt like warm jelly. *Ugh!*

Screaming came from behind me as he released his hold. The good news was I could breathe again. The bad news was it didn't matter. A cross to my chin loosened the grip on the axe and it was finally ripped away. The pistol whip to my left temple sent me to the floor, where someone kicked me in the ribs for good measure.

Blood distorted my vision as I looked up at a foggy image of one of the guards lifting his boot to stomp on my face.

I'm not sure if it was a product of so many concussions at once or I was already dead and I imagined this in the afterlife, but a black ball of fur streaked across my vision like a lightning bolt.

Once second the boot was about to descend on me, the next the boot along with its owner was gone.

I sat up, trying to clear my vision as I understood what

was going on. Mrs. Grundy's hellhound, the one she called Odin, had his jaws around a guard's throat, ripping out his vocal cords. It was graphic to say the least and made my stomach turn.

The other four guards still on their feet looked stunned.

Suddenly, one fell to the floor with his head snapped to the side.

"You didn't think I was going to let you come alone, did you?" Evan asked, revealing himself behind the fallen guard. "The wolf tagged along. I don't care what he says. I was here first."

The remaining three guards backed up, drawing the weapons that had previously been holstered. Odin and Evan were on top of them in the blink of an eye.

Mad laughter, the likes I had never heard before drew my attention to the opposite side of the room where Shannon battled Winston Bloodstone. Like my own fight, theirs had been brief yet fierce. Bloodstone's clothes were in tatters, his face a mess of flesh as his body healed the damaged Shannon's rifle inflicted.

Shannon's left arm hung useless at her side. With her right hand, she gripped the katana handle, keeping Bloodstone at bay. He played with her, circling his prey with glee.

"A human with one good arm?" Mr. Bloodstone laughed. "You know what I think? I do remember your sister. You look like her. It was that whore in the Midwest, right?"

Shannon roared and lunged at him. He sidestepped her attack, opening a shallow cut across her forward with sharp nails I had yet to see on any vampire.

She was going to need help. With Odin and Evan busy, I was the best chance she had. I tried moving for my axe, but every muscle in my body screamed in pain.

Get up, Jonny, I coached myself in my head. *Get up one more time. She needs you. Get up!*

That was when I remembered the snuf packets in my pocket. Bloody hands reached into my pants pocket, coming back with the two paper packets. I ignored the warning labels, ripping both packets of the blue stuff open, shoving them at my nose, and inhaled sharply.

Now I may have lied before. I have tried my fair share of drugs, but who hasn't, right? The snuf hit me like nothing I had ever experienced before. It was like having a cocktail of crack, caffeine, adrenaline from a giant, and that stuff they injected Uma Thurman with in *Pulp Fiction* shot straight into my brain.

Pain receded to a memory. I felt focused, stronger, and faster than ever before. Heck, I even felt like I could freaking fly at the moment.

I jumped to my feet, grabbed my axe, and headed for Winston Bloodstone.

"You'll die alone like your sister," Bloodstone taunted Shannon, who bled from half a dozen shallow cuts he inflicted as he dodged in and out of her reach. "And in time, I'll forget you like I did her."

"She's not alone, dirt bag," I said, joining Shannon, who struggled to stand. "And Captain Insano's about to open a can of you know what."

Bloodstone squinted at me as if he recognized me but was trying to figure out from where.

"Do I know you?" Bloodstone finally asked.

"Oh yeah, I met you at a party a few nights ago." I grinned through blood-stained teeth. "I just filled out my HR paperwork to work with V Model Management today, actually."

I was willing to talk more at the moment. I had so much energy, I couldn't keep it all in. I bounced up and down on my toes and from side to side like a boxer. My jaw clenched over and over again as if it had a mind of its own.

"You know my roommate Evan Woods," I continued. "He

used to work for you too. I say 'used to' since we're about to kill you."

Bloodstone's black eyes fixated on me. His mouth opened in a snarl. Without words, he lunged at me. He was fast, but for the moment, high on the gift basket of drugs Mrs. Grundy gave us, I was just as fast.

We clashed, each scoring a blow. I brought the half-moon blade of my axe to bear where his left arm met his shoulder. The blade hummed red on contact. Brought down on the vampire's skin with such force, it severed his arm from his body.

At the same time, Bloodstone stabbed through my Kevlar vest with his right hand. I felt his nail-like talons tear open my skin and sink deep before being ripped out again.

He howled in pain, smoke wafting from his severed stump of an arm.

I fell to my knees, the pain from his inflicted wound dampened thanks to the snuf, but I knew I'd feel it shortly. Already the drug was beginning to wear off. I wasn't as sharp as I had been moments before. The packaging did say the effects were meant to last only a short time.

Bloodstone yelled to the ceiling in pain.

Shannon saw her moment of opportunity and took it. One arm dangling uselessly by her side, she leapt at Bloodstone with her good arm wielding the katana like the pro she was.

On his knees, Bloodstone caught the blade of her katana with his one remaining hand. Blood oozed from his palm as Shannon pressed her weight behind the hilt of her weapon, forcing the end toward his face.

I ran over, bringing the axe I was starting to get very fond of down in a huge circular blow. I took his other arm from his body in a single motion.

Bloodstone's scream seemed more frustration and anger than pain.

"You think you've won?" he raged. "You think this means anything? The Count will see you choke on your own blood. Your victory here means nothing!"

"You're wrong," Shannon answered. "This is for my sister. Her killer's been found and brought to justice and you'll never hurt anyone ever again."

Bloodstone was about to say something else, but Shannon did this impressive slash with her katana using one arm that opened up his bowels. Intestines fell out as he watched, horrified.

Shannon did the move again, this time taking his head from his body.

I lost it. I couldn't keep my Matty Too Fatty burger in any longer. I vomited all over my boots.

Odin and Evan joined us both, staring with large eyes at what was left of Mr. Bloodstone.

"Well, I'm out of a job, but I'm glad you found rest for your sister," Evan said to Shannon. "I think wherever she is, she'd be proud."

Shannon looked over at Evan with a wince. "Thanks. I still might kill you later because you are a vampire, but thanks for coming."

"Fair enough," Evan said, coming over to me and helping me to my feet. "Need me to hold your hair?"

"I think I got it all out," I said as the last effects of the snuf wore off. "But I feel like I'm going to pass out from the pain. I think I'm going to need a doctor."

"I bet Mrs. Grundy can patch us up or at the least knows where to go," Shannon answered. "Evan, I'll get Jonny if you can pull the car to the front."

"On it." Evan dashed off.

Shannon and I supported one another as we made our way to the elevator. Odin trotted alongside me.

"Good boy," I told him. "Good magic, creature,

hellhound."

Odin grinned up at me.

"Things were moving so fast back there, I can't be sure, but did you tell your ex fiancée to get down?" Shannon wondered as the elevator doors slid closed behind us. "I think my mind is still trying to process everything that just happened."

"Uh, no, I mean, maybe," I stammered, swallowing hard. Suddenly, my mouth felt like it was full of cotton balls. I couldn't tell if that was from the snuf or I felt embarrassed like I let Shannon down somehow. I looked around for any sign of Tracy, she was gone.

"Still have feelings for her, I get it. If it makes you feel any better I saw her sneak out when you were getting your ribs kicked in and assuming the fetal position," Shannon said, pressing the button to take us to the first floor. She removed her good arm from around me, gingerly touching her left arm that she hadn't moved since her fight with Bloodstone.

Odin sat down beside us and looked at us as if to say, "We going or what?"

"Oh that's going to need to be put back in." Shannon grimaced as the elevator moved us to the first floor. "Stinky, I'm going to need you here."

"Me?" I asked that stupid question realizing she wasn't talking to Odin, so there was no one else it could have been. "I'm not really good with popping bones back in place. I mean—"

"Jonny, you just disarmed a vampire, and before that, you shoved your axe into the chest of another." Shannon looked at me deadpan. "You can do this. I need you to help me put my shoulder back in place."

I felt lightheaded, tired, even as I nodded. Shannon needed me right now and she was right. If I could take on vampires, then I could put a shoulder back in place.

"I need you to grab the wrist and then pull it forward and straight in front of me," Shannon directed. "I don't need a countdown; just do it."

"Oooooookay," I said, feeling like I was about to pass out. I grabbed her left wrist and watched Shannon's face contort in pain as I moved her arm up in the desired position. "Are you ready?"

"Just do it," Shannon growled over the elevator music serenading us to the Beach Boys.

I took a deep breath, readying myself to pull. I wasn't sure why I felt so lightheaded.

Without warning, Shannon jerked her body back, sliding her injured shoulder back into its socket.

"Son of a nutcracker!" Shannon howled, working her left arm around with a look of pain-laced ecstasy. "That's the stuff."

The elevator doors dinged open. My vision was starting to go blurry for some reason. I took a step out of the elevator and then stumbled on the tile floor of the lobby.

"Jonny?" Shannon asked, worried. "Jonny, what's going on?"

"I," I said, my breathing coming shallow and heavy. "I don't know."

"Oh, Jonny, you're bleeding. Where's all this blood coming from?" Shannon asked. She was on her knees by my side in a second, ripping off my Kevlar vest.

Already the blood was falling down my chest.

I felt Shannon taking off my shirt to see the extent of the damage. She was saying something to me now, but her face was blurry.

I looked down right before I passed out. Near my left pec where Bloodstone stabbed me with his razor like nails, a single black nail had broken off in my skin. Blood leaked from the wound like a waterline in need of repair.

THIRTY-ONE

I FELT COLD. No, more than cold. Freezing. My nipples were so hard, they could cut glass. I shook, looking around me for some kind of warmth. There was none. I lay in a snowbank.

I wasn't really used to the snow, living in Southern California and all. I sat up, wrapping my arms around my chest.

My chest.

Looking down, I saw the same wound on my left pec. It felt numb. One of Bloodstone's black talons sat in my flesh, deep and happy. The black tendrils of poison or whatever it was leaked over my body, spreading out like a spider web.

"I'd leave that in there if I were you." A voice I didn't recognize offered me advice. "Vampire poison is better left in until you're around the right hands who know how to take it out."

I wrapped my arms around my shaking body; puffs of steam left my mouth before they disappeared a moment later. I didn't see anyone.

"Who," I managed to ask past chattering teeth. "Who are you?"

"A friend or an enemy; that choice can be yours," the

voice said in an accent I couldn't make out. It was a man's voice, but was he Russian, Serbian, something else? "The trees to your left."

I looked around the area to see a copse of trees to my left. Their trunks were thick, branches laden with snow. A tall man stood against the closest tree. He moved from it now toward me.

He looked like a king. Dark hair, a short beard, and a fur cloak over his shoulders. He came toward me with a smile on his lips I didn't know if I could trust. It was like looking at a spider before it bit.

"John Hunter," the man said, fixing his black leather gloves. "I have to say I am surprised a human like you, so inexperienced, was able to destroy Bloodstone and his coven. That is very impressive."

Dread like I hadn't experienced before took me. This man, whoever he was, carried a presence with him that was nearly palpable.

"Who are you?" I asked, trying to make sense of all of this. "Where am I?"

"Bloodstone infected you, connecting us," the man said as if the explanation were simple enough. "I was the one who turned Bloodstone, so in this way, we are able to commune. We talk here in a plane not known in your world. As for who I am. You know who I am, John Hunter."

"The Count?" I asked, trying to fit the pieces together in my mind. I was still so cold. "You're a vampire."

"And who says models are dense?" The Count smiled. His teeth were straight, his eyes ice blue, not black.

I looked down at the black nail in my chest again.

"Leave it in," the Count instructed. "It's the only thing keeping you alive at the moment."

As I stood there in the freezing snow trying to make sense of this new plane of existence and who I was speaking with, I couldn't help but wonder why he was keeping me alive. I was about to rip out the black nail in my chest like an ingrown hair. If I did that, according to the man in my dream or whatever this was, I'd be dead.

"Why tell me?" I asked. "Am I supposed to believe that you're one of the good guys? Count, whatever your last name is."

"How rude of me, of course." The man gave a flourishing bow. "My name is Count Victor Jovanovic. I have no desire to see you die, John Hunter. Too long have my kind been hunted by the Court and the hunters they contract. I was hoping you might be a bridge to fill that gap."

"I think what we have here is a case of mistaken identity," I said, rewrapping my arms over my chest in an attempt to keep warm. "I'm not contracted by the Court. I didn't know any of this even existed more than a few days ago."

"And that is why you would make the perfect emissary between both our kinds," Victor remarked, taking off his fur cloak and placing it around my shoulders.

I flinched. I wasn't sure if what happened here in this other reality happened in the real world. I sure as heck didn't trust Victor, but neither was I in a position to decline warmth.

"You've been through much, John Hunter," Victor said, taking a step back. His black boots crunched on the layer of snow on the ground. "I know who you are, where you come from. I understand how brutal an upbringing you've had. The struggle with bullies, money, and relationships. I can fix all of that. I can make you the hero of your own story."

I watched in awe as Victor swept an open arm to our left. The snowy terrain shimmered then shifted from ground laden snow to a two-story mansion. A long driveway led up to a grey home with white trim. A Bentley and a Porsche sat parked near the front door.

Tracy was there waving to me with a sincere smile on her face. That same smile I had come to know and love before she was twisted and corrupted.

"Everything you've ever wanted, John Hunter," Victor continued. "Everything you've ever wanted and all I need you to do is agree to bring peace to our two factions. Vampires hunting humans, the Court hunting vampires; it's a vicious cycle that must be stopped."

I don't know how he managed to get in my head, but he knew about my past. Every detail of the house is what I daydreamed my own would look like one day, it even had a nice wide yard, and of course, Tracy.

"One thing I learned a long time ago is that nothing's free," I said, looking from the image back to Victor. "What you're selling is too good to be true."

For the first time, Victor's generous façade cracked for just a moment. I saw his jaw muscles tighten, his eyes go from that ice blue to black, and then back again.

"I want peace," Victor crooned. "Take time to think about my offer, for I will not ask again. I just need someone in the Court who sees things like I do. That's all."

"You mean a spy?" I asked, finally getting down to the actual word. "You want me to spy on the Court for you. Nothing in my life has ever come easy because I've never chosen the easy way out."

I told him, letting his cloak drop to my feet. I didn't care about the cold anymore. Anger erupted in my chest. Anger at Victor for trying to manipulate me and anger at myself for being so naïve and even entertaining the idea.

"I will kill you," Victor threatened, letting his eyes go pure black now. His flashy white smile morphed into a mouth of razors. "You could have had it all and instead you've chosen death, John Hunter. I am coming for you."

Victor lunged at me so fast, I had no chance at all.

THIRTY-TWO

"AHHHHHHH!" I sat bolt upright as the image of Victor's maw of sharpened teeth lingered in my head. I finally understood what that bat felt like before Ozzy Osbourne bit its head off.

My heart hammered in my chest. With awareness came an aching brutal cold pain from my chest. As soon as I sat up, I regretted the act, cringing with the massive amount of agony seizing my body.

"Hey, hey, it's okay, it's okay," Evan said, looking at me through the rearview mirror. "When you're out of the woods, remind me to make fun of you for screaming like that. For now, are you okay?"

Shannon turned around in her passenger-side seat, looking back at me with concern in her eyes. "We're almost there. Mrs. Grundy gave you something to hold off the infection. She said you'd make it."

"What?" I asked, so confused I didn't know where to start. I grasped my bearings. I sat in the backseat of Evan's BMW with Shannon in the passenger-side seat and Evan behind the wheel. "Mrs. Grundy? Where are we going?"

"Going to go visit the Muffin Man on Dreary Lane, little guy," Evan said without cracking a smile. "You've been out hard. We took you to Mrs. Grundy first, but she couldn't do more than slow the poison."

"She said there's a doctor that can help." Shannon picked up the story. "We're on our way to his office now. He's supposed to meet us there."

My chest tightened with every breath. I didn't want my friends to see me squirm in pain, but it really sucked. Each movement sent a cold ice pick through my chest.

"If you need to cry, it's okay, buddy," Evan said. "I'll cry with you."

"I'm not going to cry," I said through gritted teeth. "Just hurry."

"We're almost there. GPS says the next left and then the office should be on the right hand side. 2259 Dreary Lane."

I guess Evan wasn't kidding about the Muffin Man. We pulled into a well-lit strip mall. The late hours meant the parking lot was mostly empty, save for a few random cars in the lot.

In between a ninety-nine cent store and a CVS stood an unmarked building with a warm cream trim and glass exterior. White blinds were drawn behind the windows, but a light inside told us someone was present.

"Uhhhh, Shannon?" Evan asked, turning off the engine. "Are you sure this is the right place?"

"This is the address she gave us," Shannon confirmed, checking her phone again. "Maybe we should give her a call to make sure? This doesn't seem right."

"Come on," I said through a grunt in the back seat. "Let's just go. If she said this is it, then this is it."

I didn't know why the two were being so hesitant. I'd faced down a coven of vampires, been stabbed, and had a vision or dream or whatever it was with Count Jovanovic. I wasn't worried about going into the wrong office at this point, if it was the wrong office at all.

It wasn't until Shannon helped me out of the vehicle and we walked up the sidewalk that I realized why my friends had been so hesitant.

On the outside of the door in white lettering read Mallory Muffin MD, Obstetrician-gynecologist.

Evan was already knocking on the door.

I leaned heavily on Shannon, rethinking my life choices.

"Actually, maybe this isn't the place," I huffed. "Are you sure that address is right? I think we need to call Mrs. Grundy and confirm."

Before anyone could agree or dismiss my request, the white blinds behind the glass door shifted. A bolt clicked and the door opened. A middle-aged man with a warm smile and bad comb-over beckoned us inside.

"Oh, you must be the ones Mrs. Grundy called about. Please come in, come in," Dr. Muffin greeted, waving us into the waiting area. "We have no time to spare. The side effects of the concoction Mrs. Grundy gave you are nothing to be brushed under the rug. Sure, it slows the spread of the poison, but no one wants numb tongue."

"Thide effects?" I asked as my tongue refused to form the words. "Numb tung?"

"Uh oh," Doctor Muffin said, motioning us forward again. "Come in, come in, I have a room waiting for you."

I tried to work my tongue around the inside of my mouth, but it felt two sizes too big. On top of that, my mouth was suddenly so dry.

Shannon, Evan, and I walked into a wide waiting room with calm mood lighting. On the corner table sat a diffuser steaming what smelled like mint and enough of Oprah's *O* magazines on the table to start a bonfire.

"Were you followed?" the doctor asked, looking out from

behind his curtain through the glass door. "Does anyone beside Mrs. Grundy know you're coming?"

"Thno," I said past my tongue.

"No, we're safe," Evan said, shaking his head. "I was checking the mirrors at every turn. Only Mrs. Grundy knows we're here."

"Good, good." Doctor Muffin waved us along to follow him. "I need to get going on our patient here before the rash starts spreading."

"Wrath?" I asked, forgetting the pain in my chest for a moment. "Wha wrath?"

"A rash is the second side effect that will take place, given the antidote Grundy administered. She did the right thing to slow the infectious spread, but that rash is nothing to joke about," Doctor Muffin said as we followed him into a well-lit room.

The room, much like the waiting area, was painted with calm cream and white. A picture of a smiling woman looking up at a clear sky might have put me at ease if I wasn't worried about a supernatural rash appearing at any moment.

I was directed to sit in a padded reclining chair with my feet in stirrups and my head tilted back.

"Don't worry, don't worry the rash won't pop up where you think it might," Doctor Muffin said, snapping on gloves and a magnifying glass apparatus that connected to his glasses. "If it does come, it'll start on your scrotum and work its way out from there."

"Don't worry. I got you, Jonny," Evan said, holding my hand. "Squeeze as hard as you need to."

I looked over to see a reassuring smile on my best friend's face. I knew he was trying to make light of the situation despite the events taking place around me to put me at ease.

"All right, all right, all right, party people," Doctor Muffin said, cutting down what was left of my shirt with a pair of scissors. "Let's let the Muffin Man do what he does best."

"You call yourself the Muffin Man?" Shannon asked with a raised eyebrow. She stood close on my left side but didn't offer me a hand to hold.

"Oh, the irony isn't lost on me," Doctor Muffin answered. "Muffin Man, Dreary Lane? I get it. Oh, you've got a high-level vampiric infection going on here. I'm going to have to pull out the nail, then clean and cauterize the wound."

If I could talk, I would have asked him what he meant by cauterize, but my aching numb, cold feeling was beginning to warm and feel hot as the temperature of my body increased.

One second I was practically shivering, and the next I felt like I was standing in the middle of a roaring volcano.

"All right, I'm going to need some help here." Doctor Muffin looked between Shannon and Evan. "Who here's not squeamish around blood and who wants to hold him down?"

"Holth me down?" I asked, doing a half sit-up, which was incredibly awkward since my feet were above my head in these metal stirrups.

"I can help," Shannon said, clenching her jaw and looking at me with concern.

"I'll hold him," Evan said, placing a firm but gentle hand on either of my shoulders.

"Good. Here," Doctor Muffin said, retrieving a pair of clamps and handing them to Shannon. "When I tell you, you pull the nail out smooth and straight. I'll be right behind you with the holy water and brand."

"Hey, guyths, guyths," I said as panic set in. "I'm feeling beddur. Theriouthly, I'm feeling beddur."

"Stay with me, Mr. Hunter," Doctor Muffin said, placing one end of a clamp on the end of the black nail in my chest and handing the other end to Shannon. "This is going to get worse before it gets better."

I didn't want to be afraid. I didn't want to scream and wrestle Evan to get off me because I let fear best me. I wanted to be that tough guy in all the movies. I wanted to take the brand with a smile and a swig of whisky.

Truth be told, I'd never broken so much as a bone before much less have a full-blown supernatural operation. Once when I was a kid, I had to get some teeth pulled, but that was it.

"Hey, hey, look at me. Look at me, Jonny." Shannon's voice held so much strength, I couldn't help but obey.

I looked at the Valkyrie incarnate to see tears of intensity in her eyes.

"Thank you, thank you for helping me give my sister peace," Shannon said, swallowing hard. "Thank you for giving me peace."

Tears splashed down my cheeks not from pain but understanding the level of torment that Shannon had gone through all these years. Understanding it and now realizing this burden had been lifted from her. I was just happy I was able to help play a part in her healing.

"Pull it now," Doctor Muffin shouted.

Shannon held my gaze. Evan pressed my shoulders down. With one rip of the pliers, Shannon tore the nail free.

The pain was horrific but bearable. I grunted, holding the scream. The holy water Doctor Muffin poured over the wound next was unlike anything I had ever encountered. It felt like molten hot lava being poured directly into my soul.

THIRTY-THREE

"RAWWW!" I screamed, or more like heard myself scream. It wasn't a decided physical reaction. More as if my body was like "What the heck are you doing to me, man? We need to get out of the Muffin Man's house of horrors."

Evan held me down. A cold sweat covered my brow as my internal temperature shifted again, back to being cold. Or was I warm? My face felt hot, but the sweat was practically frigid.

"Now it's going to really hurt," Doctor Muffin warned me with a sad smile. Hold on to something firm in your mind, Mr. Hunter. This isn't going to tickle."

I saw Doctor Muffin place a flask with the symbol of a cross behind him on the counter and lift a smoking hot rod. The rod couldn't have been more than ten or twelve inches. He held on to a handle on one side. One the other, the metal glowed with a reddish-orange hue.

Oh please let me just pass out, please just let me pass the heck out, I thought to myself. *Come on, John, just pass out. Just pass out.*

It just wasn't in the cards for me. I could hear the skin

around my chest cooking as flesh sizzled against heated steel. Shannon removed a blade from her boot and shoved the handle into my mouth before I could swallow my tongue, if that were even possible now.

I roared again, but this time, between my swollen tongue and the wooden knife handle in my mouth, it came out more like a rumble.

When Doctor Muffin removed the brand from my body, I was a pile of exhausted pain. I let the knife drop from my mouth, still totally coherent as the fiery hot pain dulled to distant agony.

"You with me, buddy?" Evan asked, moving himself from pressing me down and back to my right side. "Jonny, you still with me? Are you in shock? Answer me. Who's my favorite Pokémon?"

"Pikachu," I said, actually able to pronounce the word without working past a tongue fit for a giant.

"My man," Evan said, giving me a hug.

I moaned as his body pressed against my wound.

"Oh, right, sorry, sorry," Evan apologized, taking a step back.

"It looks like the wound is setting nicely," Doctor Muffin said, removing his glasses and taking a closer look. "Yes, yes, the vampiric poison was washed away and the brand sealed the wound."

"I feel like I should tell you thank you, but after my marathon of pain, I'm having a hard time with that," I admitted, trying to sit up.

"I do what I can," Doctor Muffin said with a reassuring smile. "OBGYN by day and doctor to the supernatural at night. It pays the bills."

"How did you get involved in all of this anyway?" Shannon asked.

"Oh, you know, classic story of a pack of werewolves jumped me going home one day. I was saved by a hunter, but she was injured in the fight. I patched her up and then things went from there once word spread," Doctor Muffin explained. "It's great money and exciting. And I get to make so many new friends. My psychiatrist says I need friends."

I removed my feet from the stirrups. As I sat up, I found myself grateful I didn't feel any itching in my nether regions.

"Your body has been through a lot, Mr. Hunter," Doctor Muffin said, reaching into his pocket and handing me a lollipop. "You need rest."

"What's this?" I asked, looking over the red clear-wrapped piece of candy. "Is this some kind of supernatural medication that's going to make me grow a tail as a side effect?"

"Oh, that's a good one, good one." Doctor Muffin chuckled, slapping his knee. "John Hunter, you're a comedian. No, no, my friend, just a lollipop."

I moved to my feet, supported by Shannon and Evan. The latter took off his designer sweater and draped it over my naked torso. It seemed like a small act, but I knew how much that meant to him. The sweater was one he'd picked up during a photo shoot in Rome.

"Oh snap, is that permanent?" Shannon asked, looking at my chest.

I followed her gaze down to my left pec where a brand of a fierce wolf head now stood out against angry red seared flesh.

"The brand was needed to combat the infection," Doctor Muffin explained. "You see, the werewolves and the vampires are natural enemies. Although that rivalry is dead and buried over millennia of fighting, old truths remain truths. The seal ensured the poison in Mr. Hunter's body would be stopped."

I wasn't really sure how I felt about getting a brand of a

wolf on my left pec, but it was done now. I really didn't have a say in it if it was going to save my life.

We walked back into the waiting room where Doctor Muffin bid us a farewell.

"We don't owe you anything?" Evan asked, surprised. "I mean, you came here in the middle of the night and saved Jonny's life. I want to give you something."

"Oh, no, no, it's all billed through the Court." Doctor Muffin waved away Evan's offer. "We have a direct billing system set up. You know, the IRS wants their share of everything and all."

"You pay taxes on this?" Shannon asked incredulously. "How does that even work? I mean—"

Shannon's next words were cut off by multiple pairs of headlights penetrating the blinds and car doors slamming shut.

I squinted past the bright lights, unable to make out anything through the white curtains.

"Oh no." Doctor Muffin sighed, heading around his counter to the phone and dialing a number. "Here we go."

"Who is it?" I asked as the footsteps grew closer. "Vampires?"

"Worse, feds," Doctor Muffin said, pressing the phone to his ear. "You were right. They're here. Understood."

A heavy hand rapped on the door so hard, I thought the glass was going to shatter.

"That was Mrs. Grundy," Doctor Muffin informed us. "She's on her way. There's no need for violence at the moment; these are government officials. They've probably just been putting together what happened tonight."

"Open up, Mallory," a not unfriendly voice said from outside. "We know you're in there. We're just here to talk. No one's in any kind of trouble."

"Feds, like the government?" I asked, buttoning Evan's

designer sweater to make sure they wouldn't be able to see the brand. I looked to Shannon for answers.

"Don't look at me, Stinky." Shannon shrugged. "I had no idea the government was a part of this or the Court, for that matter. It's new to me too."

"The government has a division, very Men in Black," Evan said with a long sigh. "They police the supernatural. I've run into them a handful of times. Very self-important, law-abiding type. Not bad, but, well, preachy."

"Doctor, we're not going to ask again," the voice said on the other side of the blinds. "I don't want to have to break into your establishment. Will you please open the door?"

They sounded polite enough to me. They were right; I couldn't imagine it would take much to shatter the glass on the front door then reach in and undo the lock.

"Yes, yes, I'm coming," Doctor Muffin called, raising his voice. He lowered his tone next as he walked to the door and addressed us. "Don't worry about me; they know all about my operation. I'd advise waiting until Mrs. Grundy gets here before you commit to anything."

Before I could ask any other questions, Doctor Muffin flipped the lock and in poured black-suited men and women. Evan was right; they were very Men in Black, right down to the black ties and weapons.

I was no expert on weapons. Shannon, on the other hand, let out a low whistle. Some handguns and rifles I recognized; others were straight out of sci-fi novels with dull silver exteriors and red sights.

For the moment, no one pointed their weapons at us, but I realized that could change in a second. At least four of the agents passed us as they went deeper into the office securing the space.

"Thank you, Doctor," an older man with a thick white beard and full head of hair addressed Doctor Muffin. "I had no desire to damage your door. We've always had a good relationship, you and I."

"Yes we have, Agent Bentall." Doctor Muffin nodded. "You know what I do here. I'm doing the same thing tonight just healing those who have been wounded by the supernatural."

Agent Bentall nodded, looking over at us.

Right now, Evan, Shannon, and I stood to the rear of the waiting room, well, waiting to see what would happen next. Shannon drummed her fingers on the hilt of the knife she tucked into her waistband.

"We received reports of weapon fire from a downtown location," Agent Bentall explained. "Looks like someone took out a coven. We're just following the rabbit hole to see who did it. I thought if anyone was hurt in the process, they would've come here."

"We did it," Shannon said, cutting through all the layers of conversation that would lead Agent Bentall to that conclusion. It wasn't like he didn't already know. "We took out the coven. The doctor was just helping tend to our wounds."

"Very good." Agent Bentall strode forward. He extended a warm hand in greeting. "My name's Agent Steve Bentall. I'm with SOAP."

"SOAP?" I asked, shaking the man's hand.

"Supernatural Observation And Policing," Agent Bentall explained. He stopped when he shook Evan's hand as if he recognized him. "Have we met?"

"No, but I'm sure I'm on some government watch list," Evan said as if it didn't faze him. "I'm a vampire. One of the few who just takes what he needs and doesn't kill or turn. I get a visit from SOAP from time to time making sure I'm in check."

"Right," Agent Bentall said, releasing his hand.

"All clear," a gruff voice said, coming back from the rear of the office. I hadn't realized the size of the man before, but now I got a better look at him. It was like someone shoved a hybrid gorilla and rhino in a suit. The man was massive with shoulders larger than my head.

"Thank you, Agent Lees," Agent Bentall addressed the bodybuilder. He turned back to us. "I didn't know there was a new hunting team operating in Los Angeles."

"Oh, we're not really a team," Shannon said.

"We just started," I answered at the same time.

We looked at each other in confusion.

"Sounds like the kids have some business to work out amongst themselves," Evan joked with a smooth transition into what we were all thinking. "Are we in any kind of trouble here, Agent Bentall?"

"Trouble?" Agent Bentall repeated the word as if he had never said it before. "Trouble, no, I wouldn't say that. You helped us actually. That coven has been on our radar for some time. Sooner or later, we would have had to step in."

"Oh good, so he's not going to try to hurt us?" Evan asked, looking at Agent Lees, who glowered at us from behind Agent Bentall. "Because he really looks like he wants to hurt us right now."

"Who, Agent Lees?" Agent Bentall asked, looking over his shoulder. "No, that's just his face. He always looks like that. Isn't that right, Agent Lees? How are you feeling?"

"Just peachy," Agent Lees growled.

"He's harmless unless you piss him off," Agent Bentall explained. "But let me get right down to it. SOAP is always looking for new assets to deploy in the field. As you can imagine, it's a big supernatural world out there. There are times we're dealing with alien threats and a zombie infestation at once. Then a drunk elf decides to do some magic he should not be doing at a bar and we have more than we can handle. We like to partner with teams such as yourselves to help."

"You want to recruit us?" I asked incredulously. Of all the crazy things I thought I might encounter this night, working with the feds wasn't one of them.

THIRTY-FOUR

"BENEFITS ARE NICE, and the pay is great, comes with vacation days, a 401k, and the best dental plan money can buy. Show them your teeth, Lees," Agent Bentall said over his shoulder.

Lees bared his teeth. Sure, they were straight and beautiful, but the guy really freaked me out. It was like he enjoyed showing his teeth to us a little too much.

"I need to sit down," I said. My body was exhausted from the night's events and the whole branding thing to get rid of the poison. All I wanted to do at the moment was fall asleep to some reruns of *Golden Girls*.

Shannon and Evan guided me over to a soft grey chair. I sank deep with a heavy sigh.

"Can I get anyone some chamomile tea or perhaps hibiscus?" Doctor Muffin asked. "I think I may even have some elfish-made honey almonds in the back."

We all looked at the man with deadpan stares.

"Or not, or not." Doctor Muffin shrugged. "Just asking."

"As much as we appreciate your invitation," I said,

looking back at Agent Bentall, "the Court has already offered us a position. I'm not sure we can."

"Of course they have." Agent Bentall frowned. "The Court has been an itch I've been wanting to scratch for a long time."

I think Agent Lees even let off a low growl.

"Aren't you two on the same side?" Shannon chimed in. "I mean, it sounds like you want the same thing."

"We are—required to work together at times," Agent Bentall chose his words carefully. "SOAP is government-led with structure and we approach the supernatural based on science and fact. The Court is more, shall we say, mystical in their dealings."

"Hello in there, hello?" Mrs. Grundy's voice sounded from the front door where a pair of agents blocked her entrance. "Agent Bentall, be a dear and tell these fine SOAP agents to let me enter."

I was shocked Mrs. Grundy had been able to arrive so fast. Doctor Muffin had barely made the call. No way she was able to get here from Haven Apartments this quick.

"If you haven't signed anything with the Court, a verbal agreement will do for SOAP until we can get something on paper," Agent Bentall said, ignoring Mrs. Grundy for the time being.

It all felt wrong. If I trusted my gut, it said Agent Bentall wasn't a bad guy, but neither did I want to get sold on a pressure sale. If I really listened to my gut, it said I needed some food at some point as well.

"Sorry, no can do," Shannon answered first, throwing a thumb in my direction. "You see, this one's been through a lot tonight, and to be honest, even when he is on top of his game, his decision-making skills are questionable at best—"

"Hey, I'm right here," I blurted, nodding along with Shannon until the last few words exited her mouth.

"She does kind of have a point," Evan said.

"And I'm not going to agree to anything until I see a contract," Shannon finished.

"Steven," Mrs. Grundy said from the front door. "If you don't tell these kind young agents to let me in, I'm going to age them in front of your eyes and suck their best years right from their souls."

Agent Bentall looked furious at us and then took a deep breath. "Let her in."

"Wait, she can do that?" I asked, looking from Shannon to Evan and Doctor Muffin for an answer.

Shannon and Evan shrugged.

Doctor Muffin nodded with large eyes.

Mrs. Grundy walked into the room slowly, any hint that she just threatened to suck the life out of anyone gone like a plume of smoke in the wind.

"Agent Bentall, Agent Lees," Mrs. Grundy addressed the men with a smile I couldn't tell was fake or real. "How so very SOAP-like of you to come in after a job is complete and try to poach my hunters."

It was comical really. Agent Bentall stood a head taller than the old woman and Lees practically towered over her. None of this seemed to intimidate the woman as she continued.

"Mallory, thank you for taking such good care of our hunter," Mrs. Grundy said to the OBGYN. She walked over to me and pulled down my sweater just enough to see the wolf brand on my wound. "Oh my, did we have to go with the sigil of the Pack on this one? They won't be pleased. You know how territorial they can be."

"It was the only sure way to make sure he didn't die," Doctor Muffin answered. "I could have rolled the dice with some orc widow's sage, but I didn't want to chance it. Oh,

I'm being so rude. Mrs. Grundy, would you care for some tea? Perhaps lemon or ginger?"

"Thank you, Mallory, that would be wonderful." Mrs. Grundy smiled. "Oh and if you have any of those elvish almonds? They were delicious."

"Yes, of course, coming right up," Doctor Muffin said with a smile. "I do love to entertain."

As the doctor got up to bring the requested items back to Mrs. Grundy, I saw flecks of my blood still on his shirt. I liked the doctor, don't get me wrong, but there was something a bit disturbing about a man that could be cauterizing wounds one second and putting out tea on the next.

"Well, isn't this nice," Agent Bentall said without meaning any of the words. "If these are your hunters, Mrs. Grundy, you know the proper paperwork has to be filed with SOAP. I'm not going to make a thing about it since we're all on the same side here, but get your house in order or I will."

"Promises, promises, Agent Bentall." Mrs. Grundy chuckled. "You act as though we don't let you have anything. You just signed that young immortal, didn't you? The reporter?"

"That's classified, ma'am," Agent Bentall said, fishing a card out of his suit pocket. He handed it to me. "Here's my information in case you change your mind."

I accepted the card more out of habit than anything else. I didn't plan on using it. To be honest, at the moment, I didn't plan on much outside of sleep and maybe a pizza.

"Oh, and before you go I must thank you for the assist in St. Louis," Mrs. Grundy said to Agent Bentall. "If it wasn't for SOAP sending assets, the wizard might not have made it out alive."

"I can't tell if you're being sarcastic with me or not." Agent Bentall gave her a raised eyebrow. "If you're not being sarcastic, you're welcome. If you are being sarcastic, you better thank your magic butt we were there when it counted the most."

"Me? Sarcastic?" Mrs. Grundy placed a hand on her chest. "Why, never."

"Mmm hmm," Agent Bentall said. "Well, we'll leave you to it. Be cautious out there. You know that was one of Count Jovanovic's covens you took out. He's not going to sit by the sidelines and let this one go."

"Noted," Mrs. Grundy said with a wave as the SOAP agents filed out of the room.

"Oh, your tea and almonds," Doctor Muffin said, coming back with a tea cup and a handful of almonds on the saucer.

"Thank you, Mallory," Mrs. Grundy said, blowing on the steam wafting from her cup.

"Wait a minute, so the Court and SOAP do work together?" I asked, trying to parse out the information into categories past my fatigued thought process. "It didn't sound like you two like each other much."

"We're on the same side when the world is on the line, but the Court is much, much older than SOAP," Mrs. Grundy informed us. "They didn't come into existence until George Washington founded them in seventeen ninety. Since then, they think they run the supernatural world, when in reality, the Court has been around a millennium longer."

"I'm sorry, did you just say George Washington?" Shannon stuck a finger in her ear and twisted it around a few times. "Because it sounded a lot like you just said George Washington founded SOAP."

"Well, they weren't known as SOAP back then; they've gone through different leadership and names as you can imagine, but SOAP is what they're known by now," Mrs. Grundy paused here to take another sip of her tea, savoring the taste. "Mallory, you make the very best cup of tea I think I've ever had."

"Pleased that you're pleased, my friend," Doctor Muffin said with an approving smile. "Are we still on for game night next week? I've invited the gnomes this time."

"Oh, of course," Mrs. Grundy answered. "I wouldn't miss it."

"Wait, wait, wait," I said, feeling drunk, I was so tired, but I couldn't let this next question go unasked. "You said the Court is older than SOAP? How much older? Did you say a millennium?"

"There we go," Mrs. Gundy said with a smile. "Now you're onto it. Smarter than you look, John Hunter. Smarter than you look."

"Thanks, I think," I replied, not sure if that was a compliment or an insult.

"The Court has been around since the beginning of our time. We rely on what you could call magic more than physical weapons," Mrs. Grundy explained. "There's a much longer explanation, of course, but it's nearing three o'clock in the morning and if I'm not mistaken, Doctor Muffin has patients to see first thing."

"Oh, no bother, no bother at all," Doctor Muffin said, stifling a yawn. "I enjoy the company."

"Be that as it may, our young hunter needs rest," Mrs. Grundy said, handing the doctor an empty teacup and palming the almonds. "Thank you, Mallory. Please send us the bill."

"Always a pleasure," Doctor Muffin said, looking over at me as Shannon and Evan helped me up. "And you get some rest, young man. Expect the wound to be sore for a week or so, but you'll heal nicely."

"Thank you," I told him as we walked from the building.

"Come see me tomorrow once you've eaten and rested, both of you," Mrs. Grundy said to Shannon and me. "We have much to discuss."

"Do you want a ride?" Evan asked as our elderly neighbor headed off through the door and down the walkway.

"No, I'll be fine. I prefer a good stroll at night."

"How'd she get here so fast without a car?" Evan asked under his breath. "Sorceress."

"Can we debate the magic of Mrs. Grundy another night, Bloodsucker?" Shannon asked Evan. "Let's just get home. I feel like I could sleep for days."

"Right," Evan said, clicking the remote on his key ring to unlock his black BMW. He opened the back door for me to get in and visibly cringed.

My blood was all over his back seat and carpet. Evan liked nice things, from his handmade kimonos to his leather massage chair and vehicle. I could see his jaw tighten in the glow of the parking lot lights.

"I'm sorry," I told him. "I'll clean it."

"No, no," Evan said, taking a deep breath as he closed his eyes for a moment. "This is a me thing. This has nothing to do with you, Jonny. I have to deal with my OCD. You are so much more important than a, than a…"

I looked over to see Even lift a fist to his mouth. I thought he was going to cry.

"Than a special-ordered Italian leather back seat and Persian carpet," Evan managed through his fist. "You're more important. These are just things, incredibly nice, expensive things that I love."

It sounded like Evan was trying to convince himself more than me.

"Oooookay then, ladies," Shannon said, hopping into the passenger-side seat. "Can we get a move on, then? I'm not getting any younger here."

THIRTY-FIVE

WHEN WE MADE it back to Haven, I was so delirious, I think I mumbled a good night and thank you to Shannon. Evan helped me up and I fell into my bed more than went to sleep. Lucky for me, there were no more visions or dreams of Victor.

When I finally did wake up, there was a line of drool connecting the corner of my mouth to the pillow. A stream of afternoon light entered the room through closed drapes.

I stretched in bed then grunted, feeling an aching soreness spread from my left pectoral around my whole body. I was almost afraid to look down at my chest as memories of the night before crashed through my mind like a tidal wave.

Looking down, I saw my skin as a mess of angry red with a wolf brand pressed into my flesh. The wolf was looking at me head on with slanted eyes like someone had just pissed in his cereal.

Movement from my left jolted me to action. I moved so fast to a sitting position, my chest screamed at me in sore agony. Right now, pain would have to wait. The black wolf-like dog sat in the corner of my room, staring at me through yellow eyes.

I blinked a few times then pinched myself to make sure I wasn't in another kind of dream state. As far as I could tell, this was real life. How Mrs. Grundy's hellhound had gotten into my room was another story.

What was his name? Mrs. Grundy had called him Odin?

"Odin?" I asked, swallowing hard at the massive jaws and teeth staring back at me. "Is that your name, Odin?"

The hellhound tilted its head to the side, just staring at me.

"Um, I'm not really sure what the deal is with hellhounds, but thank you for saving me back there," I said. "I mean, you had my back against the chimera and the coven. I don't know if you're even understanding me, but can I get you a treat or something as payment?"

At the word "treat," the hellhound's ears perked up.

"Oh, there we go," I said with a smile. "There's a word we can all get behind. Let me shower and then we can find some treats together."

Usually, I looked forward to a shower. Not this time. I found a new definition of pain every time I moved my torso. I couldn't handle the water hitting my wound either. I stood with my back to the water and did my best to wash my chest with a cloth.

When I got out of the shower, I settled for a pair of gym shorts and a loose-fitting shirt that didn't rub across my new brand.

I checked my phone and found a myriad of text messages. One was from Evan telling me he had to be on set, but he'd be back later that night. The next was from Shannon, asking if I was awake yet. The last from a number I didn't recognize that read, "Be sure to stop by my apartment before you do anything rash like getting stabbed again, Grundy."

I responded to the texts as Odin and I walked to the kitchen and helped ourselves to a meal of eggs, bacon, and Black Rifle Coffee. Well, I drank the coffee. Odin seemed content with more bacon.

While my body worked, my mind also processed everything, from Tracy's escape, to the brand I now wore, and of course the dream I had of Count Victor Jovanovic.

I was shoving another forkful of eggs in my mouth when I heard a knock on my door. Normally, I'd be suspicious. But after the supernatural events of the previous night, I was downright sure there was a minotaur on the other side about to kick in my door.

"Open up, Stinky," Shannon said through the door. "It's silly texting back and forth when I'm right below you."

I let out a breath I didn't know I was holding before going over and letting Shannon through the door.

She walked in with her arm in a sling. She wore black pants, athletic shoes, and a black tank top. A few scratches and bruises marked her face and arms, but she looked happy despite this.

"Is that bacon I smell?" Shannon stopped in her tracks, looking at Odin. "Wow, you let the hellhound in here?"

"I think he let himself in or maybe Evan did," I answered. "I'm not really sure. I need to find a book on hellhounds; heck, the supernatural realm in general. Too much is going on for me to be able to process it all. I need to take notes."

"Seriously," Shannon said, heading over to grab a piece of bacon off my plate. "So you ready to head over to Grundy's? Up to it? How are you healing?"

"It feels like a gorilla used my chest as a trampoline." I grimaced as I tried to stretch. "But at least I'm not poisoned anymore. Hey, I need to tell you something."

I told Shannon about my dream in the back of Evan's car while I was unconscious. She munched on the bacon like popcorn as I related my story. Her eyes got bigger and bigger until, at the very end, I thought they were going to pop out of her head.

"Holy meatballs, why didn't you say any of this last night?" Shannon asked incredulously. "I mean, to the Muffin Man, Mrs. Grundy, me, Evan, even the SOAP agents."

"Oh, I don't know, maybe because you were ripping poisoned vampire nails out of my chest while some mad gynecologist poured holy water on me and used a wolf brand on my skin." I shrugged, taking another sip of my coffee.

"Fair enough, fair enough," Shannon allowed, reaching for another piece of bacon. "You should really tell Grundy about this. I mean, if anyone would be able to tell what that means, it would be her. And we need to watch our backs. It sounds like there's a pissed off count coming our way soon."

"I hope not. I need a vacation," I answered, shaking my head. "I mean, I need a break and I need to get back to work. My modeling life is pretty much non-existent. Evan said my old agent was a vampire as well. Once he gets wind of all of this, I don't think he's going to send me on any other casting calls. That leaves me with Tacos Culos Locos and Lyfter."

"Easy there, we'll figure all of this out," Shannon reassured me. "Also, you need more bacon. Bacon makes everything better, am I right, Odin?"

Shannon crouched and let the hellhound sniff her fingers. Odin wasn't exactly the bound forward with licks and tail wags type. Physical contact seemed to make the hellhound uncomfortable. As soon as Shannon's hands reached for his ears, he backed away a safe distance.

"What's wrong with him?" Shannon asked, confused. "Dogs usually love me."

"Well, he's a hellhound, not a dog," I reasoned. "Beats me; he's not really mine. He just comes and goes as he pleases."

"Okay, well, let's head down to Mrs. Grundy's and get our minds blown with some supernatural knowledge," Shannon said, waving me over to the door. "Oh, and I have your axe, war hammer thingy in my apartment. You shouldn't leave your toys everywhere."

I had totally forgotten about the supernatural weapon. What had that giant vampire called it? Was it the steel of the gods? Or metal of the gods, maybe?

I followed Shannon out the front door. Odin came with us. Of all the things I could be worrying about at the moment, my bank account filled the back of my mind. Rent would be due next week.

Sure the money from Nate for clearing out the chimera would help, but that wouldn't solve all my problems. There were utilities and things like car insurance and cell phone service to worry about too.

The three of us walked down the steps and crossed the courtyard to Mrs. Grundy's house. The same mat with runes matching my weapon's handle greeted our feet.

Shannon raised a hand to knock on the door. Without warning, the door creaked open. Not in the welcoming mom's cooking dinner kind of way, but in a slow, creepy, creaking way. Odin huffed something then bolted inside the dark apartment.

The house was darker somehow. Even though outside it was just after lunch without a cloud in the California sky, the inside of the apartment was pitch black as if light didn't dare enter.

"Mrs. Grundy?" Shannon called, taking a step inside. "Mrs. Grundy, are you home."

"What are you doing?" I asked, grabbing Shannon's arm.

"Um, I'm going inside," Shannon said with a raised eyebrow as if I were being unreasonable.

"Nope, nope, not doing it, not doing it again," I said,

shaking my head. "Been down this road, got stabbed, poisoned, and branded. Nope, not going into the apartment of doom."

"John, please," Shannon said, rolling her eyes. "She's probably in the restroom or taking a nap or something and just forgot to close the door."

"Oh, really? Oh really?" I asked with a finger snap I didn't know I had in me. "Or maybe there's a horrifying creature of the supernatural realm we don't know about waiting to consume our face skin in there. Did you think about that? Did you ever think about that, Selfish?"

"Well, I'm going in," Shannon said, taking another step into the impossibly dark interior of the apartment. "You can stay out here if you want."

"Uh uh, no, uh uh," I said with a heavy sigh, already knowing I wasn't going to let her go in alone but still coming to grips with the truth. "She's walking inside. She doesn't even care. It's like she doesn't even care. And there she goes."

Maybe you should have taken that SOAP contract, I thought to myself. *At least that way, you'd have some kind of health insurance right now walking into the apartment of nightmares.*

"Mrs. Grundy?" Shannon called out as I followed her into the family room. "Mrs. Grundy, it's Shannon and John. You told us to come over? Are you home?"

Thick drapes covered the windows. As far as I could tell, the furniture in the family room looked undisturbed along with the table in the sitting area and the kitchen.

Odin sat next to a closed door down a hall to our left, whining.

I could feel goosebumps run up and down my spine like I was being watched. I wished we had stopped by Shannon's apartment to get the war hammer. I looked for something, anything to use as a weapon.

I grabbed for the first thing I saw: a whisk on the counter.

"Really?" Shannon asked.

"Hey, I'm in here because of you. We're about to face down a demon of the—"

"Oh the seven hells!" Mrs. Grundy yelled as the door Odin sat in front of swung open in a rush.

THIRTY-SIX

MY HEART NEARLY STOPPED. I held the whisk high, ready to do what? I wasn't really sure, whisk something or someone to death.

"What, what is it?" Shannon asked, going into a stance with her fists ready.

"Tacos Culos Locos breakfast burrito." Mrs. Grundy coughed, closing the door behind her. She used her other hand to bat air back and forth in front of her nose. "That stuff is delicious, but my, my, does it go right through me at times. John, what are you doing with my whisk?"

"Oh, oh nothing," I said, lowering the cooking utensil to the counter. "We were just worried about you."

"Well, you should be more worried about the plumbing," Mrs. Grundy said with a chuckle to herself. "We may need to call Mr. Hyde to send the super in after that one. Man, talk about—"

"Okay, okay, we get it," Shannon cut in, placing her hand by her hip. "We get it. You dropped a deuce. We're here to talk about the Court."

"Yes, of course. Be a dear and close the door, John," Mrs.

Grundy said, entering her living room and taking a seat on her overstuffed recliner. "There's a draft coming in."

I didn't feel any kind of draft, but when a supernatural, possibly sorceress tells you to do something, you just nod and obey.

Odin came over to join the group in the family room as I locked the front door and took my own seat next to Shannon.

"Where are your other dogs—the other hellhounds," Shannon corrected herself. "I don't see them."

"Remember, I don't own the hellhounds; they come and go as they please, much like Odin here." Mrs. Grundy smiled fondly at the large black beast. "I have faith Warden and Cerberus are where they are needed most at this time. If I don't see them again, then I can be grateful for the time I did spend with them."

I moved my hand without thinking to reach for Odin and scratch his head. He was sitting right next to me and it just felt right. I loved animals and always wanted a dog growing up.

My father said we couldn't afford to pay for one and he was probably right. Currently I'd held off owning a dog with our apartment living and me being gone so much.

As soon as my fingertips touched Odin's ears, he moved away, looking at me with distrust in his eyes.

"Odin's been through a lot in his former life," Mrs. Grundy explained. "Don't take offense, John. He'll warm up."

"Former life?" Shannon repeated. "He was a regular dog before?"

"Abused, starved, and neglected, I'm afraid." Mrs. Grundy sighed. "He came back to this world as a hellhound once he died to finish whatever work was meant for him. I see now that work is looking after John."

"Me?" I asked, despite knowing the answer. "I mean, I love dogs, but why would he be sent to watch me?"

"Time will tell," Mrs. Grundy said. "I can't tell the future, John. I'm not a mind reader, you know."

"No, actually, I don't know," I stated, feeling the pressure of the last few days welling inside of me like some kind of overflowing dam. "I don't really know who or what you are or about this Court. I do know that I'm out of my main source of income and I need to get to work Lyfter driving or sign twirling if I'm going to make rent this month."

"Always so concerned about money." Mrs. Grundy clucked her tongue. "You know there are more important things than money."

"Spoken like someone who hasn't had to worry about money their entire life," I responded. I heard myself and I didn't like what I was saying, but it was the truth.

"Well, you'll be happy to know that, as hunters, you are rewarded with bounties once you eliminate or complete certain missions for the Court," Mrs. Grundy said as calm and cool as ever. "Taking out that coven of vampires and Mr. Bloodstone will amount up to quite a decent sum for the pair of you."

"We weren't technically employed by the Court to take them out," Shannon reminded both of us. "I mean, we kind of just went after them."

"Details that can be overlooked," Mrs. Grundy remarked. "Each vampire had a price of two thousand dollars on their head and the coven leader a five-thousand-dollar bounty. Reports came in that there were twenty vampires killed plus the leader, amounting to a forty-five-thousand-dollar bounty. I just need your bank account information to send the money."

I sat there blinking then had the urge to stand up just to get some of this pent-up energy out. Even my half of forty-five thousand amounting to twenty-two thousand five hundred dollars was more than I ever had at one time. Heck, that might be more than I had ever had.

I wasn't sure if I was having heart palpitations or maybe some kind of panic attack, which was a weird reaction to have, since this was a good thing. With this amount of money, I didn't have to worry about rent, food, or bills for a very long time.

"You okay, Stinky?" Shannon questioned. "You look like you're having some kind of moment over there. This is good news."

"Oh, I know, I know," I said as a wave of relief hit me like a surge of cold ocean water. "I've, uh, I've just never dealt with that much money at once before."

"Well, get used to it," Mrs. Grundy said with a groan as she stood from her recliner and shuffled over to the kitchen. "I have contracts for you both to be signed on as official contractors to the Court. We'll need your blood to sign the pact and social security numbers and such."

I was still in a daze thinking about the money about to hit my account. I missed the part about the blood sample.

"Blood?" Shannon asked.

"Just a little supernatural humor," Mrs. Grundy cackled as she moved to the kitchen, reached into a drawer, and brought out two stapled contracts and a pair of pens. "Take your time going through them, of course. There's no hurry. I want you both to feel good about this."

I accepted mine. It was kind of disappointing for a supernatural contract. I was suspecting cracked and fragile parchment with maybe a feather pen to use to sign it. What I held in my hand was stiff eight by eleven white paper and Times New Roman font staring back at me.

"Can you tell us a little more about the Court?" Shannon asked as she started reading through her contract. "I mean, like where are they and why are they monitoring the supernatural in the first place?"

"Fair enough, fair enough," Mrs. Grundy said, answering Shannon's question but looking over at me. "First, John is disappointed at his contract's appearance."

"What?" I asked, looking up. "I didn't say anything."

"Oh, John, that face says it all," Mrs. Grundy said with a wave of her hand. "Take a look at it now."

I looked down at the pen and paper in my hands and nearly dropped them both. Like some kind of weird David Blaine magic trick, the white paper in my hand was now old, cream, and cracked. The ballpoint pen wasn't a feather, but rather some kind of ancient calligraphy pen, dripping with ink.

"What the..." I said, allowing my voice to drift off. "Sorcery. What are you, Mrs. Grundy? I mean, no offense, but you're a witch, right? You can do magic?"

"Watcher is close enough to sorceress, yes, I do suppose so," Mrs. Grundy said, moving her head from side to side as if she were weighing words in her head. "Perhaps you are ready to know more. Perhaps I'll show you now."

I stood at the island in Mrs. Grundy's kitchen, looking on in awe as the room darkened around us as if someone in fact dimmed the lights. The ceiling lit up in a display of stars that began to shift and move as Mrs. Grundy told us a tale I knew I'd never forget.

"The Court's official founding date is unknown, however we do know it was founded near the beginning of the creation of the world. Back when myth and legend did not yet exist but were fact. A small group banded together to put demons, monsters, evil spirits, and everything else in check," Mrs. Grundy explained as the stars overheard morphed into hydras, giants, dragons, and other beasts. "Over time, our numbers have grown. We were there when the Minotaur was put in his maze, when Fenrir was chained, and the sword drawn from the stone. The Court stands throughout mankind's history as the shield to this realm."

More images formed then dissipated from tiny stars of light in the ceiling. There were epic battles, bloody conflicts, and men and women slaying monstrous beasts that ranged from leviathans to goblins.

When the light show was over, the stars overhead were gone, and the normal lights in the apartment were then turned back on.

I stood in silence, just coming to grips with all the information being relayed. The inner geek kid inside of me wanted to smile and say I knew it all along. The adult in me was terrified that the stories were true.

"You won't be alone," Mrs. Grundy reassured us. "The Court has Watchers like me to guide you, their own teams in the field as well as other hunters we contract. We're stronger together. Our network spans from teams in Croatia to Australia."

"I mean, I'm in," Shannon said with a shrug. "You had me at each vampire was worth two thousand bucks a piece. I don't want anyone to have to suffer and end up like my sister."

Both women looked at me.

"I don't know how I can say no," I began slowly. "It's strange, but I feel like this is actually something I can be good at. Maybe this is what I was meant to do."

"We all have a road set before us." Mrs. Grundy nodded. "It's up to us to choose to walk it or not."

I went over to the kitchen table and sat down with my contract as I began to read through it page by page.

It was all standard stuff, until it wasn't. Questions I expected like home address and waiving the right to sue the Court soon turned into promises I wouldn't hold the Court responsible for the three Ds: decapitation, dismemberment, and disembowelment.

"Oh," Shannon inhaled sharply from across the table where she too took a seat. "You have the bounties just listed here?"

"Where?" I asked, craning my neck to see her contract.

"Page eleven," Shannon said, reading down a list of beings and the dollar amount next to them. "Unicorns? You want me to kill a unicorn? They're not good, like in My Little Pony?"

I widened my eyes, not believing the number placed next to the unicorn as its bounty.

"Ten thousand dollars? Ten thousand dollars to kill a unicorn?" I asked incredulously. "I'll bring you Pinky Pie's head for that amount of money."

"Pinky Pie wasn't a unicorn," Shannon corrected. "You're such a nerd."

"Not all supernatural beings are devouring human souls; that should be remembered at all times," Mrs. Grundy said from her spot at the kitchen island. "Your friend Evan is a good example of that. To say all vampires deserve death is an ignorant blanket statement. Just like saying all unicorns need to die. Usually, unicorns are a docile bunch, but every once in a while when they get out of line and start goring humans, they need to be put down."

I flipped to page eleven in my contract, going down the list of supernatural creatures ranging from krakens to the mothman. My jaw couldn't drop any further. I was going to be rich if I could bag even a few of these.

The section on vampires reminded me to tell Mrs. Grundy about what I witnessed while I was passed out from blood loss in the back of Evan's BMW.

I interrupted my read-through of the contract to tell her

the same story I told Shannon back at my apartment. I didn't leave anything out.

Mrs. Grundy pursed her lips. A worried expression etched itself in the creases of the woman's forehead.

"We should expect a retaliation," Mrs. Grundy cautioned. "The Count is a very powerful vampire. He's not just going to stand by and let one of his covens go up in a flash without retaliation. You both should be prepared."

"I feel like I need a gun or something," I said honestly. "That war hammer is great and all, but if I could get my hands on a magic machine gun or something like in the movies, that would be great. Hey, remember that gun Scarface carried at the end—"

"Perhaps training would be more in order, rather than something you might shoot somebody you don't mean to with," Mrs. Grundy broke in with a caution.

"That's what I told him," Shannon agreed, flipping to the back of the contract without reading the rest of the pages and signing her name. "Well, I'm done."

"You're not even going to read the whole thing?" I asked incredulously. "I mean, we could be signing away our souls here. No offense, Mrs. Grundy."

"None taken, but we don't want your souls." Mrs. Grundy chuckled. "Your bodies in this life fighting for the light will be enough."

Just then, Odin, who seemed fine licking his privates in the family room, jumped to attention. Bristling, he went to the door sniffing harder than I had when taking in the snuf. Which reminded me I need to get more of that magic powder from Mrs. Grundy. A low, menacing growl came from the hellhound as he stared down the front door.

THIRTY-SEVEN

"WHATEVER HAPPENS NEXT, you stay in this apartment," Mrs. Grundy said in a very serious unlike Mrs. Grundy tone. "There are enough ancient runes and spells on this place to keep out one of the ancient ones. Let me handle this and stay in the apartment."

I for one was not about to argue. Odin lowered his front paws to the floor, sniffing under the door while a growl rumbled from somewhere deep in his chest.

A light knock that somehow sounded familiar to me echoed in from the other side of the door.

"I need to start carrying some kind of weapon on me wherever I go," Shannon mumbled under her breath.

Mrs. Grundy reached the front door and looked through the peephole. She turned back to frown at me before opening the door.

To my surprise, Tracy stood there, wringing her hands. She wore a black jacket and wide-brimmed hat with dark sunglasses. She looked in past Mrs. Grundy to where I sat at the table.

"Yes?" Mrs. Grundy asked, blocking her view. "May I help you?"

Odin growled low and slow.

"Yes, yes," Tracy said, clearly distraught. "I—I'm looking for Jonny? I checked his apartment, but he's not there. The manager said he saw him walk over here. May I come in? It's so hot out here."

"No, you may not," Mrs. Grundy stated, not in an especially unkind way; more of a matter-of-fact way. "I'm sorry, you are not welcome in my home."

"Because of what I am?" Tracy asked.

"Because of who you choose to be," Mrs. Grundy corrected.

The whole time I sat at the table, a war raged in me. Part of me wanted to go back to what I knew. Tracy was familiar. Sure, she hurt me, but didn't all relationships have their ups and downs? Maybe this was a chance to get back together. Maybe this could be a fresh start for us. She needed me. That much was clear.

I rose from the table.

Shannon caught my wrist in a vise-like grip.

I looked at her.

"She's using you," Shannon said, shaking her head. "Jonny, this doesn't feel right."

"I—I just—I'll just talk to her," I said, trying to justify my own actions. "Tracy—she's not a bad person, maybe a bit selfish and conceited at times. She does park in handicapped spaces when she's in a hurry, but she's not evil."

I pulled my hand free and went to the door.

Tracy's lips turned up in a slight smile when she saw me. "Jonny, I'm so glad you're here. This old woman won't let me in. I need to talk with you. Please, I just want to talk."

"Okay, okay," I said, edging past Odin and Mrs. Grundy.

The former gave me a look that asked how much paint I'd been huffing to do this, the latter shook her head.

"Be careful," Mrs. Grundy stated. "Don't trust her, John."

I nodded before leaving the apartment and joining Tracy in the courtyard.

I wanted to give her a hug, maybe even hold her, but the events of her dumping me after our engagement were still too fresh.

We just stood there staring at each other for a moment. I saw the drapes at the kitchen window move and Mrs. Grundy and Shannon stared out at us.

Tracy shrugged deeper in her black coat away from the sun's rays and stepped into a shadow.

"Can we go somewhere to talk?" Tracy asked uncomfortably. "That woman looks like she wants to kill me. Both of them actually."

I followed her gaze to look back at Mrs. Grundy's apartment, where Shannon ran her pointer finger slowly across her throat then pointed to Tracy. She even did the "I'm watching you" thing where she aimed her pointer and middle finger at her eyes and then at Tracy.

"Sure, yeah," I said. "We can go up to my apartment or maybe just a walk. A walk around the gates."

"A walk sounds good," Tracy said with a sad smile.

I led us both out of the gates with Odin trailing a safe distance behind to keep a watch. I imagined Shannon and maybe even Mrs. Grundy were going to follow as well.

The idea this could be some kind of trap ran through my mind, but I didn't see anyone outside our gates. Plus, it was during the day. I imagined an attack in broad daylight by a creature who preferred the dark would be difficult.

I opened the rusted wrought-iron gate for Tracy and then joined her as we walked side by side slowly down the sidewalk.

"I don't know where to start," Tracy began. "The last few days have been so wild. I'm confused about what happened. What I am. What I want."

"So you're turned, then?" I asked. I already suspected but wanted to hear it from her. "Bloodstone. He turned you, didn't he?"

"Yes," Tracy admitted. "He did before—before you killed him. Jonny, what are you now? Some kind of supernatural hunter?"

"Something like that," I answered, not really sure myself.

"I heard you, you know, when you came in to kill Bloodstone," Tracy said as we reached Rami's storefront. "I heard you yell for me to get down before you killed everyone in that room. I barely escaped with my life and that was because of you. You killed them all but let me live. There still must be a part of you that cares for me."

I looked past Tracy to the Girl Scouts who stood behind their table in front of Rami's Kwiki Mart. Both young girls had their mouths open. The same mother from before placed the palm of her hands over one of the young girl's ears.

"Hi, it's me again." I waved to the group of horrified cookie slingers. "Sorry you had to hear that."

I turned and slowly began walking back to Haven with Tracy by my side.

"Jonny," Tracy said, placing her hand on my chest. My chest was still sore from the night before and my new brand, but it burned under her touch in a way it hadn't before. "You can believe me or not, but I do care for you. There's still a small part of me that wants you."

I stopped looking at Tracy, so confused, I was starting to get pissed off. She wants me, she doesn't want me, and now she kinda wants me.

Screaming tires from around the corner grabbed my attention as a blacked-out SUV way too nice for this neighborhood rocketed around the corner. The vehicle was either lost or spelled bad news for me.

The brand burned even hotter on my chest. I pulled away from Tracy, looking to her for direction.

The sound of the charging vehicle didn't seem to bother her. As if she expected it.

"I'm sorry, Jonny," Tracy said, grabbing on to my wrist. "They made me do it. They got to me this morning."

I tried to pull back as the blacked-out SUV bore down on us, but Tracy was too strong, which was really ironic. Soaking wet, Tracy couldn't be much more than a hundred and twenty pounds. Right now, in her vise-like grip, I felt like all the circulation to my hand was being cut off.

"Tracy, Tracy, what are you doing?" I asked, trying to pull my wrist free. "Tracy, it doesn't have to be like this. What about all the things you just said? You don't have to go along with whatever they tell you to do."

"But I do, Jonny," Tracy said, just standing there as if my struggling wasn't even registering on her meter. "That's what you're not getting here. I'm one of them now and they want you to be too. You can be one of us. We can be together forever."

My heart was pounding a mile a minute as the SUV screeched to a halt and three people dressed in black with black ski masks over their face unloaded.

The mother at the Girl Scout stand screamed something I'm not going to repeat here, but I had no idea mothers could put words like that into such a long string of profanity. It was practically poetry.

With all of my weight, I leaned back, trying to rip free of Tracy's grasp and head back to the supposed safety of my apartment complex.

Fire, not just warmth or heat, activated from the brand on my chest and traveled down my arm. Tracy screamed. She finally released her hold on me and sent me reeling backward.

Her hand smoked black and charred as she screamed half in pain, half in anger.

I only made it a few steps before the first man in black tackled me. I hit the ground so hard, the air was knocked out of me. He hit me so hard, I knew we weren't dealing with humans here.

If I had to guess, the Count was in town, and this was his way of repaying me for what I had done to Bloodstone's coven.

"Get his hands," a gruff voice spoke in my ear. "Let's go—"

"Excuse me, excuse me, young man?" Mrs. Grundy's calm voice broke through the tense moment. "Will you please unhand my hunter? I'm going to need his services for many years to come, I think."

From my spot on the sidewalk, I had to crane my neck up to see her. We were just in front of Haven Apartments with the familiar iron gate to my right. The entrance was still a few dozen yards in front of us, but Mrs. Grundy and Odin were walking toward us on the street.

I'd wondered where the big, black hellhound had gone. Now I knew he had gone back to call in the cavalry.

"Secure him and get him in the SUV," the same gruff voice said. "I'll deal with the old woman."

Hands twisted to an unnatural degree, I felt a zip-tie placed over my wrists. Maybe I should be struggling more at the moment or yelling some profanity like the Girl Scout mom who was on the phone now with 911 still screaming to the good Lord above. However, I was more interested in what Mrs. Grundy was about to do against three vampires.

"Listen, old woman," the vampire approaching her said.

"Take your dog. Go back inside. I'm sure old reruns of the *Price is Right* are on for you."

"You are extremely rude," Mrs. Grundy said, still approaching. She was within feet of the man now. "Someone should teach you some manners."

I was pulled up to my feet, blood flowing from a split lip where I had face-planted on the sidewalk.

"Who? You?" the man asked Mrs. Grundy with a laugh.

"No, child of the night. I'm a Watcher. You're not going to be alive long enough to learn," Mrs. Grundy said in that same calm voice. "I'm just going to kill you."

THIRTY-EIGHT

THAT WAS when things got really crazy.

The head of the man talking to Mrs. Grundy crunched inward like someone stomping on a soda can. One second his back was to us, and the next he dropped to his knees then fell to the ground, lifeless.

I wish I didn't see it happen, but I even heard his skull being broken inward.

The two remaining vampires behind me hesitated for a moment. Bad idea. It seemed Mrs. Grundy was through messing around.

I felt a spray of blood hit the back of my head as sirens sounded somewhere in the distance. The mother in charge of the two girls selling Girl Scout cookies screamed another obscenity.

I was knocked to the side as the last vampire ran to the black SUV. The driver in the SUV apparently had seen enough. He was already gunning it in reverse back down the street, trying to get away before Mrs. Grundy played squeezy ball with his skull.

Tracy also seemed to have had enough. She ran faster than any human I had ever seen to catch up with the SUV.

The last would-be vampire kidnapper streaked toward the fleeing SUV but not fast enough. Mrs. Grundy used her—I'm not really sure what she was using, to be honest—magic, telekinesis, the force—to kill the last fleeing vampire just as he ran by the Girl Scout mother.

CRACK

His skull cracked into his brain and this one was particularly juicy. Bone broke through the black ski mask he wore, spraying blood in all directions.

Girl Scout Mom stood there shaking in her white dress as a spray of brain matter covered her, spray tan to gel nails.

Tracy made it to the SUV as the driver curved around the corner and slammed it into drive. More tires squealed as they made their getaway.

The sirens were louder now. I knew the cops would be here in minutes and I didn't really want to have to explain what happened.

I worked my way to my feet, which was much harder than it sounded, since my wrists were still zip tied-behind me.

Shannon bolted out of the apartment's gates, holding a rocket-propelled grenade. I was no gun nut, but I'd played my fair share of *Call of Duty* to know what that was.

"Where are they?" Shannon asked, looking around for something to fire on. Her eyes strayed over the three twitching bodies on the ground and then to me. "Stinky, are you all right?"

"Mrs. Grundy saved me," I said, swallowing hard as the Watcher took her time coming to me and freed me from my zip-tie. "Thanks for that, by the way."

"For what?" Mrs. Grundy gave me a wink. "I'm just an old woman."

The sirens were upon us now as squad cars surrounded the street.

"Shannon, Shannon, best to put the rocket-propelled grenade launcher down now, dear," Mrs. Grundy advised. "I'll deal with this."

I half suspected the police to come out of their vehicles with guns drawn, ordering us to the ground. Heck, if I was a police officer answering a call where three people had their skulls cracked like eggs and a chick holding a rocket launcher, I'd do that.

That was when I noticed the vehicles weren't ordinary police units. They were unmarked vehicles with small flashing red and blue lights on their dashboards.

Agents dressed in black suits and ties stepped out, weapons drawn but not pointed for the moment.

I saw Mrs. Grundy go to an annoyed-looking Agent Lees and begin talking with him.

Shannon was reluctantly placing her weapon at her feet like a disappointed kid told she couldn't take her favorite toy with her on the road trip.

The two girls selling cookies were shaking and reasonably terrified at what they'd seen. The mother just stood there, still soaked in brain matter. She too quivered.

I wasn't sure if it was my place or not. Probably not since I was in no way qualified, but I couldn't just stand there and let the woman and girls quake in fear.

"Hey, hey, it's going to be okay. It's over," I said, going over to the group with my best reassuring smile. I tasted blood on my lips from the fall when I was tackled. My bloody grin probably wasn't the most comforting image.

The woman looked like she was in shock, just standing there not saying a word.

"Hey, hey, I've got some money now; why don't I buy more than one box of cookies?" I said to the girls, trying to get them to snap out of their shocked state. "It's okay, it's okay. I'll take some of those lemon ones and anything with peanut butter on it."

One of the girls swallowed hard but nodded and moved to fill my order.

I went to the mother next. I wasn't sure why the guy who had his skull crunched next to the mom had so much fluid to spare. Maybe he did his crossword puzzle and Sudoku every day. Whatever the case, it was like a red sprinkler had hit the mother. Flecks of blood and brain matter fell down her lips and balayage hair.

"Hey, you've got a little, you have a little something right around there." I gestured to take in her entire face and body. "Let me help. I can help. We just need a tissue or a wet wipe or something."

I looked to my left where Rami had exited his store now that the situation had deescalated. He looked at me with an open mouth and a dozen questions on the tip of his tongue.

"Rami, Rami, can we get a wet nap or maybe some sanitizer here?" I asked politely. "Anything really; paper towels would work. We can be flexible."

Rami just nodded with his mouth still open and headed back inside his store.

"Here, Mom, here." One of the girls offered up a tissue from her pocket.

"Great, this is going to work, thank you," I answered, taking the tissue for the mother. "We're going to get you nice and clean. We're going to get those cookies sold and turn this day around."

I began dabbing the tissue around her mouth and eyes trying to soak up the viscera on her face. That seemed to finally break the woman out of her shock. She turned on me, her face transforming from dazed to downright angry.

"Ahhhhh!" the woman screamed, hitting me with her cell

phone in one hand and purse in the other. "Get away from me. Get your hands off me!"

"Okay, okay," I exclaimed, backing up with hands extended. "I was just trying to help."

"Geesh, what's this one's problem?" Shannon asked, joining us at the cookie stand. She grabbed a box of Samoas, ripped it open, and took a bite out of one.

"Um, excuse me," one of the two Girl Scout cookie representatives said with her hands on her hips. "You have to pay for that."

"Awww, that's cute, aren't you adorable?" Shannon said, looking at me. "Put it on his tab; he's got some money now."

I paid the Girl Scouts for my two boxes and Shannon's Samoas, all the while dodging death stares from the mother. A SOAP agent I didn't recognize had come over to the mother, informing her she had been witness to a very dangerous confrontation with domestic terrorists.

When the mother asked why their heads had exploded, the agent very calmly explained they had a sniper on the roof that was gone now but had managed to take out the threat.

I finished paying for my cookies and walked over to find Mrs. Grundy speaking with a very agitated Agent Lees.

"You and your kind know the rules," Agent Lees grumbled. "You keep your activity out of the public eye. We're always having to come to your rescue and clean up your messes. I'm getting tired of it."

"Well, I'm going to ignore the fact that you referred to us as 'my kind'," Mrs. Grundy said, looking over at me with a smile. "John here was being attacked and we stepped in to offer aid. What else were we supposed to be doing? Let the Count take him?"

"We don't know it was the Count for sure," Agent Lees corrected her. He looked at me with disdain. That same kind of look you give your shoe after stepping in poop.

"How were you guys so close?" I asked, honestly wanting to find an answer to the question. "I mean, that mom made the call and you were here in minutes."

I looked around the scene where SOAP agents had blocked off the street. Already there was a team cleaning up the bodies. Multiple agents were speaking with any witnesses, explaining to them what they thought they just observed.

"SOAP was watching us," Mrs. Grundy asserted, peering around the massive Agent Lees. "Where's Agent Bentall? I thought he'd be here himself."

"That's classified, ma'am," Agent Lees said in his same low monotone voice. "We were close by monitoring you. We suspected an attempt would be made on the lives of those responsible for tracking down Bloodstone's coven. We were right."

"You were right, but also late," Mrs. Grundy pointed out, raising an eyebrow. "One of my hunters could have been killed or taken."

"Sounds like your hunters need to learn how to take care of themselves," Agent Lees said, looking at me with that same air of disgust. It probably didn't help that I decided to open up one of the boxes of cookies in my arms and start shoving Tagalongs in my mouth. I really needed to stop with the stress eating.

"Noted," Mrs. Grundy said, looking around at the many agents working busily to clean up any trace of the incident. "Well, it looks like you and your team have things in control here. Always nice seeing you, Agent Lees."

Agent Lees made a huffing sound.

Mrs. Grundy turned to leave, but I thought if we were going to be working with SOAP, I should at least make an effort to try and be polite.

"Good seeing you again, Agent Lees," I said, extending my hand.

Agent Lees regarded me with cold, dark eyes. He didn't even move a muscle to accept my handshake. He just stared at me.

"Okay then, well, good luck with everything," I said, not knowing what to do. I patted him on the shoulder. My eyes went wide when I saw a chocolate stain on his pristine black suit jacket.

Agent Lees saw my eyes go wide and moved to look down at his suit.

"Agent Lees, I'd like to give you these cookies as a peace offering," I said quickly, shoving the cookies in his direction. "Yeah, if we're going to be seeing more of each other, I want us to have a good working relationship."

Agent Lees narrowed his eyes but took the cookies.

"I'm not sure what kind of game you think you're playing here, but this is serious." Agent Lees scowled. "This is life and death here. It might be fun and adventures to you, but daily, SOAP agents are putting their lives on the line to risk everything to keep humanity safe."

"I don't think it's a game," I said, backpedaling to the front gate. "It's not a game, thank you by the way. Thank you for the service."

I'd done enough. I speed-walked back into the gate to catch up with Shannon and Mrs. Grundy. Most everyone in the apartment complex was either out for the day or too cautious to step outside. The few people in the apartments who were brave enough to watch from the ground floor looked at the three of us with questions.

"Agent Lees needs to work on his people skills," I grumbled as Shannon, Mrs. Grundy, Odin, and I stepped into Mrs. Grundy's apartment. "Thank you, by the way, for saving me back there."

"You'll do it one day for me." Mrs. Grundy shrugged off the compliment and closed the door behind her.

"I knew that skank was good for nothing, I knew it," Shannon said, shaking her head with a heavy sigh. "John, I'm sorry but your ex is a real piece of work."

"Don't I know it," I replied, feeling the emotional knife driven harder into my gut. "She set me up."

"I hate to interrupt whatever internal realization you're having at the moment, John, but Agent Lees wasn't wrong when he said you need to learn how to fight," Mrs. Grundy warned. "It's time the two of you met Michael."

THIRTY-NINE

"I CAN'T BELIEVE you're insisting on reading every word in that contract," Shannon said from the driver's seat. "It's all going to be the same. Promise not to talk to anyone about what we do, if we get injured we can't hold the Court responsible, and so on and so on."

"Well, excuse me, I actually like to read what I'm committing to for the foreseeable future," I said from my seat in the back of Shannon's car. "Like this page thirteen sub paragraph two under the resuscitation clause. Hunter gives Court and associates permission to close interdimensional port with hunter trapped inside if world ending event is imminent. I don't want to be trapped in another dimension. I don't care if the world is ending; you leave that portal open long enough for me to get out."

"It's totally fine he reads the entire contract," Mrs. Grundy commented from her seat beside Shannon. "I encourage every hunter to do so. Knowledge is power. Besides, the interdimensional portal clause was added because there was a freak accident once a very long time ago. The odds of that happening again are slim to none."

Shannon maneuvered around afternoon traffic as people were closing shop and getting off work. While most were on their way home to figure out dinner, I was going to weapons training with another Watcher Mrs. Grundy only called Michael.

Apparently, Mrs. Grundy was well versed in other things, but hand-to-hand combat and weapons training was best left for someone else. Shannon reassured Mrs. Grundy she could teach me, but Mrs. Grundy insisted even she would be able to learn from this Michael.

Eventually, Mrs. Grundy directed us to a flower shop on Grand and Seventeenth. It was a clean, well-lit place with a halogen sign out front that read Halo's Bouquet above the front door with the emblem of a sunflower next to it.

"Uh, Grundy?" Shannon said, parking her car and looking out the front window with a raised eyebrow. "You can't be serious."

"Oh, I can be." Mrs. Grundy gave a knowing smile as she opened her car door. "Michael was the best warrior the light had this side of our universe. He's the one we need."

"What are 'oozing creatures of the nightmare realm'?" I asked, nose still in the contract. "Should I be worried about that clause?"

"Just your typical demon spawn," Mrs. Grundy reassured me before closing her door.

I followed the two women inside the store. The interior of the flower shop was open and smelled wonderful. I was more of an aromatic-coffee-aroma-loving kind of guy myself but I had to admit the flower shop smelled great.

Vibrant orange arrangements gave way to purple, rose, reds, and yellows of every shade and hue. I couldn't help but smile at the idea a master warrior was to be found among such delicate flowers.

I heard talking coming from a counter to the rear of the

shop. A man not much larger than myself spoke with a trio of older women. His long, dirty blond hair was pulled back from his face in a man bun. A few days' worth of stubble showed on a square jaw.

He held an arrangement in his right hand and pointed out facts with his left.

"I think your daughter will be really happy with the outcome," the man said with a genuine smile. "She's more than welcome to come in tomorrow and I can show her options for her wedding day. I'll be here bright and early."

"Oh, Michael, thank you," one of the older women gushed, letting her hand stay on his muscular forearm too long for friendship. "I don't know how you managed to stay single."

"Wow, who is that?" Shannon asked, eyeing the man behind the counter like a piece of meat. "Is that Michael?"

"Have some respect," Mrs. Grundy said, unamused. "Michael was bathing in the blood of the ancient ones before your bloodline began."

Michael caught sight of us and stood up straighter. He cleared his throat, addressing the women in front of him. "Thank you again for trusting me with your business. I have to be closing now, but I'm looking forward to talking with you tomorrow."

"So are we." One of the women giggled.

The three women moved toward the front door, one of them fanning herself, the others laughing.

"Mrs. Grundy," Michael greeted, moving around the counter and wiping his hands on his green apron. "You know you're always welcome in my store, but if you've come for the reason you always come, you know the answer's no."

"Michael, Michael, no one is asking you to re-enter the fight," Mrs. Grundy said to the shop owner. "They need guidance and you're the best."

"There are others who can train them," Michael insisted, not even glancing at Shannon or me. "Take them to Hephaestus or Osiris. I'm done with that life. Now, you're welcome to stay and look over the flowers if you like. I can recommend a nice arrangement for your kitchen."

Michael turned and walked back to the counter, clearly disturbed by our presence, despite not even having said anything to Shannon or me.

"Are you sure this is the right guy?" I asked, trying to be optimistic. "He looks like he's pretty set on not fighting and arranging flowers for the rest of the night."

"He can arrange my flowers any night," Shannon muttered under her breath.

"What?" I asked.

"What?" Shannon answered.

"He's the right man for the job," Mrs. Grundy said with a sad sigh. "Like many of us, he's just been through a lot. John, you should go talk to him."

"Me?" I asked, raising my eyebrows. "I don't know anything about flowers, or fighting, or whatever it is he's been through."

"You might be surprised," Mrs. Grundy told me with a knowing smile. "Just be yourself. Tell him what's happened to you."

"I don't mind going over there and talking to him," Shannon offered, all of a sudden standing straighter. She started fixing her hair. "How do I look?"

"You look like you're about to wander around this shop looking at flowers with me while John goes and talks to Michael," Mrs. Grundy declared. "John, if you would? Time is not on our side."

I scratched the back of my neck as I headed over to speak with Michael. I didn't really know what I was supposed to say to the man. He had retaken his position behind the counter, creating an arrangement of flowers in a clear glass vase. At the moment, he had a sunflower in one hand and a daisy in the other.

He had to know I was coming but chose not to acknowledge me.

"So, nice flowers you have there, man. I mean, seriously, I think you have a great shop," I started, already mentally kicking myself for how poorly I was doing. What was I even doing here?

"Thank you," Michael replied, not looking up at me. "Grundy send you over to try and talk me into helping?"

"I could say something clever here and try to break the ice, but I'll just say yes instead," I admitted. "She said you can help us train and get ready for a fight to come."

"No can do," Michael said, turning the vase to see the flower arrangement from every angle. "That is behind me now. I've lost enough."

"I don't blame you," I told him. "I've only known the supernatural existed for a few days now and I've lost more than I thought I would be able to bear. My fiancée was turned into a vampire, I got a wolf brand on my chest, and now I'm supposed to use this war hammer gods' steel weapon thing to fend off an oncoming vampire count. Listen, I'm sorry to have bothered you. I'll try to get Grundy and Shannon to leave."

"Did you say steel of the gods?" Michael asked, stopping what he was doing halfway into inserting another sunflower in the arrangement.

"Uh, yeah, I think that's what it was called," I said, turning around. "It has runes on it and hummed red when I sank it into a vampire I was fighting the other day. I've only used it once, so I'm not really sure what else it can do."

Michael just stood there staring at me for way too long. The situation became awkward real fast.

"So then, I'm just going to go," I said with a nod. "Okay, good talk. Next time I need flowers, I know where to come."

I turned around thinking that was the weirdest interaction I had when mentioning god's steel. But then again, how many interactions had I had talking about the weapon?

"No luck?" Shannon asked, adjusting herself in her tank top. "Maybe I should go over."

"He did enough." Mrs. Grundy looked at me approvingly. "John did enough. Come on; let's go now."

"Uh, but I didn't get him to train us," I said, confused. "I barely talked to him."

Mrs. Grundy opened the front door for us, ushering us back to the car.

Shannon walked out first, as confused as I was. I was about to exit next when I heard a voice call out, "Grundy, is what he said true? Did the god's steel activate for him?"

"It did, Michael," Mrs. Grundy answered. "I can only imagine what that must mean to you."

Shannon and I both looked back into the store. Michael stood there in the middle of his shop. Even through his green apron, I could see his muscular physique tense. His hands balled into fists. The muscles near his jaw line clenched.

"Train them for her and that's all I ask," Mrs. Grundy reassured him. "No one's asking you to fight again. If you can't bring yourself to do it for you, then do it in her memory."

Michael swallowed hard. Eventually, he gave a nod.

"All right, for her," Michael consented, walking toward us. He waved us inside. Once we moved back into the store, he closed the door, locked it, and switched the open sign in the window to closed. "Follow me."

"Oh, I think I'll stay here and enjoy the flowers," Mrs. Grundy said, shooing us forward. "I'd only get in the way."

Michael didn't seem to care either way. Shannon and I

followed him past the counter to a back room where a door led to an underground storage area. The steep flight of steps gave me vertigo as we headed a full story underground.

Bright lights showed me this wasn't an underground storage area at all. Shannon sucked in a breath and I think I might have done the same when I realized where we were.

A training facility with two large rooms opened up in front of us. One area held black mats and sparring equipment; on the other side was a medieval armory, not of this world.

Axes, swords, shields, spears, clubs, and a plethora of other weapons sat on the wall. Michael removed his green apron and lifted a great two-handed sword from its place on the wall with reverence.

He handled the sword like I had seen him hold the flowers.

"Hunters, prepare yourselves," Michael said, looking from his blade to us for the first time. "Now you train."

FORTY

TO BE HONEST, I was getting kind of hungry and I was usually best in the mornings. Michael handed me a wooden axe shaped just like the real one I used the day before. Shannon chose a wooden katana.

Michael whispered something to his blade before placing it back on the wall and selected a wooden sword that mirrored his real one.

"Forget all you think you know and just let yourself be taught," Michael instructed, eyeing Shannon, who twirled her wooden sword with practiced ease. "Also, do not be frightened. I lost this eye a long time ago in battle. I use the prosthetic to make my customers feel at ease."

"Your eye?" Shannon asked.

"Say what now?" I answered.

Michael reached into his left eye socket and popped out his bright green eye like he was taking a Pop Tart out of the toaster.

"Oh, oh," I murmured, raising a hand to my mouth. Now I was actually glad I hadn't eaten.

"I feel more comfortable in my eye patch, but that tends

to raise too many questions," Michael explained, going over to a small table. He placed the eye in a drawer and reappeared with a worn brown eye patch in his hand.

"Wow, I can't look away," Shannon said as we both gaped into the empty socket where his eye used to be. "You lost it in a fight?"

"I lost it and so much more that day," Michael said, securing his eye patch. "But that is a story for another day. Now we train."

And train we did for hours and hours. I was still sore from my brand the night before. I wasn't really sure I should be doing this at all. Didn't Doctor Muffin tell me I should be resting? The main reason I pressed on was because Agent Lees and Mrs. Grundy were right. I needed to learn how to fight.

I thought about how easily Tracy had grabbed me. It took nothing for the other vampires to throw me to the ground and tie my hands behind my back. If I was going to be a hunter, I needed to be able to defend myself. I couldn't count on Odin, or Shannon, or Mrs. Grundy to always be there bailing me out.

Michael was a great teacher, spending equal time on weapons and hand-to-hand training. He was kind and fair. I could tell as my admiration grew for the man, Shannon's was decreasing.

Going into this, Shannon thought she was going to stand toe to toe with the warrior. She didn't say it, but I knew that was what she was thinking. Michael took her down every time, be it as they sparred or with their wooden swords.

"Again," Michael called to Shannon as she lifted herself off the floor. "Your attacks are powerful enough but not well-thought-out. This is a chess game, not checkers."

"I'll show you checkers," Shannon grunted, doing a kip-up as she regained her feet and charged, trying to take Michael off guard. It didn't work out well for her.

Shannon struck out with her thinner katana-shaped weapon in a flurry of blows. Michael moved his weapon with an ease that reminded me of how water flowed smooth and even.

At every turn, Shannon's sword was blocked. Sweat ran down her forehead as she looked for an opening that didn't exist. Michael refused to give her ground as the sharp staccato sound of wood against wood filled the underground room.

Out of nowhere, Michael struck out with an open palm, slamming his hand into Shannon's chest. She gasped and fell back onto the mat.

"Speed and ferocity isn't everything," Michael said, moving to offer her a hand up. "Timing, openings, be patient."

Shannon ignored the offered hand and rose to her feet on her own.

I was up next and already taking Michael's words to heart.

"Your weapon is something special, John," Michael said, looking at the wooden axe in my hand as if it were the real thing. "It has a great history and is capable of wonderful things in the right hands. It activated for you, so I know your hands were meant to wield it once more. It has a name."

"The war hammer has a name?" I asked.

"It does," Michael answered. "Anew she pan is set."

"Oh," I said, already forgetting what he just said and how to pronounce it. "Amew chingatha soup."

"No, Anew she pan is set," Michael repeated.

"That's what I said," I argued. "Almore he panga isn't. I'm saying what you're saying."

Michael actually broke out in a full smile I had yet to see. For the first time since I met him, I got the feeling I was able to see the real Michael, not whatever he was pretending to be in the flower store above.

He was ready with a smile, strong and a great leader. I found myself wondering what happened to him to make him recoil so far into himself.

"She would have liked you," Michael said. "Why don't we just go with the translated title the weapon carries in English. The weapon is known as Blood Rage."

"Oh, oh my goodness, Blood Rage," I repeated.

"And I will teach you how to wield that weapon as if it were an extension of your own body," Michael said. "Let's begin."

I can only explain what happened for the next few hours as a marathon of pain. At times Shannon and I both took instruction from Michael; other times he worked us one on one and allowed the other to rest. Other times, we sparred against one another.

By the time we were done, I was covered in sweat, sorer than when I walked into Halo Bouquet, but I did have a better foundation in both hand-to-hand combat and using Blood Rage.

I felt better about throwing punches and grappling. I felt like I could actually block an incoming strike with Blood Rage now. I even learned a few combinations with the weapon, using both the shaft and the head of the war hammer in an attack.

"That's enough for today," Michael said, calling a halt to our training. "We need you up and prepared to work tomorrow morning. If we're going to do this, we train from five am to seven am, an hour for hand-to-hand and an hour for weapons. You'll have to do physical fitness exercising on your own."

"Tomorrow morning?" I asked, checking my phone, there were two worried texts from Evan and a missed call. It was almost seven now. I texted him back all was well, still doing the math on how many hours of sleep I could get tonight.

"You'll need all the training you can get to not die," Michael said, trotting up the steps. "Tomorrow, bring your actual weapons to work with. Also, it might be a good idea to take some kind of weapon with you now wherever you go."

"I'm beginning to realize that," Shannon said, having lost all her initial interest in Michael. "We'll be here at five."

We exited the underground torture chamber and walked out into the brightly lit front room. Mrs. Grundy was there with a pair of glasses perched on the edge of her nose, scrolling through her phone.

"Well, how did they do?" Mrs. Grundy asked.

"Too early to tell," Michael answered. "We'll see them again tomorrow, bright and early."

"Wonderful, thank you, Michael," Mrs. Grundy said, patting his muscular shoulder. "She would be very happy. You know that."

Michael just nodded as we exited his store.

"So what's the deal with that guy anyway?" Shannon asked as we entered her car. "I mean, I can put some of the puzzle pieces together. He used to fight a lot, and what, he lost an eye and a girlfriend?"

I leaned closer to the two in the front seat to hear every word.

"Michael can decide how much he'd like to tell you," Mrs. Grundy replied. "It'll be good for him to recount the story whether he knows it or not. Right now, we should be talking about some Matty Too Fatty burgers with extra chili cheese fries, oh, and a diet cola."

"Diet, huh?" Shannon asked. "Not going to worry about the calories in that burger and fries, but you're going to pump the brakes at the soda and get a diet?"

"I have to draw the line somewhere, dear," Mrs. Grundy

said good-naturedly as Shannon headed to the preferred burger joint. "I texted Evan. I have his order as well. We can go back and share a meal together."

"The Bloodsucker likes burgers?" Shannon asked with a half laugh. "Of course he does."

"He's a part of this as well," Mrs. Grundy reminded Shannon. "I understand you're going to view him from behind a certain pair of glasses because of your hate for his kind and what happened to your sister. Evan, however, should be given some credit. To rage against what you are on a daily basis is a battle few of us must face. I've only known a handful of vampires in my time that have sworn off killing or turning humans. It takes a substantial strength of will."

Shannon listened but didn't say anything.

We made it to the drive-through and back to Haven Apartments without incident. My legs and chest, heck, my whole body screamed at me as I exited Shannon's car. I remembered to take the contract with me.

"Still haven't signed, I see," Mrs. Grundy noted as we walked into the apartment complex. She carried the drinks in one hand and opened the gate for us with the other. "You will."

"I was thinking—" I started.

"That sounds dangerous," Shannon joked.

"I was thinking," I began again. "Should I be training, given these secrets and a war hammer called Blood Rage if I haven't even made a commitment to become a hunter? I mean, what if I decide this life just isn't for me?"

"You'll sign," Mrs. Grundy said knowingly.

"But I mean, what if I don't?" I asked. "Last time I committed to something, I had my heart torn out of my chest and then she tried to kidnap me."

"You'll sign," Mrs. Grundy said again, fishing for the keys to her apartment and letting us inside. "On another note, both of you need showers. I can smell you and the odor isn't exactly sunshine and rainbows."

"Seriously," Shannon agreed as we sat down at Mrs. Grundy's table. "Usually, it's just John that has it going on, but I smell like a gym bag."

Evan joined us a few minutes later and we dug into the calorie-filled goodness with abandon. I wasn't sure how Evan and Shannon were going to get along, but Evan was his usual cheerful self and Shannon seemed to rein in any negative comments after the talk with Mrs. Grundy.

I realized then that I had been missing this for a long time. Just having friends. It was only Evan and me before Tracy came along and then mostly just Tracy and me. I couldn't remember the last time I actually had a group of friends all sitting together.

"Uh oh," Evan said around a mouthful of fries. "Jonny has his emotional thinking face on. I recognize that face. What are you thinking?"

Shannon and Mrs. Grundy looked at me for an answer.

"I just—this," I said, looking at each of them around the table. "I guess I really didn't know how much I missed having friends. I wasn't exactly popular in high school. This might be the most friends I've had all together."

"Family, dear," Mrs. Grundy corrected, patting my hand. "Friends that are more like family."

"Seriously," Shannon said, sucking on her straw. "I was just going to make fun of you right now or say something funny but also mildly offensive about the vamp at our table, but I'll refrain. Since my sister died, I haven't had many friends either. I guess my cousin Rylee is the one I'm closest to now."

"I don't get out much as you can imagine," Mrs. Grundy added. "But my hellhounds keep me company when they're around. They seem to be out again now. No doubt needed elsewhere at the moment. It can get lonely."

We all looked at Evan.

"What?" Evan asked. "I'm great, super busy with work, I mean, I was until the owner of my modeling agency was murdered by you fine people, but he had it coming. I'm thinking of opening my own business as these final shoots I've been contracted to work wind down. I am happy I can share who I really am with all of you, even if one of you tries to decapitate me every so often."

"Might try again later. I'm still deciding." Shannon smirked.

"Fair enough," Evan answered.

"Well, this has been a very nice night for me, but you two need to shower and get rest if you're going to be up and be ready to train tomorrow morning," Mrs. Grundy said, looking at me and Shannon. "You must be prepared when Victor makes his appearance."

"Wait, who?" Evan asked, almost jumping out of his seat.

"Count Victor Jovanovic," I clarified, taking in Evan's clearly disturbed appearance. "He came to me in a dream. What's wrong?"

"Jonny boy," Evan said after chewing on his bottom lip for a moment. "There's something you have to know."

FORTY-ONE

I FELT a sense of doom spread from Evan, across the table of empty wrappers and used ketchup packets, and descend on my shoulders.

"Jonny, the Count's not someone to be taken lightly," Evan warned, as worried for me as I'd ever seen him. "This isn't your run-of-the-Hollywood vampire or even coven leader like Bloodstone. He's one of the older ones. Way more powerful than even me."

"Older ones, huh?" Shannon asked, shaking her head. "That sounds ominous."

"It's not a joke," Evan said, looking at Mrs. Grundy. "You know this. Why are you encouraging them to fight him?"

"Not encouraging," Mrs. Grundy asserted. "Preparing them for what is to come. The fight comes our way whether we like it or not. It is our job to prepare."

"We'll be okay," I reassured my friend. "We're training now. We're going to start carrying weapons."

"I've also looked into warding our apartment complex after our little visit today," Mrs. Grundy shared, trying to appease Evan. "I thought just protecting my apartment would be enough, but apparently not. I'll work on it more tonight, setting runes and stones in place to keep out the darkness. This place will become a fortress."

"Well, that's well and good, I'm sure, but I'm talking about anything that happens outside of here," Evan said, clearly still worried. "The Count has a reputation to keep. He'll come for them outside of this apartment. Jonny, you don't know how the vampire hierarchy works here. The Count's not going to let this one go."

I understood where Evan was coming from. I knew he was just worried about me, and to be honest, I was kind of worried about myself. Bloodstone nearly killed me and we had the drop on him.

This time around, the Count could attack anytime and anywhere. He would be the one springing the trap now. I also knew I was tired of running from bullies. My entire life I crossed the street to walk on the other sidewalk when I saw them coming, I avoided eye contact and just took the butt of their jokes. Maybe this time, I could actually stand up to one.

"I can't just run, Evan," I told him. "I don't want to."

Evan knew about my past. He was one of the few people who understood the bullying I endured when I was younger. I could tell he still didn't like it, but at least now he understood.

"Train hard," Evan told me. "He'll more than likely come himself when you're out at night. That's when he's the strongest. I'll reach out to a few of my contacts and see if I can get any more intel."

"Well, this has been a nice brotherly moment, " Shannon said, stretching in her seat. "I'm going to head up to my apartment for a shower and then go to bed. Tomorrow comes early as fu-"

"I'll work on warding Haven," Mrs. Grundy said hurriedly to interrupt however Shannon was about to finish that sentence. "This place will be more than secure when I'm through with it."

We parted ways, Shannon promising to bring Blood Rage with her in the morning when we drove back to Halo Bouquet. When Evan and I got back to our apartment, he opted for video games while I hopped into the shower then set my alarm for four thirty am and passed out into blissful peace.

My dreams were plagued with memories of being bullied in school. I remembered the beatings, the verbal degradation, and public humiliation. My family always struggling with money, me being overweight and socially awkward. I was the perfect target.

My phone alarm went off when I was in such a deep sleep, I didn't know where I was. It took me a moment to look over at my nightstand and reach for my phone.

I blinked a few times, staring at the ceiling fan in my room. My chest was still sore from two days ago, but now my legs and arms were sore as well, thanks to the workout plan Michael had us on.

I went through my morning routine of brushing my teeth, dressing, and drinking water like a zombie. I didn't know how I was going to get through the training Michael had in store for us today. I just knew I had to find a way. It was this or run. I was tired of running. I was tired of being used and thrown to the side.

I dressed in workout clothes since I thought that would be most fitting for what was about to happen. I had just enough time to throw in a K-cup of Black Rifle Coffee in my Keurig machine before heading out.

I walked from my apartment, heading down to Shannon's unit. I was pretty cheery in the morning. It seemed Shannon was not.

She was just walking out of her door as I reached her

floor. She wore a black tactical backpack with her katana handle sticking out of the top. My war hammer in her left hand as she locked her apartment door.

"Hey, good morning," I said, shivering a bit in the crisp morning air. The sun wasn't even out yet. Most of the apartment windows around us were dark as the sane people slept in. "How'd you sleep?"

Shannon turned to look at me like she was about to bite my head off. I'd seen that look before when a snake is about to unhinge its jaw and eat a mouse whole. Her hair was up in a messy bun, there was no time for makeup, and bags hung under her eyes.

"Oh gosh, you're one of those morning people, aren't you?" Shannon griped, handing me the war hammer. "I hate people like you. I just want to punch you in your grinning face, like all the time."

Instinctively, I took a step back. I didn't think Shannon was actually going to hit me, but she'd done stranger things before. I mean, the woman did have a rocket-propelled grenade launcher in her apartment.

"Come on; let's go. Just don't talk for a few minutes. Give me a chance, you early morning freak," Shannon groused, walking by me and plucking my coffee cup from my hand in the process.

"Well, you need it more than me," I said, justifying the act to myself. "I'll drive."

Shannon wasn't kidding. We walked to my car in silence. My Mustang rumbled to life coughed, wheezed, and then we pulled out of Haven Apartments.

There was barely any traffic at all. We made it to Halo Bouquet in record time. Shannon had remained content to sip on her, or rather, my coffee in silence. She was looking better now. A few of those bags under her eyes had disappeared and she didn't seem so pissed off.

We exited the car, going up to a dark Halo Bouquet store front. I squinted to see inside and knocked on the door.

"Oh good, maybe it was cancelled this morning," Shannon said. "I'm all about training, but this early morning nonsense is going to be the death—"

Shannon stopped herself as Michael appeared on the other side of the glass door with a ready smile and his own cup of coffee. He opened the door for us and waved us inside.

"Good morning, you two. Let's get to work," Michael said, eyeing the weapon in my hand. "Today's going to be a good day."

"Oh lord have mercy," Shannon said, walking in. "Another one. It would be my luck I get not one but two morning people in my life."

"Nice cup," Michael said, looking at the mug in Shannon's hand.

"What?" Shannon asked, examining the words on the cup for the first time.

I'd received the cup as a gag gift from Evan a few years ago. Sure, it may have been inappropriate, but it was funny. Shannon read it and looked at me deadpan.

"Really?" Shannon asked. "Do you want me to kill you in training today? It's like you're asking for it."

"I don't know, I like it," Michael said, locking the store door behind us and waving us to follow. "Come on; we're burning time."

Much like the day before, the training routine was one part hand-to-hand combat, one part weapons training, and all pain. My body was asking me what it did to deserve to be put through the wringer like this. I didn't really have a good answer as sore muscles fatigued and new definitions of pain were discovered.

Michael set Shannon on drills with her katana against a

wooden opponent on one side of the room. He motioned for me to stand in front of him with Blood Rage.

"May I?" He motioned to the weapon.

"Yeah, of course," I said, handing him the war hammer.

Michael took it carefully, handling it like he would a flower. His hands ran up the weapon handle. He touched the top of the weapon, steering clear of the honed edge and gripping the opposite end that was more of a sledgehammer.

I knew this was my chance to get some answers out of him.

"This weapon clearly means something to you," I said as I watched him hold the weapon close. "Did it belong to you or someone you knew?"

"It belonged to my wife before she fell in battle," Michael said barely above a whisper. He ran his right thumb over the runes on the wooden shaft. "She made it. For the longest time, it was thought only she would be able to wield it. It wouldn't activate for anyone else, but now Grundy tells me it answers to you."

"Oh, I'm so sorry to hear about your wife," I said, not really sure what else to say but thinking these were the right words for the moment. "The runes and blade turned red when I was fighting vampires with it. If that's what you mean by answering to me."

"It's a good weapon," Michael said, swallowing hard. "It served her well and didn't fail her, even in her final moments. It will serve you well."

"If this is some kind of family weapon and it means that much to you, maybe you should keep it," I offered. "I mean, there's a dozen other things I can use to fight. If I can get Shannon to let me use one of her guns or something, that might be better suited for me."

"No, it chose you for a reason," Michael said, snapping out of some trance-like state. He handed me back the war hammer. "I'm not sure why it would choose someone as ill-suited and inept as you, but it has and I trust it."

"I think there's a compliment in there somewhere," I said, accepting the weapon. "Thanks?"

"Don't thank me yet," Michael said, stretching his arms and then cracking his neck from side to side. "Let's begin."

FORTY-TWO

BY THE TIME we were done with our second day of training, I thought for sure I pulled my butt muscle or cracked my tailbone. I was drenched in sweat again but feeling a little more comfortable with the idea of breaking holds and grappling as well as maneuvering around a fight with Blood Rage.

Shannon was learning quickly as well, not getting hit by Michael in the first few seconds of the fight. Once she almost scored a hit of her own, almost. Michael was untouchable, even with only one eye. I couldn't imagine what he was like with both in action.

When we ended the day, instead of heading back up to the store, Michael held us back for a moment.

"I'm beginning to see what Grundy has found in the two of you," Michael told us with an approving nod. "She always has had a knack for discovering talent. Has she repeated the code to you?"

"The code?" Shannon looked at me for confirmation. "I don't think so."

"Nope, definitely not," I answered.

"The code of the Court goes like this. It's repeated by

Watchers and serious hunters alike. After I say a line, you say 'send me'," Michael instructed. "When the world of men stands defenseless against the dark."

"Send me," Shannon and I said in unison.

"When the ancient ones come to reclaim their throne," Michael continued a little louder now.

"Send me," Shannon and I answered louder, matching his volume.

"When all hope is lost and no one can see the way!"

"Send me!"

"And when the light trembles to regain its feet, who will go?"

"Send me!"

The room reverberated with our shouts. I could feel goosebumps on my arms and a rush of heat rise to my face as my heart beat picked up tempo.

"Well done, hunters," Michael answered.

"Well, I just feel like I should be honest," I said, breaking the magic of the moment. "I haven't signed the contract yet."

"You will," Michael answered, unfazed by my admission. "You will."

"Why does everybody keep telling me that?" I muttered under my breath.

Michael walked us to the front door. It was seven in the morning and the sky was just beginning to change from complete darkness to a greyish gold.

"You have a lot of sunflowers in here," Shannon said as we walked outside the store.

"They were her favorites," Michael shared with a sad smile before waving goodbye and closing the door behind us.

"Man, I feel so sorry for that guy," Shannon said as we drove back to the apartment complex. "I mean, to love someone and then have her taken away like that. It must feel like hell. I can't imagine someone you loved just gone. I loved my sister, but I get that it's a different type of love one has for their spouse."

"I can," I answered. Realizing what happened to Michael and his wife wasn't what happened to Tracy and me, but I felt like I could relate in a small way.

"I mean, someone you wanted to spend the rest of your life with just never coming back? That must feel like taking your heart and putting it in a blender."

"It does," I said.

"Geesh," Shannon said. "Why am I always attracted to the ones with issues?"

I didn't really have an answer for her and neither did I want to engage in the conversation further.

When we got back to the apartments, Shannon and I agreed to take the morning to rest and recover. Then she'd run me through a physical exercise, including cardio training, which I was less than enthused about. After that, she promised to show me some of the more modern weapons and how to shoot them at a local range.

I ran into Evan as he headed out the door for his work day.

"Hey, man," Evan said, placing his designer sunglasses over his eyes. "I'm glad I caught you before I left. I wanted to tell you I'm sorry about last night. I kinda freaked out when I heard the Count was involved."

"No reason to apologize, man," I told him with a shake of my head. "I appreciate you being worried."

"It's just I've never really had someone good to talk to about all of this," Evan said, adjusting the keys in his hand as if suddenly they were very interesting to him. "You're like a brother, Jonny. The closest thing to family that I've got. I just don't want to see anything bad happen to you."

"Hey, nothing's going to happen to me," I told him with a reassuring smile. Evan was usually the happy-go-lucky one, cheering me up. "I'm good. I'm going to train hard and learn as much as I can and heck this whole hunter thing might not even be for me."

"Who are we kidding, you're going to sign that contract," Evan said without hesitation.

"I might not."

"Please, the John Hunter I know is going to sign that contract," Evan stated as fact. "You're just waiting to feel good about it and responsible."

"I might not," I said as Evan clapped me on the shoulder with a smile and started walking down the hall.

"You are," Evan called back.

"Who knows, maybe not," I shouted as Evan disappeared down the stairwell.

"Oh, you will," Evan shouted back.

I went into my quiet apartment for another shower, breakfast, and sleep. If Shannon was going to put me through a workout, I needed all the recovery time I could get. My body was used to the gym, not weapons training and hand-to-hand instruction.

I passed out hard on the couch to a rerun of *Golden Girls*. It was the one where Betty White's been dating a small-statured doctor and is embarrassed to bring him home to the girls, one of my favorites.

I woke to the sound of my phone going off. Reaching blindly for it on the coffee table, I didn't even bother to see who it was, still half asleep.

"No, I already know who I'm voting for," I said, still in slumber land. "Stop calling me."

"Jonny, it's me," Tracy said.

Hearing her voice woke me up faster than a bucket of ice water hitting my face. I sat bolt upright, blinking rapidly as I tried to make sense of what was going on.

"Tracy?" I asked, still coming out of my mental fog. "What's going on? Why are you doing this?"

"Jonny, I wish I could explain to you without everyone interfering," Tracy said. "We should talk."

"Uh, well no, last time we tried to talk, you were about to kidnap me and then Mrs. Grundy started cracking vampire skulls like she was about to make an omelet, or did you forget?"

"I know. I'm sorry," Tracy said, sounding like she was so flustered she might cry. "This whole transition has been so confusing for me. Then you killed Bloodstone, who was going to be my mentor, and made it so much worse."

That was just like Tracy to turn the tables and make things clearly her fault sound like my fault. Was this what Evan and my mother had seen? How could I have missed it?

"I don't know what they're doing to your mind, but this isn't you, Tracy," I said, trying to come up with a solution. "I can talk to Evan or Mrs. Grundy. Maybe they know of a way to help. We can bring you in and—"

"So you won't just come out and talk with me?" Tracy asked again, this time shifting her voice from desperate to angry.

"I'm pretty sure you're not thinking clearly right now," I told her. "If I go meet you somewhere, I feel like another black SUV is going to pull up and take me."

There was silence so long on the other end, I thought maybe she had hung up.

"I was afraid you were going to say that." Tracy sighed like she used to when they were all out of her shoe size at the most expensive outlet in town. "For what it's worth, I'm sorry, Jonny. I didn't want it to come to this."

"What are you talking about?" I asked, confused. "Come to what?"

"Jonny?" Evan's voice came through the line, exhausted and full of pain. "Jonny, don't come. Whatever they say, however they're baiting you, don't come. They're going to kill you."

"Evan?" I asked, jumping up from my sofa and beginning to pace. "Evan, what have they done to you? Are you okay?"

Panic swelled in my chest. I felt sick.

"We picked up your friend today," Victor's voice sounded on the other end of the phone. I recognized it from my dream. "Since your little Watcher warded your apartment and we can no longer come to you, I thought this would be the next best thing."

The blood in my veins ran dry. Panic turned to anger and then doubt. How was I going to get Evan back unharmed if Victor had him?

"Don't hurt him," was all I managed to say at the moment.

"It's not him I want," Victor answered. "No SOAP, no Watchers, I want you and the other hunter who took out Bloodstone's coven. You tell anyone else, he dies. Sunset at V Model Management top floor. You tell anyone else besides your fellow hunter, he dies. You don't come, he dies. You try and trick me, he dies."

"Don't come," Evan shouted from somewhere behind, Victor. "Jonny, don't—"

He was cut off by a heavy thud and a groan.

The line went dead.

FORTY-THREE

I FELT empty and without hope as I related the news to Shannon. We stood in her apartment as I felt that same feeling of defeat I did when I was younger being bullied. There was no way out that I could see now besides Shannon and I walking into a trap.

Shannon took it all in stride, her muscular arms crossed over her chest, just listening and nodding.

When I finished, I thought for sure she had finally gone off the deep end. She was just standing there smiling.

"Shannon?" I asked, confused. "I think you may not have just understood what I'm saying here. I know you don't like Evan, but—"

"No, it's not that," Shannon interrupted, waving away the idea. "John, don't you see this is good. This is our opportunity to put what we've learned to use and kill the Count."

I stared at her, blinking, wondering exactly how suicidal she was.

"We've been training for two days," I said, holding up two fingers on my right hand. "Two days, Shannon. You heard what they said. The Count is way more powerful than any vampire we've come across yet. Bloodstone almost killed me. On top of that, we don't have any more light grenades or snuf. Man, I could really go for some more snuf right about now."

"Easy, druggy," Shannon warned. "We may not have that, but we have our weapons and that axe of yours is a force to be reckoned with."

"I feel like we really should get Mrs. Grundy or Michael or even SOAP involved," I said, beginning my pacing again. "I mean, how would Victor know we contacted them? Are they watching us now? Do they have our phones tapped?"

Shannon shrugged. "I don't know, but I wouldn't risk it."

Odin walked around the corner, nearly giving me a heart attack. The hellhound grinned with his tongue falling out the side of his mouth.

Shannon didn't seem fazed.

"When did he get here?" I asked.

"A few minutes before you." Shannon shrugged. "He still shies away when I try to pet him, but he wanted to hang out, I guess. I heard him scratching at the door. He's just been in here licking himself."

My mind transitioned from the near heart attack I had from seeing Odin, back to a way to save Evan. As confident as Shannon seemed, I knew the odds of us walking out of there alive was nil. Who knew how many vampires the Count had in there.

Odin padded over to sit right in front of me. He looked at me then at the door and back at me again.

"I don't know what you want, buddy," I told the wolf dog. "Do you need to use the restroom? Do you need out?"

Odin panted and blinked at me a few times. He stared at my pocket where my cell phone sat then lowered to the floor.

He placed his paws over his head and neck area shimmying backward as if he were trying to remove the leather collar around his neck.

"What's your hellhound doing?" Shannon wondered with a raised eyebrow. "This is weird. Is he trying to take his collar off?"

"He's not my hellhound," I said, sounding like Mrs. Grundy in my own ears. "Maybe he wants his collar off?"

Odin got up, rolling his eyes, and went to the kitchen. He jumped, placing his two front paws on Shannon's counter, and picked up a pen. He came back and dropped it at my feet.

Light bulbs flashed in my mind as I realized what the hellhound was saying. "Oh, good boy, good boy, Odin," I said, reaching out to ruffle his ears.

Odin backed out of reach before I could touch him. Memories of what Mrs. Grundy said about Odin being neglected before reminded me of his emotional scars.

"Okay, we're not there yet," I said, picking up the pen.

"You can send a message to Mrs. Grundy using Odin," Shannon said, nodding in understanding. "I bet we could put it in his collar. With all the fur, if someone was watching our apartment, they wouldn't be able to tell there was a note in there."

Shannon didn't wait for me to agree or not. She opened a drawer in her kitchen and pulled out a white pad of paper.

I wrote a quick note to Mrs. Grundy, taking as much care as I could when working on my handwriting to ensure it would be legible. The note read. "The Count has Evan. Shannon and I are going after him tonight at sundown at V Model Management, top floor. He said if we bring or tell anyone else, they'll kill Evan. Please follow carefully. Also, this is John in case there's any confusion. Hope you have a great day, John Hunter."

"Let me see that," Shannon said before I had a chance to fold the letter and stick it under Odin's collar.

I was so used to texting, even that short time writing left my hand cramping. I flexed my fingers as Shannon shook her head.

"I can barely read this; seriously, your penmanship is horrible. It's like ancient Egyptian hieroglyphics." Shannon didn't look up from the note but reached for the pen in my hand. "Give me the pen and I'll make it legible."

Odin and I looked at one another. I shrugged and he licked his lips and panted. Shannon finished a moment later with her tongue sticking out the side of her mouth, a few last pen marks on the paper.

"There we go," Shannon said, folding the paper and placing it securely in Odin's collar.

It occurred to me then that was the closest the hellhound had gotten to either one of us petting him. I'm not sure what abuse the animal had endured at the hands of its previous owner, but my blood boiled just thinking about it.

Odin looked uncomfortable but managed not to run away as Shannon finished.

"All right, buddy," I addressed the hellhound, opening the door for him. "I'm not sure if you can understand me, but try not to look too obvious going to Mrs. Grundy's house. If they are watching us, they'll see you leave this apartment. Maybe do a few rounds, pee on some stuff or something."

Odin looked at me and I swore he rolled his eyes before heading out. I closed the door right behind him. My mind was already working on what needed to be done next.

I looked at the time on my phone, which I realized didn't really mean much, since I had no idea when the sun was going to set.

"We have a few hours to get ready," Shannon said,

tapping her pointer finger against her chin thoughtfully. "We should use that time to prepare."

"I like that idea, but prepare how exactly?" I asked, shaking my head. "We don't know how many vampires Victor is going to bring. We're for sure walking into a trap. They're not going to let any of us out of there alive."

Shannon stopped tapping her chin and looked over at me with a frown. "If you don't think we're going to get out of there alive, why would you go in the first place?"

"Evan's my friend," I answered matter-of-factly.

"Most people have lots of friends." Shannon shrugged.

"I don't," I responded quicker than I could think. The words just came out and I knew they were nothing but the truth.

"Tragic," Shannon said, waving me to follow her to the room I knew was filled with weapons. "Well, come on, Cinderella. We have a ball to get ready for."

I followed Shannon into her armament chamber, amazed once more of how many weapons and how much ammunition she could pack into a single room.

Guns of all shapes and sizes lined the walls with ammunition boxes on the floor in the corners. Bladed weapons were in one section, while medical supplies and the like were stationed in a glass cabinet marked with a red cross.

Shannon was already busy taking items off the walls that included her katana, body armor, and handguns. She loaded up my arms as she talked.

"The biggest thing we have going for us right now is that last time we had to be careful because we weren't sure who was human and who was a vampire. This time around, we can bring the big guns because everyone's going to be out to suck our blood."

"That's one way to look at it," I said, huffing as Shannon stacked something that looked like a shotgun on steroids into my arms. "Shannon, the only reason I told you about this is because I knew you'd be pissed if I went without you and would probably never talk to me again."

"You got that right," Shannon agreed, checking a magazine before placing it on the growing mound of death in my arms. "You did the right thing. If you tried to leave without me, I would have caught you anyway. I put a tracker on your phone."

"Haha, good one," I answered.

Shannon just blinked at me a few times.

"You're kidding, right?" I asked. "I mean, you're not really tracking my phone, are you? That's a serious invasion of privacy."

"Maybe I am and maybe I am," Shannon said without showing the slightest bit of regret. "Hey, don't look so down; it's your lucky day. I'm going to let you shoot a gun this time."

My eyes lit up like it was Christmas.

"Now you're talking," I cheered, following her into the front room where I gently laid down my arms full of boom. "I've always wanted one of the machine guns like in *Predator*. You know, keep my finger on the trigger and yell as loud as you can?"

"I think that was *Point Break,*" Shannon said, laying out the weapons in front of us in the family room. She picked up some kind of large machine gun and aimed down the sights.

"Oh nice, that's perfect for me," I said, reaching for the weapon.

"No, no, no, no," Shannon said, bringing the weapon closer to her chest. "Marly's mine. You need something a little more accident-proof. Here."

Shannon reached for a revolver and handed it to me. The weapon wasn't exactly what I was expecting. It was a behemoth as far as revolvers went, but I wanted something with a hundred round magazines or even some kind of mini-gun.

"It's not the size that counts," Shannon said, beginning to instruct me on how to use the weapon. "This is a Smith and Wesson .500 Magnum. I've designed the rounds myself to carry a little extra bang. Check the barrel."

The weapon itself was no joke; the handgun was heavy. Shannon was right. Around the barrel was some kind of added circle or mount.

"The most powerful UV light money can buy," Shannon explained. "Go ahead, give it a try."

The extra barrel around the weapon made the thing look like some kind of futuristic weapon. Next to the trigger guard, there was a switch. I flicked the thing and a beam of circular light shot out so bright, I almost blinded myself just looking at it.

"Hey, be careful where you point that thing," Shannon said, dancing out of the way. "That light's no joke. I aimed it at a piece of paper for a few seconds, and the paper heated up so much, it started burning."

I could see what she was talking about. Just moving the weapon around the room, the intense white light followed along like a laser.

"You think this'll kill a vampire?" I asked. "And what do I do after I run out of ammo?"

"That's what speed loaders are for. You should probably practice reloading on the move before we go. I'm not sure if it'll kill a vampire for sure, but I am sure that when you put the UV light and a round from that weapon in them, they're not getting up anytime soon. Especially if you hit them in the head."

"Noted," I said, feeling the excitement and the weight of the moment at once.

The rest of the afternoon was spent going over our battle

plan, practicing dry firing my weapon, reloading with the speed loader, and Shannon doing her best to let me know what I could anticipate when I fired the hand cannon.

We drilled for hours, ate, tried to rest, but we were too amped up.

In the back of my mind, I prayed Evan was still all right and that Odin had made it to Mrs. Grundy.

FORTY-FOUR

THE RIDE from Haven Apartments to V Model Management was packed with traffic like most afternoons in Los Angeles. The trunk was full of our gear, including body armor, blades, and guns.

I tried playing more Rachel Platten to lighten the mood, but Shannon wasn't having any of it.

"What was that code Michael had us repeat this morning?" Shannon asked. "The one where we said, 'send me' like some kind of cult chant."

"Something like when the night is the darkest, send me," I answered.

"When all hope seems lost," Shannon continued.

"Send me," I answered.

"When fear seeks to cripple us," Shannon said one last time in a low voice.

"Send me," I answered.

We both sat in my rumbling Mustang, quietly lost in our thoughts.

"I can't believe I'm actually going to save a member of the

supernatural race I swore to hunt down and kill," Shannon said with a sigh. "Fate has a twisted sense of humor."

"If it makes you feel better, I won't tell anyone," I answered.

We pulled into the empty V Model Management parking lot. Since the first confrontation with Bloodstone killed him and most of his staff, the place was pretty much shut down. I couldn't imagine SOAP wanted anything to do with the crime scene after a day or two. They already knew what happened. There was no mystery here.

The sun was just lowering behind the tall Los Angeles buildings. A reddish-pink hue clung to the air.

There was no real point of being discreet. It wasn't like Victor and his crew didn't know we were coming. I rolled right into the deserted parking lot and parked the Mustang.

Shannon and I both exited the vehicle in full view of the building. There was little question as to if Victor and his vampires and Tracy were watching or not. I could practically feel their eyes on me as I popped my trunk and began to gear up.

I saw Shannon turn and offer a one-finger salute to the top level of the building. She must have been feeling their eyes as well. I donned my body armor along with the high neck guards Shannon constructed.

A belt wrapped around my midsection with my new revolver, and five speed loaders full of ammunition. I had no idea if I'd get through all the rounds, but Shannon convinced me it was better to have it and not need it than need it and not have it.

I carried the axe in a sling over my shoulder. It was strange as I handled the weapon and understood more of its past. It was like I could almost feel what it was thinking. Like Blood Rage carried a spirit of its own inside. Right now, as I felt the hard wood in my hands, I felt calm and a reassurance that when it was time, the war hammer would do its job.

Shannon was loaded out much like me for armor with her red handkerchief around her throat. She carried her katana on her back. A pistol on her hip with a knife on the other side and her rifle in her hands.

"You remember the plan?" Shannon asked as we headed inside the building. "It's going to go down fast."

"We watch each other's backs," I repeated. "Get to Evan as fast as we can so we have another fighter on our side. Call out your reloads. Man, I could really use some snuf right about now."

"You and the snuf," Shannon grumbled.

We walked into the recently abandoned building. Not to our surprise, the front glass doors were unlocked. An eerie silence followed us through the lobby and to the elevators. Inside, the lights were off. Only the last rays of the dying light coated the walls and floors.

The elevators weren't working, so we were sentenced to taking the stairs to the top. We climbed the stairwell, checking and rechecking our corners. Shannon insisted I take the lead because she didn't want to accidentally get shot in the butt.

The Smith and Wesson felt good in my hands. Not as good as Blood Rage, but comforting knowing I had a way to fight back the vampires waiting for us.

"You know, I think your sister would be proud of you," I said as we climbed from the first to the second floor. The emergency lights in the stairwell were the only things to see by for the moment.

"Stop," Shannon said without even so much as a thank you.

"What?" I asked. "I'm being serious here."

"Oh, I know you are," Shannon answered. "I don't want

you to get all mushy on me because you think we're about to die."

"I'm going to live through this. I don't know about you," I retorted. "I'm being serious, though. I never got to know her, of course, but I couldn't imagine she would be anything but proud of you and what you've become."

"You still haven't signed your contract, have you?" Shannon asked after a comfortable silence. She wasn't going to interact with me about her sister. Maybe the thought was still too painful, but she heard me and that was enough.

"Nope," I answered. "I thought that if I lived through this, I may or may not. I'm still weighing my options as a sign twirler in a chicken costume."

That one actually got a chuckle out of Shannon.

We moved from floor two to three without seeing or hearing anyone. I wanted to flick on my UV light to help light the way, but that was an ace up my sleeve I wasn't prepared to share with our enemy just yet. We needed all the surprise advantages we could get.

The top floor was six stories up. It wasn't until we were moving from floor three to four we caught that light sound of someone humming.

I looked back at Shannon, who shrugged before I moved on again. The humming wasn't only eerie but bothered me in the way only a tune on the tip of your tongue could. I recognized the melody, that much was clear, but the answer as to exactly what it was, was just out of grasp.

I moved on, clearing floors four and five. I caught sight of the person humming the tune as we approached the final level.

"No need to point the weapons at me," the man said with a smile that didn't reach his eyes. "We're all friends here for the time being."

This man wasn't the Victor I knew from my dreams. This man was actually tall with short dark hair and a suit.

"The Count's expecting you," the man said, waving us forward. "You can bring your little guns with you if you want, but they're not going to do much good. What's that on your back? Gods' steel?"

The man didn't wait for a response. "Ohhh, very impressive. I'm sure you're so proud of yourself for that."

I wanted to think of a smart remark, but like so many times before, the words just failed me. I knew I'd think of the perfect comeback later that night or the next day if I lived that long.

"Who are you?" Shannon asked as we followed the man inside. He sauntered and then bobbed his head as if there was a song being played only he could hear. "And how much drugs have you done in your day?"

"Oh, I think I like you," the man said, doing a spin and snapping his fingers. "My name is Eldric. Although you're not going to be alive long enough to use it."

We walked into the center of the room where another man I did recognize stood with open arms. Count Victor Jovanovic.

He was just as I remembered in my dream. Tall with dark hair and ice blue eyes. He wore dress shoes, pants, and a shirt with a fur cloak over his shoulders. Next to him was my Tracy; no, not mine anymore. She had chosen a different path.

Tracy stood next to the Count in a red dress, makeup done like she was getting ready for a photo shoot.

"Welcome, welcome," Victor said with open arms and a smile. "I'm glad you hunters decided to come."

The room was empty besides the trio. The only light came from the moon washing in through windows. If Evan was around, I couldn't see him.

"Where is he?" I asked, biting back my fear.

"No pleasantries?" Victor asked, feigning insult. "You Americans, always so straight to the point. We are not alone."

From out of a side room, a man and a woman supported a bound Evan between them. Dried blood crossed his face where cuts were already beginning to heal thanks to his vampiric biology. His wrists were bound with two sets of handcuffs.

"Sorry, Jonny," Evan said through a split lip. "I should have seen this coming."

"So here we all are." Victor smiled at Eldric, Tracy, Shannon, and me. "We meet at a crossroads predestined for us before the beginning of time even. We were always meant to meet in this way and this is the only way it could have happened. Wondrous, isn't it? And now the illusion of two paths face us, although we know only one can ever be chosen. Join me, Tracy, and Evan in the realm of the immortal. The age of the ancient ones will come. Believe me. Sooner than you think. Be counted among us. Work to overthrow the Court and SOAP. It is they who are the real enemy."

"Jonny," Tracy said, taking a step toward me. "Jonny, we've been through a lot, you and I, and this is all very new to both of us. Will you trust me? One more time, will you give me that chance? I made mistakes, but we were good together once. We loved each other. I still love you."

It wasn't like I didn't know I was being manipulated. I could see that much clearly. However, there was still a little part of me I was beginning to hate that wanted to go back to Tracy. I understood then what kept people in abusive relationships. It was the other side promising to be better. It was fear of the unknown and being alone.

Tracy mistook my hesitancy for compliance. Shannon did the same.

"Oh, you got to be kidding me," Shannon snapped, taking a step to move in front of me. She pointed the end of her barrel at Tracy's forehead. "One more step, you skank, and I'm going to put enough lead in you you'll be too heavy to move, vampire or not."

"Is this what you want?" Tracy asked, giving Shannon a murderous stare then glancing at me. "Is she the partner you want to spend the rest of your life with? Or with me? We can have everything we ever wanted. V Model Management needs a new owner, Jonny. That can be us."

"That and so much more," Victor crooned. "We will usher in a new era. The supernatural are poised to make a resurgence in this dimension. The ancient ones are awakening. You must feel it."

"Heeees thinking about it," Eldric said in a sing-song voice with a wicked smile on his thin lips. "Wheels are a-turning."

"What do you think, Jonny?" Tracy asked. She moved around Shannon and ran a hand down my cheek. "Come be with me again."

"I think that my whole life I've been beaten down," I responded slowly, straining every word. "I think I've been used and manipulated since high school and maybe even further back. I think right now I'm tired of being used. I think right now someone's asking me that all hope is lost and who will go."

Victor, Eldric, and Tracy all looked to one another, a bit confused. Even Evan wore a frown. Shannon was the only one with a wide grin.

"Send me," Shannon answered.

"Give us Evan like you said you would," I told Victor. "Or I'm going to start unloading and I'm not even kidding when I say I'm not qualified to use this gun. Who knows what's going to happen."

"So sad," Victor growled between gritted teeth. He actually thought I was going to join him. "Eldric, kill them both."

"He's a sorcerer!" Evan shouted and tried to lunge forward. His captors restrained him, dealing several blows to his head and stomach.

"I was hoping we'd be able to dance tonight," Eldric said, cracking his knuckles. "Let's party, shall we?"

FORTY-FIVE

EVAN'S SHOUT was enough for me, and apparently, Shannon to aim our weapons at Eldric as he began to twist his hands into a series of patterns. Dark blue energy wafted from his palms.

Shannon opened fire on him with her rifle, sending a burst of rounds in his direction. Her rifle sounded like a fireworks of sharp cracks that sent my ears ringing.

I leveled my revolver and squeezed, not pulled the trigger like Shannon taught me. Holy bananas, I was ready for the recoil, but it was still a shock to my entire body. It was as if the weapon wanted to break my wrist. My whole body rocked backward, even with both hands around the handle. My palms felt numb.

The Smith and Wesson was more like a massive boom than the cracking sounds coming from Shannon's rifle. I squeezed the trigger three more times in quick succession, my ears hating every stroke of the trigger.

Before I could see what was left of Eldric, I caught motion from my left. Tracy, who had stepped back, now rushed forward, making a beeline for Shannon.

Shannon saw the same thing I did. She managed to pivot to her left and fired off a round before Tracy barreled into her.

Both women went to the floor. I aimed my revolver down on the back of Tracy's head.

Can you do this? I asked myself. *Are you really going to put a bullet in the back of your ex-fiancée's skull?*

Before another thought could enter my mind, what felt like cold hands gripped my wrists. I looked down to see what looked like blue wafting smoke of some kind circling my wrists.

I followed the coils of smoke back to Eldric. The magic or energy or whatever he was channeling came from his palms. The rounds Shannon and I fired at him stuck in the air in front of him as if an invisible wall kept them in place, impeding their forward progress.

Grunting, I tried to force my hands up and get another shot at the sorcerer. Nothing. My hands were secured to my sides. Already a numb, tingling sensation ran down my palms as circulation was cut off.

I lost hold of the revolver. It clattered to the ground as I was forced to look at Eldric. I could hear Shannon and Tracy really going at it behind me. There was nothing I could do in that moment.

Eldric gave me a smug smile I wanted to punch right off his stupid face. He manipulated my bonds, forcing me to my knees.

The war hammer in my back was warm. I could feel the heat, even through the Kevlar I wore. It was ready. If only I could get to it now.

"This all just seems so silly." Victor sighed as he walked toward me. His pointer finger transformed to a large black talon in front of my eyes. "You could have been my informant to the Court. You could have been my inside man and had it all. Your own company, your own coven, the woman of your dreams even."

A third bluish smoky tendril came out of Eldric's palms and wrapped around my throat. The cold hold cut off all but a raspy gasp of oxygen every other breath, just enough to make me panic but remain coherent.

"I'm going to make you suffer before you go," Victor said, kneeling beside me. He brought his black talon inches from my eye. "I'm going to take your eyes, then your—"

A snarling mass of black fur rocketed into the room like a freight train of claws and teeth. Odin showed up out of nowhere, streaking straight for Victor.

My mind couldn't process the events unfolding fast enough. Victor moved three, maybe four times faster than any human. Odin lunged for him, flying over the blue bonds keeping me in check.

Victor caught the hellhound by the throat with both hands, lifting him off the ground then slamming the hellhound to the harsh wooden floor.

"No!" I croaked, trying in vain to free myself from Eldric's hold. It was no use.

I could hear Evan shout something.

Odin whimpered in pain as Victor showed off his impressive strength, lifting the massive hellhound off the floor and slamming him back down over and over again.

On the fourth impact, Victor released his hold on the hellhound and sent a boot down on his ribs. There was an audible crack as Odin's tongue lolled out the side of his mouth.

I couldn't imagine what the hellhound was going through, knowing his past. Maybe he was reliving events that haunted him even now. I felt anger, I felt rage, I felt heat coming from the weapon on my back as well as the brand on my chest.

"Rawww!" I was a man possessed. I heard myself make

the roar, but it didn't sound like me. It sounded like some kind of animal. Using every ounce of strength in my arms, I slowly began raising them from their forced places at my sides.

Eldric looked at me, confused, and then at Victor. He pressed his hands forward, sending more of the black and blue swirling energy in my direction.

I saw the ghost of my own pasts. I saw the bullying. I saw Odin gasping for breath. I heard Evan and Shannon crying out.

Inch by inch, my shaking hands reached for Blood Rage at my back.

"How is he stronger than you?" Victor asked, still seeming somewhat amused and not worried in the slightest. "I thought you were the best, Eldric? Why am I paying you so much if you can't even restrain a human?"

He said that last part like it was an insult.

Eldric, on his end, didn't respond. Instead of arguing, he gritted his teeth and leaned in.

My right hand reached behind my shoulder and grasped the handle of the war hammer. It didn't matter that I couldn't breathe. When I touched the weapon, a sense of peace hit me that everything was going to be okay.

As soon as I brought the weapon out, the magical holds on my wrists and neck dissolved and struck the war hammer instead. The blade on the weapon shone red as well as the runes on the handle.

Eldric's dark blue energy cracked and snapped against the red blade as Blood Rage shielded me from the attack. I couldn't help but think of when the Sith in Star Wars used their lightning attack, only to be held at bay by the light sabers of the Jedi.

I struggled to my feet, keeping a hold on the weapon in front of me and a confused Eldric at bay. The icy cold grip around my wrists and throat was gone, but the pressure against Blood Rage threatened to rip the weapon from my hands.

"Impressive," Victor said with that sure smile of his. "But you're still a human."

Victor came over and hit me in the face so hard, I thought for sure I'd lose consciousness. He hit me twice and I fell to my knees. Pain exploded in my skull, and my vision blurred.

There wasn't much I could do in the form of defense. Eldric pressed his attack as well. If I lost hold of my weapon or swung it toward Victor, I'd leave myself open for Eldric.

"What is he?" Eldric asked past his grunts.

"It doesn't matter," Victor said, smashing another fist into my face that left a sheet of blood covering my vision. "He's dead now."

I knew I was about to die. I wasn't sure how I had held on to my conscious state this long.

"Rawww!" Victor let out a scream.

Odin had dragged himself across the floor close enough to get a mouthful of Victor's left ankle. The hellhound bit deep. Blood poured from his jaws.

"No!" I screamed as Victor reached back a handful of talons to end the hellhound.

His hand descended in slow motion but never reached the injured hellhound. Instead, a voice drew all of our attention.

"Victor!" Michael's familiar voice shouted in a challenge. "Victor!"

Everyone in the room looked over to see the owner of Halo Bouquet in the doorway with a long blade in his hand. A brown eye patch covered his left eye. His blond hair was pulled back in a ponytail.

Mrs. Grundy walked out from behind the large man, her two other hellhounds, Warden and Cerberus, with her.

Eldric immediately cut off his attack, focusing now on the

newcomers. Victor did the same. With a painful grunt, he tore his leg free from Odin's mouth, leaving a trail of meat and blood.

I dragged myself through a mixture of my own blood, Victor's, and Odin's, to be by the hellhound's side. Odin whimpered as I drew near, slapping his large black tail on the floor a few times.

"Easy, buddy, easy, buddy. I'm here, I'm here. You're not alone," I said, stroking the animal's cheek and jawline.

"Michael," Victor said, still seemingly not worried about the arrival of the two Watchers. "I heard you retired. Something about flowers and weddings?"

"I'm making an exception for you," Michael said, not willing to play Victor's games. "Tonight, I put you in the ground forever."

"Like your wife?" Victor asked with a laugh. "Sorry, that was low. Perhaps uncalled for. I heard she squealed when they took her."

"They didn't take her; she died," Michael ground out through gritted teeth. He lowered his stance and lifted his weapon in a two-handed hold, ready to charge. "Don't let her name leave your mouth, vampire. She deserves better than that now, even in death."

"Oh, you think she's dead?" Victor laughed like the maniac he was. "You really do, don't you? She's not dead, Michael. She was taken and her mind tortured."

The calm flower shop owner I had come to know was gone. Michael's entire body shook with rage. He was past words now. Michael moved so fast, it was difficult for my eyes to track.

I saw Eldric raise his hands as if he were going to try and blast Michael. A beam of bluish-black energy shot from off Eldric's hands but never made it to Michael. Mrs. Grundy stepped in the way with a wave of her own hand that dispelled the attack.

"That's not going to happen, son," Mrs. Grundy said as if she knew the man. "I failed you. I should have taught you better. I'm so sorry."

"I don't need your pity, Mother," Eldric scoffed, raising his hands as blue energy formed in each palm. "I'm more powerful than you now. I'll show you."

FORTY-SIX

MY MIND WAS BEING BLOWN at the moment. If Victor could be believed, then Michael's wife was alive and Eldric wasn't your run-of-the-mill sorcerer. He was Mrs. Gundy's son.

I wanted to ask a dozen questions and watch both fights unfold at once with a bucket of popcorn with extra butter. There was no time. With both Victor and Eldric busy, I was finally free to look at Shannon and Tracy.

Shannon seemed like she was able to hold her own for the time being. She was on her feet, katana in hand, bleeding from a cut above her hairline and a bruised left cheek, but still able to fight.

I looked over at Evan. He had been struggling against his captors, but handcuffed with two of them to hold him down and beat him, there wasn't a chance. Right now, Evan was on the floor being used as a doormat by the two vampires over him.

"I have to go," I told the hellhound in my hands. "Odin, I don't know if you can understand me, but thank you. I have to go help a friend. I'll be back."

Odin whimpered something. Warden and Cerberus

skidded to a halt beside me, the former nuzzling Odin with a whine, the latter gently pushing me off as if to tell me it was okay, Odin wouldn't be alone.

I struggled to my feet, getting a better grip on Blood Rage. The blade shone bright from the sharpened crescent moon blade on one side to the sledgehammer head on the other.

The idea of sneaking up and impaling one of the vampires over Evan seemed less than honorable, but I was playing with the hand I was dealt. I moved forward, bringing the war hammer up and around behind me in a full circle as I ran.

Michael had shown me how to leverage the war hammer and the way to swing the weapon to get my full weight behind the impact. Either the vampires didn't see me approach because they were too busy playing hacky sack with Evan's head, I was actually faster than I thought, or a combination of both. In a matter of seconds, I was on my feet, crossing the distance, ready to take on the pair of vampires.

I brought Blood Rage back in a perfect arc. The weapon landed dead center in the skull of the female vampire with her back toward me. The red axe blade bit so deep, it nearly severed her skull in two.

The impact of the weapon sent tremors down my arms and into the rest of my body. Blood Rage seemed hungry; it glowed brighter on contact.

The vampire in front of me quivered before she dropped as if her body was still realizing it was dead.

Finally, the vampire slumped to the ground. The remaining vampire, Evan, and I all looked at one another.

"I don't think she's walking that one off," Evan croaked.

The last vampire's eyes transitioned to black. His fingernails lengthened as he pounced. I had enough time to rip Blood Rage free but not enough time to attempt another attack. I was tackled so violently to the floor, my teeth chattered.

The vampire landed on top of me, unhinging his jaw to take a bite out of my neck. Blood Rage acted as a barrier between us. I pushed up on the weapon, trying to keep the supernatural creature at bay.

I was beyond exhausted from the night's events, my own blood loss, and the training I endured the previous days. I felt the vampire pressing down on me, slowly bringing the war hammer against my chest.

The smile on the vampire's face faded as Evan appeared behind him, placing his still handcuffed wrists over the vampire's head and neck and pulling back violently.

The vampire was dragged off, allowing me to regain my feet. Evan, for his troubles, received an elbow in the stomach and then the vampire hurled him off. Evan crashed to the floor in a heap.

The war raged around me as Mrs. Grundy battled her son, Tracy and Shannon squared off, and Victor took on a pissed-off flower shop owner.

I rushed in, this time ready. The vampire swiped at my face with his right claw. I ducked, bringing the sledgehammer end of my war hammer down on his knee cap. The vampire howled in pain as his knee was shattered. He fell to a single knee, about to curse me before I brought the war hammer back around in a full circle and connected with his jaw.

His face reminded me of watching a boxer get punched in super slow motion, except in his case, it didn't go back to normal after the hit. The vampire collapsed, unconscious. I brought the axe high overhead, blade down to decapitate the vampire before it could think to try and get back up.

Blood Rage whistled through the air as if it approved of the last action.

"Wow, where did you get that thing again?" Evan asked, struggling to his feet. "Do you need a permit for that or something?"

"Or something," I said, motioning to his wrists.

"Oh right." Evan stood and pressed his arms against the wall.

I set up the swing perfectly and severed the chains connecting his two metal cuffs.

"Nice hit," Evan said, shaking his hands free. He looked at the battle raging around us. Out of the three fights, Shannon now seemed to be faring the worst. Two more cuts had been opened on her shoulder and another on her neck. She was slowing and breathing heavy.

Tracy circled her like a predator waiting for its prey to tire a bit further and go in for the kill.

"Are you thinking what I'm thinking?" Evan asked.

"Sure, but where are we going to get enough snuf and C4 to do that?" I asked. "I mean, at this hour especially."

"What? No," Evan said, shaking his head. "It's time to finally get our payback on the demon seed of Satan."

I looked over at where Tracy and Shannon squared off again. I wasn't sure if I could kill Tracy; in fact, I was pretty sure I wasn't going to be able to kill her. However, I was equally sure that I wasn't going to let anything happen to Shannon.

Evan and I ran forward to help.

Unlike my previous blindside attack, Tracy saw us coming. Her pitch-black eyes, elongated teeth, and black nails showed me what she really was now and just how much she had embraced the idea.

"Don't make us do this," I told Tracy. "I don't want to kill you."

"No, please try something dumb," Evan goaded her. "I really would like to kill you."

Shannon was breathing hard, resting on her katana. Right now, the blade was pointed in the floor as she leaned on the handle.

I made my way over to her, never letting my eyes leave Tracy.

"You okay, partner?" I asked her.

"Oh yeah, just great. Might watch some Netflix and grab some Matty Too Fatty's later tonight. You?"

"So this is what you really want?" Tracy asked, looking at Shannon with disgust. "You traded me in for a girlfriend hillbilly with a samurai sword?"

"You would make this about you." I sighed, shaking my head. "Shannon's my—my partner, not like a life partner; just my friend. You broke us up. You chose all of this."

There was a sound like thunder so loud, it caused us all to look. I turned my head just in time to see Eldric vanish in a thunder clap of black and blue smoke. At the same time, a scream left Victor's lungs as Michael pinned him to the floor with his sword.

I saw her go. Maybe I could have stopped her. Maybe I could have shouted a warning for someone to grab her. Mrs. Grundy was probably fast enough or Evan.

At the same time, I understood and hated myself as Tracy took the opportunity to slip away toward the exit. I caught her eye; at least, I think I did. All black with no pupil or iris to speak of, it was difficult to tell.

Then she was gone.

"Hey, Tracy... Where did she go!" Shannon asked, snapping back to our present situation.

"She must have slipped out the fire escape," Evan said, looking at me and then toward the door. "We might be able to catch her."

"I don't think I'd be able to catch an armadillo right now," I answered, not lying in the slightest. "I'm beat."

Evan held my stare, opened his mouth, and then closed it again. "All right."

I knew it. He knew it. Tracy was one of the bad ones. The

Court had no empathy that I'd seen thus far for vampires behaving badly. She'd be killed. While I wanted to stop her, I knew I couldn't let that happen.

Maybe there was something wrong with me, or I was wrong for not wanting to kill Tracy, but she was different.

"Is that all of them, then?" Shannon asked, using my shoulder to lean on. "Did we get them all?"

"All but one," I said as Michael twisted his sword blade into Victor.

Another scream of pain lifted toward the ceiling, only to die into groans a moment later. I aided a hobbling Shannon over to the grisly sight. Mrs. Grundy met us there.

Michael had pinned Victor to the floor with his blade. The sword went into Victor's left pectoral, right under his shoulder, halfway to the hilt. Victor coughed up blood. The red fluid contrasted dramatically across his pale skin. The bluish-grey light of the moon sent its rays into the top floor of V Model Management, illuminating our surroundings.

"Tell me you lie," Michael demanded, pressing a booted foot into Victor's chest. Both hands on the hilt of his sword, he twisted. "She died that day. You are a liar."

"Am I?" Victor wheezed. "Then why am I still alive? Yes, she fell that day, but she didn't die. You didn't think there was anything left to bury, but there was. He brought her back. He brought Ja—"

Michael ripped out the sword from Victor's body in one single motion then stabbed him through the opposite side of his chest.

"I told you not to use her name, filth!" Michael shouted amidst a torrent of tears seeping from his eyes. His voice cracked. "You don't get to say her name. Do you understand me? You don't get to say her name!"

Mrs. Grundy put a hand on Michael's shoulder. She didn't pull him back or offer words. She just placed her weathered, wrinkled hand on him to let him know she was there.

Victor coughed and howled in pain once more. I wish I could say I felt sorry for the man. Should I? Should I try and stop this? Michael was torturing Victor after all. Was this what the Court was about? Did I want to be part of this?

"I was there, at the battle of the Morning Star," Michael screamed at Victor. Tears splashed freely down his face. If he was embarrassed to cry in front of us, he showed no sign. "I saw her burned alive! I held what was left of her to my chest. Her bones burned me. I feel that same burning every time I think of her. Every day of my life since."

"But she's not," Victor rasped. "Yes, she was burned, but the bones you found belonged to someone else. She was taken by him, tortured, twisted, and now she serves another."

I looked at Michael, not knowing what to say or do. Michael looked like he was in a trance. He stood there blinking as if he were caught in some kind of mental stasis.

"Where is she?" Mrs. Grundy asked for him. "If what you say is true, then where is she?"

"Wouldn't you like to know?" Victor spewed a laugh that was cut short from more coughing and blood coming from his lips. "She is out of your reach."

I knew what Michael was going to do even before he lifted the blade free of Victor's body. Michael ripped the weapon upward in a move that came with a wet sloshing sound as it exited Victor's body.

Michael's eye was alive with righteous indignation. For a moment, he seemed ten feet tall with a wild mane of blonde hair and the face of fury itself.

"Stop, maybe he can help," I shouted. "Maybe he can tell you where your wife really is. You're supposed to be one of the good guys."

Michael turned his head toward me. I wanted to shrink and wither under his stare, but I refused and stood my ground instead.

"I'm a Watcher, not a saint," Michael spat, returning to his victim. He slammed the pointed end of his sword lengthwise across Victor's exposed throat. The blade nearly chopped off the entire head of the vampire. Michael rocked it from side to side as he withdrew the edge, making sure the head was completely severed from the neck.

Blood pumped from the wound, painting the ground red.

Count Victor Jovanovic was no more.

A bark reminded me of our one ally that hadn't fared so well. I pivoted, rushing over to Odin and dropping to my knees. Warden and Cerberus whined sadly.

"Hey, hey, we're back," I said, ruffling the black dog's ears. "Mrs. Grundy, do you think you can heal him. Odin? Odin?"

The large hellhound wasn't moving. I tried rolling his big head into my lap. There was no sign of life, not even a slight rise and fall of his chest.

I felt empty inside. I felt anger, glad Michael had killed Victor. I remembered Odin coming in to try and save me. He was dead because he was willing to put his life on the line for me.

"Oh, buddy," I murmured, clenching my jaw. I felt my eyes burn with the promise of tears. "You came for me. You came to save me. Thank you. I'm so sorry I couldn't save you."

I sat on my knees, rocking the wolf dog.

Mrs. Grundy coughed into her hand.

Evan cleared his throat.

Everyone minus Michael stared at me.

"Will you have some respect?" I asked, swallowing hard. "He's dead. Odin's dead."

"I hate to be the one to break this to you, Jonny, but hellhounds are already dead," Evan said, coming over and patting me on the shoulders. "They were dogs that came back. It's not like they can be doubly dead or killed again."

I blinked back tears, trying to understand what Evan was saying. I felt Odin move in my arms. The big black wolf dog inhaled sharply then blinked open yellow eyes and got to his feet.

Cerberus and Warden growled and howled, happy to see the third member of their pack moving once more.

"You're okay?" I asked hesitantly. "Odin, you're okay?"

Odin shook himself from head to tail as if he were waking up from a deep sleep. He yawned and then went to town sniffing the room.

"I think he's going to be okay," Shannon said. "I think we're all going to be okay."

FORTY-SEVEN

AFTER THE EVENTS of that night, Mrs. Grundy called in SOAP to clean up our mess. As you can imagine, they were super pissed. I can't say that I blamed them either. Mrs. Grundy, on the other hand, seemed to enjoy making the call.

I was beginning to see how the Court dealt with SOAP and why the relationship was so stressed. I would probably hate the Watchers too if I was always cleaning up after them.

While we waited for SOAP to arrive on scene, I had a moment to talk to Mrs. Grundy alone. Shannon was receiving help from Evan binding her wounds, which was ironic, since they had both caused each other harm just nights before. Michael moved to a window overlooking the city as he cleaned his weapon. The brooding man had a lot to think about and I didn't envy him his position.

"Was that Eldric guy your son, I mean, your actual son?" I asked Mrs. Grundy, deciding to do away with the small talk. "Is he a sorcerer too?"

"Yes and yes." Mrs. Grundy sighed. She went over to a sofa and patted the space next to her for me to take a seat.

"As you're beginning to see, members of the supernatural realm have our issues as well. Everyone has their own family drama, it seems. Eldric is my son. He chose a different path, as you can tell. He's a mercenary of sorts, offering his services to the highest bidder."

"Oh, I'm sorry," I said, sensing just how much hurt and pain were in Mrs. Grundy's words. "I can only imagine how that makes you feel."

"Mmm hmm," Mrs. Grundy said, beckoning to me to get a better look at my own cuts and bruises. "I'm sorry about it too, but all I can do now is hope and pray that he sees the light. I don't think anyone is past saving and that means there's still hope for my Eldric, as slim as that hope may seem at the moment."

"Ouch." I winced as Mrs. Grundy checked out a bruise on the left side of my face.

"You'll be fine. We'll get you patched up in no time."

My eyes drifted over to Michael, who stood with his back toward us, gazing out the window. His sword was clean now. Despite this fact, he continued to rub it down and polish it in the light of the moon.

"I feel so bad for him," I said to Mrs. Grundy. "Do you think what Victor said is true? Do you think Michael's wife is still alive?"

"The world we live in is stranger than fiction," Mrs. Grundy answered. "All I know is that if she is still alive, Michael will find her."

I wasn't sure if this was the right time to ask Mrs. Grundy, but I figured it was as good a time as ever.

"Why did you give me her war hammer?" I asked. "I mean, you sent me Michael's wife's weapon knowing it was hers."

"Blood Rage hasn't been used since the old times because

it didn't have an owner it would answer to." Mrs. Grundy shrugged. "When I met you. I knew you were the one. Call it intuition, discernment, or something else, but it just felt right, John Hunter. It felt right for you to carry it next. Maybe that's what this was all leading us to? This moment where Michael could find out his wife was alive."

I nodded along with Mrs. Grundy's words, wondering how much I really understood and how much she still wasn't telling me.

"You should go talk to him," Mrs. Grundy said, nodding over to Michael. "He could use a friend. Friends aren't really something he has many of these days."

"Are you sure?" I asked, indecisive. "I think he might want to be left alone."

"Oh, of course he wants to be left alone," Mrs. Grundy said with a knowing smile. "But what one wants isn't always what one needs, now is it?"

I had to give her that much as I thought about Tracy and my own actions in letting her slip through my fingers.

I rose from my seat and headed over to Michael. The broad-shouldered man saw me coming in the reflection of the glass. His cheeks were still.

"I don't know what to say," I said honestly. "Thank you for coming to help us. I know you don't want to fight anymore. If there's anything I can do to help you find the truth about your wife, anything. I know I'm just a human hunter, but I will. You just have to ask."

Michael just stood there with his back toward me. I couldn't tell through the reflection if he was looking at me or not. I stood there wondering if I should have said something different, something more comforting.

I was about to interpret his silence as wanting to be alone, when he finally spoke.

"You know she loved to fly?" Michael said so quietly, I almost missed it. "She was a force to be reckoned with, yes, but there was so much more to her. What if Victor was telling the truth? What if she's needed me out there all this time and I've been cutting rose stems thinking she was dead?"

"Then we'll find her," I asserted. "I don't know how but we will. We'll figure this out. You can't dwell on the past and the what ifs and maybes that's all out of our control and behind us now. Right now we can take action and find the truth."

Michael slowly turned toward me. He stared into my eyes so deeply, I thought he was going to bore a hole right through me.

"I see why Mrs. Grundy knew Blood Rage would activate in your hands, John Hunter," Michael said. "Thank you. If I have need of your assistance, I will call. I'm not going to rest until I find out the truth about Jael. If she is alive, I'll find her."

"I know you will," I answered as Michael turned to go.

It was then the first sirens sounded in the distance. Mrs. Grundy took out her phone and looked at the time. "SOAP's getting slower or traffic must have been bad."

Michael left without another word. I was thinking we should get the heck out of Dodge as well, but Mrs. Grundy insisted we stay to greet SOAP and let them know what happened here.

Apparently, as much as there was a working rivalry between SOAP and the Court, there was also a mutual respect.

Agents Bentall and Lees entered the top floor of V Model Management with an entourage of agents wielding both weapons I did and didn't recognize.

Lees looked as pissed off as ever. Bentall was a bit more relaxed, as if he expected as much.

"I wish I could say it was good seeing you again," Agent Bentall said as we waited for his agents to secure the room. He looked over at the bodies and then back to us. "You know, Victor was one of the heads of the vampire sect. He wasn't just a coven leader. He could have told us a few things we needed to know if you kept him alive long enough."

"Some things can't be helped." Mrs. Grundy shrugged. "I did call you, however, and even waited for you to arrive. That must count for something."

"It does," Agent Bentall said with a playful smile on his lips. "It would have meant more if you told us the whole truth that Michael's back in action."

If Mrs. Grundy was surprised to learn that SOAP knew about Michael's involvement, she didn't show it. One thing was for sure, Mrs. Grundy would have made one heck of a poker player.

"I don't control Michael," Mrs. Grundy replied nonchalantly. "He's older than I am and has seen so much more. He goes and does what he deems fit."

"Word was he and the Court had a falling out," Agent Bentall pressed, digging for information. "Is he working on his own now or on behalf of the Court?"

"Whatever may or may not have happened between Michael and the Court is between Michael and the Court," Mrs. Grundy countered. "What's that term you and SOAP so easily throw around?"

"Confidential," I chimed in.

"That's right. Thank you, John." Mrs. Grundy looked at Agents Bentall and Lees. "That's confidential."

Lees fixed me with a stare that said we were not friends. It almost hurt my feelings.

Evan and Shannon were speaking with a few other SOAP agents, giving them the rundown on what happened. I saw Lees going over to the two vampires I had taken out with Blood Rage.

I got the feeling Mrs. Grundy and Agent Bentall needed to speak alone for the moment. I strolled over to where Lees looked down on the dead supernatural beings.

"Not too shabby, right?" I asked, deciding to try and befriend the hard-nosed agent instead of ignoring him. "I'll get better too. I just need more time to train."

"Meh, it looks sloppy." Agent Lees shrugged in his massive suit jacket. He pointed at the first vampire I had ambushed. "This one looks like it was taken out with a cheap shot from behind. The other one has a mark around his throat like someone choked him with something. Humans aren't strong enough to choke a vampire, so it looks like you had help with this one. Mediocre at best."

"What?" I asked, actually offended. "First off, how did you read all of that from this scene? Second of all, I am highly offended you called this mediocre. Third of all, I want my Girl Scout cookies back."

"Can't, already ate them." Agent Lees patted his stomach, while still looking down at the bodies in front of us. "I'm also going to send you my dry-cleaning bill."

"You ate the entire box already?" I asked incredulously. I intentionally ignored the dry-cleaning comment. "I'm not even mad; that's impressive."

"Ate both of them, actually," Agent Lees said. "I did a better job on those boxes than you did on these vampires."

"Well, joke's on you. Those cookies are packed with empty calories and artificial ingredients," I said, placing my hands on my hips. "Someone's going to have love handles in the morning."

"I don't have love handles," Agent Lees said, finally looking at me with a scowl.

"But don't you?" I asked, backtracking in case I pissed him off a little too much. "But don't you?"

I turned but not before I saw Agent Lees' enormous hands go to his sides and start feeling his hips when he thought I wasn't looking.

FORTY-EIGHT

THAT NIGHT, I stumbled into bed feeling like one massive bruise. Evan kept thanking me for what I had done, but I didn't really think I was the hero he was making me out to be. There was just something that needed to be done and I did it. I slept like a baby, free of the cage of my past.

The next morning, I woke to a series of huffs and impatient pants. Pulled from a dream I couldn't remember, I woke to Odin's familiar yellow eyes in my face.

I wasn't sure how the hellhound had gotten in. To my memory, he wasn't inside last night. I really needed to do some in-depth research on how hellhounds worked. So far, I knew they couldn't be killed and somehow they could get into places that were locked up tight.

"Okay, okay, I'm up, I'm up," I lied, rolling over in bed. My body ached at that simple action. Cuts crossed my face and bruises over my whole body reminded me the cost of what being a hunter really meant. On the nightstand next to my bed, my phone lit up like a Christmas tree.

There were messages from Mrs. Grundy, Shannon, and to my surprise, Michael. Shannon was inviting us all over for breakfast. Shockingly, even Evan was on the text. Mrs. Grundy was wondering how we were feeling and Michael announced training would resume in two days' time after he got back from an out-of-town appointment.

There was a gentle knock on my door.

"Come in," I called to the closed door.

"Are you decent?" Evan asked from the other side. "I've been through enough lately. I don't need to undergo retinal scarring on top of it all."

"Please." I snickered. "You're usually the one gallivanting around in that robe of yours with whatever model you're dating at the time."

"It is a kimono," Evan corrected, opening the door wearing said kimono. "From Japan, no less. Please have some respect."

I couldn't take him seriously as I laughed and rose from bed.

Evan gave off a good-natured chuckle, looking over at Odin with a frown. "How'd Cujo get in? I didn't let him in."

"I don't know." I headed for the restroom to relieve myself and brush my teeth. "That's a Grundy question."

"You get the text about breakfast at Shannon's this morning?" Evan inquired through the closed bathroom door.

"Yep, you going?" I asked.

"I don't know. It's kinda weirding me out," Evan said. "What if this is all some kind of ruse to kill me by putting garlic in my omelet?"

"I thought you said garlic doesn't affect you," I answered, going over to the mirror, washing my face, and not really fixing my hair; just making sure it wasn't absolutely out of control. "Besides, I don't think she's going to kill you. She's had plenty of opportunities thus far."

"I'm just kidding about the garlic," Evan replied. "But you know what? You're right. I think I'm starting to make some headway with our female hunter friend. She might not be so eager to drive a stake through my heart now."

"Or chop your head off with her katana," I added around a mouthful of suds as I brushed my teeth. "Maybe this is the olive branch. It can't be easy for her after what happened to her sister. This is some real headway to healing for her."

I opened the door to the bathroom to see Evan with a thoughtful expression on his face.

"What's that look?" I asked. "Are you about to get emotional?"

"You're the emotional one, for the record, and no," Evan said with a sigh. "I've just been doing a lot of thinking about —well, I'll tell you at breakfast. Let me go throw on some clothes."

Evan exited my room, leaving me to put on my jeans, Converse, and a plain black shirt. Odin seemed content to wait for me as I dressed. I met Evan at the front door a few minutes later. He was wearing slacks and a button-up dress shirt as if he were going to a meeting. There was a briefcase in his right hand.

"You planning to put on a presentation at breakfast?" I asked him. "I already tried selling Mary Kay. That is like a cult, by the way. I don't know if everyone there is drinking the Fresca or it was just my area manager, but they were promising me everything from vacations to cars. After a year, I was given a cup."

"Nope, no Mary Kay today, my good man," Evan said, waggling his eyebrows. "This is something else. Come on; I'll tell you all at breakfast."

Odin and I followed Evan out the door and down to Shannon's apartment. I was about to knock when Mrs. Grundy's voice greeted me with a "Come in."

"How does she do that?" I muttered as I stepped into the apartment.

"Anyway, that was the second time I was thrown in jail for trespassing," Shannon said.

"We've all been there, dear," Mrs. Grundy answered before sipping a steaming cup of coffee.

Shannon worked in the kitchen, flipping pancakes, scrambling eggs, and turning sausage on her stove. Mrs. Grundy sat at the kitchen island as content as ever.

"Good morning, ladies," Evan said with a smile.

"Good morning, Evan, John, Odin," Mrs. Grundy returned his greeting.

"Stinky, Bloodsucker, thanks for coming," Shannon said, looking up from her work in the kitchen.

"Still with the Bloodsucker, huh?" Evan asked.

"Don't push it." Shannon gave Evan a raised eyebrow. "I'm still coming to grips with you actually being in my apartment. And why are you dressed like you're going to try and convert me to your cult?"

"I'll behave," Evan promised, taking a seat next to Mrs. Grundy. "Once everyone is settled, I have a bit of a business proposition for all of you."

"Speaking of business, John," Mrs. Grundy said to me from her barstool seat. "You haven't signed your contract with the Court. No pressure, but until you do, we can't pay you. There's another four thousand coming your way after last night."

"Right, I have it here," I said, pulling the folded contract out of my back pocket I'd stuffed there before we left for breakfast. The paper was stained, wrinkled, and torn in a few places from me always carrying it around, reading and rereading sections.

Maybe I was making a bigger deal about the contract than I should, but it was a big deal to me. To me, it represented more than a new job. It meant that I was for the first time in my life going to be the one protecting the weak. I'd been the victim throughout my whole life, whether it was bullying, relationships where I was used, or a pawn in someone else's business campaign.

Signing the contract meant I was done with those things. To me, it meant I was willing to put myself in harm's way to help those who would be victims.

"It's a calling," Mrs. Grundy said, reading my hesitancy. "You're not wrong to be so reluctant."

"Breakfast will be ready in a few minutes," Shannon said, handing Evan and me each a cup of coffee. She gave me a pen along with my cup. "Come on, partner. I'll do this by myself if I have to, but you're a good meat shield to throw in the way."

I looked up from my contract to see the smile on Shannon's face. She was still limping a bit from her fight with Tracy the night before. There was a bandage on her neck and fresh cuts on her face.

"I don't think I could go back to my old job now that I know the truth," I admitted, putting my coffee down on the kitchen island. I flipped to the back of the contract and used Shannon's pen to sign my name.

"Oh, thank the lort." Mrs. Grundy gave off a long, relieved sigh. "Given all you know and all you've seen, I was going to have to kill you if you refused to sign now."

I looked up with a smile and laugh on my lips.

Mrs. Grundy stared back deadpan.

"Wait, you're kidding, right?" I blurted, wide-eyed. "You're joking. That was a joke. Tell me you weren't going to kill me."

Mrs. Grundy just took a sip out of her coffee cup.

"Well, now that we officially have two hunters signed with the Court, I would like to take this time to make my presentation," Evan said, opening his briefcase and handing all three of us identical folders.

As much as the smell of sausage and coffee worked up my appetite, I was actually eager to see what Evan had been hinting at all morning. I looked down on my dark grey folder that had three words written on the cover: *Hunters for Hire*.

"Going forward, I know you two are going to be busy working on cases for both the Court and other business that comes your way," Evan said, talking with his hands and making eye contact with each of us. "I was planning on opening my own modeling agency, but then I started to wonder what it would mean to open a business that employed hunters who could do some real good for the supernatural community."

"You want to be our boss?" Shannon asked with a raised eyebrow. "Because, Bloodsucker, I can tell you right now that's not happening."

"Nope, nope, not boss," Evan corrected. "If you'll open your binders to page two, you'll see a partnership plan laid out for the three of us to work together as equal members in the company."

I followed along with Evan's directions, turning the pages. There was a cool logo of the face of a wolf that kind of looked like Odin and the brand on my chest. Paragraphs and bullet points of a well-thought-out business plan and partnership filled the document.

"I can handle things like finances, finding us an office to work out of, contracts and such while the two of you focus on training and hunting." Evan looked at Mrs. Grundy. "I wouldn't really be a member of the hunting team or member of the Court; just a business partner."

"I understand and don't see an issue with it," Mrs. Grundy said. "You wouldn't be doing any of the hunting yourself?"

"Have you seen this face? It's made for business deals and reassuring clients," Evan said. "I'm more likely to use heavenly facial creams from Paris than have fists slammed into it."

"Understood," Mrs. Grundy said with a nod. She looked at the two of us. "If this is what you two want, I don't see the Court having issue."

"Hunters for Hire, huh?" Shannon asked. "I kinda like it. Stinky?"

"If we are going to go down this path with the Court, then I'd want to do it with the two of you," I said, looking toward Shannon and Evan. "I think the three of us are going to make a great team."

Odin, who had been sniffing for sausage up to this point, barked.

"The four of us," I corrected myself, reaching down to ruffle the hellhound's ears out of instinct. "The four of us are going to make a great team."

For the first time since I knew the animal, he didn't pull away when I touched him.

EPILOGUE

"I DON'T KNOW! I told you, I don't—"

I shoved his head back into the dirty sink of water. He splashed and flailed in vain as I held him there. I didn't feel sorry for him.

Besides, I knew I didn't have much longer. Already the other regulars at the bar were starting to take notice. I walked in like I owned the place, heading straight for him. From there, it was easy enough to grab him, throw him over the bar top, and fill the sink with water.

The bar on the edge of the city wasn't hard to find. The place was rundown and a locals only kind of place, save for the roving biker pack that frequented it. Inside, it was dark and smelled like piss and cigarette smoke.

The werewolf I held under the water was one I'd known before to be a less than upstanding member of the supernatural kind. The only reason I wasn't attacked by the rest of his pack now was my reputation. Right now, it held them at bay, but for how long was yet to be seen.

"Feel like talking?" I asked, ripping the werewolf in

human form up from the water. "Next time, you stay in for a full minute. Where is she?"

"Wait, okay, just wait a minute," the man pleaded, sputtering and coughing up rancid sink water. "Give me a second to breathe."

Locals in the place who didn't know what was going on fled. Others who were members of the supernatural started to surround me, reaching for weapons both from this world and other worlds.

I kept my focus on the informant in front of me. If anyone had information about what had happened to my wife, it would be Treg. The werewolf knew everything that went on in the supernatural world. If an elf so much as sneezed, he'd be the first to tell the orcs for the right amount of cash.

"Let him go," the bartender demanded, lifting a shotgun to the right side of my head. "I'm not going to tell you again, you one-eyed freak. Let him go."

He was younger and human, probably some poor soul the owner found who was cheap labor. The kid was only doing his job. I might have done the same in his shoes.

Other members of Treg's pack, seeing that I was at gunpoint, unholstered their firearms and surrounded me. No one wanted them to turn. A werewolf turning in front of humans would be sure to incite news headlines and gain the attention of both SOAP and the Court. Since I wasn't on official Court business, I didn't want that either.

"You don't know what's going on here," I told the kid holding the shotgun to my head. "I don't want to hurt you. Put the gun down and mind your own business."

"I can't do that," the kid said, swallowing hard as he nervously regripped the shotgun in his hands. "Now I said let him go. Last chance."

Treg waited to see what would happen next. Looking in his dark brown eyes, I could tell he knew something. He was just waiting to see if he would get off the hook thanks to the interference of this kid. I'd been around long enough to tell all the signs if someone was going to make the move to violence or not.

Without warning, I grabbed the end of the shotgun with my right hand and lifted the barrel to the ceiling.

BOOM!

The shotgun went off, sending a shower of wooden splinters down on us like spent confetti at a New Year's Eve party. I bent the barrel upward, leaving the shotgun in an L-shape as Treg ripped free, leaving his black leather jacket in my grip.

"Get him!" Treg yelled to the rest of his pack as he bounded over the bar top.

I jumped over the counter after him as weapons went off in the room with sharp cracks. The bullets bounced off me like hard rain. It didn't feel great when I was hit, but it was more of a nuisance than any real pain.

Anyone not willing to get into the fight had cleared out by this point. It was me and the Pack and Johnny Cash playing over the jukebox now.

Treg made for the door. I was prepared to go after him and ignore the attack of his pack until one of them thought it would be a good idea to step into my path. I clotheslined the werewolf so hard, I nearly broke him in half.

The other werewolves were finally understanding that bullets weren't going to put me down. Loyal to their alpha to the point of sacrificing themselves, they came at me at once.

I slammed a boot into the chest of the next one, who held a knife the length of my forearm in his hand. His feet left the ground as he flew backwards into another member of his pack.

One of the werewolves still on his feet grabbed me around the neck. Yet another threw all reason out of the window and started to make the change into his supernatural form in front of me.

I wasn't afraid to take on a pack of turned werewolves. I just didn't have the time. I grabbed the ear of the werewolf behind me and ripped it right off the side of his face. His grip immediately slackened as he howled in pain. I turned, grabbed his face, and head-butted him so hard, he lost his footing.

I turned back to the door as I heard the sound of a motorcycle revving to life.

You can't let Treg get away, I yelled at myself. *He knows where she is. He knows.*

It was just my luck the largest werewolf had just turned, ripping through his jeans, boots and leather jacket, to reveal a black werewolf who bellowed a challenge in my direction, sending flecks of spit onto my face. Bad idea to lean in and roar at me with your mouth open.

I'd been holding back the whole time. I didn't want to kill any of these guys. I wanted answers. Hearing the motorcycle outside reminded me how little time I had. I lunged forward, slamming my right fist into the creature's jaw so hard, his lupine head snapped to the right and cracked his neck.

I was past him and ran for the door. I caught a glimpse of the kid behind the bar holding his L-shaped shotgun. His mouth was open and he had pissed himself.

There was no time to stay and help talk him down. He'd need a healthy dose of medication and probably a few psychiatrists' sessions after today.

I ran out the front door to see Treg taking off down the dirt parking lot and headed for the road.

I powered everything into sprinting after him as if my life, as if her life, depended on it. For a moment, I almost changed. It was something I hadn't done in so long, I wasn't sure if I still knew how. I decided against it. I could reason with the Court this far. If I were to change and a bystander saw me, that would land me in some trouble.

My boots touched down, only to leave the ground a moment later. Arms pumping by my side, I moved to intercept Treg before he reached the main road and could really let the throttle open.

Luckily for me, he had to restrain himself a bit to make the sharp turn onto the road from the parking lot. I lunged forward in a flying tackle, laying into the motorcycle as hard as the man.

My left arm and shoulder wrapped around the handlebars, but my right arm caught Treg by the shoulders. We fell together into the asphalt on the side of the road so hard, the lights on the motorcycle shattered on impact.

"We could have done this the easy way," I said, getting to my feet with Treg in my right arm. He had the sense not to change. He knew it wouldn't matter, even if he did. There were some of us so old, we could remember when the first werewolf was created. I was one of those who could.

"Michael, Michael, you're supposed to be better than this," Treg pleaded. "What are you doing? You're supposed to be one of the good guys. This—this isn't you."

"It's not who I want to be," I told him, dragging him back to the bar parking lot by his left ankle. "But it's about who I'll become if it means finding her."

"It doesn't have to go down like this," Treg implored as I laid him in the center of the parking lot full of gravel and knelt on his chest. "I can't. Even if I knew something, I can't tell you."

I nodded, understanding what I would have to do to find her.

"I want you to look in my good eye, Treg," I said, staring down at him. "I want you to know that sooner or later I'll get my answers from you. That can be now or that can be after hours of pain. I want you to look in my eye and believe me. It's not what I want to do, but it's what I will do to find her."

Treg went pale, working his jaw up and down without a sound coming out. I made a show of reaching into my right pocket for an instrument of torture.

"Okay, wait, wait," Treg gasped as I kept my weight on his chest. "Michael, I don't know much. I don't know much, but if it ever gets back to him that I'm the one that told you, he'll torment me for a millennium."

"If you don't tell me what you know," I answered, "I'll do that to you now."

"Okay, okay." Treg swallowed hard. "I don't know if it's your wife, but word has it that there's an ancient one making the return to our realm. He has followers and one of them is a member of your species. A woman who's as old as you."

I blinked a few times, taking in what this could mean. When you're as old as I am, you get to be good at discerning when someone is telling you the truth and when someone's pulling your chain. Treg was all truth.

"Where, what are these followers called?" I pressed.

"I don't have a location; all I hear is whispers on the street, of a group calling themselves the Chosen," Treg said. "Please, that's all I know. That's it."

I was already off him, pulling the chewing gum out of my pocket as my mind worked over the information. An ancient one coming to our realm summoned by the Chosen and my wife could be one of them?

I popped in the piece of bubble gum and began chomping away. I could find them. I would find them. I had a lead for the first time and the hope of seeing my wife again filled my heart with joy.

"You were, you were just bluffing?" Treg asked, getting up from the ground and dusting off his pants. "You were going to torture me with bubble gum?"

"What kind of Archangel would I be if I tortured you?" I asked, already heading for the road and the downed bike I was about to borrow.

"Hey, that's pretty messed up, man," Treg said to my back. "You can't take them alone, even if you were an angel. Word is the Chosen are recruiting an army of supernaturals. You can't do it alone."

"Who says I'm alone?" I asked, righting the motorcycle and revving the engine. "I know a few hunters I can hire."

JONNY, Shannon and Evan will be back in the next Hunters for Hire book "Town Lore." Available at store.jonathan-yanez.com or at your favorite book retailer.

STAY INFORMED

This is your personal invitation to join the community we call our Pack. Below are two ways to stay in touch via email or Facebook. Either way we'd love for you to be a part of our family.

For updates about new releases, as well as exclusive promotions, visit my website and sign up for the VIP mailing list. Head there now at **www.jonathan-yanez.com**

We also created a special Facebook group called "Jonathan Yanez' Reading Wolves" specifically for readers, where I show new cover art, offer giveaways, and run contests. Please check it out and join whenever you get the chance!

BOOKS IN THE HUNTERS FOR HIRE UNIVERSE

1. Hunters for Hire

2. Town Lore

3. All Valley Tournament

4. Godmothered

4.5 darkest Night

5. Devil May Care

6. Dying of the Light

www.ingramcontent.com/pod-product-compliance
Ingram Content Group UK Ltd.
Pitfield, Milton Keynes, MK11 3LW, UK
UKHW040053031225
9335UKWH00003B/499

9 798215 878132